T4-AQI-526

INSUFFERABLE PATIENT

"You were worried about me?" Jubal asked.

"Worried about you?" Maggie cried. "I was scared to death!"

Jubal felt a smug satisfaction begin to soften his agony. She was worried about him.

"Come here, Mrs. Bright," he said, holding out his hand.

Maggie wiped her eyes and sniffed. "Why?"

"Come here."

He was speaking softly and looking at her in a way that drew Maggie to him like a magnet. She knelt by the bed next to him and her hand, of its own accord, sneaked out to brush the hair away from his forehead.

Jubal liked that a lot. "Thank you for worrying about me, Mrs. Bright."

One Bright Morning

 ALICE DUNCAN

HarperPaperbacks
A Division of HarperCollinsPublishers

HarperPaperbacks   *A Division of* HarperCollins*Publishers*
10 East 53rd Street, New York, N.Y. 10022

Cover illustration by Jean Monti

First printing: January 1995

Printed in the United States of America

HarperPaperbacks, HarperMonogram, and colophon are trademarks of HarperCollins*Publishers*

❖ 10 9 8 7 6 5 4 3 2 1

Many thanks to Linda Hart, who got me hooked on Romance novels. If it weren't for Linda and my poor arthritic feet, I'd probably still be dancing instead of writing. Infinite thanks also to Meredith Brucker for her unfailing support. And, of course, to Monica Stoner for saving Mr. Smith's life, bless her heart.

1

Maggie had the blasphemous thought that God was seriously at fault when He created women.

"He made a mistake," she muttered to the rough log ceiling when she awoke for the fifth time. Only this time, unlike the prior four, she had to get out of bed and start her day. The cold gray dawn was cracking.

She pushed the quilts aside and shivered as icy air hit her. Pain stabbed through her skull in piercing, furious shafts when she went to thrust her arms into her heavy wrapper and stuff her feet into her slippers. Thick woolen stockings already covered her legs; she had worn them to bed for warmth. The cold made the ache in her head even worse. She glanced toward the window, hoping to get a glimpse of the day, but the glass was frosted over. Her breath hung in the morning air like a soft cloud.

"Maybe it wasn't a mistake," she grumbled. "Maybe He hated His mother, and He's punishing all women in order to get even."

Her teeth were chattering by the time she stumbled out to the kitchen to stoke up the fire and heat the coffee. Every time her teeth chattered, her head throbbed. She lit the oil lamp, hung it on its peg by the door, and, in spite of her miserable headache, appreciated the comfortable yellow glow it cast.

She realized her earlier thought didn't make any sense. "I guess He couldn't have had a mother before He invented women, could He?"

Maggie was honestly puzzled about that. But there was nobody to ask, now Kenny was dead. Not that he had ever answered her when he was alive. He would just look at her with his big sweet calf eyes and smile at her tenderly with his big sweet smile. She missed him terribly, even if he hadn't been much for conversation.

At least Kenny had loved her. That was some kind of miracle. Maggie's was a life that had been powerfully short on miracles. She should have known it wouldn't last.

Her fingers were already stiff with cold when she cracked the ice in the bucket on the porch, put a pot of water on to boil for mush, and set last night's coffee on the stove lid to heat.

"Damn it," she said, as she prepared breakfast. "Why would God create a body that can't function for seven days each month and then make her do it anyway?"

Her little daughter started to fret in the bedroom, so Maggie squared her shoulders, put on a smile, and tried to look happy when she peek-a-booed into the room.

Annie saw Maggie, stopped crying, hiccuped, and then laughed at her mama, who was making a silly face. She pulled herself up in the crib her daddy had

built for her and held out her chubby arms, which
were swathed in thick flannel.

In spite of how poorly she felt, Maggie laughed and
walked over to her little girl to pick her up. Annie
looked like a roly-poly muffin, swaddled as she was.

"How's mama's best baby this morning?"

"Mama's bay," Annie confirmed, and hugged her
mother tightly around the neck.

"I love you so much, I can hardly stand it, baby girl.
And we're going to be all right. You just see if we
aren't." Maggie knew she was trying to make herself
feel better with those words. The kitchen was warmer
than the bedroom, so she carried Annie in there and
laid her down on the table to change her diaper.

Annie's sweet little face looked wet and red and
miserable. So did her sweet little bottom. Annie was
just fifteen months old. Maggie wiped the tears off of
her baby's cheeks, kissed her soundly, changed her
diapers, rubbed her chafed behind with glycerin, tickled her tummy, and bundled her up again.

"I miss your papa, Annie honey. He loved you so
much, and you'll never even remember him."

Maggie shook her head sadly as she settled Annie
into the lovely high chair Kenny had built and lowered the wooden tray he had fashioned on hinges so
the baby wouldn't fall out and hurt herself.

It didn't look as though the water would ever boil.
Maggie and her daughter sang a little back-and-forth
tune while she poured herself a cup of not-quite-hot
coffee. Then she swallowed it with a shudder. Sometimes coffee eased the pain of these God-awful headaches.

She was startled by a loud thump on the kitchen
door.

"Mercy sakes, what's that?"

Annie offered her mama a toothless smile, and Maggie grinned back.

"Ozzie?" she called.

Nobody answered.

The thump came again. This time it was followed by an odd scrape, as of wood sliding against wood.

Maggie planted a quick kiss on her daughter's curly head and went to the door.

Somebody had told her about zombies once. Whoever it was said that zombies were the undead, and that's pretty much what Maggie felt like as she trod miserably over to the kitchen door and opened it.

She expected to find a drunken Ozzie, propped against it with a stupid grin on his face, and she was prepared to lecture him soundly. Ozzie Plumb was her hired man, and if a more useless individual existed on this earth, Maggie had yet to meet him. She'd fire him and hire somebody else, but she didn't know how to go about it. Anyway, there wasn't anybody else in this part of New Mexico Territory to hire. And even if there was, who would work for a woman, except another bum like Ozzie?

"Oh, sweet Jesus!" Maggie breathed, at the sight that greeted her eyes.

A big roan horse stood there. It seemed to loom from out of the misty dawn, and it was peering at her with solemn brown eyes. Astride the horse was a man unknown to Maggie. The stranger had apparently reached out to bang at her door with the stock of the rifle that now dangled from his fingers. As Maggie stared at him, the rifle slipped out of his slack grip and hit the frozen dirt. Blood dripped from the fingers that had held the gun.

The stranger's long duster and left trouser leg were soaked with blood as well. It had begun to congeal in the cold February dawn, and Maggie saw the glint of ice crystals where blood had dripped down to the stranger's boot and over the side.

"I'm awful sorry, ma'am," the man breathed through white lips. He was drooping at an odd angle in his saddle.

As Maggie watched in horror, his eyes slid shut. He slumped over his horse's neck as he passed out and would have fallen onto the frozen earth, but his duster caught on the saddle horn and he couldn't.

"Oh, sweet Jesus," Maggie murmured again.

She swallowed the sick feeling in her gut and reached for the man's shoulders. The fellow was leaning perilously, and Maggie didn't want him to fall.

"Ozzie!" she hollered. "Ozzie, get your worthless butt out here right now!" The sound of her own loud voice ripped through her pounding head like a bullet, but she tried to ignore it.

She'd have to tend to this person, she guessed, whoever he was. At least that was one thing she knew how to do: nurse people. When Kenny had been kicked by a horse, she'd had to learn. And then he had died anyway, two months later. Sometimes life just wasn't fair.

She could hear the baby beginning to fuss in the kitchen, but Maggie couldn't stop to see to her. This poor stranger might die right here, half out of his saddle, if she didn't do something fast.

"Ozzie!" she bellowed again.

"I'm comin'," came a thin, warbly voice.

Maggie had managed to support the stranger's broad shoulders in her arms by the time Ozzie made it to the kitchen side of the house. He was a small man with a skinny lined face that ran toward florid. Right now he looked a little green. Maggie figured he must have spent most of last night drinking in town.

"This man's hurt. Help me get him inside."

"Great God almighty," said Ozzie. "Whoozat?"

"I have no idea!" Maggie snapped. "Help me get him inside."

Ozzie went over and helped her lower the man out of his saddle. Then they carried him into the house and rested him on the floor. The fire Maggie had built in the kitchen stove had already warmed the place up considerably.

"Hold him there, Ozzie. I'm going to fix my bed so we can lay him on it."

She didn't look to see that he obeyed. Fortunately, Maggie possessed a stronger will than Ozzie did, and he generally did what she told him when he was inside the house and in her line of sight.

"Who dat?" Annie asked her mama. She had stopped fussing and stared at the unconscious man curiously.

"I don't know, baby, but he's bad hurt."

Annie eyed the stranger again. "Bad hurt," she said. Her little voice sounded sad.

Maggie raced into her bedroom and ripped the sheets off the bed. Then she reached into the chest in the corner and took out the oilskin sheeting from when Kenny got kicked by the horse. Quick as lightning, she spread the oilskin onto the bed and tucked fresh linens over it, then dashed out to the kitchen again.

"Help me, Ozzie," she commanded. And Ozzie did.

They carried the stranger into the bedroom and laid him on Maggie's bed. She wished it were warmer in the room, but that couldn't be helped. She'd just leave the door open so the heat from the kitchen stove would warm it up.

In the meantime, she quickly applied a tourniquet of rolled linen to the poor man's right arm and determined that his left leg was also bleeding. She folded up another pad of linen, discovered with some exploratory prods, where the blood was seeping out of his leg, and strapped the pad tightly over it.

"I'll be right back to figure out exactly what's the matter with that leg," she muttered to her unconscious patient.

Then she piled him with quilts and blankets, hoped he wouldn't die before she could attend to him, and hurried back to the kitchen with Ozzie.

"See to the stranger's horse first, Ozzie. Then run to the Phillips' place and tell Sadie I need help. Then go to town and fetch Doc Pritchard. If you don't do all of those things and do 'em fast, Ozzie Plumb, don't you even bother to come back here. And if you don't do those things and *still* try to come back here to get your stupid guitar, I'll bust it. Swear to God I will, Ozzie. So you just do as I say."

A practiced expression of hurt settled onto Ozzie's wrinkled face. "Now, Miss Maggie, would I fail you?"

"Yes. Now you git. I'm going to settle the baby and then tend to this stranger."

"Yes, ma'am."

Maggie eyed him narrowly and decided he probably meant it. Since she didn't trust him out of her eyesight, however, she quickly marched outside to Ozzie's shack next to the barn and confiscated his guitar while he tended to the stranger's horse.

When he led Old Bones, the mule, out of the barn,

Maggie lifted up the guitar. "You see here, Ozzie? You just do what I say, or I'll smash this guitar into a billion pieces and feed 'em to you."

The icy air was creating infinite numbers of little new pains in her head, sharp and brittle, all stabbing into her skull, but she did her best to pretend they weren't there.

Ozzie still looked hurt. "Jeez, Miss Maggie, I'm goin'."

Maggie just snorted and turned back to the house.

"Sometimes I purely don't know why life is so blamed hard, Annie," she muttered as she rummaged around in her kitchen cupboard.

Annie apparently thought her mama had said something very funny, because she laughed at her and thumped on her wooden high-chair tray.

Maggie grinned at the baby because she couldn't help it. She opened a tin and handed Annie one of the hard biscuits she had made out of graham flour and arrowroot from a recipe in a *Farm Wife's Journal.* The magazine claimed they were good for teething babies.

"Here, sweetie, you chew on this. Mama has to tend to a sick man."

The biscuit would at least keep Annie occupied while she tried to do for the stranger, Maggie figured. Annie banged happily on her tray, and Maggie sighed when she looked at the pretty chair Kenny had made.

"Your daddy was so good to us, Annie girl." She felt like crying all of a sudden.

Whenever Maggie had her monthlies and these detestable headaches, she succumbed to moods. She knew it was weak of her, but she just figured it was her nature to be weak.

Annie gurgled as she gummed her biscuit. She smiled

at her mama, and Maggie smiled back. "I love you, baby girl."

She could see Kenny every time she looked at Annie. The baby had his sweet nature, as well as his shiny, curly light-brown hair and big brown eyes, and she was pretty as a picture. Maggie sighed again and began foraging in her medicine chest.

Maggie had spent most of her first seventeen years trying to appease her aunt and uncle, without succeeding. Then, in 1876, Kenny Bright had wandered through southern Indiana, fallen hopelessly in love with her, married her, and brought her here to his farm in Lincoln County in the New Mexico Territory. She thought her luck had finally changed, but now she realized that was not quite the case.

By the time Kenny got kicked by the horse, he had taught Maggie enough so she could keep herself and the baby alive at any rate, barring unforeseen Indian raids, outlaw incursions, drought, flood, or fire. Those things were liable to happen at any time, Kenny or no Kenny. She had a cow and a mule and a vegetable garden and chickens and Annie. And Ozzie, for what good he did her.

"And now I've got me a gun-shot cowboy."

Life on a farm had sounded nice to Maggie. She liked animals and she didn't mind hard work, although she was a small woman. Life on a farm in Lincoln County, however, was nothing like life in a snug little town in southern Indiana.

"This damned territory," she grumbled as she ripped clean linen into bandage-sized strips.

Until she moved to New Mexico four years ago, Maggie had never uttered a cussword in her entire life. It had never occurred to her. Now these words occurred to her every other minute. That was just one more reason she was glad Aunt Lucy wasn't here. Aside from the fact that Maggie and her aunt hated each other, the older woman would have blistered Maggie for even thinking a cussword.

The water she had set to boil was bubbling now, so she poured some into a clean pail. Then she grabbed a tin of alum from the cupboard, gathered up her linens, some soft flannel squares, a knife, and her scissors, and looked around to see if she had missed anything else she might need.

"Lordy, I thought these days were over." Frowning, she surveyed her kingdom.

"Wish me luck, Annie," she told her daughter.

Annie gurgled and gnawed on her biscuit with gusto.

Maggie hooked the oil lamp over her arm, took a deep breath, and stepped into her bedroom.

"Oh, Lord, please help me." Some of her stoicism deserted her when she peered at the man passed out on her bed. "He looks dead already."

She stared down at the stranger for a moment. He was a good-looking man, or would be if he wasn't as pale as a frosty window. He had thick, sun-bleached brown hair. She couldn't tell what color the man's eyes were because they were closed, but his eyelashes were long and dark. That figured. Men always got the nice lashes.

He had thick stubble on his chin and cheeks, as though he hadn't shaved in a few days, and he was taller than Kenny was. Maggie could tell from the way his legs dangled over the end of the bed. She wondered if that would prove to be a problem, since she figured his leg to be gun-shot, but decided she'd just have to cross that bridge when she came to it.

Taking one more deep breath, she squared her shoulders, laid her tools out, and began unbuttoning the man's duster. If he'd been hit in the chest, that was the wound she'd better tend to first. She didn't know much about gunshot wounds although, Lord knew, there were enough of them to go around in this territory. Somebody was always getting shot up. She'd had to dig a bullet out of Ozzie's arm once when some gunplay had erupted in a saloon in town.

"I swear. If it isn't the Apaches, it's the bugs. If it isn't the bugs, it's the prickles. If it isn't the prickles, it's the animals. If it isn't the animals, it's the outlaws. And if it isn't the outlaws, it's the weather."

She eased the stranger's duster off his shoulders and noticed there was a folded paper sticking out of his shirt pocket. Maggie opened it up and grimaced when she saw that half of it was soggy with blood. It was a WANTED broadside.

Maggie looked at the picture on the poster and then peered down again at the stranger on her bed. After surveying the two critically for a moment, she decided with some relief that they weren't the same man. The man on the poster was a mean-eyed black-haired fellow named Jack Gauthier, and according to the description he was five-foot-seven. The man hanging over the end of her bed was much taller than that and had brown hair. Maggie shoved the WANTED poster out of the way.

"You look like a strong one, anyway," she muttered as she peeled the shirt off his heavily muscled arms. "We'll wash you up some and then see where I have to dig, *if* I have to dig. Lord, I hope I won't have to, especially if you got yourself a chest wound." Maggie said a short prayer that Doc Pritchard would be sober if and when he got here, but she didn't hold out too many hopes.

When she had his arms and chest washed off, she realized the hole was in the stranger's right shoulder, just above the armpit. That seemed encouraging. At least it had missed his heart. Assuming he had one. Maggie wasn't one to take much on faith anymore.

The stranger moaned when she pressed around the wound after she had bathed him, but he didn't open his eyes. Maggie's mouth set in a grim line. She hated this so much, poking and prodding and hurting people. It made her insides curl up into tight little knots.

And her headache wasn't any better either. Sometimes the pain was so bad her eyes blurred, but she just blinked hard and kept working.

She found where the bullet was lodged and knew she'd better try to take it out. Depending on what the man had been shot with, he could die of lead poisoning if the bullet wasn't dug out quickly, even if the wound wasn't bad enough to kill him on its own. She sterilized her knife over the fire in her lantern, dunked it in hot water, and then swallowed hard.

"You just hold on, mister. This knife is sharp and it shouldn't take me long."

She flinched when she pressed into the wound with her fingers, trying to ease the bullet up. But she managed to get it loose, the knife did the rest, and she picked the bullet out with tweezers. The stranger groaned some, but he didn't yell or kick or wake up. That was some kind of blessing, anyway.

She cleaned up around the wound, sprinkled it with alum, packed it well, and wrapped it tight. After a critical survey of her work, she didn't think anything vital had been touched by bullet or knife.

"As if I could tell if it was."

Then she stood up and quickly stretched the crick out of her back. She would have to tackle that leg now. Lordy, what a way to start the day.

She listened for Annie, heard her cooing contentedly, and squatted down beside the stranger again, pondering what to do next.

"I wonder if I'll have to cut that boot off you. They look like a good pair." Always poor, Maggie didn't want to ruin a good boot if she didn't have to. "Besides, if you live, I don't suppose you'll appreciate having your boot slit down and spoiled."

Having decided to try to get the boots off without cutting, she moved to the foot of the bed and gently picked up the stranger's left leg. She tugged gently, and the boot slid off the man's foot. The inside was bloody, but Maggie didn't have time to look at it too closely because a grunt startled her into looking up. Although the sound didn't seem to come from the direction of the bed, Maggie knew she and the stranger were the only two people in the little house who could possibly make a grunt like that; it had to be him.

It wasn't. There was an Indian standing in her open bedroom doorway. She was so startled that she screamed.

Then she squeezed her eyes shut for a second. "Oh, no! Why me, God? Why are these things happening to me?"

"It's all right, ma'am," the stocky man at the door said in a very deep voice. "I didn't mean to startle you."

Maggie brought a hand up to wipe the straggling hair away from her forehead and realized too late that the hand was covered with the stranger's blood and she had just smeared it all over her face. This had been a trying morning, and she was very nearly at the end of her tether.

"I'm real sorry, ma'am," the man said again. "I knocked, but you was busy and I reckon you didn't hear me."

Maggie figured her headache had sent her over the edge and she was now crazy. She knew the man speaking to her so calmly from the door of her own bedroom was an Indian. He looked like an Indian, with long braided hair, dark red-brown skin, and black eyes. He wasn't naked like an Indian, thank God; he had on cowboy clothes, which some Indians wore. But he sure didn't talk like an Indian. She figured that just meant God was playing more tricks on her.

Maggie was hugging the gun-shot stranger's boot to her breast in fright. She couldn't figure out what to do. There were no weapons nearby, nothing with which she could defend herself or the unconscious stranger. Was the man at the door the person who had shot him, come here to finish the job? Then she realized he was talking to her again.

"I apologize for scarin' you, ma'am," he was saying. "I followed the trail to your house. That there's my partner." He gestured to the man on Maggie's bed.

Through her headache and her tumbling thoughts, Maggie was barely able to comprehend his words; they seeped through her panicked brain slowly. All at once she realized she was clutching a bloody boot and thrust it away from her in revulsion.

"Ugh!"

"Here, ma'am, please let me help you. You shouldn't be doin' this all alone." The fellow stepped farther into the room.

"No!" Maggie's voice held barely suppressed panic. "Who are you? What are you doing here?"

The man stopped. He seemed to have an infinite supply of patience. Maggie wished she had a little bit of it.

"My name's Dan Blue Gully, ma'am."

Suddenly Maggie remembered Annie. "Where's my baby?" she shrieked, her eyes wild.

The man sighed as though he was used to this kind of reaction from white people. "She's in her high chair in the kitchen, ma'am, and she seems real happy. She sure is a pretty little thing."

He looked behind him, and Maggie saw that he smiled at something. A horrible image of her beautiful Annie, scalped in her high chair, flashed through her fevered brain. Maybe this person and the stranger on her bed were vicious criminals. God knew, there were plenty of those wandering around in Lincoln County. It was all too much for her, and she began to weep hysterically.

The expression on the Indian's face was one of mingled concern and aggravation. "Are you all right, ma'am? I know I gave you a start, but I'm not violent. Swear to God I'm not. Honest."

Maggie couldn't stop herself. Huge, shuddering sobs were making her head ache even more, and the pain had concentrated, as it usually did eventually, behind and around her left eye.

"No," she finally managed to choke out, "I'm not all right. There's a dead man in my bed, and my baby's been murdered, and I'm crazy, and there's an Indian in my kitchen. And I have a headache!"

The man walked over and took her by the shoulders. She wanted to turn tail and run and tried to pull away from him, but he gently and firmly led her out to the kitchen and sat her down next to Annie, who was still working away on her arrowroot biscuit. She had managed to soften a good deal of it with drool and was smearing it into her soft curls delightedly.

Annie gurgled at Dan Blue Gully and he grinned at her. Then he squatted beside Maggie, dipped a rag in some water at the sink, and wiped off her bloody face and hands. He kept her hands in his when he was through doing that.

"I can tell you got a bad headache, ma'am, and I'm right sorry. But I have to help my friend in there. We've been partners for so long I've forgot when I didn't know him, and I don't aim to see him die. I appreciate your tryin' to help him, and I may need you again. You chew this and drink some water, and I hope you feel better in a little while."

He opened a leather pouch and handed Maggie a piece of bark. She had no idea what it was. Her tears had stopped, but her head was now pounding so badly she could barely lift it. She stared at the man beside her, and the numb realization that her hands were no longer caked with blood registered dimly somewhere in her consciousness.

She was afraid to disobey him for fear he would harm her and her baby. She only hoped that if he planned to kill them he'd do it quickly. And soon. The sooner this headache was gone, even if it took her with it, the better.

Dan Blue Gully pumped a mug of water and brought it to her. "Chew on that piece o' bark, ma'am. It may help your head. And drink water with it. Otherwise, it might make you sick. I got to get to work now."

With that, he turned and went back into the bedroom.

Maggie sat in the chair. She was normally a fighter, but right now she couldn't even see straight, much less fight. Her headache had become so bad she didn't think she could stand up without falling over in a faint.

"Oh, what the hell," she finally muttered. "If it poisons me, so much the better." She began to chew.

It was about ten minutes before she again had a coherent thought. She suddenly realized how absurd this whole situation was. Here she was, sitting in her kitchen chair, chewing on a piece of bark and drinking water, while her baby sat gurgling in her high chair, gumming a biscuit and smearing glop into her hair, and an Indian operated on an unknown, nearly dead man in her bedroom.

She almost laughed before she realized her headache was gone.

Maggie stared at the remains of the bark in her hand in pure awe. She had never in her whole life had one of these headaches just up and go away.

She shook her head experimentally back and forth. There was no pain. Not a shard. Not a wince. She turned her gaze on her baby. Annie was smiling at her and looked as though she could use another biscuit.

"Ho, Mama," the baby cried.

Maggie cleared her throat. "Hello to you, pretty Annie."

Very carefully, she stood up. She didn't want the pain to come crashing back into her again, sneakylike, and knock her cockeyed.

Nothing.

She shook her head once more. Then she looked

over to the bedroom door, half expecting to see the
Indian laughing at her wickedly. Or the devil. There
must be some mistake. Something good had finally
happened to Maggie Bright.

She decided not to argue with the fates. If the devil
were playing tricks with her, she might just as well
enjoy the few pain-free moments allowed her before
the bolt of lightning struck again. She looked with
disgust at her blood-caked shirtwaist.

"Ugh, Annie. Your mama's a mess."

"Mama mess," the baby replied.

She took a tentative step toward the bedroom, then
another. By the time she had made it to the doorway,
she almost believed her headache was really, truly
gone. She peeked into the room.

The stranger lay naked on the bed, and Dan Blue
Gully was kneeling beside him on the other side, giving Maggie a splendid view of the most powerfully
built male body she had ever seen. She squeezed her
eyes shut and gasped. Dan looked up at the noise.

"Feelin' better, ma'am?"

Maggie decided it was impolite not to look at him
as she spoke, even if it meant eyeballing him over the
most personal part of the stranger on her bed.

"Y-yes. Thank you," she stuttered. She opened her
eyes wide and then shut them tight again.

The naked stranger on her bed didn't look at all
like Kenny looked the few times Maggie had seen him
without his union suit. This man's thighs were huge
and looked like iron. Iron covered with curly golden
hairs.

"If you're feelin' better, ma'am, I could use a little
help in here," Dan Blue Gully said.

"Of course." Maggie cleared her throat. "Mr. Blue

Gully, I can't hardly believe it, but that piece of bark actually cured my headache. I don't know how to thank you."

"That's all right, ma'am. You probably saved my partner's life. That's worth some bark, I reckon."

"Well, I just want you to know how much it means to me, 'cause it does. It means a whole lot. Just let me take care of the baby for a second and I'll be right back."

Maggie fled back to Annie.

"Oh, Lord Jesus, Annie. Now I've got to go into my bedroom and face a naked man *and* an Indian."

Annie sucked on the last of her biscuit and grinned. She had goo all over her face and hair, and Maggie itched to clean her up, but she didn't have time.

When she remembered Ozzie, she cursed him. "I really will break that man's guitar if he doesn't get back here pretty quick." She handed Annie another arrowroot biscuit. "Here, baby, I guess you might as well paste on another one of these."

The baby gave a tinkling little laugh, and Maggie kissed her. Then she straightened up, sighed deeply, and headed back into her bedroom.

Dan Blue Gully had covered the stranger's private parts with a sheet by the time Maggie reentered the room.

"Thank you, ma'am." He glanced up as Maggie stepped inside. "Could you hold his leg still? I've got to dig out the bullet."

Maggie swallowed hard. "All right."

"You did a real good job on his shoulder," Dan said, as he poised his knife over the man's thigh.

"Thank you," Maggie whispered. She couldn't watch.

Dan Blue Gully worked in silence for a second or

two as Maggie held the stranger's left leg steady. It felt very hard and hairy. Kenny had been hard and hairy too, but Kenny's was a wiry hard, not a bulky, muscled hard like this unconscious man whose massive thigh she cradled in her arms.

She discovered that when she opened her eyes, she was staring straight at his sheet-covered privates. Lord, the bulge they made was big too. Maggie didn't want to think about it, so she turned her head to study Dan Blue Gully.

He had a nice profile, Maggie decided. His features were sharp and lean, not puffy like some of the Indians she had seen in town, those who had given themselves over to strong drink. As she recalled Ozzie Plumb, she reminded herself that addiction to intoxicating spirits was not by any means confined to the Indian segment of the population.

Her gaze had a tendency to slide back to the stranger's bulge, so Maggie decided to talk to Dan Blue Gully in order to keep herself occupied.

"Like I said, that piece of bark you gave me truly worked wonders. Nothing I've ever tried before has ever helped one of those headaches."

The Indian grunted. He didn't say anything until he had pulled the bullet from his friend's leg. It came out with a gush of blood that nearly made Maggie gag. Then he said, "I did hear that stuff works pretty good."

Maggie cleared her throat. "What—what is it, Mr. Blue Gully?"

Dan Blue Gully shrugged. "Don't know."

Maggie's eyes widened. "You don't know?"

"No. My aunt, she give it to me. She's a healer over in Arizona. Married her a Hopi, so the relatives kicked her out. That bark comes off a willow tree they got there. Grows by a river."

He grinned at Maggie, and she realized he had a nice smile. She offered him a tentative smile in return.

"Well," she said. "It worked, and I surely do thank you." Then, because she couldn't think of anything else to say, she added, "You're not a Hopi?"

Dan Blue Gully gave a little snort. "In New Mexico? Naw, I'm Apache. Mescalero. No Hopis around here."

Maggie was puzzled. "Then how did your aunt meet one?"

"Army run us out of New Mexico Territory into Arizona," he said, as he blotted blood away from the wound.

"Oh." Maggie didn't quite know what to say to that. Then she thought of a good question. "What's this man's name, Mr. Blue Gully?"

She eyed the stranger again. His face had relaxed into smooth lines since he had given up the conscious state for stupor.

"Jubal. Jubal Green."

"Green? Well, that's interesting," said Maggie, more for conversation than anything else. "He's Green and you're Blue. You're a colorful pair." She thought about chuckling and decided against it.

Dan Blue Gully looked at her blankly and then shrugged. "I was born on his place." He smiled ironically. "Of course, the Greens come to live there a long time after the Blue Gullys, because the Mescalero have been there for centuries, but I figure it ain't worth fighting about anymore. Anyway, Jubal and me, we sort of raised each other."

Maggie only swallowed and nodded.

Dan had been nimbly working on Jubal Green's

thigh during their conversation. He sprinkled something over the wound and packed it tight, then bandaged it up with the clean linen strips that Maggie had set aside for the purpose.

"How—how did Mr. Green get shot?"

"Saving my life."

Maggie wondered if she had misunderstood. "Did— um, did you say saving your life, Mr. Blue Gully?"

"Yep. We trade off." He gave her a big grin.

Maggie felt terribly confused. This Dan Blue Gully didn't seem to be one to tell a body a whole lot at a time. Then she remembered the WANTED poster.

With a nod toward the table where the broadside still lay, she asked, "Were the two of you looking for the criminal on the poster?"

Dan Blue Gully looked over to see where Maggie was indicating. "Kind of."

Maggie decided to ignore that "kind of." "Why?"

The Indian looked at her somberly for a second or two. "French Jack killed Jubal's family."

"Killed his family? His wife and children?" she whispered. "How terrible." Maggie felt like crying at the thought.

"Nah. Killed his brother and sister-in-law. They all lived on the spread. In west Texas. Near El Paso. Called Green's Valley Ranch."

"Oh." Maggie still felt sort of sick. "Why did he do that?"

The Indian shrugged. "It wasn't personal."

Maggie gaped at him. "Not personal?" Maggie didn't think she could come up with too many things more personal than killing someone's family.

"Naw. He was bein' paid."

"Paid?"

"That's right. Another feller wants us dead."

Maggie swallowed hard. "Why?"

Dan shrugged again. "He's crazy."

Just then Maggie heard a crash at the kitchen door. Was Ozzie back?

"Maggie!" It was Sadie Phillips, shrieking.

Maggie suddenly wondered if asking for Sadie had been a good idea. Sadie was a very nervous sort of person. It was rather pleasant to be around this stolid Indian. He seemed so calm. She sighed.

"I'd better go talk to my neighbor, Mr. Blue Gully. She's come to help."

Dan grunted a *humph*. It didn't sound like a happy *humph*.

"I'll—I'll get rid of her," Maggie stammered.

Dan smiled at her and nodded. "Good idea."

2

"*Maggie, what on earth* is going on? Ozzie said something about a bleeding cowboy come knockin' at your door and you took him in and laid him out. Is he dead?" Sadie's voice was low and throbbing with excitement.

"No, he isn't dead." Maggie eyed Sadie curiously. "Why are you whispering, Sadie?"

"Why, if you had a dead man in here, I didn't mean no disrespect."

Now Maggie really regretted having sent for her.

"He isn't dead yet, Sadie. He's bad hurt, though. We had to dig two bullets out of him, and he's unconscious. I know he lost a lot of blood."

Maggie remembered the bloody boot and shuddered. She figured she'd best take care of that next, before the blood dried and ruined the leather completely.

Sadie had backed up some and was now looking at Maggie with wide, horrified eyes. Maggie didn't know what was wrong, but she sure hoped Sadie wouldn't shriek again.

"What's the matter, Sadie?"

"Your dress," Sadie said in a low, dramatic whisper. She pointed a theatrically quivering finger at Maggie's shirtwaist.

Maggie looked down at her bodice and sighed.

"Oh, yes. I got some blood on me, I guess. I'll have to clean it up when I have time." She shook her head in perturbation. "Blood leaves stains, too. Oh, well, it can't be helped. I'll just soak it in cold water and soda powder when I get a chance."

"Vinegar might help, ma'am," came the deep, rumbling voice of Dan Blue Gully from the bedroom doorway.

Sadie looked up, and then she did shriek.

Maggie grimaced, recalling her recent headache and hoping it wouldn't decide to come back.

"Please don't scream, Sadie," she said in a tight voice. "You'll upset the baby. This here is Mr. Dan Blue Gully. He's the wounded man's partner, and he's been helping me. Or I've been helping him."

Since Maggie was incurably honest, she didn't want to usurp any credit due Mr. Blue Gully, but she really wasn't sure how to express their relationship.

"He's an Indian!" Sadie whispered.

Maggie wondered if Sadie thought that fact had escaped her attention. "I know."

"But—but, he's an *Indian*." Sadie was visibly trembling.

"It's all right, Sadie. He's not a *wild* Indian. Mr. Blue Gully is a friend of the injured man, Jubal Green. They're from a spread near El Paso. Some criminal named French Jack shot him because they were looking for him because he was looking for them. French Jack killed Mr. Green's family. Not his wife and children, but his sister and brother-in-law."

"Brother and sister-in-law," Dan Blue Gully corrected her conscientiously.

"Right. Brother and sister-in-law."

Sadie just stared at Dan Blue Gully, her normally squinched-up brown eyes opened wide in terror.

"It's all right, Sadie," Maggie said again.

She wondered what on earth to do with the woman now that she was here. Finally she took her by the arm and led her over to Annie. Maybe Sadie could be useful in spite of herself.

"Would you please watch Annie for me? I've got to tend to Mr. Green a while longer. All I've been able to give the baby for breakfast so far is a couple of biscuits. Maybe you could clean her up some and get a little milk down her from the back porch. If it isn't froze hard."

Sadie sat with a thump and stared up at Maggie.

"Sadie?"

Maggie hoped Sadie wouldn't go into hysterics. She'd heard that happened sometimes with ladies who possessed fine sensibilities. Maggie didn't figure she herself had any sensibilities at all, but she wasn't sure about Sadie.

"I-I—" Sadie swallowed hard. "All right," she said, and turned her attention to Annie.

Annie said a chipper, toothless "Ho, Say!" to Sadie.

That won a delighted smile from her mama, but Sadie didn't even notice Annie's greeting.

Maggie sighed and turned back to Dan Blue Gully, who was watching them with serene brown eyes. He stepped aside so Maggie could enter the room before him, and Maggie wondered why all men weren't that polite.

She walked with him over to the bed, and they both looked down at the unconscious Jubal Green. He was quite a specimen, all right, thought Maggie. He surely took the shine out of what she remembered of Kenny. Then she shook her head at her disloyal, wicked thoughts.

"What should we do now?" she asked.

Dan didn't answer her. He was looking down at her with a puzzled frown. Then she realized that this was her house and he most likely figured it was up to her to say what happened next. She cleared her throat.

"I mean"—she started over—"I guess he'll have to stay here for a while. Will you wait here with him?"

Dan Blue Gully still didn't answer immediately, and Maggie wondered if she was making herself clearly understood. This had been such a confusing morning. She pressed a hand to her forehead. Maybe she had a fever and this was all some kind of a vision caused by brain waves. Maggie had read about brain waves.

"You got a man?"

The question startled Maggie into a little twitch of surprise. Dan Blue Gully was still staring down at her, but his expression was unreadable.

"He—he died," she stammered.

Dan uttered a "Hmm" that didn't tell her a thing.

Silence reigned once more. It loomed over them like a palpable thing, until Maggie began to chatter in reaction. She plucked at Jubal's bedclothes as her tongue ran on like a locomotive.

"He died three months ago. Got himself kicked by a horse. Never was much good with horses. He was a fine man, though. His name was Kenny, Kenny

Bright. Kenneth Anthony Bright. He was born in New York, but he moved to the territory after the war. His whole family came out here, though some of them stopped before they got this far. Don't say as I blame them much. It's pretty rough out here. I don't know if I'd be here if it wasn't for Kenny. He married me in Indiana and brought me to this farm. It's real hard living here in the territory. I never farmed before. I'm not much good at it. And then there's Annie. I don't know if it's good to raise a baby all alone like this. And there's also a lot of rough types always wandering into Lincoln. But it *is* pretty here. And the place is mine. That counts for a lot."

Maggie ran out of breath and stopped talking. Like an engine losing steam, her words just sort of chuffed out and died. She felt her cheeks get hot with embarrassment and hoped it was too dark in the room for Mr. Blue Gully to notice.

Then Dan said, "I had to cut the britches off Jubal. He won't be usin' them no more. Your dead man got any britches he can wear?"

Maggie wondered if he had heard a word she had said. Then she wondered how he could have avoided hearing them, they had all tumbled out so loud and fast. She swallowed hard.

"Kenny was a lot smaller than Mr. Green, I'm afraid. I don't know if they'd fit him."

"You any good with a needle and thread?"

Maggie didn't answer for a minute as she considered the question. Dan Blue Gully seemed to home right in on the important things. Cut straight to the nub, he did.

"Oh," she said finally. "Oh, sure. I guess I could let some out for him."

He nodded. "That would be right nice, Mrs. Bright," he said. "Otherwise, Jubal'll have to ride out to kill French Jack buck naked."

Maggie stared up at him in surprise. "You mean you're still going after him?"

Dan just looked at his partner and nodded.

"Oh."

"Can I leave Jubal to your care for a day or so, ma'am? I think he'll be all right, if you keep them wounds clean and sprinkle 'em with this powder." He dangled a hide bag with a leather drawstring in front of Maggie.

Maggie smiled. "Your aunt in Arizona?"

He didn't smile back, just nodded again. Then he said, "You got to clean them wounds twice a day and sprinkle this stuff on 'em. Wash 'em with warm water. Not hot. Not cold. Just tepid. Sprinkle this stuff on 'em and bind 'em tight. Not too tight."

"Right," said Maggie, memorizing the instructions.

"This here's a different kind of bark that's good for fever. Boil it up in some water. Better do that now, because I expect he'll be feverish before very long."

"Right," Maggie said again, and went to do exactly that. She put the bark in a little pot of water and set it on the stove to boil. Then she returned to the room.

"Er, Mr. Blue Gully, do I feed him that bark and water like—like tea?"

Dan Blue Gully considered the man on the bed for a moment before he spoke. "Might have to spoon it down him, if the fever's bad. He might not know enough to drink it."

Maggie looked at the naked man on her bed and felt so inadequate all of a sudden that she almost cried. "What about that bark you gave me for my head-ache? Can I boil a piece of that up for his pain?"

"Better not do that yet, ma'am. If he don't hurt, he might move around too much."

"Doc Pritchard should be here soon if Ozzie found him. If Doc's sober. If Ozzie's sober."

Dan frowned. Maggie looked up in time to catch that frown, and it worried her. The man looked fierce when he frowned.

"I don't think I want a white doctor messin' with my friend, ma'am," he said after a moment or two.

Maggie was about to protest but was suddenly assailed by the recollection of Doc Pritchard reeling down the street in Lincoln and shut her mouth. Mr. Blue Gully might have a point.

"Well," she said diplomatically, "I don't suppose Doc Pritchard is any worse than most doctors."

"But you see, Miz Bright, Jubal Green and me is more than just friends. We grew up together. We were kind of like each other's family. We're like brothers, like kin. I don't know as I want anybody dealin' with him unless I trust him. I trust you. I don't know who this Doc Pritchard is, but if he might be drunk, I don't want him messin' with Jubal. You understand me, ma'am?"

Maggie understood him. She nodded. "Yes."

Neither one of them spoke for a few moments.

"I'll tend him," Maggie said at last. "I won't let Doc Pritchard touch him. I promise."

Dan smiled. "Thank you kindly, ma'am."

"What will you do?" Maggie asked.

"Got to keep track of French Jack," he said. "I don't suppose he's gone far."

Maggie's eyebrows shot up.

"Don't you think he'd try to get away from the scene of his crime?"

Dan Blue Gully shook his head. "French Jack's bein' paid by a man who hates Jubal Green worse than anything else in the world. He'll want to make sure Jubal's dead so's he can collect his pay. He won't go far."

The more Maggie thought about this information, the more it didn't make her feel particularly good. Her brow crinkled up.

"Mr. Blue Gully," she began.

He grunted.

"If this French Jack person is after Mr. Green, do you really think it's a good idea to leave him here? I mean, with me? Alone? With nobody around?"

The Indian looked at her with a level gaze. "You worried, ma'am?"

Maggie swallowed. "Well, yes. Yes, I guess I am worried. I mean, if this crazy man is after your partner who is lying here gun-shot and unconscious, don't you think that might be a little dangerous for us? For all of us? For my daughter and me? And Mr. Green too?"

"Don't worry, ma'am," Dan Blue Gully said. "I'll be watchin'."

Maggie looked at him with dismay. He'd be watching? She cast a glance at Jubal Green and sighed. Well, Mr. Green sure wasn't going anywhere, that was for certain. He'd be lucky to survive.

Ozzie came back shortly before Dan Blue Gully left. He barged right in the back door without knocking. Not that Maggie expected politeness from Ozzie. Still, it always irritated her that he didn't knock. She spoke sharply to him when he lurched into the kitchen.

"Will you ever learn to knock, you useless bum? And you took your sweet time, didn't you, Ozzie?"

Ozzie looked hurt, as he often did. That irritated Maggie too. If he weren't such a no-good loafer, he wouldn't have so much to look hurt about.

"Well now, Miss Maggie, I told Sadie Phillips you needed help, like you told me."

"You did that, all right."

Sadie and Annie were now in the bedroom, where Sadie was dressing the baby and Annie was giggling.

Maggie was trying to clean up after the various operations that been performed in her bedroom. Jubal Green was sleeping—or unconscious—in her bed, and she and Dan Blue Gully had managed to get one of Kenny's old nightshirts over his head, so he was at least decent.

She had covered him with two quilts and promised Dan that she would watch very carefully for fever and do precisely what he told her to do in case it struck. Maggie had decided that anybody who could cure one of her headaches was a person whose advice was worth following when it came to medical matters.

Now, as she washed out rags and bandages and Ozzie lounged at the kitchen table, Dan Blue Gully was checking his friend over one last time before he left to search for French Jack.

"Did you find Doc Pritchard, Ozzie?"

She felt just a tiny bit guilty for sending Ozzie after a doctor she no longer needed. Then she decided she had nothing to feel guilty about. After all, she hadn't known an Indian would show up and take over the show when she sent Ozzie out earlier.

"He was passed out in the saloon." Ozzie still looked downcast.

"Humph. And I suppose you had to hang around the saloon, waiting for him to wake up."

Maggie's tone was unmistakable. She thought both the doctor and Ozzie were worthless, disgusting specimens of humankind. She was sure Ozzie had spent a good hour or more guzzling bad whiskey while pretending to wait for the doctor to rouse himself.

"Well now, Maggie, it were a long thirsty ride to town," whined Ozzie.

Maggie just eyed him with contempt and continued scrubbing lye soap over the bloodstains on the sheet she held. The water, when she dunked the sheet, turned a deep scarlet. This Jubal Green, whoever he was, had fighting-red blood, she thought. It would be a shame if he didn't make it.

She glanced over to Ozzie again and saw he had turned paper-white as he stared through her bedroom door. She figured the reaction must be from his first glimpse of Dan Blue Gully and thought contemptuously that at least Sadie had had the guts to scream. She nodded over at the doorway.

"Mr. Blue Gully, this here's my hired hand, Ozzie Plumb. Ozzie, this is Mr. Dan Blue Gully. He's a friend of the gun-shot man, whose name is Jubal Green."

Ozzie just stared at Dan Blue Gully. Maggie noted that he trembled, which was just like him. She supposed if the Indian had been hostile, Ozzie would have fainted.

Dan's head jerked toward Ozzie. "He work for you?"

A loud sniff accompanied Maggie's reply. "He's supposed to."

Dan nodded. "You need help here," was all he said. Then he looked hard at Ozzie. His eyes narrowed slightly, and he pointed a long brown finger at him. "You help her," he said.

His voice held no more inflection than it usually did, which meant it was fairly flat, but Ozzie shrank back into his chair. He looked as though he might throw up.

"Yessir," he whimpered.

Maggie was impressed. There was a lot more to this Indian than met the eye. Which reminded her of something. She wiped her hands on her apron.

"Mr. Blue Gully?"

He turned to look at her and nodded slightly.

"Would you mind leaving another one or two of those bark pieces with me? Usually these headaches come in twos and threes. I'd surely appreciate it, if you have enough to spare."

"Oh, sure, ma'am," Dan said. "Should have thought of that myself. Guess I was too worried about Jubal. Here you go, ma'am." He handed her a little bundle of bark in a leather pouch.

"I don't quite know how to thank you. You can't know what this means to me," she said softly.

The thought of receiving relief from the agony she suffered two or three times a month was almost overwhelming. There were tears in her eyes, which made her feel a little silly.

He shuffled in embarrassment. "Shucks, ma'am, it's nothing. My aunt, she give 'em to me. I can get more if you need 'em later. Hell, them trees grow right there in Arizona."

A tear slipped out of Maggie's eye, and then she really felt silly. "It's not nothing to me, Mr. Blue Gully."

"Well, ma'am, if you take good care of Jubal for me, I'll make sure you have all the bark you need for the rest of your life."

"Oh, I'll take care of him. Can't do anything else. After all, he's in my bed."

Maggie gave him a little smile after her small show of levity. Dan only looked puzzled.

"Well, guess I'll be off now, ma'am. I'll be back soon."

Although Maggie wondered what "soon" was, she didn't ask. Instead, she turned to Ozzie, who still clutched the edge of the kitchen table with quivering fingers.

"Go on and chop some wood, Ozzie. You haven't chopped wood for days, and we're almost out. What do I pay you for, anyway?"

Ozzie started to protest, but when he glanced up to see the squat but intimidating form of Dan Blue Gully standing next to Maggie, his words died unspoken.

"Yes'm," was all he said as he scrambled to his feet.

"I'll call you in when breakfast is ready!" she hollered after him.

"Yes'm," he said again.

"You stay for breakfast, Mr. Blue Gully. With so much going on here, food's real late in getting prepared this morning."

"I better not, ma'am. Got to catch French Jack's trail, if it's not too late already."

"Afraid he'll get away?"

"No, it ain't that, ma'am. French Jack ain't goin' nowhere until either me and Jubal's dead or he is. I just want to know where he is so he can't sneak up on us."

Maggie looked a little sick. "Oh," she whispered.

She glanced toward the bedroom and decided she didn't particularly want French Jack to sneak up on Jubal Green right now either, since he was lying unconscious in her bedroom and the only way to him was through her.

"That's a good idea," she added, in a strangled voice.

Dan Blue Gully touched her arm. "Don't worry, ma'am. I won't let him hurt you or your little girl."

Maggie looked up at him with worried eyes. "Thank you," she said, but there was uncertainty in the words.

Dan shook his head at her a little sadly and seemed to take note of her exhausted eyes, rimmed with purple circles, set in a face with cheeks sunken from not enough food, too much work, and too little sleep.

"You need some rest, ma'am," he stated.

Maggie sighed and turned toward her stove. "I guess so."

Dan shook his head again and took his leave.

Sadie quickly agreed to keep Annie at her house for a couple of days, since it looked as though Maggie was going to be occupied as a full-time nurse for a while. Maggie felt a little disappointed when her little girl happily toddled out of the door, holding Sadie's hand.

"Go wi' Say," Annie announced with a big smile.

"Well, you don't have to look so danged happy about it," her mama told her with feigned sternness.

In truth, she hated like the devil to see her baby go away, even for a couple of days. Annie was all Maggie had in the world, and she couldn't bear to be parted from her.

"She'll be just fine, Maggie. You know she loves to play with the twins." Sadie and her husband, Pig, had two little boys just six months older than Annie.

"I know," said Maggie, and that didn't make her feel very good either.

Annie would probably be better off if Sadie kept her forever, she thought grumpily to herself. At least the Phillipses had a profitable pig farm and each other. All Annie had was Maggie.

She sighed when she bade Sadie and Annie goodbye at the door. Then she realized she hadn't heard the steady *chop-chop-chop* from the rear of the house for a while and stepped around back to see what Ozzie was up to.

He was up to a nap, as usual. Maggie's nerves finally snapped. She picked up a chunk of wood and hurled it at the man snoring next to the wood block. The wood hit Ozzie square in the small of his back and Maggie smiled in satisfaction.

Ozzie sat up with a bellow of rage and thunked his head on the handle of the ax, which he had embedded in the block before lying down to snooze. One hand rubbed his head while the other rubbed his back, and he looked over at Maggie with a terribly hurt expression on his wrinkled face.

"Either you finish chopping that wood by four o'clock this afternoon, Ozzie Plumb, or you get the hell off of my place," Maggie shouted. "For God's sake, Ozzie, I need you now more than ever. I got me a gunshot man to tend in the house. I can't always be after you to do the work I pay you to do. And don't forget, you miserable son of a sow, I still have your damned guitar."

She whirled around to stomp back to the house before Ozzie could do more than flap his mouth.

Ozzie wasn't a quick thinker even when he was awake, or he might have mentioned the fact that Maggie didn't own a clock. Instead, he glared at Maggie's back for several seconds, all the emotions common to weak men crossing his face, from anger, to a craving for revenge, to perplexity. Finally he hauled himself up and resumed chopping wood.

The aroma of fresh-cut pine followed Maggie to the house. It was one she liked a lot, and it mingled nicely with the fragrant woodsmoke that billowed from the chimney. She paused at the door to look around, and the scene that met her eyes was one of deceptive peace and beauty. In fact, Maggie thought, if she weren't so blamed exhausted, she might even enjoy it.

Even now, during the tail end of a hard winter, the woods were beautiful. Piñon and mesquite lined the clearing in which Kenny had built their home, and the front of the house afforded Maggie a grand view of the field where he had grown corn. Maggie couldn't plant corn alone, so it would soon revert to meadowland.

A little branch of the Hondo River ran beside the house, making water easy to come by—the only thing easy to come by around here. The stream was so insignificant that nobody had bothered to name it yet, but Maggie always thought of it as Bright's Creek. She thought of Kenny every time she fetched water. Building the house near the stream was most likely the smartest thing Kenny had ever done.

The house itself could more appropriately be termed a cabin, since it was put together out of thick rough-hewn logs, but Kenny had called it a house, and that was all right with Maggie. It had a kitchen, a bedroom, and a small parlor, and if that wasn't a house, Maggie didn't much care. It was hers and she loved it, in spite of the hardships she faced to keep it.

There was a screened-in back porch where they could keep milk cold in the winter, and a dugout that could be accessed from the porch. She stored her fresh and preserved vegetables in barrels in the dugout. Kenny had built shelves on the porch, and Maggie still had jars and jars of preserved fruits, vegetables, pickles, and jams from her garden's reapings during the summer and autumn, in spite of winter being almost over.

Maggie was a good gardener and a good preserver. In her underground storeroom there were even a couple of pumpkins and several squash, half a barrel of potatoes, three strings of onions, an almost-full string of garlic, and two strings of chili peppers still waiting to be used.

She was proud of her food stores. Of course, the fact that she had only herself and Ozzie and little Annie to feed made life easier in that regard. She would have given up any amount of her well-stocked larder to have Kenny back, though. She missed him. Life was sure easier with a good man around to do some of the work. Ozzie didn't count.

When she got back inside the house, she sat at the kitchen table, put her face in her hands, and closed her eyes. She was so tired. She vaguely heard the sound of chopping, as Ozzie resumed his labors, before her eyes closed, her elbows folded up, and she fell asleep at the table.

Maggie hadn't been asleep very long before a low moaning sound began sliding around in her muddy brain and dimly penetrated her exhaustion. Consciousness was a long time in coming, though. When her eyelids finally creaked open, they felt as though they did so through a layer of thick gum.

At last a deep, miserable groan and a hoarse cry sent Maggie shooting out of her chair so fast it fell over with a loud crash.

"Oh, my God!" she cried, running over to the bedroom door. "Oh, my God," she said again, her heart slamming against her ribs like hail during a storm.

Jubal Green was bright red and thrashing back and forth on her bed. His fever had come upon him with a vengeance.

Maggie put her hands to her cheeks and just watched him for several seconds, her mind not yet having caught up with her body. When it did, she realized she couldn't have slept much because she still heard Ozzie chopping wood. To the best of her knowledge, Ozzie never worked more than fifteen or twenty minutes at a stretch.

"Oh, God, I wish I was stronger," Maggie said. "Please, God, make me strong for this poor man."

She remembered Dan Blue Gully's instructions and quickly tore the quilts from Jubal Green's body. Kenny's nightshirt was soaking wet with sweat. Maggie dashed to the kitchen and pumped some fresh cold water and took it back into the bedroom.

"Oh, Lord, Mr. Green, don't die on me. Please don't die," Maggie whispered to the unconscious man.

She felt his forehead before she sponged him off. He was hot as a firecracker.

"Oh, Lord." It was a short prayer that time.

Maggie bathed Jubal's head in cool water, dried him, and struggled to get Kenny's soaking nightshirt off. She couldn't keep herself from eyeing his body as he lay on her bed, shimmering in sweat. He was something to look at, all right. Quickly, she drew a fresh sheet over him.

"No quilts while you're sweating," Maggie said, trying to concentrate on her nursemaiding. "That's what Mr. Blue Gully said."

By this time, Dan Blue Gully had assumed the position of a god of medicine in Maggie's worried mind. She needed something to believe in or she was afraid she'd lose Jubal Green and herself, too. In spite of the food stores, it had been a hard winter, and she was nearly at the end of her strength.

Jubal Green seemed to calm down some under her tender ministrations. He stopped thrashing, at least.

"All right, Mr. Green," Maggie said when he lay still. She stroked his forehead. "I'm going to get you some of that bark tea. Don't you move, now." Even though she knew the poor man couldn't hear her, she spoke to him firmly.

She got a cupful of bark tea and a spoon and took them back into the bedroom, knelt beside the bed, and lifted Jubal's head. It was heavier than she had expected. Very carefully, she spooned a little of the tea into his slack mouth. It dribbled out. Maggie almost cried.

"Oh, please, Mr. Green. Please help me here."

She tried again. The tea dribbled out again. This time Maggie did cry.

"Damn it," she said. She set his head back down and wiped her eyes with the back of her hand.

She stared at him and cursed again with frustration. He was such a handsome man. His sun-streaked thick wavy hair ruffled over his forehead and looked pretty against her pillow. He just lay there, eyes closed, sick as a dog, and he wouldn't drink his tea. Flat on his damned back.

That gave Maggie an idea. She lifted his head again so that his mouth dropped open. Quick as she could, she shoveled in a spoonful of bark tea and laid his head back down.

Jubal gagged a little, then swallowed, and Maggie very nearly laughed out loud. She continued to spoon tea between his lips. It was awkward, and Maggie guessed that if she were a clever person she could have figured out an easier way to get the tea in him, but it worked, so she did it anyway.

As she fed him, she recalled the cry that had ultimately awakened her from her nap at the kitchen table. Maggie could have sworn that Jubal Green had cried out the name "Sara."

"Now I wonder who Sara is to you, Mr. Jubal Green," Maggie said, to keep herself company. "Is she a sweetheart? Mr. Blue Gully says you don't have a wife."

She considered the man whose head she cradled in her arms. His deep fevered flush had tamed down some and left him more nearly his normal complexion. At least Maggie assumed it was closer to his normal complexion. When she had first laid eyes on him, he'd been pale as death. Of course, Maggie's own senses had then been swimming in a wash of agony, so she couldn't be sure of anything.

Now as she watched him, she saw a face that was lean and tanned under its stubbly beard. "You're sure good-lookin' enough to have yourself a sweetheart."

There were little white lines around his eyes, the kind that come from creases that don't get tanned when a person's in the sun a lot. Maggie had most often seen those creases on the faces of people who smiled a lot, and she hoped Jubal Green was one of those smilers.

"Although I don't suppose it will matter in the long run what kind of man you are. When you're well again, you'll up and go away and that will be that." She didn't know exactly why the realization saddened her.

She supposed she was just a bit tired. After all, because of her headache, she hadn't slept at all for thirty hours.

She continued to spoon bark tea into Jubal Green's mouth until the cup was empty. That was probably enough for now. She felt his forehead again, realized his fever had gone down a lot, and chalked up another score for Dan Blue Gully. The Indian really knew his medicine.

Then she stood up, put her hands on her hips, and stretched out her aching back. Stabbing pains radiated from her spine. She groaned. She'd been bent over and tensed up for a long time.

"I guess I'd better make up some rich soup for when you're well enough to take nourishment, Mr. Jubal Green," she told the sleeping man.

She reached down and felt his naked arms. They were a little cool, so she put a quilt back over him. His biceps were also hard as rocks, Maggie realized, as she tarried a bit to stroke them lightly.

She decided not to bother with another of Kenny's nightshirts for a while. Not only was it a pain to put on the sleeping man by herself but she found she rather enjoyed looking at him this way. He was quite something.

Maggie blushed when she realized she was staring at Jubal Green's hairy chest. She couldn't quite get her eyes to drift any lower than that, and anyway she had kept the sheet on him from the waist down. She wasn't altogether sure she wanted to see that bulge again. Still, she had to admit he was very well favored in that department.

"Don't want you to catch a chill," she told him as she carefully smoothed the quilt up over his shoulders.

Maggie realized the sound of chopping could no longer be heard from out back and sighed heavily. That meant she'd have to go out back and bully Ozzie Plumb some more, she reckoned. Much to her disgust, she was getting right good at bullying that man.

She smoothed her hair and rubbed the back of her neck, got herself a drink of water from the pump, and stepped outside. She walked around to the back of the house, then stopped in horror. Ozzie Plumb was draped over the woodpile, dead, a shotgun blast having ripped his back open.

3

Maggie didn't even remember getting herself back into the house. She only remembered staring at that gigantic bloody hole in Ozzie's back, sucking in a shuddering breath, turning on her heel, and running hell for leather in the other direction. She paused inside the door with her back pressed against it and sobbed in fright.

With shaking hands, she slammed the bolt down.

"Great God!" she gasped. "O God, please help us!"

She managed to make it to the kitchen table before her knees gave out and she collapsed.

"O, Lord, please tell me what to do now. How could I have missed hearing the sound of a gun?" she asked herself in her frenzy. "I was probably so blamed busy with Jubal Green that I wouldn't have heard a train if it hit the house. What on earth am I supposed to do now?"

She had absolutely no idea. She was afraid to go

out there and try to wrestle poor Ozzie's body somewhere, even if she knew where to wrestle it. When
Kenny had died, the whole community had more or
less expected it, and they had already made arrangements. But this time, nobody except Maggie knew
Ozzie was dead.

Well, he would probably freeze overnight, she rea-
soned. That ought to keep him. She didn't know what
she'd do after that. She'd just have to think about it
later.

"I'm sorry, God," she said aloud. "I'm sorry I yelled
at him so much."

And there wasn't only Ozzie's lifeless corpse to
consider, there was the strange man who was possibly
dying on her bed. She couldn't very well leave him
and go fetch help.

"I mean, it wasn't even Ozzie they were after," she
whispered into the warm kitchen air. "They just killed
him out of spite. It's Jubal Green, the man on my bed,
the man who can't move, who isn't even conscious,
that they really want. If I leave the house again, they're
liable to shoot me, and then sure as check they'll kill
him too. Oh, God. I wish Mr. Blue Gully was here."

The only bright spot in this whole terrible scenario,
as far as Maggie was concerned, was that Annie had
gone with Sadie. Then she sat bolt upright in terror.

"O God, please let Annie be safe!"

The awful possibility that Sadie and Annie might
have been ambushed before they got back to Sadie's
place crossed her mind. She tried to dismiss it with
the sensible notion that Sadie and Annie had left
hours and hours ago, a long time before Ozzie had
been shot.

But then the fear overtook her again. "French Jack

could have got them first and then come back here for Ozzie," she mumbled.

Maggie told herself she'd better get a firm grip or she and Jubal Green would both be in deep trouble. Then she decided she'd better take a detailed survey of her home to determine just how secure it was and what she could do to make sure French Jack couldn't get inside. The back porch was a worry, since it was only screened in.

Very carefully, she made her way to the window and peered out. She could see nothing except what was supposed to be there: earth and trees and the meadow beyond. Daylight was barely holding on to the edges of the woods, giving the piñon branches a deep golden overlay to their dark green needles. Maggie figured it must be about four o'clock.

"The time I told Ozzie to have the wood chopped by." She had to dab at her moist eyes. "Stop it," she commanded herself. She mustn't allow herself to get weepy again. Her life and that of Jubal Green might depend on her keeping her emotions in check. I wish to God I could see, she thought.

In truth, Maggie's eyesight was not the best. That fact bothered her often. Kenny had gone all moony about her blue eyes—back in the days when they really were pretty, before she got so dragged down. He told her over and over again how beautiful he thought her eyes were. But Maggie always figured she'd rather have eyes she could see out of than eyes that were good to look at.

Kenny's Spencer rifle lay on a rack over the fireplace in the parlor, and Maggie carefully removed and loaded it. She made it a habit to clean the rifle once a week, just as Kenny had taught her to do, whether she used it or not, just to keep her education up to date. Kenny had taught her to shoot the gun, too. She wasn't much of a shot, but she didn't figure French Jack had to know that.

"Let him find out for himself," she told the rifle, giving it a little pat for luck.

It made her feel better to realize she wasn't completely helpless.

She remembered Jubal Green's guns, then, and tiptoed into the bedroom. The rifle he had knocked against her door was lying across a chest against the wall, and Dan Blue Gully had put a Colt revolver there as well, its leather holster neatly folded. A pouch next to the weapons contained extra ammunition, and Maggie suspected there was more in Mr. Green's saddlebags, which were stacked next to the wall.

His pocket watch and chain also lay on the chest, in a tidy little coil. Maggie thought sadly that she actually would have been able to berate Ozzie for not finishing chopping the wood on time, after all, but she didn't allow herself to dwell on that unhappy thought.

She gathered the weapons and ammunition together and took them into the kitchen. There she fetched Kenny's gun-cleaning box out of the cabinet and carefully cleaned each gun and loaded it.

Then, holding Mr. Green's Colt revolver in her sweaty hand, she took a deep breath, backed herself against the kitchen wall, and edged over to the door to the screened porch. She devoutly wished the door had a window so she could peek through it to see if someone lurked on the porch. Carefully she unlatched the door and peered through it. No shots rang out, so she braced herself for her foraging expedition.

Maggie had already made a mental inventory of her

needs, which she repeated over and over to herself in order not to forget anything. Her plan was to be as efficient as she could possibly be when she braved the porch. She didn't fancy being shot lingering over the potato barrel.

She waited until she judged the light to be low enough to provide protection without concealing anything that might be hunkered down outside. Then she pushed the door open, propped it with a book so it wouldn't slam shut and cause her to have to fumble with it on her way back in, and dashed onto the porch and into the dugout. In less time than it usually took her to sneeze, she had gathered everything she figured she would need for the night and raced back into the kitchen.

Her arms were piled full, and a couple of onions and a turnip fell and bounced across the floor, but she had done it. She offered up a tiny little prayer of thanks as she dropped the rest of her armload onto the table and relocked the door.

Working very quickly, she peeled and chopped an onion, threw it into a pot of water with a couple of chopped carrots, a chopped potato, and a meaty beef bone, and set the pot on the stove to cook up into a healing soup for Jubal Green.

Then she stepped into the bedroom to check on her patient. He was burning up once more.

"Oh, dear Lord, Mr. Green, how am I supposed to tend to your soup if I have to be sponging you off all the time?"

She removed the quilt from him yet again and realized she needed another sheet; the one that covered him was sopping wet. She wasn't about to tend him while his privates were exposed, so with a weary sigh she threw the wet sheet into a corner, fetched a clean one, covered him from his waist down, and began the sponging and drying ritual once more.

After she had blotted him dry, she went to the kitchen to dish him up another cupful of bark broth. This time, he seemed to be able to swallow it without her having to raise and lower his head for each spoonful. Maggie took that as a good sign.

Over the course of the next few hours, however, his fever showed no sign of abating.

"I guess fevers are always worse at night," Maggie murmured to herself and the wall as she bathed his head with cool water once again and tried to stop him from thrashing about. She was having to physically restrain the man from chasing the demons his fever-induced hallucinations had brought on. "Lord in heaven, I hope French Jack doesn't decide to attack us now."

Eventually the fever was replaced by chills, and she had to pile quilts on a shivering Jubal Green, whose teeth were now chattering loud enough to wake Ozzie Plumb from the dead. Maggie had stopped even trying to keep the tears from trickling down her cheeks.

"Lordy, Mr. Green, if you can just lie there and not die until I can get back from the kitchen, maybe I can get some hot broth down you. That might warm you up some."

Maggie didn't stop to consider if she should try to do anything for herself. Her limbs were aching and stiff from exhaustion, and her eyes felt as though they had been glued into their sockets and then had sand thrown into them. She knew she had to eat something or collapse, so she drank a cup of the same broth she brought to Jubal Green and grabbed a hunk of stale bread to chew on her way back into the bedroom.

She was so exhausted and sore that she didn't even notice the tears still leaking from her eyes. It was almost as though she had stopped feeling anything. She didn't have time to listen to her body. She just kept lifting the spoon to Jubal Green's mouth. Every swallow was a victory, every dribble a defeat.

An hour and a half later, Jubal Green's soul began a slow, slogging climb through a painful, mysterious black morass into semiconsciousness. For some time he had been dimly aware of a struggle going on around him and in which he was involved, but only from a great distance. That struggle somehow seemed not to involve him directly but was being waged valiantly around him and on his behalf. Sorting it all out was too confusing, so he decided not to bother.

When his eyes slowly cracked open, he saw nothing that was familiar to him. He was also in excruciating pain.

The thought that he might be dead flitted vaguely through his mind, only to be immediately rejected. *Too much pain. If you're dead, you don't hurt.*

Then he frowned and wondered how he knew that. After all, he'd never been dead before. And to the best of his knowledge, no other living soul possessed any first-hand knowledge about whether or not pain persisted after life ended. Jubal Green only knew for sure that there was an inordinate amount of pain during life itself. If he was still alive.

His thoughts began spinning around and making him dizzy, so he stopped thinking. He concentrated instead on seeing.

When his eyes had had a chance to focus in the

dimly lit room, he found he was too weak to lift his head or even turn it to check out his surroundings. Instead, he took a painful survey of the length of his body, which seemed to stretch out forever in front of him.

He was surprised to find that he was naked and had a bandage wrapped around his chest. He couldn't see too much of that particular bandage because it was so close to his chin, and he didn't have enough strength to raise his head. There was more white linen encircling his thigh.

The entire right side of his upper body hurt like fire, and the whole left side of his lower body felt as though somebody had beaten him with a steel mallet. The rest of him didn't feel too good either. He couldn't have moved even if he'd been in the mood to, which he wasn't. He felt remarkably lazy. Jubal Green had never felt lazy before to the best of his recollection, and he hoped it wouldn't become a habit. He was used to getting things done. Jubal scorned lazy people.

What had he been doing before he woke up in this strange place?

Slowly he became aware that there was a head resting on his belly. He frowned. That didn't seem right, somehow.

He squinted down what seemed like miles and miles of his own naked flesh to concentrate on the tousled honey-blond head that lay there. The head was actually butting up against his waist, in the little crook where it joined his hip. Jubal Green didn't think that was quite proper and he wondered if he'd been sporting with a whore before he went to sleep. He couldn't quite remember, but it did seem out of character.

He had a foggy recollection that he and somebody—

oh, yes, it was Dan Blue Gully—had been doing something important. Jubal Green never sported with whores when he and Dan Blue Gully were doing important things. They were always very single-minded when they were working.

Still, he couldn't account for that head.

Maybe I am dead, he thought. Maybe that's an angel.

That didn't make sense either, and his frown deepened.

Just then Maggie gave a deep sigh in her sleep and turned over. She had been holding Jubal Green's legs down because he was thrashing so hard she was afraid he'd reopen his thigh wound and bleed to death. When his struggles had gradually ceased, her exhaustion overcame her and her eyes had just shut as she sat there, her arms still draped over Jubal's right leg, and her head lying practically in his crotch. By that point she hadn't even noticed the impropriety of her position.

When he saw Maggie's face, Jubal immediately rejected his angel theory. Angels didn't have tangled hair, huge dark rings around their eyes, smears of blood and sweat on their faces. They didn't look as though they had been dragged, kicking and screaming, through the fires of hell.

Maybe this is hell, he thought. That would certainly account for the pain.

He tried to concentrate on Maggie's face.

Can't be hell, he decided.

Because that face was a good one, even if it was dirty and tired-looking. And, while he wasn't at all sure about himself, he didn't figure a face that good would have landed in hell.

His right hand, the hand attached to the shoulder

that was presently consumed by a raging inferno, was resting near that good face, and Jubal found the strength somewhere to lift the hand and place a finger on its soft cheek. He gently stroked the cheek twice. That activity took every single remaining ounce of his energy. Then Jubal Green's illness overcame him, his hand fell, and he slept once more.

It was the sound of gunfire that woke Maggie up. She jolted awake and up onto her feet in one motion that was so sudden she nearly blacked out and toppled over onto her patient. She managed to keep upright by clinging desperately to the table beside the bed. Then she was horrified at what might have happened had she actually fallen onto the invalid. It didn't bear thinking of.

"Oh, my God, I'm sorry, Mr. Green," she whispered.

When she could move without falling down, she dashed into the kitchen to try and figure out where the gunshots were coming from and where they were being aimed. She picked up Kenny's Spencer rifle just in time to hear a bullet slam into the side of her house and briefly thanked God that Kenny had built the house out of thick piñon logs.

Then she got furious. How dare those men shoot at her house! She didn't have anything to do with their problems. She was just trying to keep one of them alive.

Maggie couldn't remember ever feeling such a combination of rage and indignation before in her life. She crept over to the kitchen window, raised it slightly, and peeked outside, making sure she didn't give anyone who was out there enough of a target to aim at.

Daylight was just beginning to come over the forest. The trees still looked black, but their pointy tops could just be perceived, outlined against the gray sky. Maggie strained to pick out men among the trees and then gave up the effort in disgust.

"My eyes are so blamed bad, I couldn't see anybody in those stupid trees in broad daylight," she grumbled to herself.

She saw the flash of light just before the sound of the shot reached her, and a split second after the sound of the shot came the *thunk* of another bullet in the side of the house. Maggie smiled a nasty smile.

"You son of a bitch," she said to her unknown adversary, and she aimed as well as she knew how and pulled the trigger.

The rifle's recoil nearly knocked her across the kitchen floor, and the sound almost deafened her. That startling result of her effort at self-defense, however, was not enough to block out the satisfying cry of pain that wailed across the clearing from the woods. She grinned triumphantly.

Then another flurry of shots assailed her ears, followed shortly thereafter by the thundering of hooves. She was shaking with terror when she heard Dan Blue Gully call out to her.

"Mrs. Bright! Mrs. Bright!"

She peeked out of the front window to see Dan Blue Gully on a big sorrel horse sliding to a stop across the bare winter yard in a spray of dust and pebbles. Dan Blue Gully was off the horse and running toward the house before the horse had finished skidding. Another horse and rider were following fast on his heels, and Maggie hoped that person was a friend too and not an enemy.

Whoever the second rider was, Maggie was overjoyed to see Dan Blue Gully again. She had the door open by the time he reached it.

"Are you all right?" He grabbed her by the shoulders in a grip that Maggie knew would leave bruises. She scrunched up her face in pain, and he eased his hold. "Sorry, Mrs. Bright. Are you all right?"

"I'm all right, Mr. Blue Gully. And I'm so happy to see you, I can hardly see straight."

Maggie almost giggled when she realized she could hardly see straight even before he showed up.

"I'm real, real sorry, Mrs. Bright. French Jack got by us when we doubled back. I thought for sure you was dead when we rode up and heard the shots. Who was it shot his partner?"

Dan knew better than to expect Jubal Green was well enough to defend the little cabin, but he couldn't imagine anybody else shooting that well.

"Me," said Maggie proudly.

"You?"

"Yes." Maggie's face, through the grime and exhaustion, was beginning to reflect the tiniest bit of offended pride. "Kenny taught me how to shoot, Mr. Blue Gully. I'm not much good because I can't see worth a darn, but—well, I guess I got lucky."

Dan just shook his head as he peered down at her. She looked as though it had been a rough night.

"I think that shot was more than luck, Mrs. Bright. You got him right in the butt. He won't be able to ride for a month."

The Indian grinned and Maggie blushed.

"I'm real sorry I left you, ma'am," he said.

"Well, I guess I'm all right. I don't know about your friend, though." A sudden fear for Jubal Green almost swamped her. She hoped Dan wouldn't be angry or upset with her. She'd done the best she could.

"Well, let's take a look."

They both walked toward the bedroom, Maggie trailing a little behind Dan, worry making her footsteps drag.

Dan stared incredulously. Jubal Green looked almost good. He even had a little color in his cheeks. "My God, ma'am, what did you do to him?" he asked in amazement.

"Oh, dear," Maggie whispered. "I tried to do what you told me. I had to change the thigh bandage one extra time because he flung his leg around so bad it began to bleed again. I sponged him off a lot and poured bark tea down him, and soup, and—oh, God, Mr. Blue Gully, I'm sorry."

She was too tired to stop the tears of remorse that slid down her cheeks. She was sure she had killed Jubal Green with her poor nursing.

Dan frowned at her. "You're *sorry?*"

Maggie nodded. "Is he dead?" she whispered.

"Dead?" Dan stared at Maggie in amazement. "Ma'am, I didn't expect him to look this good for a week or more. I don't know what you did, but I swear you must be magic. He looks wonderful."

Maggie blinked several times, certain she had misunderstood.

"I did all right?" The words stumbled out of her mouth so softly that Dan had to strain to hear them.

"You did more than all right, ma'am. You did—you did superior," he said. He wasn't used to talking to women and didn't quite know how to go about it.

Maggie looked up at him with astonishment evident in her big tired eyes. "Thank you," she murmured.

"Thank *you*, ma'am," said Dan Blue Gully.

He took in Maggie's ragged appearance. The poor woman needed rest, that was obvious.

"Ma'am, you got French Jack to back off for a while. Now I'm going to take over nursemaiding Jubal, here, and I want you to clean up and rest. All right?"

Maggie stared at Dan numbly and nodded. She didn't trust herself to speak. Nobody had ever said she had done anything superior before in her life. That made her want to cry even more than thinking she had killed Jubal Green did.

All at once a terrible fear shot through Maggie's heart. She had clean forgotten about Annie. She must be a terrible mother to have forgotten her own daughter, she thought, guilt almost swamping her terror for Annie's safety.

"Mr. Blue Gully, I'm worried about Annie," she blurted out in a rush.

"Annie, ma'am?"

He peered down at her in confusion. Then he remembered. "Oh, your daughter."

Maggie's head bobbed up and down; she didn't dare speak for fear her voice would crack. She wasn't sure how much more she would be able to take without falling down in hysterics.

"I saw your daughter last night, ma'am. She and that shrieker lady were walking into a cabin a mile or so down the road to Lincoln. She looked right happy."

Maggie's knees nearly buckled with relief. "Thank God," she whispered. "I was afraid French Jack got them."

Suddenly, another man burst into the house, and Maggie whirled around with a tiny shriek.

"They's a dead body on the woodpile," the new man said.

Maggie stared at him in fright for only a second before she realized he must be the one who had ridden up behind Dan Blue Gully.

"A dead body?" Dan looked at Maggie, a question in his eyes.

"Ozzie," whispered Maggie. "French Jack shot him last night, I guess. I don't know who else would have done it."

"It's been a bad time for you, ma'am, ain't it?" Dan Blue Gully asked softly.

Maggie could only nod. It had been real bad.

"I'm sorry we brung bad times on you," he added.

Maggie just looked at him. She was too tired to form a coherent response. Besides, it was true. They *had* brought bad times.

Dan took her gently by the arm and led her to a kitchen chair. "You sit right there, ma'am. Me and Four Toes will take care of everything."

"Four Toes?" she repeated in a tiny voice.

"Oh, right," said Dan Blue Gully. "This here's Four Toes Smith."

He gestured toward the second man. Maggie could now see that the tall newcomer was another Indian, but she was too tired to ask what tribe he originated from. She hoped that wasn't impolite.

Four Toes Smith nodded at Maggie and touched his hat, which was a greasy floppy-brimmed model with a pheasant feather sticking out of the beaded ribbon that encircled it.

Maggie nodded back and sat down, and Dan looked around the kitchen for a minute, then slopped up a big bowl of Maggie's soup. He figured out where the bread was kept and hacked her off a big piece.

Then he set the food before her. "Here, ma'am, you eat this. You need to eat something."

Maggie did indeed look as though a strong wind might carry her off.

Dan Blue Gully and Four Toes Smith conferred for a few minutes; then Four Toes headed out onto the back porch.

"He's going to fix you a bath in that tub on the porch, ma'am. That will make you feel better."

Maggie was eating. She hadn't realized how ravenous she was until she'd had a chance to sit down and think about something other than keeping Jubal Green and herself alive. She couldn't remember ever being so hungry. She was so busy shoveling soup and bread into her mouth she didn't ask the first question that flashed through her mind at Dan's words, which was where she was supposed to bathe with her house full of strange men. It was, after all, still winter, so the porch would be too blamed cold.

It turned out she didn't need to worry. Four Toes Smith rigged a curtain out of two bedroll blankets in a warm corner of the kitchen. Then he carried in the heavy tub as though it weighed a mere pound or two and set it down behind the screen.

Maggie and Kenny used to have to struggle to get that tub into the kitchen. During the summer, Maggie would bathe on the porch because it was easier. It was too cold for that during the winter, though, so she usually only gave herself thorough sponge baths. A tub bath would be a rare and welcome pleasure.

"Thank you very much," she murmured. Four Toes began to heat water on the stove and Maggie's cup overflowed. She'd never had anybody heat bathwater for her. She was infinitely grateful to be spared the backbreaking work of filling the tub.

Before she took her bath, she tiptoed into the bedroom to fetch clean clothes and check up on Jubal Green. Dan Blue Gully was sitting next to the bed, staring at his friend's face.

"How's he doing?" Maggie whispered.

Dan Blue Gully shook his head slowly, as though he couldn't quite believe what he was about to say.

Maggie immediately feared for the worst.

"He's doing good, ma'am. It's because of your fine care, and I thank you. I don't know what I'd do without Jubal Green. Him and me has been partners for-damned-near-ever." He looked up quickly and amended his words. "I mean we've been together a long time, ma'am. I didn't mean to swear."

Maggie was so relieved she actually smiled. "It's all right, Mr. Blue Gully. I understand. I'm just glad I could help." She didn't bother to tell him that she herself had taken to swearing like a drunken cowboy during the last few months.

Maggie took her clean clothes behind the screen with her. When she sank into the tub, she thought this must be pure bliss, to be able to bathe in her own warm kitchen and not have to think about anything at all for a while. Soon she fell asleep in the tub.

4

While Maggie dozed in her bath, Jubal Green came fully conscious for the first time since French Jack's bullets had knocked him senseless.

Dan Blue Gully still sat at his side. He was staring at Jubal's face with a frown, and that was the first thing Jubal saw when, with a monumental effort, he forced his heavy-as-lead eyelids up over his bloodshot eyes.

"Jesus Christ," Jubal whispered when he saw the Indian's ferocious scowl. "Whatever it is, I didn't mean it."

Jubal had a faint, misty memory of waking up once before and finding an angel in his bed. No, he corrected himself. It hadn't been an angel. It had been a—what? A whore? No. And not a devil. He decided that particular memory was buried too deep and would require entirely too much energy to dredge back up to investigate, so he quit trying.

He had no trouble at all in recognizing Dan Blue Gully, who gave an enormous start at his friend's words.

"You're awake," Dan said, emotion making his voice bland and toneless. Strong feelings always did that to Dan Blue Gully, which was one of the reasons nobody in the world except Jubal Green ever knew what he was thinking.

"What happened?" Jubal asked, though he was almost afraid to find out. Whenever Dan sounded like that, Jubal knew that whatever happened was really, really bad.

"French Jack shot you."

Jubal frowned so hard at his friend's words that his head began to ache, so he stopped frowning and merely glared.

"No, he didn't," he said at last.

"Yes, he did."

"Hell." Jubal sounded disgruntled. "I never let myself get shot before."

"Weren't your fault."

"Like hell."

Jubal Green didn't believe in chance accidents or luck, good or bad. He knew he must have done something stupid to let French Jack shoot him. After all, now that he thought about it, he remembered it was French Jack that he and Dan were after. He was supposed to have shot French Jack, not the other way around.

"They must've got another man to ride with 'em, because we followed their trail and two of 'em doubled back, but French Jack, he fooled us both and shot you."

"Hell," Jubal said again.

"I chased the decoys, and when I figgered out what they'd done I went back for you, but he'd already got you so I shot one of 'em and followed your blood trail here."

Jubal didn't react to Dan's gruesome revelation but looked around the room in which he lay. He was certain he had never seen it before.

"Where am I?"

"Little cabin in the woods near Lincoln. It's Mrs. Bright's farm."

"Mrs. Bright?" Jubal didn't recollect knowing a Mrs. Bright. He looked at Dan with a big question in his eyes.

"Mrs. Bright. She took you in and saved your life," said Dan.

Another frown greeted those words. Jubal couldn't recall ever meeting anyone by the name of Bright.

"Who's Mrs. Bright?"

"Widow lady. Lives here with her daughter. We're about ten miles outside of Lincoln. French Jack's still around, though. He shot her hired man. So she up and shot *his* hired man." Dan Blue Gully grinned at the recollection.

"She shot him?"

"Right in the ass." Dan actually chuckled.

Jubal's expression settled into a frown of pained concentration. He was troubled by flittery, shimmery images of a rumpled angel with stringy blond hair and a kind, tired face. Was the person attached to those foggy mental pictures the one who shot French Jack's colleague? It didn't seem likely. He would have shaken his head in an effort to clear it of those strange memories, but everything hurt too much to shake.

"I hurt like hell," he told Dan.

"I bet you do," said Dan with another grin. "You got shot all to blazes."

That wasn't exactly what Jubal wanted to hear. He gave his friend a murderous scowl. Then he remembered Dan's earlier comment.

"You say this Mrs. Bright saved my life?"

Jubal Green had never known a woman who was good for more than one thing, and a man only wanted that one thing every now and again. Well, a man might want it more often than that, but he only needed it every now and again.

But Dan Blue Gully was firm on that point.

"She saved your life," he said, and Jubal knew he meant it.

"Hmm," he muttered. "I'll have to thank her, I guess." It didn't sound as though he relished the prospect.

"You better," said Dan. "She worked herself damned near to death for you, you ungrateful son of a bitch." The words were said mildly and were laced with a liberal dose of fondness.

Jubal looked up at him curiously. Dan Blue Gully sounded suspiciously as though he actually respected this Mrs. Bright, and that was a reaction Jubal would have found astonishing if he'd had the strength. Neither Jubal Green nor Dan Blue Gully had discovered very many people who were worth respecting in the course of their lives, and thus far those few people included no women. And he wasn't forgetting his mother, either.

"What's she like?" he asked.

Dan thought hard about Jubal's question. All that heavy thinking required him to stare at the wall across from Jubal's bed for a good two or three minutes, until Jubal was so frustrated he would have hollered at him if he'd had the energy.

"Well?" he finally demanded. He chalked his short temper up to his having been badly wounded. Generally speaking, he was possessed of an abundance of patience.

"She's got a big spirit. Her spirit's stronger than her body," he said at last. That was all.

Jubal glared at Dan for a few moments, until he realized his friend didn't have anything more to add. He sighed heavily. "Hell, Danny, you're talking like a goddamned Indian again," he said, with the barest hint of a grin.

Dan looked down at Jubal with relief. Any lingering doubts about his friend's health and possible recovery had just been banished from his mind.

"I *am* an Indian," he said.

The two men grinned at each other like a couple of idiots until Jubal Green drifted off to sleep again.

Maggie finally woke up when the bathwater got cold. She was shivering as she washed her hair, dried herself, and put on her clean clothes. It felt good to be clean again, although she was so exhausted she couldn't quite keep her balance when she pushed the makeshift screen aside and stepped into the kitchen.

Dan Blue Gully caught her before she hit the floor in a faint.

"Lordy, ma'am, you'd better get some rest," he murmured.

He carried her into the bedroom and laid her on a pallet he'd made for her against the wall. Then he went out to the kitchen and gave Four Toes Smith a few instructions, and while Maggie slept the two Indians went to work.

When Maggie woke up again, it was deep night. She yawned and stretched and then curled back up and hugged her pillow. She felt good and wondered why. It had been so long since she'd felt good she'd forgotten what it was like. She lay there for another couple of minutes before the events of the past couple of days sifted through the pleasant fog of well-being that engulfed her and reclaimed her attention. Then she sat up on her pallet with a gasp of dismay.

"Oh, my sweet Lord," she breathed.

She looked wildly around her and couldn't figure out exactly where in her house she was. The last thing she recalled was being in the bathtub. She felt her hair and discovered that it was dry.

"Oh, my land," she murmured again. "I must have been asleep for hours, and I don't know how I got here. I don't even know where 'here' is."

She knew she couldn't be in her bed because, last she remembered, somebody else was there. When her pulse stopped hammering in her ears and she had calmed down some, she took a careful survey of her surroundings.

It was nearly pitch black in the room, but a kerosene lamp, turned very, very low, squatted on the bedside table and cast its feeble light upon the bulky form sleeping in her bed. Maggie finally figured out that Dan Blue Gully must have made her a bed on the floor. She appreciated that.

"I guess I needed some rest," she commented softly to herself. She wondered how long she had been sleeping.

Very carefully, she rose from her pallet and stepped toward the bed to check on the health of the invalid she had abandoned.

A quick stab of guilt shot through her at that thought, but she tamped it down almost immediately. After all, she hadn't abandoned him until help had returned. She half expected to see the hunkered form of Dan Blue Gully sitting on the chair by the bed, but he wasn't there.

Maggie stood beside the bed, staring down at Jubal Green. He looked a little better tonight. She sighed. He was a handsome devil, all right. She hoped he made it. It would be a shame for such a handsome man to die in her bed. Or for anybody else to die there either, she amended guiltily.

It was so dark in the room and Maggie was still so fuddled with sleep that she didn't notice Jubal Green's eyes slit open and stare up at her.

It's that angel again, he thought groggily. This time she looked distinctly less scruffy. Jesus, I wonder if I really am dead.

Then he remembered Dan telling him about something bright. He couldn't remember the words, but they had something to do with a bright woman shooting French Jack in the hand. Or was it the ass? He peered at Maggie's face, which was, at that moment, catching the soft glow of the kerosene lamp rather artistically. Her burnt-honey hair was clean and shimmered in the low, flickering light. Jubal was a little puzzled.

He couldn't tell from where he lay whether Maggie looked bright or not, but she looked very peaceful to Jubal and not at all the sort of female who would want to shoot people. Still, she had to be the woman who had helped him.

Maggie was startled when she felt Jubal's hand clutch hers where it dangled at her side.

Jubal frowned at her reaction to his touch, but he decided not to take exception. He didn't have the energy, and anyway, according to Dan, he owed this woman a large portion of gratitude.

Instead of becoming surly as he usually did around women, he whispered, "Thank you, ma'am." There. That was polite of him, wasn't it?

He couldn't figure out why the blasted woman's eyes looked like they were suddenly full to overflowing. Jubal Green hated like hell when women cried at him. He scowled and dropped her hand.

"You're welcome, Mr. Green," Maggie whispered back to him.

In spite of the frown Jubal was aiming at her, she smiled down at him.

While Jubal wasn't entirely satisfied, he decided her smile was enough for now. He couldn't seem to keep his eyes open any longer anyway.

Maggie wiped her tears away as Jubal drifted back into sleep. "He's going to make it," she breathed to herself over Jubal's sleeping body. "He's going to make it."

She didn't know why she was so happy or why, when she was so happy, she felt like bursting into tears, but both of those conditions prevailed within her at the moment. She decided she'd better calm down before she went into the kitchen in search of Dan Blue Gully.

It was her physical needs, which she had forgotten all about and which were becoming perilously insistent, which finally propelled Maggie out of the bedroom and into the kitchen. As soon as she passed through the doorway, she stopped dead in astonishment.

The kitchen was Maggie's favorite room in the house.

It was always warm and welcoming and smelled pleasantly of the herbs that she bundled and hung up to dry. But she hadn't expected it to be warm and welcoming at the moment, since she had not had time to tidy it up. And then, instead of cleaning the kitchen as a proper farm wife should, she had apparently been sleeping for hours and hours.

Yet when Maggie stepped into the room, it looked just like home should look. In fact, it looked a good deal better than it usually did.

Someone had swept and mopped the floor, and there was a neat stack of freshly chopped wood in a basket by the potbellied stove. The stove itself gleamed. Maggie had been meaning to clean it for weeks and hadn't had the time. She would have made Ozzie do it, but she could never find him when she needed him.

Her soup simmered on the immaculate stove lid, ready for anyone who wanted it. It had been joined by two beautifully roasted chickens, a pan full of golden corn bread, and a huge pot of greens.

"Greens!" whispered Maggie, awed that anyone could have found them in February.

Three quarters of one of the chickens had been consumed already, and Maggie's eyes strayed from the stove to the table, where Dan Blue Gully and Four Toes Smith sat. They had just eaten, a fact that was obvious to Maggie from their satisfied expressions and the dirty plates and full coffee cups that sat in front of them.

"Good evening, Mrs. Bright," said Dan formally.

"Good evening, Mr. Blue Gully," said Maggie.

"Ma'am," Four Toes Smith said, by way of greeting, and then ducked his head bashfully.

Maggie nodded and smiled at him.

"Feel better, ma'am? More rested?" asked Dan.

"Yes, thank you."

"Four Toes fixed us up a good meal, Mrs. Bright. Four Toes and you. That soup goes real good with the chickens and greens and corn bread."

"Where on earth did you find greens?" Maggie couldn't help asking.

"Woods," said Four Toes in a muffled undertone.

Dan jerked a thumb at his friend. "He kin find food anywhere, ma'am. It's a gift."

Maggie figured it must be.

"Sit down and have some, ma'am. It's real good." Dan stood up and pulled out a chair for her.

Maggie's stomach took that opportunity to growl, and she realized just how hungry she was.

"Thank you," she said. "But first I need to use the privy." She felt embarrassed to be speaking aloud of such things, but she needed to know the answer to her next question. "Is it safe to go outside?"

Dan nodded. "Four Toes will go out with you, Mrs. Bright. He'll stand guard."

That didn't appeal to Maggie a whole lot but, on the other hand, she guessed it was better than being shot by French Jack while sitting on the toilet, so she did not protest.

She felt much better when she returned to the kitchen after her trip out-of-doors. "Mr. Green looks better today. How is he doing?" she asked Dan.

He nodded. "Pretty good."

For some reason Maggie felt nervous. That it was natural for her to be somewhat ill at ease under the circumstances, what with a gun-shot stranger occupying her bed and two strange Indians her kitchen, didn't occur to her. Being Maggie Bright, she chalked her discomfort up to that weak flaw in her character for which her aunt used constantly to chide her.

"Is there something I should do for him?" she asked.

"Eat," Dan said in a low rumble.

"He's sleeping," added Four Toes. "He don't need nothing right now."

Maggie looked from man to man and glanced at the chickens, which were perched delectably on the stove, beckoning to her in all of their succulent basted glory. Her stomach growled again. That gave her all the incentive she needed, and she fixed herself a plate of food and joined the two men at the table.

"I'm afraid we've sort of taken over your place, Mrs. Bright," said Dan.

Maggie opened her mouth to protest politely but decided against such an overt lie. "That's all right," she said instead.

The chicken was absolutely delicious. She had to stop herself from stuffing it into her mouth as if she were some kind of starving bum.

"Well, ma'am, I'm glad to hear you say you don't mind us taking over your place like we done, but I'm afraid we may be causing you a good deal of trouble."

Maggie thought about telling Mr. Blue Gully that he could take over her place with her blessings if he continued to clean up and cook, but she didn't.

She was chewing, so she couldn't respond immediately, and Dan continued. "You see, French Jack is camped out there somewheres, and I'm afraid to leave you alone here now until we get him. We can't move Jubal yet, and I know French Jack ain't going nowhere as long as Jubal's here." His eyes told Maggie as much as did his flat voice: Nothing.

She didn't answer, because she didn't know what to say.

"Four Toes kilt a couple of your chickens for supper," Dan mentioned then. "I hope that's all right. We'll pay you for them. He also wrapped your hired man up and set him in the barn. Ground's too hard to dig in yet. Anyways, thought you might like to tell any kin he's got so's they can have a funeral."

"He didn't have any kin," said Maggie, "but I suspect his friends in town might like to bid him good-bye."

She refrained from mentioning that most of those friends were Ozzie's drinking pals from the saloon, who'd probably be too drunk to remember to go to the funeral but who would be more than happy to toast his memory with bottles of whiskey.

"There's a little cemetery outside of town. This is a very good supper, Mr. Smith," she added to Four Toes. She was shocked when the Indian blushed at her praise. She never knew Indians could blush.

"Thanks, ma'am," Four Toes mumbled into his cup of coffee.

When Maggie finished her dinner, she felt better than she could remember feeling in months. She was full of good food that she hadn't had to cook herself and she was almost well rested.

She also thought it was sort of nice to have a couple of men around the house to do things, even if they were strangers. The fact that the entire population of her little home was apparently under some kind of siege, though, put a tiny damper on her enthusiasm. That got her to thinking about how Annie was doing with Sadie, and she started worrying again.

"Um, Mr. Blue Gully?" she began timidly.

"Ma'am?"

"I'm a little worried about my daughter."

"Oh," said Dan.

He didn't continue, and that "Oh" didn't help Maggie much.

"What if Sadie decides to bring her back? Do you suppose French Jack will try to hurt her?"

Dan appeared to be considering Maggie's question carefully. The effort required him to stare at the kitchen wall for a long time, and Maggie was beginning to wonder if he'd heard her when he finally responded.

"I believe he would," he said.

Maggie's heart nearly stopped beating for a second. She stared at Dan, trying to figure out what to say next.

Nothing profound occurred to her, and she finally blurted out, "I can't let him hurt my baby." There were tears in her eyes and a quiver in her voice.

"No," Dan said.

It sounded as though he was agreeing with her, but since he didn't elaborate, Maggie wasn't sure.

She was becoming very frustrated: indeed, almost angry. The thought of something happening to her sweet Annie terrified her. The tension inside her was building so fast she was on the point of shrieking at Dan Blue Gully when he spoke again.

"I'll go get your baby tomorrow, ma'am. I won't let nothing happen to her."

That took the starch out of Maggie's anger immediately, although the frustration still remained to a degree. She wondered if all Indians were as phlegmatic as this one.

"Thank you, Mr. Blue Gully. I'd appreciate that. I'll be really happy to get my little girl back again."

"Sure thing, ma'am. I'll go first thing in the morning."

Maggie had plumb forgotten it was still night. Realizing it made her sleepy again, and she yawned.

"What time is it?" she asked. Then she felt a little silly since she didn't have a clock in the house.

But Dan apparently wasn't bothered by that. He took an engraved silver watch from his pocket and looked at it closely.

"It's one thirty in the morning, ma'am. You probably ought to get some more sleep. You'll have to tend to Jubal while I'm gone tomorrow. Four Toes will be here to stand guard."

Maggie yawned again, nodded, and headed back into her bedroom. On her way over to her little pallet on the floor, she stopped by Jubal Green's bed once more.

For a long time, she simply stood there, staring down at him. He looked peaceful somehow, a fact that vaguely puzzled Maggie. She didn't think a person who had been shot twice and nearly died from it had any reason to appear peaceful.

She brushed her fingers across his forehead to see if he was feverish. His skin felt warm but not hot. Her hand strayed across his brow, down his face, and paused to stroke his stubbly cheek. She justified that action by telling herself she wanted to make sure she hadn't been mistaken about his feverless condition.

When her hand slid down the side of his neck to rest on his naked shoulder, she finally admitted to herself that she missed having a man in her bed and wanted to remind herself what one felt like. She sighed. Jubal Green's skin felt good. It was warm and firm and somehow comforting. Maggie brushed away a tear.

"Damn Kenny and that stupid horse," she whispered.

In the dim recesses of his healing body, Jubal Green felt a cool hand stroke his forehead and cheek and wander down to his shoulder. It felt really good. Soft. Sweet. He wanted that hand to continue to caress his body. For some reason, it seemed to be giving him strength, which was silly because the caress was so gentle. Peace. Maybe that was what it was giving him. He couldn't quite make himself wake up so that he could think about it.

He hated it when the peace-giving stroking stopped and the gentle hand went away.

When Maggie finally withdrew her hand from Jubal's body, she saw him frown. That worried her and she hoped she hadn't hurt him.

She woke up feeling pretty perky when dawn cracked a few hours later. By the feeble winter light that peeked through the window, she brushed and braided her hair and peered out into the day. It looked so peaceful out there; not at all as though there might be villains lurking.

Since she had slept in the clothes she had donned after her bath and felt rumpled, she fetched a clean calico dress from the wardrobe Kenny had made. The thought of Kenny and the wardrobe made her feel a sudden wistful pang. He could sure build things, Maggie acknowledged, even if he couldn't handle horses.

She cast a glance at the bed and wondered if it would be indiscreet to change clothes in the sick man's room. But Jubal seemed to be sleeping, and Maggie knew Dan Blue Gully and Four Toes Smith were ensconced in the kitchen and Ozzie's shack. So she shrugged her shoulders, whipped off yesterday's wrinkled frock, and tossed the clean one over her head.

It was the early-winter-morning sun whispering across his eyelids that woke Jubal up. He didn't know where he was at first and tried to yawn and stretch. Although that had seemed at first to be a perfectly sensible reaction to waking up, he immediately realized what a terrible mistake it actually was. The only reason he didn't bellow in pain was that he couldn't seem to get his mouth to work. By the time his wits had gathered themselves together, he remembered that he had been shot and was now lying in some bright lady's house with Dan Blue Gully. That seemed very odd to Jubal.

He couldn't lift his head very easily because it hurt too much, but his eyes creaked to half mast in time to observe Maggie brushing her hair by the window. The chilly February sunbeams bathed her in their silvery light and imbued her with an otherworldly quality that made Jubal shut his eyes and open them again in order to make sure he wasn't mistaken: there really was a female brushing the tangles out of her hair in front of his window.

Even before he figured out that Maggie was indeed a corporeal being and not a mere figment of his sick brain, his insides told him it was a good thing to have this female brushing her hair in front of his window when he awoke in the morning. He knew his insides liked it because of the odd feeling of contentment that washed over him, in spite of the many excruciating aches, pains, and throbs that plagued him.

Jubal actually smiled a little bit when Maggie

shrugged off her wrinkled frock. He had a nice view of her slim body in its camisole and drawers. Maggie wore no corset or chemise, a fact that might have shocked a more conventional gentleman than Jubal Green.

But Jubal didn't mind at all. In fact his smile broadened in appreciation of Maggie's feminine form displayed so pleasantly before his interested eyes. He was disappointed when she pulled a clean dress over her head. Maggie was a little on the thin side, he noted, but she still looked pretty good. Soft. Womanly. He liked that.

Jubal nearly chuckled out loud at the realization that he was finding a woman appealing. As if he could do anything about the attraction in his present condition. His eyes slid shut on the thought and he dozed again.

Maggie straightened up her pallet and laid her wrinkled dress aside. It was clean; she just needed to iron it. Maggie always did the ironing on Fridays. She stopped for a moment when she realized she had lost track of time and didn't even know when Friday was. Maybe it had come and gone already, behind her back, when she'd been busy with other things. That would throw her schedule all to flinders. Maybe Mr. Blue Gully could tell her.

Then she went over to Jubal's bedside to check on her patient's condition.

"You look much better, Mr. Green," she whispered with real relief when she peered down at him. "Why, you even have a little smile on your face this morning."

She couldn't stop her hand from reaching out to caress his forehead—to check for fever, she told herself once again.

When Jubal's eyelids suddenly opened and his sea-green eyes blinked up at her, she was embarrassed. She yanked her hand away from his face, tucked it behind her back, and blushed.

It was the angel again. Jubal still wasn't able to sort things out very quickly, but as soon as that thought crossed his mind, he knew it was wrong. He was annoyed that whoever or whatever this vision was, she had removed her soothing hand from his brow.

"You're not an angel," he said in a raspy whisper, frowning slightly at the effort it took.

Maggie thought she had misunderstood his words. She just said, "Good morning, Mr. Green. You look better today. Are you feeling any better?"

"I feel like hell," he replied, too confused at the moment to lie politely.

She looked distressed. "I'm awfully sorry," she said, her voice breathy and soft.

Jubal could tell she meant it and that made him feel a little better, although his irritation at the general state of affairs and his inability to arrange them coherently still rankled. He decided to try another tack with Maggie, since she wouldn't identify herself as an angel or a mortal.

"Are you the bright lady?" he asked, still frowning.

Maggie misunderstood. "I'm Maggie Bright, yes. That's right, Mr. Green. You rode up to my house the other day, gun-shot, and now you're staying here for a while."

"Maggie Bright," Jubal repeated, glad for that clarification at least. The name appealed to him, for some reason, so he said it again. "Maggie Bright."

Shadowy flickers of recollection assailed him once more, and he wondered if Maggie Bright was the same angel who had been sleeping in his bed at night—some night—he couldn't remember. His concentration on the subject was so intense that he wore himself out and his eyes drifted shut again.

Once Maggie was fairly certain he was sleeping, she caressed his brow again, and Jubal smiled.

When she guessed she'd had enough of petting Jubal Green's face, Maggie went out to the kitchen. Four Toes Smith again accompanied her out to the privy.

"Mr. Green seems to be a little bit better today," Maggie ventured experimentally when she got back to the kitchen in one piece.

"He's resting better and don't seem as addled," said Dan.

"Addled," Maggie murmured, pleased with the word. He *had* seemed a little addled, at that.

"Is there anything you'd like me to watch out for when you go get my baby, Mr. Blue Gully?" Maggie asked, since she considered Dan in charge of Jubal Green.

Dan looked a little surprised that she would be asking him what to do. He shook his head.

"No. Just do what you been doing. Whatever it is you do, it works. Keep him as comfortable as possible, I guess. Don't know what else you can do. If he has to—" Dan stopped, embarrassed, as he struggled to find a polite word. "If he has to relieve himself, Four Toes can help you."

"Thank you," Maggie said. Then she thought to ask, "Will you be all right, Mr. Blue Gully? Will French Jack try to hurt you and my baby?"

"Naw," Dan said. He didn't sound at all concerned. "He don't bother me none, ma'am. I know how to fool him."

Maggie pondered that for a second. "Too bad Mr. Green didn't know how to fool him too."

Dan looked vaguely irritated, and Maggie hoped she hadn't said something wrong.

"That was just bad luck, ma'am. Jubal Green's the best there is. We was tired, is why. That's never happened before, and it won't never happen again."

"Oh," said Maggie. "Well, I sure hope it doesn't. It would be a shame."

Then Dan said, "I'll go fetch your little girl now, Mrs. Bright. Do you expect she'll be scared of me?"

"Annie? Lord, no, Mr. Blue Gully. Annie loves everybody. She's just like her daddy. But I'd better write a note for Sadie. *She'll* be scared to death."

Dan remembered the shriek that Sadie Phillips had greeted him with and nodded.

The thought of her friend screaming at the kindly Dan Blue Gully tickled Maggie, and she continued to giggle a bit as she wrote the note to Sadie.

Four Toes had made a breakfast of biscuits and coffee, so Maggie gratefully sat at her kitchen table and ate after Dan left. It was the second meal in as many days that she had not had to prepare herself. She actually began to wonder if being under siege was really so bad after all.

Then Four Toes went out to the privy and she heard a shot ring out and slam into the thick log side of the house. A second or two later a barrage of gunfire shattered both the early-morning stillness and her back-door window.

"Damn," Maggie grumbled. "Kenny brought that window all the way from El Paso."

Then she heard another volley of shots and what sounded like a commotion in the woods.

Four Toes Smith called to her on the tail end of the gunfire. "Mrs. Bright! Open the door quick!"

Maggie heard somebody running madly across the hard-packed dirt, and she did as he had hollered.

When Four Toes stumbled into the house, his momentum propelled him clean across the floor to bump into the wall on the other side of the kitchen before he could stop himself.

"Sorry, ma'am," he panted. "Didn't dare slow down."

"That's all right, Mr. Smith," Maggie assured him. "I heard the shots. Are you hurt?"

Four Toes grinned a tight grin. "I'm not hurt, ma'am."

Maggie recognized his expression as one of satisfaction. "Did you shoot French Jack?" she asked, with a hopeful lilt to her voice.

"Naw," said Four Toes. "But I scared the hell out of him." He looked instantly abashed at his bad language. "I'm sorry, ma'am."

"That's all right, Mr. Smith."

It suddenly occurred to her that she was saying those words about a whole lot of things she never would have anticipated being all right with her. She supposed that's just the way life worked. You never knew what was going to happen next. At least, she decided, this episode was nominally exciting, if she didn't get shot to death.

"I guess they saw Dan leaving," Four Toes continued. "They was sneaking up to the back porch. They probably won't do that again."

"The porch?" Maggie was aghast. That was her worst fear, that their besiegers would sneak in through the screen.

"Don't worry, ma'am. We won't let them hurt you."

Although Maggie didn't say anything, she did wonder about that. So far, it looked to her as if they had a standoff going. She wondered if Dan and Four Toes were ever going to try to get rid of French Jack, or if they were planning merely to hold him at bay. The awful thought crossed her mind that the two Indians were waiting for Jubal Green to get better before they tried to rout the villains.

Good Lord, that could take months! Maggie thought unhappily.

She decided to ask Dan Blue Gully about it when he got back. Right now, she figured she'd better check up on Jubal. Those gunshots had been loud enough to wake the dead. They might even have awakened poor addled Jubal Green.

They had.

When Maggie went back into her bedroom, Jubal was glaring at her. That made her stop dead in her tracks momentarily, because he had a powerfully ferocious glare. Then she decided it was most probably not directed specifically at her. After all, he couldn't have known it would be she who would walk through the door just then, could he?

She took a deep breath and approached the bed. Jubal's scowl didn't leave his face.

"I'm sorry for the noise, Mr. Green. There's some trouble outside." Maggie decided to spare him the details since she didn't want him to waste energy worrying about French Jack.

The gun battle had awakened Jubal with a start that set his wounds and inflamed muscles to throbbing viciously. He was furious that he should be lying in this bed, helpless, and not know what was going on or be able to help, whatever it was.

He hadn't meant to frown at Maggie, really. It's

only that he had been staring at the door when she walked in and got trapped by his scowl. Then, when he saw her, his frown changed from one of anger into one of concentration as he tried to figure out who she was.

Maggie couldn't tell the difference between his various frowns, however. He just looked mean mad to her.

"Did the gunfire startle you, Mr. Green?" she asked gently.

Jubal decided that was too foolish a question to answer. What he remembered from the last few foggy days was that he'd been shot all to hell and was now in some woman's home with his friend Dan Blue Gully. If the woman were with Dan, she sure as hell wouldn't be sleeping with him, and if she was an angel, she wouldn't be here on earth. If this was earth. Besides, if Dan had gotten himself a woman, wouldn't he, Jubal Green, know about it? He and Dan were like brothers, for God's sake. Jubal couldn't have been unconscious for that long, could he?

There was also something about gentle, peaceful hands, but he couldn't sort that one out at all, so he gave up.

"Who the hell are you?" he finally asked.

Maggie was distressed at his tone. She hoped he wasn't a touchy sort of man.

Well, she thought, I guess getting shot up might make anyone cranky, so she decided to give him the benefit of the doubt.

She dipped a cloth in the bowl full of water that rested on the bedside table and began to wipe his brow.

"My name is Maggie Bright, Mr. Green," she said. "I told you last night, but I guess you don't remember."

Suddenly Jubal did recollect having been told that before.

"Oh," he said, with a bare hint of surliness in his voice.

What she was doing with that cloth felt really good to him. He looked up at her suspiciously.

"You're not an angel?" he asked, fearing the answer.

Maggie laughed softly. She had a very pretty laugh, and that worried Jubal too.

"No, Mr. Green, I'm not an angel. Just a widow lady on a farm in New Mexico Territory trying to get you healthy again."

But Jubal didn't seem to pay attention after the first part of her explanation. "Then I'm not dead?" he asked. There was just the faintest touch of fear icing the edges of his words.

Maggie smiled at him tenderly. Jubal Green touched her, for some reason. She guessed it was because he was obviously a strong man and mad as hell at his present helplessness. She supposed he wasn't a man who allowed himself to be taken care of any too often. If his size and strength were any indication, he probably did most of the taking care. That thought started an unsettling series of warm ripples flickering through her insides, so she stopped thinking it immediately.

"No, Mr. Green," she said softly. "You're not dead, thank the Lord."

He sighed weakly and looked relieved. Then he nodded just a little bit.

"You don't look like an angel," he said. That was true. Maggie looked entirely too earthy to be an angel in Jubal Green's opinion. Not that that was a bad thing.

Maggie wasn't sure if she had just been insulted or not, but she decided to let it pass if it was an insult. "Would you like a drink of water, Mr. Green?" she asked instead.

Jubal thought about it. His tongue felt as though it had been replaced by cotton wadding, and the inside of his mouth felt like flannel. Water sounded like a good idea.

"Yes."

He was horrified when Maggie stopped bathing his forehead and looked like she was going to go away. Although it took an incredible amount of effort and hurt like fire, he reached up and grabbed her by the wrist.

"Don't go," he whispered. He would have yelled, but it had taken all of his energy to grab her.

Maggie was shocked.

"I'll be right back, Mr. Green. I won't leave you. I'm just going to get you some water."

Jubal stared at her in disbelief for a second or two. Then his hand began to shake from pain and weakness, and he let go of Maggie, although he didn't want to. His hand flopped back onto the bed, and he experienced a feeling of incredible, terrible loss as he watched Maggie walk out of the room. He shut his eyes and felt gloomier than he could remember feeling since his brother died.

When Maggie came back to his bed a minute later, carrying a glass of water, his eyes were still closed.

"Mr. Green?" Maggie ventured softly, wondering if he had gone back to sleep.

But his eyes opened immediately, at the first sound of her voice. "You came back," he whispered.

Maggie smiled. "Why, of course I came back, Mr.

Green. Did you think I wouldn't? I was just getting you some water."

As he listened to her explanation, Jubal decided it wouldn't be a good idea to tell her the truth. He had believed her to be a figment of his imagination. He was really glad to know she was a real live woman named Maggie who had brought him water. He struggled in a vain effort to sit up.

Maggie was appalled. "Mr. Green, stop that right now. You just lie back and don't move. For heaven's sake, you nearly died. You can't sit up yet. Here, let me hold your head and I'll help you drink."

Jubal frowned at her for a second. Then, when her arm slipped behind him to cradle his head and she held him close against her soft bosom and leaned over to bring the glass to his lips, he decided this wasn't such a bad idea after all. His gaze never left Maggie's face, which was lost in concentration as she tried to help him drink without jostling his poor wounds. When she withdrew the water glass, he smiled.

He was still smiling as he fell asleep again.

5

Maggie was nervous until she had her daughter in her arms again. Then she actually began to relax and enjoy life for the first time since before Kenny had died.

Dan Blue Gully and Four Toes Smith worked like a couple of Trojans around the place. In two days, they had the farm looking better and running more smoothly than it had even before Kenny's encounter with the wrong end of that horse. They also replaced the shattered back-door window. Each one of them did more work in an hour than Ozzie Plumb had done in a week, and although Maggie felt a little bit guilty and disloyal to admit it, she was glad for the change. In fact, once Dan had taken Ozzie's body to town for storage until it could be buried, it was almost as though poor Ozzie had never existed.

"You know, Mr. Blue Gully," she said early one morning, as she fixed breakfast, "it may sound crazy, but it's sort of nice having you men around the place."

She blushed at her confession as she stirred the morning's cornmeal mush.

Dan didn't seem to find anything odd about her words, however. "There's too much work for you to do here alone," he said.

"I guess so." With a sigh she resumed stirring, wondering how she'd get along when Jubal Green got well and she'd lose Dan and Four Toes. She wouldn't even have Ozzie's questionable services to draw upon after these men left her.

The strange part of this whole situation was that she liked them. Dan Blue Gully was pleasant and friendly and considerate. He could also cure her headaches, an accomplishment Maggie considered as miraculous as the discovery of fire and the invention of the wheel. And Four Toes Smith was polite to a fault. In fact, he was bashful and he blushed, which Maggie thought was sweet.

She didn't know Jubal Green yet, but there was something about him that seemed to draw her to his bedside like a bee to a flower.

The injured man continued to improve. Within the week, he was well enough to sit up with help, although the effort apparently required a good deal of grunting and swearing on his part.

"Watch your mouth, Jubal," Dan said, the first time he made the attempt. "There's a lady present."

"Hell," was the only response Jubal gave to that admonition.

By the time he was sitting up, he was sweating rivers, and Maggie could tell he was in great pain. She rushed over with her bowl of water and soft cloth to blot his damp brow.

She had been inspired to add a couple of drops of her beloved lilac toilet water to the bowl of water. She didn't figure Jubal Green could object to the sweet smell, and it definitely made her feel good.

She just couldn't get over how splendid she felt since all these men had invaded her life. At the moment, Annie was in the kitchen being entertained by Four Toes Smith, who was showing her how to build things with some wooden blocks he had fashioned for her.

She settled herself next to Jubal's bed, dipped the soft flannel cloth in the scented water, squeezed it out, and pressed it to his forehead.

Jubal's eyes had been closed in agony, but they opened as soon as he felt the cool, soothing cloth. He sniffed suspiciously.

Maggie had not particularly noticed Jubal's beautiful sea-green eyes before. Now, as they stared at her with uneasy misgiving, they almost took her breath away. My Lord, he was a handsome man!

His eyes were actually hazel, Maggie realized, but they were a deep, deep hazel and they were flecked with green so the effect, when they were aimed directly at her, was stunning. And they were framed by those beautiful dark lashes that Maggie had envied before. Jubal's eyelashes were thick as grass, black as soot, and curled naturally.

A woman would pay a fortune for lashes like that, Maggie thought as she sponged his brow.

"You have pretty eyes, Mr. Green," she commented as she gently worked over him.

Jubal frowned slightly. He had finally figured it all out. This woman was Maggie Bright, a widow lady whose door he had come to after being shot by

French Jack. She had taken him in and saved his life, and for that he was grateful. It must have been she, since there were no other females around, who had floated like an angel by the window, brushing her hair in the early-morning light.

No one except for whores had ever complimented him on his eyes before. According to Dan, Maggie Bright was not a whore but was, rather, a proper lady with lots of grit and no pretensions. Jubal didn't quite know what to make of her comment about his eyes. It didn't square with what he knew about women.

"Thank you," he said, since he couldn't think of anything else to say.

"You're welcome," said Maggie with a tender smile that made Jubal's heart flutter so hard he thought it might give out.

He positively hated the fact that he enjoyed Maggie's ministrations. Pleasure in this female's touch was a flaw he was sure he would overcome as soon as he was healthy again. He was weak as a kitten now. He sucked in a deep breath of lilac, and his weakness made him say, "That smells real good, ma'am."

Maggie looked pleased, a reaction that warmed Jubal's innards.

"I'm glad you think so, Mr. Green. It's my favorite lilac toilet water. My husband gave it to me," Maggie said with a sigh, glad to have somebody to talk to. Sadie hadn't come back since the first day. Dan had told her it wasn't safe.

The idea of Maggie Bright with a husband sent an irrational surge of annoyance through Jubal's guts. He frowned.

But Maggie was staring out the window, lost in memories of happier days with Kenny, and didn't notice Jubal's frown. She just heaved another sigh, which aggravated Jubal further.

"He bought it for me in Indiana right after we were married," Maggie said. "I've saved it ever since. Don't use it very often, 'cause I never go anywhere. Besides, I don't expect I'll ever get any more when this is gone."

"Yes, you will," said Jubal Green.

The irritation in his voice surprised Maggie even more than his words did. Both quickly drew her attention from the window and back to his face. He was glaring at her for some reason. She didn't suppose it would be wise to argue with him, so she put on a perky smile instead.

"Well, now that you're all cleaned off and sitting up, I'll get your breakfast."

He didn't want her to leave his side, but he didn't say anything. Instead, he shook his head as he watched her hips sway gently as she left for the kitchen.

Hell, he thought.

He chalked up his reaction to his having almost died and decided he'd be real, real glad when he was better. He inhaled a lungful of the soft, sweet lilac scent that lingered in the morning air and knew that for the rest of his life he would think of Maggie Bright whenever he smelled lilacs. His heart ached with the knowledge.

The following morning, before daylight yawned over Maggie's little piece of Lincoln County forest, Four Toes Smith and Dan Blue Gully left the tidy farmhouse in the clearing near Bright's Creek and went hunting.

They surprised French Jack and his two companions, who were still at rest. French Jack's last mistake in this world was letting the man whom Maggie had wounded stand guard.

"Probably had no choice," Dan told Jubal as he recounted the morning's events to him a little later in the day. "They was only the three of 'em. But the butt-shot man was too weak to stay awake. We got 'em all."

Maggie, who was folding clean bandages on the chest across the room, was a little alarmed at the broad smile with which Jubal greeted Dan's words.

"All dead?" he asked with obvious glee.

"They are now," said Dan. There was grim satisfaction in his voice.

Maggie stopped folding and watched the two men while she listened.

"How?" Jubal asked.

"The butt-shot man took one through the heart. Dead in a second flat. I expect they'll be pieces of his spine stuck in that tree for a hundred years or more."

"You Indians," said Jubal with a wry grin. "Always thinking about your ancestors and your posterity."

"In this case, I guess it was posteriority," said Dan Blue Gully.

Jubal and Dan laughed heartily at Dan's joke. Maggie felt a little sick.

"What about the other two?"

"Well, as for Jack's other pal, Four Toes blew his brains all over his bedroll. I decided it wasn't worth takin' the blanket to clean it up. It was a mess."

Maggie closed her eyes in revulsion.

"And French Jack?" Jubal asked the question with relish, as though he had been saving the best for last.

Dan looked up at the ceiling for a minute and said, almost dreamily, "Well, French Jack, we figgered he deserved something special. Four Toes and me, bein' Apache and all, we decided we ought to give him a little extra care. So first we strung him up."

"Did you go through his pockets and gear?"

"Of course. Found what you was lookin' for, too," said Dan. He showed Jubal a folded piece of paper.

Jubal nodded with satisfaction. "Good. Then what?" He sounded very eager.

Dan Blue Gully had already begun his recitation of French Jack's demise by the time Jubal realized Maggie was still in the room.

"Well, first we slit his belly open and let him watch his guts fall out," Dan said.

He was warming up to his description when Jubal's deep grunt stopped him. Dan looked down at him with a puzzled expression on his face. Jubal jerked his head in Maggie's direction, and Dan turned and saw her. She was standing still as a statue by the window, linen bandages dangling forgotten from her fingers, staring at the two of them with a horrified expression on her face.

Dan looked down at his boots in obvious embarrassment.

Jubal cleared his throat. "Mrs. Bright, you probably don't want to hear this."

He knew how touchy females were. They didn't seem to be able to appreciate the finer aspects of revenge unless it was their own.

Maggie swallowed hard and whispered, "No, I don't guess I do." Then she practically bolted from the room, ran into the kitchen in a pelter, and collapsed at the table.

Four Toes had just put the finishing touches on the rest of Annie's building-brick set. As Maggie's gaze took in the sweet picture of him squatting on the kitchen floor, handing her baby a block, the full measure of men's inconsistencies struck her. Four Toes was grinning in real, tender pleasure at the little girl's ill-coordinated attempts at constructing a tower with the blocks.

"That's right, Annie. Now this one goes here," said Four Toes, as Maggie's baby succeeded in setting one block on top of another.

Annie laughed and clapped her hands. Four Toes chuckled softly.

"You're real good at this, Annie," he said, giving her chubby cheek a tweak.

"Annie good," the baby said, winning another chuckle from Four Toes.

Maggie shook her head in wonder. If she didn't know it for a certified fact, she would never in her wildest dreams believe that this man who was playing so peacefully with her baby had tortured and killed another human being earlier in the day.

"I'll never understand people as long as I live," she murmured.

Dan came out of the bedroom as she whispered the words. He shuffled uncomfortably for a second or two, then said, "I'm sorry we upset you, ma'am. I guess what we done to them men probably shocked you some."

Maggie considered denying it but decided not to. After all, they had seen her reaction to their words. It wouldn't do any good to lie.

"Yes, I guess it did some," she whispered.

Dan sat down at the table across from her. "I know it sounds mean, ma'am, and brutal, but, see, me and Jubal, we been chased and hunted by French Jack for months now, and we been chasing and hunting him back. Jubal's only brother and his family was murdered in cold blood by that man, and I figured he should pay for what he done. He's a criminal, ma'am. There's a reward's been posted on him."

Dan laid the broadside, on the table in front of her. Maggie stared at it numbly.

"And it ain't only that, ma'am. You see, French Jack, he was just a pawn. He was a crazy, mean pawn, but he was still only a pawn. The man who hired him is even worse."

The Indian laid another paper in front of Maggie. It took her a couple of seconds to realize that it was a letter. She picked it up and read it, holding it close so her poor eyes could decipher the words.

She had to read it twice because she didn't believe she had read it properly the first time. When she was through with her second reading, she looked over the crumpled paper into Dan Blue Gully's eyes with tears in her own.

"Why, this Mr. Mulrooney says he means to kill the entire Green family! 'Wipe them off the face of the earth,' it says here. He was paying Mr. Gauthier five thousand dollars to do it." Her voice held pained awe. "And you and Mr. Smith."

The Indian nodded somberly.

Maggie stared at the letter once more. "I don't understand," she muttered weakly. "Why would anybody hate another person that much?"

"Well, Mrs. Bright, it's a long story and it ain't really mine, except by—well, by adoption, I guess you might say. I expect I should let Jubal tell you about that."

Maggie just stared at him.

"There's a reward on French Jack, Mrs. Bright. Four

Toes and me, we'll haul the bodies into Lincoln this afternoon and visit the sheriff there. You're due some of the reward, ma'am. In fact, you're probably due all of it, for putting up with us like you been doing." He said that with a grin.

The Indian's last words shocked Maggie out of her torpor. "Will you be leaving now?" she asked in a faint whisper.

Suddenly she couldn't bear the idea of these two good men leaving her. They'd been here for over a week and turned her life upside down and inside out and killed three people and scared her to death, and yet she didn't want them to go.

Dan cleared his throat, as though he didn't much want to say what he had to tell her next.

"Well, ma'am, you see, Jubal, he ain't up to traveling yet."

"Of course not," Maggie agreed.

Dan didn't continue, and Maggie wondered if that was all he was going to say.

"Mr. Green can certainly stay here until he's well," she offered, though the prospect of caring for an invalid while mothering Annie and keeping up her farm single-handed made her heart sink like a lead weight into her sturdy shoes.

Dan still didn't speak. He seemed troubled, and he was apparently having a hard time looking at Maggie.

Finally Maggie couldn't stand his silence. "What's the matter, Mr. Blue Gully?"

Dan sighed. "Well, ma'am, I'm afraid it might not be as easy as that."

Easy? Maggie almost laughed.

"You see, Jubal is writing a letter to Mr. Mulrooney right now, telling him what happened."

"What on earth is he doing that for?" Maggie hadn't meant to yell her question.

Dan shrugged. "He thinks he has to, this being sort of a family feud. They write back and forth to each other all the time, Jubal tellin' Mulrooney to give it up and Mulrooney tellin' Jubal that he ain't goin' to give it up 'til one of 'em's dead. When Mr. Mulrooney gets that letter, he'll be mad as fire. There's no way he'll be able to avoid learning that you helped us. Anyway, I expect he already knows, since he's got spies followin' Jubal everywhere, and he's probably got more killers on his tail right now. Then you'll be a target too, ma'am, and Jubal and me—well, we don't want anything to happen to you."

"No," Maggie whispered miserably.

"So you see, ma'am, I know it's a bother to have us here, but we don't dare leave yet."

"No," Maggie said again, but with a little more hope.

"But we don't want to trouble you no more than we have to, so Four Toes and me, we'll help out around the place. The reason I brought Four Toes along in the first place was to do some work for you, since your other hired fellow was a no-good drunk."

The way Dan said it was so matter-of-fact that Maggie could only nod. Hearing Ozzie Plumb described as a no-good drunk by an impartial third party helped ease her guilt about having found the man so aggravating.

"Do either of you play the guitar?" she asked.

Dan seemed taken aback by this departure from the subject at hand. "No, ma'am."

"Well, I've still got Ozzie's guitar if you want to learn," she said sadly.

Dan didn't say anything for a moment or two. He

just watched Maggie as she stared at the tabletop in front of her. His normally expressionless eyes held a world of sympathy.

"Thank you, ma'am," he finally said. "Four Toes, he's kind of musical."

Dan looked a little doubtfully at Four Toes Smith, who was now sitting on the floor having a conversation with baby Annie while they built a wood-block cabin.

Maggie followed his stare and smiled at the young Indian man and her daughter.

"He's good with babies too," she said.

"Yes," agreed Dan. "He likes kids."

"Is he married?" Maggie asked.

"Naw. He don't want to live on a reservation, and if he got married he'd have to do that or be chased for the rest of his life."

Maggie looked vaguely puzzled. "Really?"

Dan nodded. "Yeah. Most white folks can tolerate one or two of us at a time, but they don't want a whole family of Indians anywhere near 'em. Four Toes and me, we've never lived on a reservation."

Maggie wasn't embarrassed, a fact she later found rather surprising. She only said, "How sad," as her gaze wandered back to Annie playing with her new friend.

"Besides," Dan continued, "Four Toes has it in his head that he ain't going to live long."

Maggie shook her head. "How odd." She stood with a weary sigh. "Well, if you two are going to get those dead men to town, I'd better pack you a lunch."

Dan smiled. "That would be real nice, Mrs. Bright."

6

When Prometheus J. Mulrooney read the wire from Jubal Green that Dan Blue Gully sent him from Lincoln, his face turned a brilliant red and he bellowed loud enough to be heard on all three stories of his mansion in New York City.

"Ferrett! Ferrett!" he roared.

He stood up, his rage propelling him out of his chair like a rocket. He was so angry that his enormous belly quivered like the jellied aspic he had consumed at luncheon. He sat down again because he didn't know what to do with himself once he was on his feet. Then he stood up once more, furious that Ferrett hadn't responded yet. Approximately ten seconds had passed since his first yell.

When Ferrett pushed Mulrooney's office door open and skidded to a halt in front of his boss's desk, his own face was red from having run up two flights of stairs three steps at a time. Ferrett was Mulrooney's secretary, and he looked like his name. He was a thin small man with thin small features that squeezed together into a rodentlike point in front.

"Yes, sir," Ferrett said in a nasal squeak. Then he saluted. Ferrett did not normally salute his employer, but he had been rattled by Mulrooney's bellow.

Mulrooney glared at his secretary and shook the wire in his hand viciously.

"What is the meaning of this?" he demanded.

Ferrett looked from the wire to Mulrooney's face to the wire and back to Mulrooney's face.

"Sir?" he asked in a reedy voice. He was shaking.

Mulrooney pinned Ferrett with a contemptuous stare. Mulrooney didn't respect his secretary. He didn't respect anybody who quailed before him, yet he employed nobody who might possibly defy him. He was, therefore, in a perpetual rage.

"You repulsive, spineless creature. Did you see this wire?"

Ferrett gulped and his Adam's apple jerked up and down. "Yes, sir."

Mulrooney slammed it down and leaned forward over his desk, supporting his bulk on two meaty forearms.

"Then you know Jack Gauthier failed."

"Yes, sir."

Mulrooney sat back down in his chair with a huge grunt. The chair groaned.

"Damn Jubal Green to hell," he muttered.

Although the words were barely discernible, Ferrett cringed at the venomous hate with which they were uttered.

Mulrooney scowled. "I thought you said this Jack

Gauthier was the best. Why the hell did he get himself shot if he's the best?"

Ferrett swallowed hard and tried to answer his boss. "Well, sir, no, sir; actually, sir, it wasn't me said that, sir. It was the agent from Texas, sir, who said that," he stammered, and added another "sir" on the end, just to make sure.

Mulrooney's eyes skewered Ferrett. The secretary seemed to shrink up even further.

"Disgusting toad," Mulrooney said.

"Yes, sir," Ferrett whispered.

Mulrooney left Ferrett to his cringing and turned to stare out his window. "Damn," he whispered. "Just a week ago Gauthier sent a wire saying Green had been shot. I thought it was over then except for those damned Indians."

Mulrooney paused to whip his head around and glare at his secretary. He wanted to be absolutely sure that Ferrett was still cowering. He was.

"I thought Jack Gauthier would solve my problems this time for sure."

"Yes, sir," said Ferrett nervously. He never quite knew when his employer expected him to comment and when he did not.

"What do you know about it, you ridiculous rat-faced worm?"

Ferrett gulped again. "N-nothing, sir," he stammered.

"Damned right," Mulrooney said, with a nod that squished several of his chins together.

He glared at the wire again. Then he shuffled through the messy pile of papers on his desk until he found what he was looking for, picked it up, and glared at it.

"It says here," said Mulrooney, "that a Miss Maggie Bright is nursing Green on her farm in Lincoln County in the territory." He paused to think. "Lincoln County's always being written about in the papers because of its violence and feuds, isn't it, Ferrett." He practically screamed the question. He liked to keep his people off guard.

He succeeded well with Ferrett, who jumped a yard in the air and whispered, "Yes, sir."

Mulrooney tapped a finger on the arm of his chair for several seconds as he pondered. Then a smile began to curl his fat lips, which did not lessen Ferrett's nervousness.

"I don't like it when people aid my enemies, Ferrett," Mulrooney said.

"No, sir," agreed Ferrett.

Mulrooney's gaze strayed out the window again. The smile didn't leave his face, but his finger stopped tapping.

"Still, even though Jubal Green lives, something good was achieved by this Gauthier fool," Mulrooney mused. "Jubal Green is the last of his line now, since Gauthier wiped out the brother and his family. Dan Blue Gully, of course, has no one. Neither does Four Toes Smith. The army helped me there."

A chuckle that sounded nearly jolly rumbled out from Mulrooney. Ferrett dared to produce a tiny little smile. The smile lasted only long enough for Mulrooney to turn his head and glare at him. Then it died fast.

"This is not funny, Ferrett, you miserable wad of slime."

"No, sir."

"His father ruined me, you piece of scum," Mulrooney

added, still stabbing Ferrett with his razor-sharp gaze.

"Yes, sir."

"He stole the woman I was to have married."

"Yes, sir."

"Stole her, Ferrett, like the miserable thief he was."

"Yes, sir."

"Marianna claimed she didn't want to marry me," Mulrooney said gazing out the window again.

"Yes, sir."

"Said she wanted to marry Benjamin Green, of all people. My partner! Usurping villain."

"Yes, sir."

"Said she wouldn't have married me even if Benjamin Green hadn't asked her. Said I was unpleasant to be around. Me, unpleasant! Can you fathom that, Ferrett?"

"Yes, sir."

Ferrett looked startled when his boss's head whipped around and he found himself withering under the furious scowl of Prometheus Mulrooney once more. Then he realized what he had just said and stammered out a quick, "I mean no, sir. No, sir, I certainly can't."

Mulrooney's eyes stayed squinched up, and he glared at Ferrett for another few seconds. "Miserable twit," said Mulrooney.

"Yes, sir," Ferrett agreed.

"It was twaddle, of course," Mulrooney continued. "Marianna was a silly girl who didn't know her own mind. I explained that to her, but she wouldn't listen."

"No, sir," said Ferrett, sure of his ground again.

"The foolish girl married Benjamin Green anyway."

"Yes, sir."

A slithery smile again took possession of Prometheus Mulrooney's face. "But I got them," he said softly.

Ferrett shuddered. "Yes, sir," he said in a shaky voice.

"They left New York for Texas. Took the profits Green had made with me and bought himself a spread near El Paso." Mulrooney stopped talking and his smile broadened, as if relishing a cherished memory.

Ferrett didn't say anything.

"They forgot all about me," Mulrooney continued, his voice dreamy. "I didn't forget about them, though. I got them, Ferrett."

Mulrooney paused. Ferrett remained silent.

Mulrooney turned and his fists crashed down on his desk. "Are you listening to me, you absurd excuse for a human being?" Mulrooney roared.

"Yes, sir," Ferrett whimpered.

"I said, 'I got them,'" Mulrooney repeated, glaring at Ferrett, who looked very much as though he might faint.

"Yes, sir," he squeaked.

"I waited until they were established and happily ensconced in their little kingdom, and then I went after them. Through my agent in Texas, I began to buy up all the land around them. They didn't know my plan. They didn't know it was me." He chuckled in satisfaction.

Ferrett swallowed. "Yes, sir," came out feebly.

"I toyed with them at first. Diverted water. Poisoned cattle. I wanted them to suffer."

"Yes, sir."

"But that got boring. Besides," Mulrooney said querulously, "that dratted Green was smart. He figured out what was happening and intervened, every single time. Damn his soul to hell."

Mulrooney's furious glower was still directed at the window, a fact Ferrett appreciated.

Mulrooney heaved a sigh that was as fat as his body. "So I killed them," he said simply, as if that made perfect sense.

"Yes, sir." Ferrett's tiny whisper barely left his lips before it died.

"But by that time they had sons," Mulrooney said, as though the Green sons were a personal affront to his dignity.

"Yes, sir."

"But I'll get them too, Ferrett. Already got one of them." He sounded downright cheerful about that.

"I've dedicated my life to this pursuit," he murmured, as though he were talking to himself. "They took away my happiness. She gave my sons to that usurping criminal, Benjamin Green. They should have been mine, those sons. They should have been mine."

Mulrooney had turned to face Ferrett again, and both his intense smile and his tiny protuberant eyes held the fervor of a crazed fanatic. Ferrett trembled.

Mulrooney's smile faded and he glared at his underling once again.

"Get my agent, Ferrett. He's got to contact my man in Amarillo."

"Yes, sir," said Ferrett. He waited for further instructions.

Mulrooney continued to glare at him.

Ferrett continued to wait.

Mulrooney's shout backed him up clear across the floor and against the wall.

"Go, you imbecile!"

Ferrett didn't waste time on another "Yes, sir" before

he opened the door and raced to do his master's bidding.

Mulrooney's agent was every bit as terrified of Mulrooney as Ferrett was. His name was Pelch.

As Ferrett took Pelch up the stairs to their employer's office, the two men commiserated with each other.

"He's in a rare mood today, Mr. Pelch," said Ferrett.

"Ain't he always," muttered Pelch.

"That's so."

When they reached Mulrooney's office door, they both had to steel their nerves before Ferrett dared venture a small knock upon the varnished mahogany. Both men winced as Mulrooney screamed, "Get in here, you idiotic fools!"

Nobody ever left Mulrooney's employ voluntarily. Mulrooney would occasionally fire people, but nobody ever left voluntarily. It was either stay and take his abuse or be fired. People who tried to quit invariably seemed to meet with unfortunate accidents. Mulrooney didn't like quitters. Neither Ferrett nor Pelch dared to leave.

Ferrett hovered outside the office door, waiting for poor Pelch to emerge. The two men often tried to bolster each other's spirits, although it was a futile task.

Pelch's eyes were downcast when he finally emerged from Mulrooney's office. Ferrett patted him on the shoulder.

The sigh Pelch heaved seemed to have been torn from an exhausted soul. He looked as though he wanted to cry as he peered sadly at Ferrett.

"How many does this make, Mr. Ferrett?" he whispered miserably.

Ferrett gave a disconsolate shake of his head. "I've lost count."

Pelch shuddered. He jerked his head toward the top of the staircase. "That man's the devil," he whispered.

Ferrett cast a frightened-rabbit look up the stairs. "That he is," he whispered back.

The two men scurried away to do their master's bidding.

During the next few weeks, Maggie felt as though she had died and gone to heaven.

All danger had passed, at least for the time being, and Dan Blue Gully and Four Toes Smith spent their days helping out around the house, since they didn't need to be protecting themselves and her from murderers. They repaired broken door hinges, fortified stalls in the barn, fixed the wagon axle that Ozzie Plumb had been meaning to get around to fixing for six months, and Four Toes even put up a fence around the little cabin's yard.

Even her monthlies held no terror for Maggie, now that she had Dan Blue Gully's magic bark to cure her headaches.

Annie and Four Toes had taken a strong liking to each other, and the young Indian spent hours playing with the little girl, a circumstance that freed Maggie's time up amazingly. Besides the building-brick set, Four Toes fashioned wooden toys for her. Annie loved playing with her carved horses, cows, mountain lions, and coyotes. He told the little girl wonderful, fanciful stories about the animals as they played.

Four Toes told Maggie he put up the fence for Annie, so she wouldn't wander away and get lost in the woods, and Maggie was grateful to him for that alone. She had worried about what she was going to do when Annie began to walk around on her own. The possibilities, from the creek to wild animals to roving criminals, scared her.

"You like flowers, ma'am?" Four Toes asked Maggie one day in early March, after he had finished installing a gate in the new split-rail fence.

Maggie had been hanging out the wash. The weather was getting on toward spring, and it was safe to hang clothes out-of-doors once more without fear of their freezing on the line.

"I love flowers. I'd like to have me a flower garden someday when I have time to tend it."

"Well, you got time now, ma'am. I can dig you a little border along the fence here. Then we can get some seeds next time we go to the mercantile in town."

Maggie's eyes, no longer sunken inside a sea of black rings, grew with wonder. "Oh! Do you mean it?"

"Sure," said Four Toes, as if surprised at her doubt. "A few hollyhocks. Maybe some cosmos."

Maggie's smile could have warmed the coldest winter day. "Thank you, Mr. Smith," she said softly. "Thank you so very much."

Four Toes dug the toe of his boot into the soft earth. "It ain't nothin', ma'am. You're two ladies here. Ladies like flowers," he said bashfully.

Maggie glowed at him and went back to hanging her wash with a song in her heart. She was going to have a flower garden! She couldn't believe it.

The song in Maggie's heart didn't take long to work its way out into the open. From his invalid's bed, Jubal Green heard her pretty voice raised in tune. She was singing "Annie Laurie" as she hung out the wash, and Jubal lay on his back and fretted. He felt left out.

Since he had never wanted to belong to anything, Jubal had never felt left out before. He didn't understand his strange longing now to be a part of the odd little family that had been created around him.

When Maggie came in to give him his lunch, he was scowling.

"Oh, my, Mr. Green, you look fierce. Are your wounds hurting you?"

Maggie was concerned, although she had mixed emotions about both Jubal Green and his injuries. On the one hand, she certainly wanted him to get better. On the other, he was a difficult patient. Not only that, but she was afraid that when he got better, he and his two Indian friends would go away. Since Maggie had not only gotten used to them but liked having them around, she didn't even want to think about what life would be like when they all went away and left her.

Jubal frowned at her. "They're not too bad." He sounded very grumpy.

Maggie set his soup and corn bread on the table beside the bed and helped him sit up. That remained a painful process, and Jubal grunted. He still looked unhappy when he was sitting up. Maggie stood back and peered at him critically, as if to assess the state of his health.

"Are you sure you're not hurting, Mr. Green? You don't look so good."

"I'm all right." He was a little mollified since she seemed to be concerned about him.

"Well," said Maggie, "let me help you eat this soup and corn bread. Maybe that will make you feel better."

Jubal grumbled his assent, and Maggie sat down

next to the bed and served him. His sour mood didn't bother her much; she figured he'd earned it. Aunt Lucy used to be in a perpetual snit and with much less reason; Maggie was used to dealing with moody people.

"Nobody's ever had to do this for me before," said Jubal, as if to assure Maggie that he wasn't normally helpless. He still couldn't use his right hand to lift anything, so somebody had to help him with things like soup that spilled easily.

Maggie's soft laugh caressed his ears. "I'm sure that's so, Mr. Green. I don't suppose you get shot up regular-like."

She was concentrating on not spilling his soup as she filled his spoon, so she didn't notice the way he was examining her.

Jubal liked the way she looked. He also liked the way she made him feel.

Maggie wasn't a beautiful woman by most standards, but she had a pretty face, with wide-set, big blue eyes, and a cute little nose that sat above a mouth that looked temptingly kissable to Jubal. He wasn't altogether sure he approved of his reaction to her, and he chalked that reaction, too, up to his weakened condition.

The fact that Maggie also made him feel good didn't annoy him quite as much, since he figured it was only natural to feel better when one's nurse was around.

"You're a good nurse," he muttered, after swallowing a mouthful of soup.

Maggie looked at him in surprise. "Thank you, Mr. Green. Actually, Mr. Blue Gully is the one who told me how to help you."

"That's not what he said to me. He said if it wasn't for you, I'd be dead."

"Did he really?" Maggie could feel herself blush. She wasn't used to hearing her praises sung, her aunt having conditioned her to expect criticism, if anything. It both pleased and embarrassed her.

"Well, thank you again," she said. She broke off a piece of corn bread and stuffed it into Jubal's mouth before he could say any more nice things about her and embarrass her further.

After Jubal chewed and swallowed his bread, he said, "And you're a good cook, too."

"Well, you know, truly Mr. Smith is the one. He goes out every day and finds things in the woods I wouldn't even know were there. He gets all sorts of greens and things I don't usually have this time of year." She nodded to herself and Jubal. "Mr. Smith's the one, all right."

Jubal was becoming right aggravated by Maggie's always belittling her own accomplishments.

"God damn it, it's not them, it's you. You're the one who saved my life, and you're the one who cooks. Now, when I say you're a good cook, I mean you're a good cook, and I don't want any argument." His voice was gruff and his expression was ferocious.

Maggie was surprised by his words. She didn't speak for a moment, an old familiar knot of frustration squeezing her chest. Long, long ago, she had learned not to argue with difficult people. Still, she was surprised at how hard it was to bite back a frosty retort. She supposed she'd gotten kind of soft, living with the easygoing Kenny Bright for so long.

She murmured somewhat stiffly, "I beg your pardon, Mr. Green. I didn't mean to argue with you."

That little comment riled Jubal even further, but he decided he didn't have the energy to set Maggie straight at the moment. He chomped down on the spoon she stuck in his mouth so hard that his teeth clanked on the metal.

When he had swallowed, he said, "You're an irritating woman, Mrs. Bright."

Maggie looked like she was going to cry. He'd rather she just yell at him. That's what Dan or Four Toes always did when he got touchy and they got mad at him.

Oh, hell, Jubal thought to himself. Why are women so blamed difficult?

Instead of pursuing the question with a member of that difficult fair sex, he said, "I want to go outside."

He didn't add that he wanted to be outside when Maggie was outside or he wanted to be able to watch her the next time she sang "Annie Laurie" and hung up the wash.

Maggie eyed him speculatively for several moments. She wasn't sure she liked Jubal Green. He said mean things, or at least things she didn't understand. She couldn't figure out why he had at first praised her and then told her she was irritating, and she wished he could be as obliging as his Indian friends.

Her long appraisal of him was making Jubal fidget, and he was glad when she drew breath to speak again.

"Well, Mr. Green, I don't know if it's a good idea for you to move around much yet. I hope you won't think it irritating of me to say that I'd like to talk to Mr. Blue Gully before trying to help you stand up."

Jubal sighed. "I didn't mean it that way, ma'am," he said.

Hell. He hadn't meant to offend her. He didn't know how to talk to women. Except for his mother, he'd grown up around men. His mother was always cringing and crying in a corner somewhere, so he'd just mainly tried to keep out of her way and not aggravate her further.

Virtually all the other women he'd been associated with since he'd grown up were whores, except his sister-in-law, Janie. He'd only known Janie a few years before she, his brother, Benny, and their daughter, Sara, had been killed by French Jack. He'd still been getting used to Janie and was sorry she was dead, although it was partly her own fault.

But he'd loved Sara. He acknowledged that fact only to himself and with an ache in his chest that he was sure would never heal. Sara had been bright and pretty and had loved him in spite of himself. Little Sara hadn't cared that Jubal was morose and broody around women. She'd just climbed up his leg and hugged him. His heart hurt whenever he thought about her.

His sister-in-law hadn't been as bad as his mother, but she wasn't easy to be around either. He'd never been near as easy a woman as Maggie Bright before. She just went about her business, smiled and sang, and didn't screech at bugs or yell at her baby. Jubal liked to listen to her and Annie. He wanted to be able to watch them, to see just what it was that mothers and children did together, since he didn't know from personal experience.

"Please talk to Danny and see what he thinks," he said politely. "I'd like to be able to get up, even if I can't get around yet. I feel—I feel lonely in here." He felt like a fool after admitting to that weakness.

But Maggie's heart melted immediately and her pursed lips relaxed. She understood lonely. She'd been lonely most of her life. She put a comforting hand over his.

That gesture surprised the socks off Jubal Green. He liked it a lot, and he liked the feel of Maggie's soft hand on his.

"I'm sorry, Mr. Green. Of course you're lonely. You're all shot up and hurting and stuck away in here while we're outside or in the kitchen doing our regular chores and leaving you out. I'm sure we can think of some way to help you."

Jubal was surprised at how natural it all sounded coming out of Maggie's mouth. It didn't sound like a puling, sniveling, weak request on his part when Maggie said it.

"Thank you, Mrs. Bright."

He had a nice smile. In fact, he had a real nice smile. It was a warm smile. When he smiled, all those little skinny white lines around his eyes crinkled up and he lost the hard-as-nails look he usually wore. Maggie felt a sudden warmth invade her heart. She really, really liked Jubal Green's smile.

"Sure, Mr. Green."

Then she finished helping him eat and went out to find Dan Blue Gully.

By the end of the afternoon, Jubal Green was ensconced on a chair out back where he could watch Four Toes Smith chop wood while Maggie planted winter kale, beets, and carrots in the kitchen garden. Little Annie was helping her mother, more or less.

Dan Blue Gully was mending the chicken coop that Ozzie had never managed to get fixed so the chickens would stay in. Dan and Maggie were swapping tales about farming. It was a subject that was relatively new to both of them.

Jubal Green breathed deeply of the crisp air. As he inhaled the fragrance of freshly chopped wood and newly turned earth, he felt just fine.

7

Four more weeks passed by without incident. "It can't last much longer," Jubal commented to Dan after supper one night.

The kitchen smelled of the good meal Maggie had just served, of freshly brewed tea, and of cinnamon, because she had spent the afternoon baking. Jubal liked the way her house always smelled of good things to eat. That was also something he had never experienced before. He was up and about now, limping, sore, and crabby, but able to get around without help.

"Do you think Mulrooney knows about French Jack killing your brother yet?" Dan asked.

"Hell, yes," said Jubal. "You don't think French Jack didn't keep him informed, do you?"

"No," Dan mumbled, "I don't guess so."

"Probably wired him every day that he was near enough to a town to do it," Jubal muttered.

"I suppose so."

"You know Mulrooney," Jubal said.

"Yeah," replied Dan. "I know Mulrooney."

"Can't be too much longer," Jubal repeated.

"No." Dan sighed. "Mulrooney's probably already got somebody else on our tail right now."

"Right."

The two men were lingering over their tea. Four Toes had gone out to the barn to see that the animals were properly tucked in for the night. Jubal didn't want to get up and go into the parlor. He liked to sit at the kitchen table, smell the good smells, and watch Maggie work. It was real peaceful in the kitchen.

Right now she was doing the washing up and singing an alphabet song with her daughter. Annie was banging on her wooden high-chair tray with a spoon, trying to keep time with the music, Jubal supposed, although he didn't know much about either music or babies. She made him grin, though.

Jubal wasn't altogether certain he approved of the warm, comfy feeling that always snuck up on him when he sat in Maggie's kitchen. It seemed somehow weak to him that he should entertain feelings of a soft nature, and Jubal was not normally weak. For several weeks now he had chalked up that particular weakness to his having been injured, but he wasn't so sure anymore. After all, his wounds were almost healed. But those contented, peaceful feelings still grabbed hold of him every blessed time he ate a meal in the kitchen or even walked into the room.

He felt even more uneasy when he acknowledged that those feelings didn't only wallop him in the kitchen. They attacked him whenever he was in Maggie's presence, and that troubled him a good deal.

But tonight he didn't want to think about his odd

reaction to Maggie Bright. He figured he and Dan had better consider what was to be done when the next contingent of thugs hired by Prometheus Mulrooney came out to the New Mexico Territory to murder them.

Jubal was scowling into his teacup. "Hell, I almost wish my mother had married that devil and spared us all this grief."

Dan eyed him speculatively. "I don't suppose you really mean that, Jubal."

"I don't know," Jubal muttered, his mood unsettled. "All she ever did was slink around the place and fret and worry and cry and stew because of him."

"Well," said his friend, "that was because he was scarin' her."

"Maybe, but for her, fretting was a full-time occupation. She didn't have time for her husband or her kids or her house or anything. She was too busy bein' scared."

Maggie had come over with the teakettle to fill the pot with water, and she listened with interest as the men talked. She was very curious about why this Mulrooney fellow seemed so determined to rid the world of Jubal Green. She felt more relaxed around Jubal now than she had at first, although she considered him a somewhat hard man. He still gave her odd warm feelings in her middle when she watched him, though. She liked to look at him when he didn't know she was watching. She got embarrassed when he looked back.

"Is that your mother you're talking about, Mr. Green?" she asked.

"Yes."

Jubal wasn't sure he should have mentioned anything about his mother in front of Maggie. Women never understood anything, especially when it came to other people's mothers.

"Those are pretty hard things to say about your own mother, aren't they?" Maggie ventured.

She felt quite shy about voicing an opinion in this matter. After all, her aunt had told her over and over again that her opinion was worthless. Her marriage to Kenny had softened her perspective on the matter some, since he deferred to her in almost everything, but Maggie still wasn't at all certain of her position among these men.

Not only that, she was almost positive that Jubal Green wouldn't appreciate her interference in what he might consider none of her business. Still, it *was* her business now, in a way, since her own life and Annie's had been imperiled by the feud between him and Mulrooney.

When Jubal turned to scowl at her, though, she was sure she shouldn't have spoken.

"Hard words or not, they're the truth," he said. "My father needed a wife. He didn't need a weeping, wailing woman clinging to him all the time and interfering with his work. All her whining took his mind off his business."

"Well," said Maggie, in defense of Jubal's unknown parent, "I suppose she was near scared to death, with that man trying to kill her."

She didn't notice Dan smile at her because she was too busy watching Jubal and being amazed at her own audacity.

"Hell," Jubal snapped. He didn't like females talking back to him. "You were scared too, but you didn't hide in a corner and bawl. You took your goddamned gun and shot that bastard in the butt. You took me in and saved my life. People can be scared and still be useful. They can be scared and still do their rightful job. And you sure as blazes didn't abandon your little girl because you were scared."

Maggie was shocked. Abandon Annie? "My God, Mr. Green, I could never do that," she said, startled into anger at the mere suggestion. "What on earth are you thinking of?"

"Well, then, there you go," said Jubal, as if she had just made his point for him.

When Maggie turned to walk back to the stove and put the teakettle down, her thoughts were troubled. She hated to argue, although Jubal Green had certainly pricked her temper. And she still believed he was being mighty hard on his poor mother.

As she trod across the kitchen floor, however, Maggie was suddenly taken up short by the realization that Jubal Green might just have paid her a compliment. She stood at the stove and thought over his words. The more she thought about it, the more she was convinced that he had actually compared her favorably to his mother.

Maggie was smiling a little bit when she turned back to face the two men at the table. "Thank you, Mr. Green."

Then she scooped Annie up out of her high chair and carried her off to the bedroom, where she prepared her for bed. She felt pretty good all at once.

Jubal and Dan sat at the kitchen table and stared after her.

Jubal looked at Dan, puzzled. "What did she thank me for?"

Dan was grinning at him. "I think she just figured out that you praised her."

"Praised her?"

Jubal tried to concentrate on the few words he and Maggie had exchanged. It seemed to him that he had been irked with the woman; he didn't remember praising her. He finally gave up and shook his head.

"Hell," he said. "I'll never understand women *or* Indians."

Dan just laughed.

In another week, Jubal decided he was ready to try to mount his horse.

"I don't think that's a very good idea, Mr. Green," said Maggie, when he let his intentions be known at breakfast.

Jubal looked up at her and was taken aback by the concern he read in her eyes.

She's worried about me! he thought. Then his surprise turned to pleasure. I'll be damned, she's worried about me! For some reason, that made him feel really good.

"It will be all right, Mrs. Bright," he told her.

But Maggie looked doubtful. "I don't know, Mr. Green. That leg wound is mighty fresh. You're still limping awful bad. It would be terrible if it opened up again."

Maggie knew Jubal shouldn't be riding yet. He was still too weak. He might hurt himself all over again, and she thought he had been hurt enough already. Besides, the mere thought of having to doctor another open bleeding wound made her blanch. She hated the sight of blood.

Jubal began to frown. He was glad she was concerned. He did not, however, care for an argument.

"I already said it would be all right," he said, his tone a trifle curt.

"I know what you said, Mr. Green," Maggie snapped back. "But I'm the one has to fix you up if you get hurt again, and I don't want to do it."

Jubal's frown deepened. "I'll be all right." With that he stomped, limping, out of the comfort of Maggie's kitchen and over to the barn. "Hell," he muttered. "I thought she was worried about me. She just doesn't want to have to nursemaid me anymore."

Then Jubal hollered at Four Toes Smith when Four Toes also suggested he wait a while before trying to get up on Old Red again. Old Red was a very large horse with a lot of spirit. At Jubal's angry snarl, Four Toes just shrugged and saddled the horse, since Jubal couldn't perform that chore by himself yet.

Dan had been riding Old Red every day so the horse wouldn't get wild, and he wasn't too fresh today. But he hadn't been ridden by Jubal for quite a while, and he was a little skittish.

It hurt when Jubal lifted his injured left leg up to the stirrup. It hurt like a son of a gun when he stuck that foot into the stirrup and braced his entire body weight on it while he slung his right leg over the horse's back. He had to clamp his teeth together in order to keep from bellowing in pain when Old Red decided to take exception to this activity and skittered a little bit.

Even when Jubal had made it into the saddle and the pressure on his left leg was relieved, his thigh still burned and throbbed like crazy. He began to wonder if this had really been such a good idea after all. He'd eat hog slop before he'd admit that to anybody, though.

Maggie watched him from the door of the house. She had intended to ignore Jubal Green and his foolishness because his stubborn attitude made her mad, but she found she couldn't bear to do that. She was too frightened for him. So she stood there in the open doorway, worrying her apron with nervous fingers, and watched. She had to squint her eyes up tight to see what was going on.

"He looks like it doesn't feel very good, Annie," she murmured to her daughter.

Annie was playing on the kitchen floor with a little wooden horse and rider that Four Toes had carved for her. "Feel good," she said to her mama.

"Stubborn man," muttered Maggie.

"Stubbun," agreed Annie.

Maggie's heart lurched when Jubal kicked up Old Red and they began to trot around the barnyard. If she squinted her eyes real hard, she could see his lips pinched together and white with pain.

Jubal was in agony. He saw Maggie standing at the doorway and wouldn't give her the satisfaction of watching him give up. So he continued to ride Old Red in circles around the barnyard, even though he was sure he'd never walk again afterward. He wished Maggie would go back into the house so he could quit this foolishness with his dignity intact.

Maggie was holding her breath. She was sure Jubal would open that dratted thigh wound again. She knew he was in pain, and her eyes filled up in sympathy.

"Damned man," she whispered.

"Dam man," Annie parroted.

That perky statement startled Maggie, and she glanced down at her child.

Oh, Lordy, I'd better start watching my mouth, she

told herself. What kind of terrible mother must she be to swear in front of her baby girl?

Jubal finally couldn't stand it another second. He was sweating with agony. His entire lower body felt as though he'd been kicked by a mule, and ferocious pains were radiating from his wounded right shoulder and down through his arm and chest and back. He decided he'd proved enough for one day and reined Old Red in with an effort that made him curse furiously under his breath as blinding pains shot through his upper body. Sweat beaded on his forehead and began to dribble down his face.

He looked around, hoping to spot Four Toes, and didn't see him. He had hoped the man would be close by to take custody of Old Red when he dismounted.

Well, that's too bad, Jubal decided. I've got to get down or I'll pass out right here in the saddle. Again. Maggie had described her first encounter with him. So he sucked in a huge breath of air in preparation for the enormous, agonizing effort.

Maggie watched in apprehension as the big roan horse came to a slow stop. Her hands went to her mouth when she saw Jubal's body heave with the exertion of slinging his right leg over the horse's back. She was already running toward the barnyard by the time his boot hit the ground.

"Stay there, Annie!" she called to her daughter as she took off.

Jubal's right leg buckled under him because he was too weak to stand. He tried to support himself by clutching at the saddle, an effort that startled Old Red into shuffling away. That jarred Jubal's wounded left leg and it also buckled, effectively trapping his boot in Old Red's stirrup.

Maggie skidded into the barnyard just in time to grab Old Red's reins and keep him from dragging Jubal off.

"Be still, horse," she said, very gently, to Old Red.

She wanted to scream her frustration and fear at Jubal, but she remembered Kenny telling her to always speak softly to horses so as not to frighten them. It was advice he used to forget on a regular basis himself, but Maggie didn't. Her heart was slamming in her chest so hard she was sure it would burst right out, but she had Old Red under control in a second.

While she was calming the horse, Jubal was furiously trying to disengage his boot from the stirrup. Since neither one of his legs wanted to work and he couldn't use both arms, he was having no luck at all in that endeavor.

He swore ferociously to himself, embarrassed that his stubbornness had caused him to do such a blamed stupid thing as get himself stuck in a stirrup. And in front of Maggie, no less. Jubal hated looking like a fool in front of Maggie Bright.

He was also in agony. His entire body was throbbing.

"Stop it, Mr. Green," Maggie said quietly but sternly, as she calmed down Old Red. "Just lie still." Her fury at him for hurting himself made her voice shake.

Jubal gave up and did as he was told. If pain hadn't completely wiped out any color he'd gained over the course of his recovery, he would have been blushing in humiliation. He lay on his back with his boot in the stirrup and silently called himself every vile name he could think of and then made up new ones.

When the horse was completely settled, Maggie tied Old Red's reins to a fence post. She was trembling when she finally knelt down next to Jubal and carefully disengaged his bootheel from the stirrup.

Jubal watched her in a haze of pain that was fogging his brain and realized that tears were streaming down her cheeks. He frowned. It didn't seem right to him that she should be crying. He was the one who was hurt.

"You just put your arm around my shoulder, Mr. Green, and I'll help you into the house," Maggie was saying. The gentleness she had assumed for Old Red was still evident in her voice because she was too worried right now to think about how much she wanted to holler at Jubal.

Jubal just absolutely hated being helpless. Still, it felt pretty good when he put his arm around Maggie's shoulder and she slipped hers around his waist. He allowed her to help him to his feet before he asked the question that was uppermost in his mind.

"Why are you crying?"

Maggie sniffed back her tears and nearly buckled under Jubal's weight as they began a slow walk back to the house. Her throat felt stuffed full of rocks, and it took her a few seconds before she could answer his stupid question. When she did speak, her words sounded somewhat strangled.

"I'm crying because I was so damned worried about you, you stubborn fool man," she said. "You could have killed yourself," she added, and her tone conveyed an odd combination of anger, worry, and fear.

Her arm tightened around his waist. Maggie could barely restrain herself from bawling right here on this man's shoulder, she'd been so scared.

Jubal couldn't think of anything to say. *Thank you* sprang to mind, and he didn't know why, especially when he realized he wouldn't have been thanking her for helping him but for worrying about him. That didn't make any sense.

He was still in exquisite pain. His whole lower body felt as though an elephant had stepped on it, and the right side of his torso was on fire.

"Ho, Mama. Ho, Juba," said Annie as they passed her outside the doorway.

Normally Maggie thought it was cute the way Annie called Jubal "Juba." Today she was so worried she didn't even notice her daughter's cheerful greeting.

Jubal said, "Hello, Annie," before he limped past her into the house.

Maggie led him through the door of the little house and on into the bedroom. She didn't stop in the kitchen. Jubal was somewhat surprised. He expected her to dump him into a chair and yell at him.

"You lie down now, Mr. Green. I'll get those boots off you and then get you some tea and find Mr. Blue Gully."

"Thank you, Mrs. Bright," Jubal said, through teeth clenched in pain.

Maggie helped him ease down onto the bed.

He felt like such a damned fool.

She had to squat down next to the bed so as not to drop him into a heap on the covers. She ended up with one arm under his back and the other encircling his chest, an intimate embrace that would have embarrassed her if she hadn't been too upset to think about it.

If Jubal hadn't been so abashed at what his own stubborn foolishness had reduced him to, he would have enjoyed the feel of Maggie's firm breasts pressing against his chest. He was sorry when she wriggled her arm out from under him and removed her other arm from his shoulder.

As soon as Maggie had disengaged her arms, she dashed to the foot of the bed to remove Jubal's boots.

"I'll take the right one off first, since that leg's not gun-shot," she announced.

"Thank you, Mrs. Bright," Jubal said again, humbly. Lord, he hated being humble. It didn't come naturally at all.

The right boot slid off easily. Then Maggie took a deep breath. "I'll try not to hurt you, Mr. Green," she said, as she picked up his left boot.

It's too late for that, thought Jubal grimly, and his whole body clenched from the jolt of his leg being lifted. But he ground his teeth together and clung like a barnacle to the mattress as Maggie wriggled the boot down his calf.

Her eyes were tearing up again by the time she had worked it off. She put the boots together neatly at the foot of the bed and wiped her eyes with the back of her hand.

"There," she said.

She wanted to scold Jubal for frightening her and making her hurt him, but she didn't know how to put the words together. How did you tell somebody that it made you want to run and hide to have to do things to him that hurt him, even though those things were going to help him in the long run? It didn't even make sense to her; she knew it wouldn't make sense to Jubal.

Jubal saw her tears and felt bad. "I'm sorry I'm causing you more work, Mrs. Bright," he mumbled. He was unused to having to make apologies and he hated it.

"Work?" Maggie repeated, astounded. "Work?" She stared at him.

"I know you don't have time to nursemaid me anymore. I shouldn't have tried to ride Old Red. I'm sorry." He was annoyed that she hadn't just said "That's all right" or something and gone on about her business.

Maggie's eyes overflowed again. The ridiculous man thought she was mad at him because he was causing her extra work! Maggie couldn't believe it, and her anger got the better of her all at once.

"My God in heaven, Mr. Green, I don't care about the work. I haven't done a lick of work since the three of you showed up here, anyway. I was scared to death you'd hurt yourself. And you did, too!"

Jubal wished to God she'd stop crying. It was breaking his heart to watch her and not be able to do anything about it. He wanted to hold her and tell her that everything was all right.

Then, all of a sudden, her words penetrated the blanket of pain and embarrassment that was nearly smothering him. His eyes narrowed in concentration.

"You were *worried* about me?"

"Worried about you?" Maggie cried, furious at his stupid question. "I was scared to death."

For some reason, Jubal felt a smug sense of satisfaction begin to worm its way into his agony. She was worried about him. It wasn't the work. It was him!

"Come here, Mrs. Bright," he said, and held out his good left hand.

Maggie wiped her eyes again and sniffed suspiciously. "Why? I have to go get you some tea."

"Come here first."

He was speaking softly and looking at her with those dratted sea-green eyes in a way that drew Maggie like a magnet. She didn't understand why she felt compelled to obey him, but she did. She knelt by the bed next to him and her hand, of its own accord, sneaked out to brush the hair away from his forehead.

Jubal liked that a lot. "Thank you for worrying about me, Mrs. Bright."

Maggie swallowed. "You're welcome," she whispered.

Jubal's gaze was caressing her face, and she began to feel real funny. Then his good hand brushed her hair back, just as she had brushed his. The touch sent whispery shivers down Maggie's spine.

"Do you feel better?" she asked to break the spell.

"I feel like hell," he murmured.

"Serves you right."

Jubal grinned. "I guess it does."

His eyes were pulling her closer and closer to his face. She knew she was going to kiss him a second before she did it. It was probably the shortest kiss in the history of the world, because the moment her lips touched his, she realized what she was doing and immediately withdrew. Then she blushed furiously and scrambled to her feet.

Jubal smiled at her as she jumped up. He couldn't figure out how he could be feeling so good when he was feeling so bad.

Maggie whirled around and ran like a spooked jackrabbit into the kitchen. She pressed her hands to her flaming cheeks as she leaned against the kitchen table, wondering what on earth had possessed her. She was shaking when she put water on to boil for tea.

"My God, I must miss Kenny even more than I thought I did," she whispered to herself and her daughter, who was galloping her wooden horse across the floor in delight.

Then Maggie attempted to recall what Kenny looked like. Try as she might, every time she managed to conjure up the lean, lanky image of her sweet-natured dead husband and picture his loving, calf-eyed grin, that image was immediately replaced by that of another man. One with rough-hewn features, green-flecked eyes, broad shoulders, sun-streaked hair, and a hard face.

"Lord almighty," Maggie breathed. "What kind of disloyal, no-good person am I, anyway? I loved Kenny. He near to saved my life. He gave me a home of my own and a beautiful baby, and I can't even remember what he looked like."

By the time the water boiled, Maggie was crying tears of regret and thinking Aunt Lucy had been right about her all along. She wiped them away disconsolately and decided she'd better try to forget about her own shortcomings for a while. Right now, she had to see what needed to be done for Jubal Green. She could berate herself about her many weaknesses later.

She wondered if the miraculous pain-killing bark that Dan Blue Gully had given her for her headaches would help ease Jubal's pain any, so she got out her carefully stored leather pouch and laid it on the table next to the teapot. Then she went over to stand at the bedroom door. She didn't dare go inside again until Dan had been found.

"The tea's steeping, Mr. Green. I'm going to find Mr. Blue Gully now."

Jubal was lying on the bed, stiff with pain. He knew he should relax, but he hurt too much to ease his muscles yet. He wished Maggie would come back in and put her hands on him again. She had such soothing hands.

"Can't you do it yourself?" he asked. "Dan's got work to do."

Maggie shook her head and didn't budge from the doorway. She had her arms crossed in front of her and looked mighty tough. She glared at him, mostly to keep herself from crying in fright.

"No, Mr. Green. Mr. Blue Gully's the one who knows about gunshot wounds, not me. And don't you dare move from that bed while I'm gone outside to find him for you."

Her voice had taken on a commanding tone to cover her nervousness and worry. She was terrified that Jubal might have reopened his thigh wound. That one was much more serious than the shoulder wound had been, and if it opened up again, infection and gangrene were real possibilities. And although they had never discussed it, Maggie was sure Jubal Green would strenuously object to amputation.

Also, while she might indeed have been able to examine the thigh, she blushed at the thought. It was, after all, one thing to hold a naked man's thigh when he was unconscious, fevered, and in danger of dying. It was another thing entirely to strip a recovering and all too conscious man whom she had just kissed and handle that man's naked thigh.

Jubal sighed with frustration. Now Dan Blue Gully was going to know what an ass he'd been too. Jubal knew he'd never live this day down.

"I won't move, Mrs. Bright," he said. He didn't add that he wouldn't have been able to get up even if he'd been so inclined. His entire body felt as though he'd fallen off a high cliff onto pointed rocks and bounced against granite outcroppings on the way down.

"All right," Maggie said. She left him with a parting sniff that Jubal believed to be one of contempt, but which had actually been necessary for Maggie to swallow her tears.

She found Dan Blue Gully out behind the barn, helping Four Toes Smith build a pen for goats. Four Toes had decided Maggie needed goats, even though Maggie wasn't quite sure why. She didn't argue, however.

As soon as he saw her, Dan put down his hammer. "Figured you'd be coming to fetch me pretty soon," he said calmly. "Four Toes told me what Jubal was up to. Fool man."

Maggie was so relieved she could barely speak. When she'd left the house, she wasn't even sure if she'd be able to find Dan. "He's really hurting, Mr. Blue Gully."

"Of course he is."

"Do you suppose that bark you gave me for my headaches might help his pain any, Mr. Blue Gully?"

Dan scratched his chin and thought. He was still thinking by the time they got back to the house.

"Ho, Dan," said Annie cheerily when they entered the kitchen.

"Howdy, Annie," Dan said, with a smile for the little girl.

Maggie was almost used to Dan's thinking patterns by this time, so she didn't repeat her question. She figured he'd answer her when he got around to it.

They were met by an uneasy glare from Jubal Green when they stepped into the bedroom.

"Danny," Jubal said by way of greeting.

Dan shook his head and grinned at the man on the

bed. Jubal was looking mighty white around the mouth and mighty sweaty around the hairline. He was in obvious pain.

"Shoot, Jubal. Don't you think we got more things to do around here than nurse you every time you pull some durn fool stunt?"

"Just check my damned leg, Danny. Mrs. Bright's already lectured me about trying to ride Old Red too soon."

Dan chuckled. "Let's get them britches off, then."

Maggie's eyes widened and she hurried to say, "I'll get the tea, Mr. Blue Gully."

Jubal watched her hasty retreat with a frown. Then he looked at Dan as the Indian worked Jubal's belt buckle loose.

"She was worried about me, Danny," Jubal said.

"Of course she was."

Jubal scowled. "I mean, she was worried about *me,* Danny. I thought she was mad because I was causing her trouble. But she was worried about me."

Dan looked his old friend straight in the eye. "And I said, 'Of course she was.'"

"You mean you're not surprised?" Then he grunted. "God damn it, Danny, take it easy."

Dan was easing Kenny Bright's made-over trousers down Jubal's legs. They were a tight fit, because the bandages wrapped around Jubal's thigh made the already bulky leg even larger.

"No," replied Dan. "I'm not surprised." He frowned when he looked at the bandage on Jubal's thigh. "You done it this time, Jubal."

Jubal forgot about Maggie for a minute. He tried to prop himself up and see his leg, but Dan gestured for him to stay on his back.

"What's the matter?" Jubal asked, worry tainting the words.

"It's bleedin'," said the Indian. He looked at Jubal and shook his head again. "You durn fool."

Jubal sighed. "Shit."

"Well," said Dan, "I'd better take a look-see."

He began to unwrap the bandages. Then he grabbed a quilt and threw it onto Jubal's chest.

"Cover yourself up," he commanded.

"Why?" Jubal asked. "You've seen me naked before."

Dan looked exasperated. "Yeah, and so's Mrs. Bright, but she ain't seen you naked for a long time and never when you've been awake—least not so's I know about it. And I don't want to maim your vanity none, but you ain't a pretty sight. I think we might could spare her, don't you?"

Jubal was annoyed and a little embarrassed by his friend's candid comment. "I guess so."

When she came back into the bedroom with a tray laden with a cup and saucer and a pot of tea, he had barely had time to contemplate the idea of Maggie seeing him naked. By that time, he was discreetly covered by her grandmother's quilt, and Dan Blue Gully had already sprinkled the wound with medicine and was rewrapping it.

"For God's sake, be careful, Danny," Jubal muttered. "It hurts like a son of a bitch."

"Yeah," said Dan. "And whose fault is that?"

Jubal didn't answer. He just glared at the top of Dan's shiny black head as Dan worked on his leg.

"Here's your tea, Mr. Green," Maggie said.

"Thank you, Mrs. Bright," was Jubal's somewhat surly reply.

Maggie didn't look at Jubal's face, a circumstance

Jubal noted with interest. Instead, she turned to Dan. When she saw that he was tending to Jubal's naked thigh, she quickly focused her attention to the floor. Jubal grinned, but Maggie didn't notice.

"What about that bark?" Maggie asked Dan. She knew she probably didn't need to remind him, but she was nervous.

Dan grunted and continued to wrap the thigh.

"Well," he said at last. "I don't know. You seen what he done today, and he was still hurting. If you give him some of that bark and he don't hurt no more, he's liable to do durn near anything."

Maggie's eyebrows shot up. She hadn't considered that.

She dared a peek at Jubal Green. He wasn't smiling anymore. His brow was furrowed, and he was sweating with pain over what Dan was doing to his leg. His face was pale, and his lips were set into a grim line.

"Well," she said, knowing what Dan said to be true but longing to relieve Jubal's suffering, "maybe if we made him promise."

Pain was making Jubal's touchy temper run perilously thin by this time. "Are the two of you talking about me?" he asked with a grunt of pain as Dan tugged on his leg.

"You know it," said Dan, grinning up at him from his chore.

"Well, for God's sake, I'm right here. What are you talking about?"

Maggie's own temper was short at the moment. Here she had tried to stop this foolish man from hurting himself, then worried herself half to death about him when he wouldn't be stopped, and then she'd had to rescue him when he had hurt himself anyway.

Then she'd made a complete idiot of herself and kissed him. And now he was complaining to Dan Blue Gully and herself, both of whom only had his welfare at heart.

"We're talking about whether to give you some medicine that might make you stop hurting, Mr. Green. But what Mr. Blue Gully said is correct. You can't be trusted," she snapped.

Jubal turned his head to glower up at her. "What do you mean I can't be trusted?" he bellowed. Nobody had ever called Jubal Green untrustworthy before, and he didn't like it.

"You can't be trusted not to do something else stupid and hurt yourself again. You already proved that!" Maggie hollered back. Her fists were planted on her hips and her eyes were spitting fire.

"Oh," Jubal muttered, only slightly mollified when he realized she hadn't meant to disparage his entire character. "That's what you meant."

"Yes," Maggie said, now angry beyond reason. "That's exactly what I meant. If I give you some of my bark, you'd better promise me on whatever you consider holy that you won't try to get up and do something else stupid and hurt yourself again." She turned to Dan. "Does he keep his word when he gives it, Mr. Blue Gully?"

Jubal roared, "Do I *what?*"

Dan laughed outright at that. Then he nodded. "Yes, I guess he keeps his word."

"You *guess?*" Jubal wanted to strangle the both of them.

Maggie eyed Jubal Green angrily. "All right, Mr. Green, I'm willing to give one piece of my bark to you if you promise me you won't get up when you feel better."

Jubal wanted to tell them both to go to hell and take Maggie's bark with them. His fury found voice when Dan laid his leg down and a monumentally vicious pain tore through him, making his entire body buck up off the bed.

"Damnation!" he bellowed.

"I guess he does hurt some," Dan said.

"I'm not moving until he gives his word," Maggie said.

"Hell!" was Jubal's response.

Rivulets of sweat were running down his face. His hands gripped the mattress as though he were afraid he would fly off it if he let go. Of course, tensing his arm muscles made his shoulder throb like thunder.

"Your word, Mr. Green," Maggie said stubbornly.

"All right!" Jubal finally hollered in defeat. "You've got my word."

Dan smiled at Maggie. "We can try one," he said calmly.

"All right," Maggie agreed.

She returned to the kitchen, opened her leather pouch, and retrieved one of her treasured pieces of medicinal bark.

Before she gave it to Jubal, she held it like a wand in front of him and said, "I want you to know, Mr. Green, that this bark is very important to me. This is the first medicine I've ever taken in my entire life that has helped me. If you waste this piece or don't keep your word about it, I'm going to get Mr. Blue Gully and Mr. Smith in here to tie you to the bed. And I keep my word too, Mr. Green. Do I make myself clear?"

Jubal didn't know whether his fury or his pain was worse. He cast a ferocious glare at Maggie Bright. "You make yourself clear," he muttered grimly.

"All right then."

Maggie handed Jubal the bark and poured him out some tea. She put milk and sugar in it, just the way he liked it, and sat beside the bed.

"Now, chew the bark and drink tea with it so it doesn't make your stomach sick." She sounded just like a nurse with a patient.

"Yes, ma'am," Jubal muttered.

Dan covered Jubal up with the quilt. He smiled at the uneasy couple as he left them to go out and tend to the goat pen with Four Toes Smith. Somehow he sensed that they should be alone.

8

The bark worked its magic on Jubal, as it had on Maggie. It wasn't more than fifteen minutes after he had begun munching on it that he noticed a big difference in the level of his pain. His sweating stopped, and his muscles, which had been tensed up in agony, began to relax.

Maggie was sitting beside the bed to monitor his progress because she wanted to be on hand if he had some kind of bad reaction. She watched him with great concern and sponged off his forehead every now and then when the sweat dripped into his eyes.

Annie had moved her field of operation into the bedroom. She was being quiet, so Maggie didn't make her go away. The little girl was still playing horse-and-rider. She had also toddled into the other room to fetch her building-brick set, which was now housed in a neat little cloth bag with a corded drawstring that Maggie had sewn for the purpose. At present she was busily creating a little pen to hold her wooden horse.

Maggie had been watching her daughter for a while, a smile playing on her lips. Now she turned her attention back to Jubal Green and found him peering up at her. He looked a little bit less tense, and his lips weren't pressed as tightly together as they had been.

"Are you feeling any better, Mr. Green?" she asked politely.

"Yes."

He really liked to look at Maggie Bright. When she'd been watching her daughter, her eyes had gone so soft and loving. Jubal had a faint memory of her pretty face hovering over him when he'd been so near death.

"I'm glad you feel better," Maggie said. She wasn't angry anymore, never having been one to hold a grudge.

"Thank you, Mrs. Bright," Jubal said softly. He wished she'd kiss him again. Only he wanted it to last longer this time. He sighed.

"What do you chew on this stuff for?" he asked Maggie then, curious. He held the remains of his bark up for her to see.

"I get awful headaches, Mr. Green. They really overwhelm me. Sometimes they're so bad, I throw up." She shook her head. "Until Mr. Blue Gully showed up with this bark, I just had to suffer through them."

Jubal had heard of headaches like that, but he hadn't ever experienced one himself. He'd always just figured the people who claimed to have them were exaggerating. But by this time, he knew Maggie Bright too well to suspect her of deceit.

"That's a shame, Mrs. Bright. What did you do with your farm and your kid when you got one of them before Dan showed up?" It didn't sound to him as though she'd be able to function at all well in the throes of one of those headaches.

Maggie sighed. "I just did the best I could, Mr. Green. There wasn't much else I could do." She looked at her daughter again. "Sometimes I wish I wasn't so weak," she admitted sadly, ashamed of the flaw that Aunt Lucy had so despised.

"Weak?" He was astounded. He was even more astounded when he realized all at once that Maggie Bright was the first woman on the face of the earth whom he actually respected. She'd earned that respect, too, and Jubal Green's respect was never bestowed lightly.

"My aunt always complained about my weakness," Maggie continued hesitantly. She was embarrassed to be speaking to Jubal this way, but for some reason she felt unable to stop herself.

"Who the hell is your aunt to complain about you?" Jubal demanded. He had a sudden angry urge to talk to this stupid aunt of Maggie's and set her straight.

Maggie looked at him, surprised at the vehemence in his voice.

"Why, she and my uncle live in Indiana, Mr. Green. They took me in when my folks died. I know it was good of them to do it, but—well, they never let me forget it, if you know what I mean." She felt a little bit traitorous to be telling him this. After all, she owed her aunt and uncle a lot. They had told her that over and over. And while in her heart of hearts Maggie detested her aunt and knew the feeling was returned tenfold, she'd never told anybody. She actually considered it just another indication of her own weak character.

"I know exactly what you mean," Jubal said grimly.

"I never could seem to please her, though," Maggie admitted with chagrin. "I was always wearing out."

There. She'd made a full confession of her weakness. Maggie had been told that confession was good for the soul, but she didn't feel a bit better now. In fact, she felt like a pure fool.

Jubal was just about to tell Maggie exactly what he thought of her aunt and uncle, but Annie tugged on her mother's apron right then, so he didn't get the chance.

"Look, Mama. Look, Juba," the little girl said.

Jubal glanced down at little Annie. Her big brown eyes sparkled with glee, and he couldn't help but grin. Annie was almost as cute as Sara had been.

Maggie smiled at her daughter. "Show us, Annie."

"See?"

Annie pulled her mother off the chair to view her handiwork, and Maggie knelt on the floor to watch. Annie had built a corral for her horse out of her building bricks. She squatted down next to the corral and put her wooden man on top of her wooden horse and made them trot around the corral. Then she made the horse stop. Then she made the man fall off the horse and lie on his back.

"See Juba?" Annie said. She smiled broadly at the two adults.

Maggie burst into laughter. Jubal expelled a big gust of air and then he, too, reluctantly laughed.

Maggie had never heard Jubal laugh before. He had a marvelous laugh. It was rich and deep, and it made her toes curl up and her heart sing.

"That's wonderful, Annie," she said when she could catch her breath.

"My God," said Jubal. "I'm going to be one of those

legends that never die and people laugh about for centuries."

"Well, that will teach you to disobey your nurse," Maggie said sassily. She rose from the floor and stood beside him once more with her hands on her hips.

Jubal grinned up at her. "I'll be sure not to do that again."

His voice was a caress, and Maggie got embarrassed. "Do you want more tea, Mr. Green?"

"No, thank you," Jubal said. Then he yawned. The yawn took him by surprise.

"You need to sleep, Mr. Green."

"I guess so." Jubal was surprised at just how exhausting acting like a fool could be.

"I'd better start supper now. Do you want me to take Annie out so you can rest?"

"Nah. Let her stay. She's not bothering me. Besides, maybe I can set her straight about a few things before she maligns me any further."

Maggie grinned down at him. "I don't know about that, Mr. Green. 'Pears to me she got it just about right."

Jubal smiled at Maggie until she left the bedroom for the kitchen. He kept smiling until he fell asleep.

When Maggie came back into the room to check up on her charges a half hour or so later, Annie had climbed onto the bed with Jubal and was snuggled up against him, asleep. He was cradling her in his good arm. Annie held her wooden horse and wooden man hugged to her chest. The pure pleasure that Maggie felt when she observed them surprised her.

Jubal and Annie dozed the afternoon away while Maggie cooked. She peeked in on them every now and then, and her heart warmed right up every time she did. She was singing softly as she stirred the chicken and vegetables she had put on to stew and began to measure out the rice. The reality that the occupants of her little house were still in danger had completely fled from her consciousness.

That reality was rudely reintroduced a second or two later when Dan Blue Gully and Four Toes Smith burst into the kitchen. They bolted the door behind them and grabbed their firearms.

"Oh, my God!" cried Maggie. "What's the matter?"

"Better get down, Mrs. Bright. Looks like Mulrooney's people are back."

Dan and Four Toes squatted in position beside the windows of the little house. For the first time, Maggie realized that her cozy home had been turned into a fortress. Without her even being aware of what they'd been doing, the two Indians had reinforced the windows, carved gunwales into the sills, and added metal bolts to the doors.

"Where's Annie?" Four Toes wanted to know.

"She was on the bed sleeping, but she probably isn't anymore," Maggie said, dashing to the bedroom.

Sure enough, Annie was sitting up, knuckling her eyes, and her little face was puckered up in preparation for a good wail. She'd been frightened by the noises in the kitchen. Maggie ran to the bed to pick her up. Jubal's hand stopped her from turning right around and rushing out again.

"What is it?" His voice sounded gravelly with sleep.

"Your friend Mr. Mulrooney's sent some more people to kill us," Maggie told him. Right now she was very angry with all of the men in her house for bringing this danger to her door, and that emotion leaked into her voice.

"Shit." Jubal still held onto Maggie's arm when he swung his legs over the side of the bed.

When she saw his huge hairy thighs, Maggie's eyes widened. Then she squeezed them tightly shut. "You're not supposed to get out of bed, Mr. Green," she choked out. "You promised."

"I know I promised, Mrs. Bright. But that was before Mulrooney's men showed up. I get dispensation when somebody's trying to kill me."

Jubal tugged on his britches. The magic bark was still working, and his leg didn't hurt too much. He limped over to the chest against the wall and grabbed his guns.

Maggie was standing in the doorway, staring at him, her insides roiling with fear, anger, and confusion. She held her baby tightly. Annie's chubby little legs straddled her mama's hips, and her fist was crammed into her mouth. Jubal strode over to them with a little less of a limp.

"The two of you stay here. Get down. Sit beside the bed and don't move."

He took Maggie's shoulders in his hands and squeezed her tight, looking at her with an intensity Maggie's startled brain couldn't quite take in.

"Maybe I can help you," she suggested in a strangled voice.

"No!"

Jubal hollered the word and Maggie winced. "Don't yell at us!" she cried, her voice a tangy blend of fear and anger.

"I'm sorry," he said, more softly. "No. You can't help. Just stay in here with your baby and keep her safe. Don't go anywhere, and stay down. Promise me," he demanded.

Maggie stared up at him and her brain registered something akin to terror. She finally nodded, knowing she'd just waste everybody's time if she argued. Besides, Jubal was right; she had to keep track of Annie.

Jubal nodded and started for the kitchen. Then suddenly he stopped, jerked around, and kissed Maggie hard on the lips. She was too startled to respond. He was gone again in a second, and she could only press her fingers to her lips and wonder what that kiss had meant.

Gunfire erupted moments later, and then Maggie was too busy being scared and cradling her daughter's small head against her shoulder to wonder about anything at all. She could hear Jubal, Dan, and Four Toes in the kitchen, discussing tactics. Maggie didn't know anything about tactics.

"Oh, Lordy, Annie, I just want all those dratted Mulrooney hirelings to go away and leave us alone. And not only that," she admitted to her daughter, willing to say it out loud because there was only Annie to hear her, "I want those three men to stay with us forever and make our lives easier."

She sniffed unhappily and sat on the floor, squashed up against the bed, and hugged Annie to her breast. Annie was frightened too, mostly because her mother was, and she didn't squirm to get free of Maggie's arms. She wriggled up closer against Maggie at each burst of gunfire.

Maggie felt a moment of sheer panic when she heard Dan and Jubal arguing. Their fussing began after what seemed like hours and hours of the noisy fighting. Actually, only several minutes had passed.

"Damn it, Jubal, you can't do it. You're crippled, for

God's sake. You'd never make it." Dan was obviously annoyed.

"It's me he wants, Danny, damn it. I'd be able to draw their fire better."

"He wants us all, Jubal; you know that as well as I do. Those men out there don't care who's who. They're just hired to kill us all, and the woman and the baby too. I ain't a cripple, so I'm going."

"Shit," Jubal said furiously. "I don't like it."

"I don't like it either, but it's got to be done, and it's got to be done by somebody who can run like hell, and you can't."

"I guess not," Jubal said. He was obviously not pleased to admit it.

"I guess you'll listen to your nurse from now on." Four Toes popped into the conversation with a grin in his voice.

"Shit," Jubal said again.

Maggie held her breath when, during the next lull in the shooting, she heard the back door creak open. She prayed into her daughter's soft curls when the silence stretched out for what seemed like decades. Then she jumped a foot when shots rang out again, and she finally gave up trying to be brave and was crying when she heard the thundering of horse's hooves and the peltering sound of running feet. Then came what sounded like a series of measured, calculated shots. A man screamed after one of those shots, and Maggie tried to cover Annie's ears with her own shaking hands.

Then there was silence. The only sound Maggie could hear was that of her own hiccuping sobs.

For some reason this interruption of her peace was much more terrifying than that first time when Jubal had been lying wounded on her bed and Dan Blue

Gully had left to track French Jack. She knew the reason for her increased terror now was that she had come to care for these men. A lot. All of them. And she didn't want them to die.

The quiet grew and grew and grew, until Maggie thought she and Annie must be the only two people left alive in the whole world.

Then, all of a sudden, there was another furious volley of shots. Maggie tried to stifle her shriek, but she wasn't sure how successful she was. Annie whimpered into her shoulder.

"All right! It's all right! All clear!" Dan Blue Gully's voice sounded faint and far away, floating over the dusky, smoky, early spring evening to the little house in the clearing. It penetrated the ringing in Maggie's ears slowly, and she only gradually realized what it must mean.

Then she sucked in a huge gasp of air that tasted sharply of cordite. She wanted to run to the kitchen to see for herself that everything really was all right, as Dan Blue Gully's words implied, but her knees were shaking so much she couldn't stand up.

Jubal Green limped into the bedroom and stopped just inside the door, looking down at the two females who were clutching each other and staring at him. Two pairs of big eyes, one a soft brown, and the other a vivid blue, held him captive. Both Maggie and Annie were petrified.

His leg hurt like crazy but he squatted down in front of Maggie. His big calloused hand reached out and stroked her cheek. Then his hand moved over to Annie's soft hair, and he leaned over and kissed the baby's head. He wanted to kiss the baby's mama, but he didn't quite dare.

He said softly, "It's all right. It's all over now."

Suddenly Maggie was in his arms. She didn't know how she got there. She only knew that with one enormous effort, she propelled herself and her daughter off the floor and toward Jubal Green, whose embrace was big enough for the both of them.

He rocked them for a long time while Maggie sobbed on his shoulder. The effects of Dan's magic bark were wearing off, and Jubal thought he was going to die from the pain in his leg and his arm. But he wasn't about to let Maggie Bright go until she wasn't scared anymore.

That took a long time, and it was only the dawning realization that Jubal Green's wounds must be hurting him that finally made Maggie draw away from the comfort of his arms.

The mood in the little cabin was very subdued when she finally served up supper that evening. The rice had cooked too long during the gunfight and was somewhat dry, but nobody except Maggie seemed to notice.

Prometheus Mulrooney's entire body quivered when he read the wire Ferrett's shaky hand had just delivered to him. The color drained from his normally florid face, he was breathing erratically, and Ferrett thought for a hopeful moment that the man might be going to suffer a spasm.

He didn't.

Instead, he slowly lowered the wire onto his cluttered desk and pinned Ferrett with a lancelike glare that set his secretary to shivering wretchedly.

"Fetch Pelch," Mulrooney said softly.

Ferrett was sure that both he and Pelch were done

for. They hadn't done anything wrong, but that didn't make much difference when their employer was in one of these moods.

"Yes, sir," he said, in a voice that squeaked pitifully.

As he made for the door, his progress was hampered somewhat by the unsteadiness of his gait. Then he was stirred into bulletlike propulsion when Mulrooney slammed his fist down on the desk and roared, "Now!" so loudly that the windows in his office shook.

Ferrett was still trembling when he and Pelch trod up the big staircase to Mulrooney's office.

"Oh, Lord, Mr. Pelch," Ferrett said in strained tones. "It must have been real bad news."

Pelch shook his head. "It's always bad news to me, Mr. Ferrett," he whispered miserably.

Ferrett nodded.

"I'm no better than a murderer myself," Pelch said, shaking his head. "I arrange for these things."

"Well, Mr. Pelch," said Ferrett, "you don't have much choice. There's no quitting Mr. Mulrooney's employ."

"If I had a shred of courage, Mr. Ferrett, I would have resigned my post months ago, when I realized what kind of person Mr. Mulrooney was."

Ferrett's brow furrowed. "I suppose that may be true, Mr. Pelch, but you have to own that you would be a dead man right now."

Pelch heaved a heavy sigh. "Aye."

Ferrett knocked on Mulrooney's door, and he and Pelch entered after a bellowed command from their boss.

Mulrooney staked them both to the floor with his furious gaze. "We're going to New Mexico Territory, you two miserable toads," he announced. His voice sounded more strained than usual.

Ferrett and Pelch exchanged a look of bewildered fright. Ferrett cleared his throat discreetly. He looked very worried about his boss's announcement.

"Do you mean, sir, that all three of us are going to the territory, Mr. Mulrooney? Mr. Pelch and me, as well as yourself? Sir?"

Mulrooney's eyes began to bug out. Little flecks of foam appeared at the corners of his mouth. He drew his brows over his eyes in a way that made both Ferrett and Pelch shrink into themselves so tightly they seemed to shrivel under Mulrooney's glare.

"What did I just say, you slimy worm?" Mulrooney said in a rasping, grating whisper.

"You—you said we were going to New Mexico Territory, sir," Ferrett whispered.

"And do you doubt my words, you disgusting scum?"

"N-no, sir," stammered Ferrett.

"Then see to it! Pelch, wire that imbecile of an agent in Texas and tell him to expect us. We should be in Santa Fe by the end of next week. Ferrett, see to arranging transportation. I'll use my own railway carriages."

"Yes, sir," Ferrett and Pelch said together.

Mulrooney eyed the wire Ferrett had handed him earlier with such a hot glower that Ferrett would not have been surprised to see the paper burst into flames.

"The idiot hired another fool, and Green and his Indian friends are still alive. So is that wretched woman who took them in. This José Escobar"—Mulrooney gestured to the wire—"was as incompetent as Jack Gauthier. Neither one of them was worth the price of the ammunition it took to kill them."

Ferrett and Pelch could only stare. Ferrett had managed to drag himself upright and now stood, trembling in agonized apprehension, next to Pelch. He was clutching one of Pelch's coattails for security.

A vile grin stretched across Mulrooney's fat face. "So I guess I'll just have to take over the job, since my hired help is incompetent," he said to his two petrified underlings.

Then he seemed to realize the two men were still there. "Well?" he thundered. "What are you waiting for?"

Ferrett and Pelch bolted for the door of Mulrooney's library like a couple of frightened antelopes.

"New Mexico," breathed Pelch when the door had shut behind them. He wiped the sweat off of his brow with a white handkerchief.

"Oh, Lord," muttered Ferrett.

They walked down the stairs slowly, their shoulders drooping, their heads bowed under the weight of their assignment.

Ferrett looked at his companion sadly. "Do you have a will made up, Mr. Pelch?" he asked.

"Yes," replied Pelch. "Do you?"

"Yes."

"Good," said Pelch.

"But I can't leave my home!"

It was a week after Mulrooney's most recent attack, and Maggie felt as though the fabric of her life had just been ripped to shreds. After several heated minutes and quite a few angry exchanges between herself and Jubal Green, her temper tantrum had still not worn itself out.

But now, as her gaze made the circuit around the table from man to man to man, what she saw in their expressions was not encouraging. She could tell they weren't going to budge.

Dan Blue Gully looked stoic, his face unreadable. Four Toes Smith bounced Annie on his knee. He was giving the little girl horsey rides. He watched Maggie with enormous compassion recognizable in his dark brown eyes, but not a shred of compromise.

Jubal Green was furious. He knew he'd just yell at her again if he opened his mouth, so he sat stiffly at the table and let Dan do the talking. He'd already said his piece at the top of his lungs, and she was still arguing.

Women, he grumbled to himself. Just when you think you like one of them, she up and gets unreasonable.

Dan Blue Gully tried to soothe her.

"It's dangerous for you here, Mrs. Bright. You and your daughter will be safer on Jubal's spread in El Paso."

Maggie's eyes darted again from man to man. Jubal thought she looked a little wild, and he had a sudden urge to scoop her up, settle her on his lap, and tell her that everything was going to be all right. Lord, those bullets must have done him more damage than he thought. He was getting soft as mush.

"But won't they just come for you there? If you go away, won't they leave me alone?"

Her voice cracked and she had trouble getting the words out. She had been furious, when they first said she'd have to go with them to El Paso, and had argued and shouted until she was nearly hoarse. Now that she was calmer and thinking more rationally, the plain truth of her feelings struck her as almost more idiotic than her fit of pique.

The truth, Maggie acknowledged against her will, was that she didn't want these men to leave. She wanted them to stay here with her and Annie, and for everything to be peaceful, and for all of them to be happy together. Maggie knew that was unreasonable, but she still couldn't help wanting it.

"I'm afraid Mulrooney doesn't work that way, Mrs. Bright. He considers anybody who helps an enemy of his to be his enemy too. He won't leave you and your daughter alone just because we go away. In fact, to tell you the truth, we're the only protection you have."

Maggie put her face in her hands and stared at the tabletop through her fingers.

"Oh, God," she whispered.

"Jubal's got a nice ranch near El Paso, Mrs. Bright. And he's got a regular army guarding it."

Dan's attempt to make Maggie feel better wasn't working.

"Well, I've got a nice farm right here, and I don't want to leave it!"

"We know that, Mrs. Bright," Dan said with a sigh. "We're really sorry about this. But we'll be able to guard you better in El Paso."

"Oh, yes? They killed his brother there," she reminded him.

"That was because his sister-in-law wouldn't listen to reason, Mrs. Bright. She was very foolish and took their daughter and tried to get to town without an escort. When Jubal's brother went after them without waiting for help, they were all wiped out."

Maggie shuddered. She knew he was right. They were trying to protect her and Annie, even if it was their fault that she and Annie needed to be protected in the first place.

But they were asking her to leave everything she'd ever had in her life, and she simply couldn't do it. This was her home, the only real home she'd ever known. Kenny had built it. She had learned love here. Kenny was still here, for God's sake, buried in the back yard. Although she'd never say it to a soul, she liked to think his spirit still lived on here, protecting them. She was sure it would break her heart to leave that spirit behind.

"My—my husband's buried here," she whispered, her words thick with tears.

Jubal's chair scraped away from the table. He stood up and he limped, scowling, over to the window and stared out into the black night. He didn't want to hear about Maggie's husband.

Dan watched him, his face expressionless. "You can come back to your farm when the danger is over, Mrs. Bright."

"Will it ever be over?" Maggie whispered bitterly.

"I sure hope so, ma'am," the Indian said.

"You *hope* so?" Maggie knew she sounded vaguely hysterical and didn't care. "You *hope* so? I'm supposed to leave my home and everything I have in the world because you *hope* so? What if I can't *ever* come back here? What then?"

Nobody had an answer for her. She gave them a full minute, eyeing each one in turn, before she exhaled in a huge sigh and resumed staring miserably at the tabletop.

Jubal suddenly turned away from the window to face the others.

"He's hiring better people, Mrs. Bright. The man we killed last week was José Escobar, a desperado who made a name for himself all over the borderlands, in

Texas, Mexico, and the territories. There's no telling who he'll send after us next. We'd all be safer on my spread."

He hated the way Maggie's blue eyes seemed to be pleading with him. That plea must be making him soft in the head, for he suddenly felt an urge to fall onto his knees in front of her and beg her to come with them. He gave his head an angry shake to clear it of those absurd notions.

"But—but this is my *home*, Mr. Green," she said plaintively. "It may not be grand like your ranch, but it's *mine*."

Jubal quelled the last of his soft feelings, and his gaze went hard. "It'll still be here when you come back, Mrs. Bright. And I don't suppose your husband will be going anywhere."

As soon as he saw Maggie's flinch of pain, he regretted his harsh words. He ran a distracted hand through his hair and murmured a soft curse.

Dan scowled a warning at Jubal, then turned to Maggie. His expression when he looked at her was compassionate.

"We won't desert you, Mrs. Bright. When this is over and you want to come back here, we'll help you. We won't just let the place go. That's a promise." He looked over to Jubal. "Right, Jubal?"

Jubal frowned at Dan. He didn't want to promise to bring Maggie back here. To her goddamned dead husband. But he knew he had to.

"Yes. That's a promise, Mrs. Bright."

All this time, Four Toes had been paying attention to Annie. Right now he was showing her a newly whittled toy. He hadn't said a word so far, but he did look up when Jubal said these words. He glanced from Jubal to Dan to Maggie and nodded.

"They keep their word, Mrs. Bright," he said.

Maggie felt as though the whole world were ganging up on her. She didn't want to leave her home; she didn't want these men to leave her. She didn't want to go back to being alone in her cabin in the woods, but she didn't want to leave that cabin in the woods, either. It was the first place on the face of the earth where she felt she belonged. It was close to being the first place on the face of the earth where anybody had ever loved her.

Besides that, what was she supposed to do at Jubal's ranch? He said he'd protect her and she believed him. But what did he expect of her in return? Did he expect her to pay him? Oh, Lord. She didn't even know how to ask the questions she had, didn't know how to phrase them. Still, she had to try.

"What—what about food?"

"Food?" Jubal and Dan exchanged a puzzled frown.

"Yes. I believe you when you say you'll protect us, but how will we eat? I won't have my garden or my chickens or anything."

Jubal's brows nearly met over the bridge of his nose, his scowl was so black.

"What do you take me for anyway, Mrs. Bright? You think we'll haul you all the way to El Paso just to let you starve to death on my ranch? It's our fault you're in danger. For God's sake, there's food there! I said I'd take care of you. That means I'll take care of you!"

"I can't pay you, Mr. Green. I have no money." Maggie was sure he still didn't understand what she was trying to say to him.

With an incredulous stare, Jubal said, his voice a near shout, "I don't want your goddamned money,

Mrs. Bright! I wouldn't take it if you gave it to me. You saved my life! Now Mulrooney wants to kill you for it. Can't you understand? Until this is over, I'll take care of you! Criminy!"

Afraid he'd grab and shake her in his fury, Jubal turned his back to the table and ran his hand through his hair once more. Good God in heaven, what kind of man did she think he was?

Maggie flinched at his ferocity, then stared unhappily at the three men for another minute or two. Then she nodded her head very slightly.

"All right," she whispered, barely shoving the words out past the lump in her throat.

Then she burst into tears, jumped up from the table, and tore out through the front door and into the black night, so quickly that the three men could only watch, startled, as she flung herself out of the house.

"Mama?" Annie said, a puzzled expression on her face, peering at the door that had slammed shut after her mother. Four Toes held her tight.

"It's all right, Annie," he whispered.

Jubal lurched away from the window to charge outside after Maggie, but Dan put a restraining hand on his arm. Jubal frowned at his friend.

"Just be kind to her, Jubal," said Dan.

"Well, what the hell did you think I was going to be?"

Dan just shook his head. "Jubal, she's a strong woman with a big heart, and we just busted it all to hell. Be careful what you say, that's all."

"Quit growling, for one thing, Jubal," Four Toes recommended with something close to a grin.

Jubal cast them both an angry glare and stomped out of the house.

The night was black as India ink and cold as winter when he stepped outside. Above the forest, stars were so thick it looked as though he could have reached up and grabbed a handful if he'd had the inclination.

Jubal didn't take any heed of the moon or the stars until he finally found Maggie. She was sitting back on her heels beside the grave of her husband.

His heart lurched when he saw her there. She was staring up into the night sky and she had stopped crying, although her eyes still looked perilously bright. He was grateful to be spared more of her tears, at least.

Although he had been angry when he left the house, when he saw her sitting there, still as stone, he suddenly just wanted to comfort her. Very quietly, he walked up until he was standing right above her. She didn't turn to look up at him, and he didn't know what to say to her.

"Kenny loved this farm, Mr. Green," she said at last.

Jubal still didn't know what to say.

"He hacked the clearing out of the forest and built the cabin and started the farm. He was so proud of the place. He might not have been the world's best farmer, but he just loved it. And then he brought me here to share it with him. He gave me my baby here, Mr. Green."

With a tilt of her head, Maggie peered up at Jubal. Her face was papery white in the moonlight, and her big, earnest eyes looked almost black against the pallor of her skin.

"I had Annie right in our house, Mr. Green. Kenny was so happy."

Jubal cleared his throat. "I think you'll like my

ranch," he said, hoping to make her feel better about the move. "It's a big place. I think Annie will be happy there." He thought his words sounded stupid and was annoyed with himself. He never had been any good at comforting women.

Maggie looked at him without speaking for a couple of seconds. Then she turned her head to stare back at the sky again. Her myopic eyes blurred all the stars together, and she wished for the millionth time she could see better. It must be really nice to be able to pick out all those individual bright spots sparkling against the dark blanket of the night. She was so unhappy she wasn't even embarrassed at her next confession.

"I loved Kenny a lot, Mr. Green," she finally said.

Jubal didn't want to know that, but he said, "I'm sure you did," rather gruffly.

"You see, Mr. Green, Kenny was the first person in the world who ever loved me. Leaving here is like—like leaving—oh, I don't know," Maggie said in despair. She really didn't know how to tell him what this place meant to her. There just weren't enough words.

Jubal didn't know how to express the feeling either, but he suddenly caught it from her and understood. Squatting down awkwardly next to Maggie, he looked up into the glittering sky with her.

"Mrs. Bright, I'm really sorry about all this. You don't deserve what we're putting you through. I wish we could just go away and have everything be the way it was before we got dumped on you, but we can't."

Maggie's stared down at her hands, which now rested on her knees. "But I don't want you to go away either, Mr. Green," she finally whispered.

Jubal quickly turned to stare at her profile. He

inhaled a quick breath of crisp air that smelled faintly of sweet lilacs and held it in his lungs.

Maggie lifted her head to look into Jubal's eyes for a long moment. Then she looked back at the sky.

"Is the sky this big in Texas, Mr. Green?" she asked softly.

"It's bigger," he said.

9

The nearest town to Bright's Farm was Lincoln, and it was there that Jubal bought a wagon and another mule to haul Maggie's possessions to El Paso. She didn't own much, so there was lots of extra room inside the wagon, even after Annie's crib and high chair and the wardrobe were loaded.

Maggie was almost resigned to her fate by the time they set out for Texas, although she still harbored qualms in her heart that she didn't dare speak aloud. She made arrangements with Sadie and Pig Phillips to take her chickens and the cow. The mule, Old Bones, would go with them and help pull the wagon.

Sadie was disconsolate and wouldn't stop crying.

"Oh, Maggie, I'll miss you so much," she sobbed into her hankie. Her little boys each clutched a hunk of their mother's calico skirt, jabbed their thumbs into their mouths, and looked worried.

"I'll miss you too, Sadie." Maggie was uncomfortable with Sadie's teary display, even though she was used to elaborate emotions from her friend.

Annie seemed to be excited about the trip.

"We go Tex," she told the twins from the comfort of her mama's hip. The little boys stared back at her with big eyes and continued to suck their thumbs and hold on to their mother's skirt.

Jubal came over to stand beside Maggie. He was ready to leave and didn't want any delays. Sadie looked up at him with teary eyes.

"Please take care of her, Mr. Green," she whimpered.

Jubal was annoyed. He hated weepy women. He wanted to yell at Sadie and ask her what the devil she expected him to do with Maggie, anyway, throw her off the mountain?

He curbed his unchivalrous impulse and merely grumbled, "We will." Then he turned to Maggie. "You ready, Mrs. Bright?" His voice was a little softer when he spoke to her.

Maggie looked around her. She felt as though somebody were thrusting a sharp stake through her heart.

"I guess so."

Jubal nodded and went over to the mules hitched to the wagon to make sure the harness was tight.

Suddenly Maggie's own eyes filled with tears and she gave Sadie a quick hug. "Take care of the boys and yourself, Sadie. I'll write."

Sadie was too overcome to do more than nod in misery. She might have thrown herself into her husband's arms, but at the moment Pig was helping Dan and Four Toes load the wagon.

Maggie wanted to take one last farewell look at

everything, so she left Sadie to her tears and her twins and carried Annie around to the back. With almost overwhelming sadness, she peered at the new goat pen Dan and Four Toes had just finished building, and the repaired chicken coop, fixed up finally so that the chickens couldn't escape. Only now there wouldn't be any chickens to make the attempt. And there would be nobody here to notice one way or the other.

She stared at the freshly spaded ground beneath the new fence where she had planned to plant flowers. There would be no flower bed for Maggie Bright now. Her throat felt thick and tight. She suspected she was succumbing to self-pity and didn't admire herself for it.

"I was happy here, Annie." She sighed. "I worked like the devil and was tired darned near all the time, but I was happy here. It was home."

"Home," Annie repeated somberly, catching the essence of her mama's mood.

Maggie plodded over to Kenny's grave. Ever since he was laid to rest there, she had tended it with love. She hated the certain knowledge that the ever-industrious weeds would now take over. No matter how tired she had been, she had always seen to the grave.

"Say good-bye to your daddy, Annie babe," Maggie whispered. A big tear slid down her cheek.

"Bye-bye, Da," said her obedient daughter.

Maggie hugged her close.

"I hope we'll be back again, Kenny." Maggie's words leaked out in a thin, strangled whisper, and she laid a hand on the wooden cross that designated Kenny's final home.

Jubal found them there. He had stomped around to the back of the house to hurry Maggie up, but when he saw her staring miserably down at her husband's grave, he stopped short. His brow furrowed and he was overwhelmed by a feeling of helplessness. He let her stand there for another few seconds; then he shook himself like a wet dog and strode on toward her.

"We'd better get going, Mrs. Bright," he said brusquely.

Maggie looked up in surprise. She had been so lost in reverie she had forgotten all about the task at hand.

"I'm sorry, Mr. Green. I didn't mean to hold you up."

"Dat's Da," Annie said, pointing to the grave.

Jubal didn't say anything. He just brushed a hand over the little girl's soft curls and wished he didn't feel so vulnerable all of a sudden.

Maggie turned and began to walk to the front of her farmhouse with Jubal. Suddenly she jerked on Jubal's shirtsleeve and stopped walking. He turned to frown down at her.

Though she hated herself for giving in to the pitiful impulse, she said, "May I just take one last look inside? Just—just to remember? Please?"

Her plea sounded pathetic the way she said it, and Jubal's mind rebelled even as his heart squeezed for her. His mind won.

"Make it quick," he snapped. Then he could have kicked himself.

"I will. Thank you, Mr. Green."

Maggie sounded so grateful that Jubal wanted to apologize for his earlier curtness, but he didn't.

Apologies did not come easily to his lips. He just sighed and followed her into the house.

The place looked empty, cold, and desolate now, with all traces of Maggie gone. Jubal watched her shuffle sadly through the few rooms and wished he could cheer her up. He wanted to tell her that his ranch in Texas was fifty times nicer than this sad attempt at a farm in the wilderness of the New Mexico mountains. He wanted to assure her that she could do anything she wanted at his place, that she could have chickens and goats and flowers and anything else her heart desired, that she wouldn't be worn out and tired all the time anymore, that he was going to take care of her.

But he didn't say anything at all. Even though Jubal couldn't fully comprehend Maggie's sentiments about this lousy little cabin on the edge of nowhere, he understood the meaning of home. He watched her say good-bye to the place and only wished he could help her.

Finally Maggie took a deep breath and said, "I guess I'm ready now." She tried to smile at him and failed miserably.

Jubal gave her a curt nod. "All right, then, let's not waste any more time." Then he gave himself another mental kick.

Maggie's voice was tight with resentment and unshed tears when she said, "I know it's not a grand ranch like yours in El Paso, Mr. Green, but it's my home and until you showed up I never expected to have to leave it. It's all I have!" That last sentence was an angry little wail, and it struck Jubal right in the heart.

"Aw, hell, Mrs. Bright. I didn't mean it. I'm sorry."

When he pulled her and Annie to his chest, Maggie tried to resist, but she couldn't because Jubal was too strong. Then she gave up and broke down. She cried and cried, until she'd made a big dark splotch on his leather vest. Annie pulled on his longish, sun-streaked hair and studied it in fascination while her mama wept.

When Maggie's sobs subsided, Jubal asked softly, "Ready now?"

Maggie nodded. "Yes. Thank you, Mr. Green. I'm sorry I got mad."

She knew, because her aunt had drilled her until she was blue in the face, that it was wrong to be angry or to make people angry. She'd been able to forget about that after she married Kenny, because he was so easygoing. But she had to remember again now. Jubal Green and Kenny Bright were two different people entirely. That was a depressing thought all by itself, let alone when combined with everything else.

Jubal wished like the devil that Maggie would quit thanking him and apologizing to him. It bothered him a lot. Hellfire, she'd saved his life, and that charitable gesture was now costing her her home. If anybody needed to be apologized to or thanked, it was her. He didn't even try to tell her that.

It was two weeks to the day after Jubal's foolish attempt to ride Old Red that the three men, Maggie Bright, and little Annie lumbered out the gate away from Bright's Farm on their way to Texas. Maggie had placed Ozzie Plumb's guitar in a corner of the wagon, tucked up with quilts so it wouldn't break.

She wondered if anybody would ever play it again.

Jubal still couldn't sit a horse for very long at a stretch, so he drove the wagon loaded with Maggie's goods with Old Red tied behind it. That hurt too, but he just gritted his teeth and didn't say a word about it. Maggie sat beside him with Annie on her lap and watched mournfully as her home faded farther and farther away into the distance.

Maggie couldn't seem to stop sighing, and every one of her sighs ripped through Jubal like the thrust of a knife. He slumped lower and lower in the seat the more she sighed.

But the funny part was that the farther away from her home they rumbled, the more Maggie's mood perked up. She thought at first she was going to cry all the way to Texas, but instead a long-buried spirit of adventure began to assert itself.

As they followed the Hondo River down the mountainside, the landscape gradually changed. It was the first week in April, and spring was getting a sluggish start this year. Only a few flowers bloomed beside the banks of the river, but Maggie showed them to her daughter eagerly from the seat of the wagon.

"Look over there, Annie," she said in an excited voice, "Pretty red flowers."

"Fowers," Annie repeated, imitating her mama by pointing with a chubby finger.

Jubal hadn't noticed the flowers, but now he peered over to his right, following Maggie's finger toward the river. Sure enough, there were some spiky red flowers sticking up, right next to a little nestled clump of tiny lavender blooms. Jubal waited for Maggie to mention those blossoms too. She didn't. He had the absurd notion that she was deliberately holding out on her daughter for some obscure reason, and that aggravated him.

"What about the purple ones?" he finally asked, with a trace of grumpiness in his tone.

"Purple ones?"

Maggie turned wide blue eyes upon him, and for a minute Jubal got lost in them. He had to clear his throat before he could talk again. "Those purple ones next to the red ones."

Maggie squinted at the river and then sighed. "I can't see them, I guess," she admitted.

Her disappointment made her words seem very poignant to Jubal.

"You really can't see those flowers?"

Maggie shook her head and hugged Annie. "I don't think my eyes are very good," she told him in a little voice, as though her poor eyesight were somehow her fault.

"Maybe you need spectacles," Jubal suggested after a minute or two.

Maggie nodded. "Yes. I think so. Kenny was going to get me some before the horse kicked him." She sounded very sad.

Jubal's brows drew together. There she went again, talking about her dratted husband. Still, he guessed he couldn't really blame her. Then a thought occurred to him suddenly.

"But you shot French Jack's partner."

Maggie grinned as she remembered that episode. It was a high spot in her life, all right. "Yes, I did," she said. "I waited until he shot at me, saw the flash, and aimed at that."

A smile quirked at Jubal's mouth. "That's the way you did it, huh?" He admired that. It demonstrated thoughtfulness and enterprise, two traits of which he approved. They were also traits he had never encountered in a female before.

Maggie nodded. She was very pleased with herself about that shot. Kenny would have been proud of her. When she stole a glance at Jubal Green, and he looked as though he was proud of her too, she felt her cheeks get hot.

"Look, Mama," Annie said, diverting her mother's attention.

Annie was getting into the spirit of adventure too, and she pointed at more red flowers in a meadow across the stream.

"I see, Annie," said her proud mama with a grin.

Jubal noted that Maggie didn't seem unhappy anymore, and he was glad. He was almost lighthearted about it, in fact. He decided to take advantage of Maggie's good mood.

"It's pretty around here, isn't it?" he said, as an experiment. Jubal wasn't used to making small talk.

Maggie sucked in a breath of fresh spring air and smiled. "It sure is. Is this land anything like where your ranch is, Mr. Green?"

Jubal chuckled. "No, it's nothing like this where I live. This is still in the mountains. I'm way down there."

He pointed toward the southwest, and Maggie squinted off into the distance. She couldn't see a thing except trees.

"Is it pretty, though?" she asked, a bit timidly. She hoped so. One thing about Bright's Farm, she thought, was that no matter how hard life got it was real pretty.

Jubal thought about her question. He hoped Maggie

would like it. It wasn't like the mountains, though. If she liked green trees all around, she'd be disappointed. He didn't want her to be disappointed.

"Well," he said finally, "it's different. It's got a river running through it, with cottonwoods along the bank. I guess it isn't like your place in the woods, but I like it."

Maggie thought he sounded a little defensive and rushed to soothe him. She certainly wasn't about to disparage his ranch, no matter how awful it looked.

"I'm sure it's a nice place, Mr. Green. I just wondered."

"Well," said Jubal, "I sure hope you like it." Then he felt like blushing and couldn't for the life of him figure out why.

"I'm sure we'll like it fine." Maggie hoped she was right.

"Fine," agreed Annie.

Jubal grinned at the little girl and realized all at once that a child could be a convenient place to rest one's attention if one was embarrassed about something else.

"You'll like it, Annie. I've got me a dog named Rover. You'll like him."

"Dog?" Annie was interested. She liked the Phillipses' dog, Pete. He was big and furry and licked her face and made her laugh.

"Yep, a dog," Jubal said. "He's bigger than you are, but he's friendly."

Maggie was smiling broadly now. She loved it when people paid attention to her daughter.

"His name is Rover, Annie," she said. "Can you say Rover?"

Annie's big brown eyes sparkled. "Wover," she said

and seemed pleased when the adults sitting with her laughed.

They camped that night by the Hondo. They would soon leave the river behind and head south, and Jubal thought it might be nice to have the luxury of easy water tonight. It would be the last water of its kind for a while, once they passed Turkey Creek on the morrow.

"There will be lots of little streamlets in places, but we aren't going to hit another big river until the Rio Bravo," Jubal told them. Then he stopped what he was doing and thought for a minute. "I guess most folks call it the Rio Grande up here."

"I didn't know they were the same river," Maggie admitted. She had just assumed there were two big rivers flowing through Texas into Mexico.

"I guess you're not alone there, Mrs. Bright." Jubal thought Maggie's mistake was a particularly female one, and for some reason he kind of liked it.

Four Toes rode up to the little camp. He'd been scouting ahead of them, watching for signs of malevolent forces. Jubal had told Maggie he didn't expect any more of Mulrooney's people to accost them yet because he didn't think there would have been time to send more murderers after them from that quarter.

"But that don't mean the rest of the no-goods who live around here won't want whatever's in your wagon, ma'am," Dan Blue Gully told her.

Dan had ridden beside the wagon while Jubal drove. Maggie watched with interest as the Indian scanned the landscape around them. He seemed very alert, and she was glad, especially after he told her about the no-goods.

"Are there lots of them around these parts?" she asked, a little worried.

Dan chuckled. "I reckon you could say that, ma'am, and not be contradicted much, yes."

Jubal, who was building the fire, grunted at Dan's words. "Shoot, every no-good who's got people after him in the States hightails it into New Mexico Territory, Mrs. Bright. It's almost like somebody tipped the country and all the riffraff rolled out here."

Jubal thought his right arm would break before he got the wood carried over to the fire. He was certain his left leg was rotting and would fall off any second now as he tried to walk around the campsite without limping. In fact, he was so sore he could barely move, but his orneriness and pride wouldn't allow him to admit it. Whether he admitted it or not, though, bouncing on the hard seat of the wagon and guiding the mules with his bum arm had taken their toll on his poor muscles.

Maggie's next comment didn't make him feel any better. "Yes," she murmured. "Kenny used to say just about the same thing, now I come to think about it."

"Got us some rabbits for supper," Four Toes said, holding out four rabbits he had shot on his scouting trip. "I'll skin 'em for you, Mrs. Bright, if you'll cook 'em."

"I'd be happy to, Mr. Smith. Thank you for skinning them. I don't like to do that very much."

Actually, Maggie hated skinning rabbits even more than she hated gutting and cleaning fish, and she hated that job a whole lot. For some reason, plucking chickens didn't bother her as much.

"Think I'll fix these pelts up for Annie, too," Four

Toes murmured, as he walked off to take care of the skinning. "I bet she'll like the soft fur."

Maggie smiled. "What a nice man he is," she mused aloud.

Jubal turned to stare at Maggie, and his face held an expression that was half bemusement and half aggravation. Dan noticed that expression and laughed.

Maggie peered at the two of them, puzzled, for a second or two, but neither one of them seemed inclined to enlighten her about what was funny. In fact, Jubal turned to glare at Dan. That was when Maggie noticed that Jubal was grimacing as he moved stiffly around the campsite.

"Are your wounds paining you, Mr. Green?" she asked.

Jubal heard the concern in her voice and his mood softened some. He had become quite cranky when she went directly from mooning about her dead husband to praising Four Toes Smith.

"Some," he said, and then Dan accidentally bumped his leg with a log he was bringing over to the fire, and Jubal let out a ragged bellow of pain and nearly fell over.

Maggie jumped up from where she had been setting up cooking things and ran over to him. Supporting him by his good arm, she held him tight and began to scold.

"Mr. Green, you stop moving around right this minute. You come over here and lie down, and I don't want an argument."

Jubal didn't swear at her because he saw that her expression held genuine concern, and he knew it was for him. He grimaced, his leg still throbbing painfully, and started to protest, but Maggie put her other hand over his mouth before he could say a word. Her hand was surprisingly soft and smelled a little bit like lilacs.

Instead of the words of protest he had been going to say, when Maggie withdrew her hand he found himself murmuring, "You smell good." Then he felt silly.

Maggie flushed a little bit, and her face looked almost golden in the last rays of the afternoon sun. Jubal liked looking at her. Her soft breast pressed against his good arm as she led him over to the quilt she had laid out, and he liked that too. He allowed her to help him lie down and wondered if he was getting so soft he'd never recover.

"I'll help you get your boots off, Mr. Green, and then I'm going to see if Mr. Blue Gully thinks it's a good idea for you to chew on another one of those bark chips of mine."

She gave him a firm nod, as though she wasn't about to take any guff from him, so he decided not to give her any. He'd already built up the fire, and his two friends were setting up the rest of the camp. He guessed he could lie down and play invalid for a little while. His mood had lightened unexpectedly with Maggie's nagging, and he found that circumstance odd in the extreme.

"Yes, ma'am," he said with a small grin.

Maggie eyed him suspiciously, but he just smiled at her. His smile sent a funny swimmy feeling shimmering through her middle, and she couldn't watch him while she pulled off his boots because she was too nervous. That alarmed her. She tried to cover her nervousness with chatter.

"Tomorrow you're going to have a cushion to sit

on, Mr. Green. I'll fix you up something, either rolled blankets or a bed pillow or something."

Jubal was too busy gritting his teeth to answer her.

Annie had been sitting on a log, playing with a corncob doll and yawning occasionally. When she noticed Jubal lying on the quilt, however, she moseyed over and plopped down next to him.

"Ho, Juba," said the little girl.

"Hello, Annie," said Jubal.

"See my dolly?" Annie held up the corncob.

Jubal noted with interest that the doll was dressed in the same calico print that the little girl wore.

"I see your dolly, Annie. Did your mama make it for you?"

"Yes."

"It's a pretty dolly, Annie," said Jubal gently.

"Yes," agreed the little girl.

Then she yawned again and rubbed her eyes. Jubal crooked his good arm out and the baby took the invitation. By the time Maggie got back to the quilt, Annie was curled up next to him, asleep, with her doll hugged to her chest, and Jubal's hand was stroking her soft hair.

Maggie's heart clutched at the sight. This is what life should be like, she thought suddenly, unexpectedly. Annie should have a daddy to hold her when she was sleepy, and Maggie herself needed a man to tend. She hadn't realized how much she missed that aspect of marriage until right this minute.

Jubal smiled up at her when she joined them. "Your little girl likes to sleep with me."

Maggie smiled down at him. Then his eyes captured and held hers for a moment and she got all confused. Somehow, Maggie knew Jubal's words didn't quite mean what they said, but she couldn't sort out his ulterior meaning because her heart was doing crazy flip-flops. She broke eye contact with an almost physical effort.

"Yes, she seems to, all right." Her attempt to make the words sound light was somewhat strained.

She had brought an armload of nursing equipment with her, and she sat down on the quilt next to Jubal and Annie, smoothing her skirts down around her legs as though sitting on the ground in a rough camp were an everyday habit.

Jubal smiled at that. He approved. He liked unflappable people, and the fact that, except when faced with gunfire or the loss of her home, Maggie Bright was very nearly unflappable pleased him. It was another first in Jubal's opinion; Maggie was the only nearly unflappable female he'd ever met up with.

She held out a piece of her careful store of magic bark to him. "Here, Mr. Green. Chew on this and drink this water. That will help your pain."

"I don't want to take your medicine, Mrs. Bright. You'll need this stuff a long time after I'm well again, I reckon."

Maggie tried to give him a nurselike and efficient glare, but she failed completely and dropped her gaze instead.

"Just chew it, Mr. Green, and stop arguing with me. You need it right now and I don't, so—so just chew it."

She looked adorable as she tried to be stern, and Jubal grinned in spite of himself. "Yes, ma'am," he said softly, and Maggie could hear the amusement in his voice.

He took the bark from her and watched her lay her supplies out in a neat little row.

"I'm going to check your shoulder wound, Mr. Green. I want to wash it off and make sure you haven't damaged it driving the team." She couldn't quite make herself look at him while she delivered her lecture.

"Yes, ma'am."

"Mr. Blue Gully gave me this liniment to rub into the scar. He says there's plants ground up in there that will ease the aching. It smells real good, too. Then I'll rebandage the wound again so it won't get dirty. If it gets dirty, it still might fester."

"Yes, ma'am," Jubal said again.

Maggie took a deep breath. Now came the really embarrassing part. "I'll help you with your shirt, Mr. Green." She still couldn't look at him and tried to appear busy shuffling her nursing things.

He was eyeing her curiously, aware of her nervousness. He wondered if she'd be the same way around any other man, or if he held some special power over her. He hoped it was the latter.

"What about my leg?" Jubal figured it was pure wickedness that made him ask that.

Maggie turned to him, and he read her shock in her wide-eyed expression. "Well, really, Mr. Green, I—I can't wash your leg."

Even through the dusk, Jubal could see her face turn fiery red. He wished he'd had more experience with good women. He'd like to tease Maggie some more because she was so cute when she was embarrassed, but he didn't know how to go about it. That one suggestive comment about his leg just about used up his reservoir of repartee. So, rather than tease her, he got embarrassed instead.

"I didn't mean anything, Mrs. Bright," he mumbled. He swallowed a big gulp of water and bit viciously on his medicinal bark after that big lie.

Now Maggie was even more embarrassed for having suspected him of intentions of which he seemed innocent.

"Well, anyway," she muttered, "let's get this shirt off."

Jubal carefully nudged Annie aside so he could sit up, and Maggie unbuttoned his shirt for him since his hands were full. That embarrassed him too, although the feel of her fingers on his skin was heaven. A flitting, foggy thought that was almost a memory floated through his brain, about soft hands stroking him when he'd been burning with fever. He couldn't catch the image and make it stay put long enough for him to examine it, but he began to burn again with a fever of an entirely different nature. Damn. His reaction to this woman was getting out of hand.

Maggie moved to sit behind his right shoulder. She didn't really have to be in back of him, but she felt less nervous there, with him naked from the waist up. Lord, she thought, for the hundredth time, he was a well-built man! His belly was flat, lean, and corded. His shoulders and arms rippled with muscle, and he had tight, dark golden curls on his forearms and chest that gleamed in the late-afternoon sunlight.

Soaping her soft cloth, Maggie began to wash Jubal's wound tenderly. Then she decided to work without the cloth, so she lathered her hands and began to massage him with gentle strokes of her fingers. She liked the feel of him. She also liked the smell of him. As warm tendrils of feeling began to sneak around and touch embarrassing places within her, she decided it had been too long since she'd smelled that male smell or felt that pelt on a man's chest. Then, since Maggie was an honest soul, she admitted to herself she'd never actually felt this way about a man's scent or feel before. She decided that realization was better left unexamined.

Jubal's wound was still red and looked painful, but it had healed over and wasn't oozing any longer. She knew it hurt him when she washed it and she was sorry.

"I'm trying not to hurt you, Mr. Green, but if I press too hard, let me know and I'll ease up."

"You're not hurting me, Mrs. Bright," Jubal mumbled. "It feels good."

His skin was warm and his muscles were firm under Maggie's hands. She was supporting herself with one hand on his back while she soaped him with the other, and she had the sudden urge to slide her arms around his shoulders and lay her cheek against his broad back. She wanted to get right up next to him and close her eyes and breathe in his masculine essence. Her sigh of regret that she couldn't do any of those things was gusty.

"I'll rinse off the soap now, Mr. Green."

Jubal only grunted.

Her ministrations were driving him crazy. He was reacting to Maggie the way a man reacts to a woman he wants to bed. Jubal decided, as he sat there and tried to remain neutral about her sensuously rubbing his shoulder and back, that he was coming on toward one of those times when a man needed the only thing a woman was good for.

He was aghast to realize that while he was trying to talk himself into what a good idea it would be to visit one of the whorehouses in El Paso, his whole being rebelled at the notion. He didn't just want a woman;

he wanted *this* woman. He admitted it to himself with something akin to despair.

If there was one thing on this earth he didn't need, it was to care about Maggie Bright. He didn't want to want her. The Lord knew, he had a very poor opinion of women. His mother had made his father a miserable man all his married life. His sister-in-law, Janie, had gotten Jubal's only brother killed, as well as herself and their precious daughter.

He knew what a woman could do to a man if he let her get under his skin. The problem with Maggie Bright was that she seemed to be getting under his skin even without Jubal's conscious consent. That bothered him a good deal.

Maggie rubbed Jubal's shoulder and back for a long time after she knew she didn't need to anymore. But she liked the feel of him beneath her hands and didn't want to quit. She smoothed Dan Blue Gully's balm into Jubal's shoulder in front and into his shoulder in back. Then she rubbed it into the rest of his back, just in case. And she decided that while she was at it, she might as well rub it down his arms. She was surprised at how very, very hard they felt.

She finally quit rubbing him when she saw he was getting gooseflesh. Then she was ashamed of herself for letting him grow cold in the evening air. She had no idea that his gooseflesh was from another cause entirely.

Jubal's eyes were closed and he couldn't decide whether he was in anguish or ecstasy. Maggie's hands felt like silk as they spread the minty balm over his body, but his manhood was in a state fit to make a delicate maiden blush. Every stroke of Maggie's fingers tingled through him and caused much more than gooseflesh to rise in him. He felt like a fool sitting there being tended by a woman who hadn't an idea in the world what she was doing to him while his whole body seemed to throb in response to her touch.

He hoped he wouldn't have to stand up any time soon because he didn't think he could tolerate the humiliation of showing his condition to the world, even the small world of Maggie, Dan, and Four Toes. Especially to that small world.

When Maggie finally quit torturing him, Jubal slumped over in relief.

"I'm sorry, Mr. Green. I didn't realize how cold it was getting to be."

She wanted to wrap her arms around him and warm him up, which was distinctly disloyal to Kenny. Maggie sighed in dismay. She was such a weak person. On that bitter thought, she helped Jubal on with his shirt.

"Are you feeling better now, Mr. Green?"

"Yes. Thank you." Jubal could barely speak. When Maggie reached to button his shirt, he said curtly, "I can do it." He was sorry when she pulled back as though she had been stung.

"Oh, of course, Mr. Green. Your hands are free now. I'm sorry."

Jubal squeezed his eyes shut. Hellfire, he hated it that she was either thanking him or apologizing all the blasted time.

Maggie scrambled to her feet. "I'll get you another quilt to wrap around your shoulders, Mr. Green. That will keep you warm while I cook dinner."

Jubal thought about protesting but decided it wasn't worth the effort. If it made her feel better to pamper him, that was the least he could let her do.

Maggie had started across the camp to the wagon when something occurred to her. "Later on, you'll have to rub some of that liniment into your leg wound as well, Mr. Green," she said. Then she blushed and fled over to the wagon to fetch the quilt.

Jubal stared after her and thought about how delightful it would be to have Maggie Bright rub balm into his thigh. Then he cursed his stupidity. He'd stay hard all night if he kept playing with those thoughts.

10

Maggie and Annie bedded down in the wagon that night. It wasn't a covered wagon, and Maggie took pains to see that Annie would be warm enough. The worst of the winter chills were past them now, although April so far wasn't proving to be very mild. Still, Annie seemed comfortable and slept soundly.

Although the day had been filled with new experiences and it was late, Maggie didn't feel especially sleepy when she lay down to rest. Not only had she become excited about this move to El Paso, she was still vaguely troubled by the stirrings she had felt when she'd been nursemaiding Jubal. She'd never felt those stirrings before, except with Kenny.

And I didn't feel them very often then, either, she admitted to herself with a guilty sigh as she stared at her sleeping baby. She tried to make herself feel less guilty about this admission by telling herself that she'd loved her husband dearly, that she'd been a good wife, that it was only because she missed Kenny so much that she found Jubal Green attractive, but she was only marginally successful.

When Maggie looked up and beheld the sky, her senses were so overwhelmed by the starry majesty that she completely forgot she had been busy chastising herself. "Oh, my goodness," she breathed softly, and wished Annie were still awake so that she too could witness this incredible splendor.

She discovered that if she squinted very hard and pulled the edges of her eyes toward her scalp with her fingers, she could pick out the individual stars much better. They still blurred together a bit, but not nearly as much.

Using her newfound aid to sight, Maggie sat up in the wagon and squinted around the campsite. It was too dark now to discern anything much except one lone man squatting on a log beside the campfire, posted guard. Light from the low, flickering flames licked him up and down erratically, and she couldn't make out who it was. She pulled the edges of her eyes so taut that the lids nearly met over her eyeballs while she tried to determine which of her three traveling companions was on duty at the moment, but it was to no avail.

Whoever it was, he was big. It had to be either Mr. Blue Gully or Mr. Green.

Maggie sat cross-legged on the wagon bed for several minutes, trying to decide whether to get down and chat with him or not. She couldn't sleep, and it would be nice to talk to somebody. It was, after all, her first night away from home since she'd married Kenny four years earlier, and she'd been alone a lot since Kenny's death.

If she knew for sure it was Dan Blue Gully there by the fire, she'd hop down in a minute. She felt really comfortable around Dan and had no trouble at all making conversation with him.

If, however, it turned out that the man was Jubal Green, Maggie didn't know what she'd do.

On the one hand, she very nearly pined to be with him, a fact that caused her no end of guilty stirrings. On the other hand, whenever she was in his company, she felt nervous and twitchy and never quite knew what to say—though, they seemed to get along pretty well now that he was no longer a fussy invalid. In fact, the only serious problem with their being together was the compulsion that occasionally overtook her to fling herself into his arms.

"Oh, bother," she finally muttered to herself. Shoving her feet into her heavy shoes, she threw a blanket over her shoulders and clambered down out of the wagon.

When Jubal caught a movement out of the corner of his eye, he was up on his feet and had his rifle cocked and lifted to his sore shoulder faster than a normal person could blink. When he realized it was Maggie, he lowered the gun and let out a soft groan that even he couldn't identify the source of.

It had taken damned near forever for his erection to go away after she'd rubbed his shoulder, and it had been bouncing back if he just thought about the sensuous way she had massaged him.

Dan was sleeping a few paces away from the fire and Four Toes was out, scouting around on a mounted patrol. None of the men really expected trouble, but they all knew better than to lower their guard. Jubal was, in effect, alone, and now Maggie Bright was coming over to torment him some more.

He watched with a glowering frown as she made her way toward him. She clutched a blanket around her with fingers that looked snowy white by the light of the stars. Her hair was braided for the night in two long braids.

Jubal had an unaccountable urge to yank on the ribbons tied around those braids, loosen them, and let her hair fall down her back in wild waves. He took a deep breath, scrunched up his eyes against the image that thought evoked, and tried to keep his face impassive as she approached.

When Maggie realized the man at the fire was Jubal Green, she stopped in her tracks, suddenly shy. Then she decided it would be more embarrassing to turn around and get back into the wagon than to join him by the fire.

Jubal noted her hesitation. It's as though she doesn't want it to be me, he thought sourly.

"I can't sleep," Maggie said with a bashful grin when she reached Jubal.

He didn't know what to say. She looked all tousled and relaxed, and he felt incredibly awkward. He gestured toward the log he had been sitting on.

"Well, why don't you sit down by the fire for a while, then," he finally managed to suggest.

With a shy smile, Maggie peered up at him. The fire was low, but it flared up every now and then when it caught some fresh pitch. One of those eruptions occurred as Jubal gazed at Maggie, and her face looked sweetly aglow in the sudden gleam of light.

Jubal didn't know whether he uttered his grunt of dismay out loud or not, but he realized with something akin to defeat that the rest of this trip was going to be awfully uncomfortable for him. Every blessed time he even looked at Maggie now, he reacted in a very embarrassing way.

"Thank you," she said softly.

She sat on the log, wrapped herself in the blanket, and sighed with contentment. For some reason, she felt very good. Part of her happy feeling, she knew, was from the excitement of doing something new. She hadn't done anything new for such a long time—except things she didn't want to do, like run the farm single-handed, holler at Ozzie Plumb, and nurse Kenny and then Jubal Green.

He put another log on the fire and sat down beside her. They both stared into the flames for several minutes. Silence, broken only by the crackling of burning logs, enveloped the two like a fragrant, cozy cloak.

"Wouldn't Mr. Blue Gully be warmer if he slept closer to the fire?" Maggie asked at last.

"He'd be a better target there, too," said Jubal, somewhat gruffly.

"Oh."

Silence stretched and grew around them once more.

Jubal couldn't stop himself from looking at Maggie from time to time. He noticed that she had an almost angelic smile on her face. Her expression was soft and sweet and bright. Maggie Bright, he thought. It fits.

Maggie's gaze left the fire and wandered up to survey the stars over her head. She was used to the woods, but they were out of the forest now, and there was so much sky up there that Maggie found it almost impossible to comprehend such vastness.

Jubal finally couldn't stand it. He had to either grab her and kiss her or talk to her.

"It's pretty out tonight." His experimental statement brought Maggie's lustrous eyes to his face, and he inhaled sharply.

"It is, isn't it, Mr. Green," she said.

Jubal cleared his throat. "Is this anything like Indiana?" He knew the answer and felt like a fool for asking, but he couldn't think of anything better to say.

Maggie laughed softly.

"Oh, no, Mr. Green. It's nothing like Indiana. Indiana—the part I'm from, anyway—is sort of . . . sort of . . ." Maggie's words trailed to a halt as she thought about what Indiana was like. "It's sort of more settled."

That soft statement earned a chuckle from Jubal. "I guess most places are more settled than New Mexico Territory, Mrs. Bright."

"I guess so," she agreed with a grin.

Jubal continued to watch her watch the stars. He wondered what a young girl who had grown up in Indiana, who had bad eyesight and terrible headaches and a little girl and no man, thought about her life, but he didn't dare ask, bold and straight out. He knew her life was harder than most, but she seemed remarkably free from bitterness, even if she did have a tendency to get weepy every now and then. He admired that, as he admired her grit. He fumbled around in his mind for something to ask her that might give him at least a little of the answer to what he wanted to know.

"Do you like it here, Mrs. Bright? I mean, on your little farm and all?"

Maggie sighed and hugged her knees under the blanket. Jubal noticed her expression turn even softer and her eyes get even brighter, and his heart began to do such crazy things in his chest that he wondered momentarily if he was suffering a spasm.

"Oh, yes, Mr. Green," she said, in a voice that was almost a whisper. "I think this is the first place where I ever was happy."

Her answer surprised Jubal. He knew she possessed, as Dan Blue Gully would phrase it, a strong spirit. But Maggie's life had been so hard that it was difficult for him to imagine her being as happy in it as she acted.

"You like it here better than in Indiana?" He tried to keep the incredulity out of his voice when he asked the question.

"Oh, my, yes. Indiana's pretty and all, but nobody cared about me there. In New Mexico, life is kind of rough, but I have friends."

For some reason, Jubal's heart was still clutching up painfully. Maybe Dan Blue Gully could give him something for it later. "You didn't have friends in Indiana?" he asked in a low voice.

Maggie studied the fire for a few moments. "Well, you see, I didn't get out much. My aunt and uncle ran a chophouse there, and I pretty nearly worked all the time."

Jubal's jaw tensed, and he made a sweep of the campsite with narrowed eyes. There it was again: that damned aunt of hers.

"That's where I met Kenny," Maggie continued in a sweet, reminiscent voice. "He came into the chophouse for supper one night on his way back to New Mexico, and we got to talking. We talked until Aunt Lucy came out to shoo me back into the kitchen."

"You loved him a lot, didn't you, Mrs. Bright?" Jubal asked. He hadn't meant to ask that. It just snuck through his defenses and burst out of his mouth without his consent.

Maggie didn't notice the strain in the question. "Oh, yes, Mr. Green," she said in a quiet, thoughtful voice. "Kenny took me away from all that misery in Indiana. He brought me here and gave me a home of my own and Annie. And he loved me."

"I'm sure he did," Jubal muttered. He hadn't meant to say that either.

"Even though I didn't know the first thing about anything. He was so sweet to me."

Jubal cast her an angry, puzzled frown, then glared at the fire. Didn't know the first thing about anything? What was that supposed to mean?

The heat from Maggie's soft chuckle seeped into Jubal's body like the warmth of a goosedown quilt. He didn't dare look at her.

"I've never been much good at anything, really, Mr. Green, but Kenny didn't seem to mind. He was so sweet."

"Not much good at anything?" Jubal did look at her then. He couldn't help it.

His brows were raised into such a high, looping arch over his green eyes that it struck Maggie as comical, and she giggled. Her giggle was almost more than Jubal could stand without touching her, so his fingers tightened around the barrel of his rifle and he tore his gaze away.

"I'm sorry, Mr. Green. You just looked so surprised."

"I was. 'Pears to me you can do damned near anything, Mrs. Bright. You saved my life, and you've been keeping yourself and your daughter right well with no help from anybody. I'd like to know what you consider something, if those two things don't count."

Maggie's mouth opened up to protest, but she

couldn't think of anything to say, so she shut it again and just stared at Jubal with surprise.

Oh, my, she thought. She'd never seen her life in exactly those terms. She'd always just used her Aunt Lucy's standards by which to judge herself. She would have to think about it later, she decided, when she could make her brain work properly. When she was away from the disturbing presence of Jubal Green.

Jubal continued to scan the campsite, more to keep himself from staring at Maggie than anything else, and she gazed into the fire. Faint and far off, barely illuminated under the stars, Four Toes Smith was riding back toward camp.

"Kenny was a sweet man, Mr. Green," Maggie said all of a sudden. Her thoughts had veered off down another unexplored turning, and her voice was low.

Jubal grunted. He really didn't want to hear about how wonderful Kenny Bright had been.

But Maggie didn't understand how he felt about listening to her sing Kenny's praises. She had never spoken about her late husband to anybody before, and it felt good to say these things out loud to another person, especially to somebody who hadn't known Kenny and couldn't contradict the conclusions Maggie had come to about him. She loved Kenny, she knew she did, yet there were some things. . . .

"He wasn't real bright," she said, and then she giggled. "In spite of his name."

Jubal's eyes, which had gone hard, lost some of their granitelike intensity when he again turned to Maggie. "He wasn't?"

Maggie shook her head and smiled. "No. He was a sweet man, though. About the sweetest man in the world. He could build things real well, too. He made Annie's high chair and the wardrobe and all sorts of things. And he was so good to us. He was such a wonderful carpenter. I guess he wasn't much of a farmer, though. And he was lousy with horses."

"It sounds like he might have had a hard time making a go of that farm," Jubal ventured, unsure of his ground, afraid he'd make her angry if he criticized her late husband at all.

But Maggie only sighed. "I'm afraid that's so, Mr. Green. I used to worry about that some, although we always had enough food because of my garden."

She stopped speaking and hugged her knees harder.

"But I never had flowers," she said with a deep sigh. "I really wanted flowers. Mr. Smith was going to help me plant some, but I guess—well, I guess I won't be having flowers for a while." She shook her head. She didn't want to make Jubal feel guilty by saying that she knew she'd never have flowers now.

Jubal decided then and there that they would pick up some flower seeds on their way through El Paso to his ranch. And maybe some spectacles too.

Suddenly Maggie sat up, and Jubal saw her eyes grow with fright. He was on his feet in a flash, his rifle at his shoulder.

"What is it?"

"Don't you see him? That man on the horse?"

Maggie was squinting very hard and pointing at Four Toes, who had by now reached the perimeter of the camp.

Jubal exhaled and lowered his rifle. "That's Four Toes." He tried to keep the exasperation out of his voice.

Maggie felt incredibly foolish. "Oh, my land! I'm sorry. I don't see too good at night, I guess."

"'Pears to me you don't see too good at any time, Mrs. Bright," Jubal growled. They were definitely going to get her some eyeglasses on their way through El Paso.

Maggie's shoulders sagged. "I suppose not," she said remorsefully, as though her bad eyesight were something she had some control over. "My aunt used to tell me I didn't eat enough carrots. She said my eyes would get better if I'd only eat more carrots. I finally ate so many carrots my skin turned yellow."

Jubal had a sudden vivid image in his mind of little Maggie Bright—or whatever her name had been then—cowering under the vicious tongue of a hateful aunt and stuffing carrots into her mouth in a vain attempt to improve her eyesight, and his insides clenched. He was sorry he hadn't tried harder to curb his annoyance. She had just scared him, that was all.

"I'm sorry, Mrs. Bright. It's not your fault your eyes are bad."

Maggie peered up at him. He seemed so tall standing beside her holding his rifle pointed to the ground and looking down at her. He actually was tall, she realized, remembering how his legs had dangled over the end of her bed.

When he sat down next to her again, Maggie sighed. She thought it must be nice to be a man and not be scared of anything.

"Did you really turn yellow?" Jubal asked. His voice held a smile and Maggie relaxed some.

"Actually, it was more of an orangey color," she said. "My aunt thought I had the yellow jaundice and called in Dr. Willis. She was real mad when he said it was too many carrots." Maggie shook her head. "I just couldn't ever do anything to please that woman."

Jubal's frown was back. He decided he disliked Maggie's aunt a great deal.

"Well, it doesn't sound to me as though she was worth pleasing. She sounds like a witch to me."

Maggie turned to face Jubal again with a combination of surprise and pleasure in her heart. Nobody had ever said that to her flat out that way.

"Do you really think so, Mr. Green? I always figured she was mean to me because I did everything wrong." She sounded just a little bit afraid to hear his answer, as if she were worried he'd tell her the truth this time, that she really was inept and incompetent.

"Of course I think so. Sounds to me as though she resented having to take care of you, so she made your life miserable. As if you had anything to do with your parents dying." Jubal sounded really crabby about it, too. He'd like to have a word or two with that stupid aunt of hers. He'd set her straight in a hurry.

Maggie's eyes opened wide. "Why, what an interesting thing to say!"

Could he possibly be right? Kenny always used to tell her that you should love your family, no matter what. And although Maggie had tried to, she had been singularly unsuccessful. It had never occurred to her until now that maybe Kenny had been wrong. This would definitely take some thinking about. In the meantime, Jubal's assessment certainly cheered her up.

"I think you might just be right, Mr. Green. Thank you."

Four Toes approached the fire before Jubal could ask Maggie why she was thanking him.

"It's real quiet out there," Four Toes told them.

"Good."

"There aren't any no-goods lurking tonight, Mr. Smith?" asked Maggie with a twinkle in her eye.

Jubal noted that twinkle and frowned. She never twinkled at him.

Four Toes chuckled. "Don't seem to be." He flung himself down on the log next to Jubal and stretched out his booted feet toward the fire. "It sure is cold, though."

"Yes," agreed Maggie. "Spring seems to be a little slow this year."

"It'll come," said Jubal.

"I hope it comes soon," Maggie said. "I'd purely love to be warm during the day."

The next morning, Jubal wondered if Maggie might be some kind of witch as he drove the wagon across the desert in weather that just seemed to get hotter and hotter all day long until it beat down upon them as though trying to give them a foretaste of hell. By the time they either had to stop for a rest or melt through the wooden slats of the wagon, poor little Annie was crying under the shade her mama had rigged up for her out of a quilt, Maggie was sopping wet with perspiration beneath her straw hat, and Jubal's leather gloves were in peril of sliding off his hands, he was sweating so much.

Four Toes and Dan were feeling the heat too.

"Criminy," grumbled Dan. "I never knew it to get so blamed hot so blamed fast."

Jubal was surprised that, in spite of the misery engendered by the heat, his muscles didn't feel as sore today as they had the day before. Maybe that was why people put hot rags on sore muscles, he mused. Still, he didn't try to talk until he had climbed down from the wagon with a grunt.

"Sure you have, Danny," he said when he touched ground. "It's like this every year, and every year you say the same thing."

Dan grinned and wiped his dripping brow. "I guess that's so."

Jubal eyed him with amusement. "I thought Indians were supposed to know everything there is to know about the weather."

Dan chuckled. "I guess my instincts got polluted living with you whites, Jubal."

Jubal laughed, but his laughter died when he saw Four Toes reach up and help Maggie get down from the wagon. He wished he could do that. His arm was too weak to lift and support her weight, though. He'd probably drop her, and he didn't suspect that would make a very good impression. He'd already done too many stupid things around Maggie Bright; he wasn't about to risk dropping her.

They had stopped by the banks of Turkey Creek, and the animals were already drinking deeply. Maggie carried her miserable daughter over to the creek, and Jubal watched her squat down beside the water and comfort her baby with the cool water. He noticed, too, that she took care of Annie before she gave a thought to herself. Now that, he thought, was the way mothers were supposed to be.

"You know," said Dan, scanning the cloudless sky above them. "It might not be a bad idea to rest here until evening and then do our traveling. The moon's full tonight, and it might be easier on Mrs. Bright and Annie. Not to mention us."

"You think so?"

Dan shrugged. "We've done it before."

Jubal frowned. "Yes," he said at last, "we've done it before. But we didn't have any women with us then."

"Can't be any rougher on them at night than it will be to travel through this blamed heat," said Four Toes, who had just dumped a hatful of water over his head.

"Mrs. Bright's not just any woman, Jubal," said Dan. "She won't be scared."

Jubal peered again at the riverbank. Maggie was now scrubbing her own face with the refreshing water while Annie sat on the bank, splashing her feet and laughing.

"Yeah," Jubal said. "I guess you're right."

Prometheus Mulrooney had been venting his frustrated rage on Ferrett and Pelch ever since their journey began.

"Nothing satisfies him, Mr. Pelch," Ferrett whispered. His features looked even more pinched than usual.

"That's true, Mr. Ferrett," agreed Pelch. "He's in a rare state, all right."

"It's been 'Do this, do that; no, you did that wrong' ever since we left New York," Ferrett said with a sigh.

"Aye. Nothing a body can do will satisfy that devil."

"And, oh, Mr. Pelch, the names he calls me. A true man would never stand for it." He shook his head as he brewed a pot of tea for his employer.

Pelch cast a sympathetic glance at Ferrett. "Well, you know, Mr. Ferrett, it's as you told me. Once you hire on with Mr. Mulrooney, you're there for life unless he takes pity upon you and fires you."

Ferrett heaved a heartfelt sigh. "That's so, all right. I wish he'd take pity on me and fire me."

"And me," Pelch said. "And me."

Both men stood in the cooking compartment of Mulrooney's specially hired train as the engine chugged them toward Santa Fe in the wild New Mexico Territory. Both men's lusterless eyes seemed to fasten upon the box of rat poison on the shelf, and both men's brains seemed to jump to the same startled thought at the same instant. They suddenly straightened up and turned to face each other.

"Oh, my goodness, Mr. Pelch." Ferrett's voice sounded as though it had been squeezed out of his mouth like juice from a lemon.

"Oh, dear, Mr. Ferrett." Pelch's whisper was low and shaky.

"Do we dare?"

"I don't know."

They looked at each other again.

Then Ferrett said, "We'd be doing the world a favor, Mr. Pelch."

"That's so, Mr. Ferrett," agreed Pelch.

Ferrett lifted a trembling hand to the box of rat poison. He brought it down and set it on the counter as though he held the weight of the universe in his hand.

"Would it be murder, Mr. Pelch?" he asked, his voice as trembly as his fingers had been.

"I don't think so, Mr. Ferrett," whispered Pelch. "I think 'execution' is a better word. That's the word they use when they hang criminals."

Ferrett nodded. "He *is* a criminal," he said, a little more firmly.

"Aye, that he is."

Pelch lifted the lid of the teapot and Ferrett opened the box of rat poison. He reached for a spoon and ladled in as much of the poison as he dared. Then he stirred boiling water into the poisoned tea until all the powder was dissolved.

Pelch put the lid back on the teapot and took a deep breath. Ferrett replaced the poison box on the shelf and turned resolutely to Pelch.

"I've never killed anybody before, Mr. Pelch," he said. His eyes looked frightened once more.

"Nor me either, Mr. Ferrett," Pelch said, and his voice quavered slightly.

Ferrett picked up the tray. "Well, here we go," he said.

"Yes," agreed Pelch. He opened the door for Ferrett. "Here we go."

Prometheus Mulrooney was pacing around his carriage like a sulky bear.

"What in blazes were you two fools doing in there for so long?" he roared as the door opened and Ferrett and Pelch entered. Both men were trembling.

"Sorry, sir," squeaked Ferrett. He put the tray down on Mulrooney's table, as was customary.

"Idiots," Mulrooney muttered.

"Yes, sir," whispered Pelch in a strained voice.

Mulrooney walked over to the tea table and sat down in a chair that barely contained his bulk. He picked up the pot and poured himself a cup of tea. Then, as was his practice, he ladled in three heaping spoons of sugar and poured in a good dollop of heavy cream. He was stirring the mixture savagely when a knock came upon the door.

Mulrooney jerked his head up and stared at the door. His florid countenance deepened until it was eggplant purple, and veins throbbed in his fleshy face.

Ferrett and Pelch looked at each other. Maybe they wouldn't need the poison. Maybe their boss would suffer a fatal stroke and save the two of them the vile necessity of doing away with him.

But Mulrooney didn't die. Instead, he stopped stirring his tea and roared, "What?"

The door opened and another frightened, quaking man entered. He clutched in his shaking fingers a piece of paper, which he held out toward Mulrooney.

"Miserable ass," Mulrooney muttered as he snatched the piece of paper out of the poor man's hand. The man turned tail and ran back out the door as soon as his errand was complete.

Even before Mulrooney finished reading the words on the paper, Ferrett and Pelch had started backing away toward the door. They recognized the symptoms their employer was displaying and wanted to be well out of the way when the eruption occurred.

Mulrooney's jowls quivered, and his eyes bulged. Even his thin yellow-white hair, which generally lay in sparse strings across his enormous head, seemed to bristle in anger. By the time he looked up from the paper to pin his underlings with a stare of fury, Ferrett and Pelch were standing flat against the door.

Mulrooney raised the piece of paper in one hamlike fist and shook it at the two men.

"Do you know what this wire says, you miserable slimy pipsqueaks?"

"N-no, sir," whispered Ferrett.

Pelch could only shake his head.

"They've gone!"

Their boss's bellow made both men jump.

Mulrooney slammed the paper onto the table in front of him. His entire body vibrated with anger.

"They've gone!" he repeated.

"G-gone, sir?" ventured Ferrett. He didn't know whether it was better to talk or not to talk. He eyed Mulrooney with fear and caution, ready to duck should his boss throw something.

"Gone. They aren't in New Mexico anymore." His furious voice then assumed a singsong quality, as though mocking Jubal Green and his band, who were trying to escape his wrath. "No. They're not there any longer. They've gone to Texas. Back to El Paso."

Ferrett and Pelch looked at each other. Pelch appeared to be almost relieved, as though he were glad his arrangements hadn't managed to get anybody else killed yet.

"But they won't get away from me," Mulrooney added, staking his two employees to the door with his vicious gaze. "No, they can't escape *my* revenge. I'll get them."

Then he turned and glared around his carriage as though looking for an outlet for his wrath. Suddenly his arm swept out and tore across the tabletop in front of him like a hurricane ripping through a small island. Everything on the table—papers, pens, books, teacup, teapot, and tray—went flying through the air and crashed up against the wall. China shattered and tea sprayed everywhere, coating wall, furniture, and papers with warm, sweet, poisoned brown liquid.

Ferrett and Pelch looked at each other with blank dismay.

Mulrooney eyed the mess he had created with fury, then slammed his porky hands down on the table.

"Well?" he roared. "What are you two blithering fools waiting for? Clean this mess up!"

When the two men finally left Mulrooney's carriage, carrying the remains of their failure away from the scene of the attempted crime, Ferrett looked very depressed. So did Pelch.

"I'll never have the nerve to try again, I'm afraid, Mr. Pelch," mumbled Ferrett, as though his inability to commit murder lightly were a miserable failing.

Pelch shook his head sadly. "Nor I, Mr. Ferrett, I'm afraid. Nor I."

11

Jubal, Dan, and Four Toes ultimately agreed that it would be better to travel at night as long as the weather was so hot. Crossing those arid desert miles would be easier on all of them, including the horses and mules, when the air was cooler.

In the meantime, they were all gathered under some cottonwoods that graced the banks of Turkey Creek and afforded the little glen a bit of cool shade. They had eaten a light lunch of hard breadsticks and dried beef. Maggie had also handed out slices of dried apples that she'd brought with them. The apple slices were tasty, and the men appreciated the fruit, which was a rare treat for them. It felt good to relax and listen to the gurgling of the little river as it tumbled over rocks on its way to wherever it was headed.

Four Toes stretched and yawned. "Well, I guess we'd better try to get some sleep now, since we're going to be traveling tonight."

"Yes," agreed Jubal.

"Well, my goodness, Mr. Smith and Mr. Green, the two of you were up most of the night too, weren't you?" Maggie asked, remembering how they had guarded the camp so assiduously.

Four Toes grinned at her. "Actually, Mrs. Bright, we all took turns. Dan here took the watch after us."

"Oh," said Maggie. "I guess I didn't realize traveling in these parts required so much vigilance."

"Well, normally it doesn't, ma'am," said Dan. "We just want to make sure Mulrooney's hired guns don't take us unawares."

"Oh," said Maggie again. She'd almost forgotten about Mulrooney.

They all lay down under the cottonwoods. Maggie spread a quilt for herself and Annie because she didn't want to get any more dirty than she already was. The men disdained such luxury but lay down with their heads on their saddles. Maggie only looked at them and shook her head and pondered the oddities of men. They were such strange creatures.

She woke up an hour or so later, wondering where she was and why she felt so content. When her eyes opened and she remembered her circumstances, she smiled. It didn't seem quite right to be so happy when somebody wanted to kill her, but Maggie was not one to worry about the inconsistencies of life.

She sat up, peered around under the trees at her traveling companions, and almost laughed when she noticed that Annie had gotten up while her mama slept and wandered over to where Four Toes lay. He had shaken out a saddle blanket for her to lie on, and she was curled up next to him now, asleep, with one of the toys he had carved for her tucked up under her chin.

Maggie felt sticky and dirty. She'd been sweating all morning, and the wagon had churned up clouds of dust that now clung to the dried sweat on her body and made her itch. It was a very uncomfortable feeling. Maggie was used to being clean, and she didn't like it. She eyed Turkey Creek speculatively. Maybe she could take a bath while the men slept.

Very quietly, she got up and tiptoed to the wagon, where she dug out a cake of the lye soap she had made earlier in the winter, a towel, clean linen, and a clean shirtwaist. Then she crept away from camp through the cottonwoods, searching out a place where she could bathe in private that was still close enough to the camp so she could hear if the men began to stir.

When she finally found a spot that was secluded enough, it was a little farther away from the camp than Maggie liked, but the thought of being clean again was so appealing she decided she just couldn't wait any longer. Maybe she'd even wash her hair. She stripped off her dusty clothes down to her drawers and camisole and waded into the stream.

"Shoot, it's cold," she muttered through chattering teeth. But she resolutely walked in up to her knees, which was as deep as the creek got in these parts. Shivering in the cold water, Maggie began to bathe.

Jubal didn't know what prompted him to crack his eyes open when he did. All he knew was that some strange feeling suddenly came over him and woke him up. It was a feeling of loneliness combined with an odd sense of danger, and all of a sudden he was wide awake. He blinked a couple of times and sat up,

trying to keep the groans of pain that always accompanied that activity to himself.

Damn, maybe I'm just getting old, was his first
sour thought. Then he decided he was probably only
dismayed because healing was taking longer than he
expected. That thought cheered him, until he glanced
over to Maggie's quilt and saw she was gone.

He was on his feet so fast he didn't have time to hurt.
He quickly glanced around their little resting area to
see that Annie was nestled next to Four Toes, Dan
and Four Toes were snoring soundly under the trees,
and the livestock was grazing near the creek.

Jubal swore silently as he yanked on his boots,
picked up his Winchester, and scanned the area for
tracks. He had no trouble picking up Maggie's, and
he followed them out of the camp and downstream,
muttering foul oaths to himself the whole time.

Jubal came upon Maggie's bathing place just as she
stood up and flung the wet mane of hair out of her face.
His breath caught, and he felt all at once as though
somebody had punched him hard in the gut.

The spot Maggie had chosen was just past a bend
in the creek where the river widened into a little pool
overhung by cottonwood branches. A couple of big
rocks sat beside the stream, and she had placed her
clean clothes neatly on one of them. She had slung
her towel over a cottonwood branch, and she reached
for it now as Jubal watched, too stunned to turn away
as a gentleman should.

Rays of sunshine streamed through the tree branches,
sort of the way they did in religious pictures Jubal had
seen in church. They splayed out like a fan over

Maggie, bathing her body in rich amber light and dancing on the rippling water like diamonds.

Unlike Maggie, Jubal had perfect eyesight, and he could see every sweet curve of her shapely body as her wet camisole and drawers clung to her skin. He swallowed hard. Her legs were long and slender, he noticed. Her belly was just barely rounded—enough to show she was a woman. Her hips were curved like ripe fruit, and her breasts—Jubal had to close his eyes hard for a second.

When he reopened them, those breasts were still just as beautiful as he had thought. They weren't large, but they were perfect, firm, round globes, and Maggie's camisole was molded over them like a second skin. Jubal had an almost overwhelming longing to taste their hardened tips.

"Oh, my God," he whispered to himself. His body's reaction to this visual feast was instant. Almost immediately, his denim trousers were nearly too tight to hold his swelling, hardening flesh.

"Damn," he murmured.

He was torn by many emotions. He was furious with Maggie for wandering away from camp by herself. He was angry with himself at his reaction to her. And, more than anything else, he wanted to stomp down there, right into the creek, pick Maggie Bright up, carry her over to the grassy bank, and have his way with her.

He had just decided that anger was the safest emotion to act upon, and was bracing himself for a good holler, when a sudden crashing noise erupted from the trees opposite the creek bank where he stood.

Maggie heard it too and stopped, frozen, having just pulled her wet camisole over her head.

Before either one of them knew what it was that had

frightened them, Jubal had torn down the bank, raced into the water, grabbed Maggie up in his arms, and flattened them both out on the ground. As they lay on the bank, stunned by fear and Jubal's sudden action, they looked toward where the sound had come from. The white flash of a deer's tail could be discerned as the animal, apparently alarmed when it came to the water to drink and found Maggie bathing, raced off through the trees.

Jubal's rifle was primed and ready for use the second he knew that Maggie was safely covered by his body. His heart was knocking a hole through his chest by the time he saw the deer, realized the harmless source of the noise, lowered the gun, and looked down at Maggie.

She was staring up at him in stark terror. "Mr. Green!" she squeaked.

Jubal shut his eyes tight and took a deep breath to keep himself from throttling her. Then he looked down at her once more and had to shut his eyes again when he realized he was lying on her in a very intimate way, and that those breasts he had so admired were naked and pressing against his chest. Her body was cool under his, and his reaction to the feel of her was even more violent than his reaction to the sight of her had been.

"Why the hell did you leave camp alone?"

Maggie wanted to cover herself, but her arms were squashed under Jubal's body. She was still pretty scared. She hadn't had a chance to calm down yet, and her heart was racing so fast she thought she might swoon. It was difficult to draw sufficient breath with which to speak.

"I wanted to take a bath. I was dirty," she whispered.

"It's not safe."

"I'm not that far from camp."

Even as she said it, she knew she had probably been at fault. She was always at fault. She didn't want to cause these nice men, who had sworn they would protect her, any worry on her behalf. Nor did she want to make the job of protecting her any more difficult than it already was. And her little bathing idyll *was* pretty far away.

Jubal knew it too. "It's too damned far to be safe."

"But it was only a deer."

"It might not have been only a deer."

"I—I guess not."

By now, Maggie was having a real hard time concentrating on their conversation. Jubal was staring down at her with those green eyes of his and making her feel hot all over. But it wasn't the same kind of hot that had baked the energy out of her earlier in the day. This kind of hot was liquid and searing and it was making her want to do things with Jubal Green that she knew a proper lady would never want to do with anyone but her lawful husband.

She could smell his sweaty, hot musk, and she liked it. His weight pressed her into the grassy bank and she felt his hardness rigid against her. That shocked her some.

"You might have been killed, Mrs. Bright," Jubal said. His voice was tight.

"I'm sorry," Maggie whispered.

That was the last thing she remembered saying before Jubal's arms tightened around her and his lips lowered to hers.

Jubal's kiss was hard, inspired in equal parts by anger, lust, and fear. His anger and fear slowly died as he drank of Maggie's sweet lips. Desire quickly drowned those other unworthy emotions.

She tasted like sweet apples and sunshine, and he couldn't seem to get enough of her. He dipped his tongue to taste of her lips more deeply, and the shimmer of reaction that swept her body nearly did him in. When he felt her arms wrap around him, he had a dim thought that they'd better stop this pretty quick, but he couldn't quite make himself let go.

Maggie couldn't ever remember feeling like this before. Not even with Kenny. Not ever, even remotely, with Kenny. She knew she shouldn't be clinging to Jubal like this, but she couldn't seem to help herself. His body was hot on hers, hot with the heat of the sun and her heat, and the combination was sending her down a road she'd never traveled.

She'd never been particularly interested in Kenny's body, but all at once she found herself wanting to rip Jubal Green's shirt right off his back so she could run her hands over those muscles she had seen, when he'd been so sick, and feel his hot skin. She wanted to caress those hard thighs she'd admired, in spite of herself, when he'd been unconscious. She remembered they were covered with sun-colored hair. She wanted to run her fingers over those hairs and find out if they were as wiry as they looked.

She found herself arching her hips against his swollen manhood and would have been ashamed if she'd had time to think about it. She writhed her breasts against him, glorying in the feel of her sensitive nipples rubbing against the heavy cotton of his shirt. She had a wanton desire to find out how they would feel against his hairy chest.

When his tongue began to explore her mouth, she

was surprised. She'd never experienced that particular intimacy before, and her lips parted a little in alarm. When Jubal's hot tongue immediately pressed its advantage and plunged into her mouth, she forgot her alarm and thrust her own tongue out to meet his.

Jubal couldn't believe what he was feeling. He'd had enough women in his checkered career, God knew, but he'd never felt anything akin to the way he felt now, as he lay fully clothed atop Maggie Bright on the cool banks of Turkey Creek. He felt as hot and hard as a pistol barrel, and he could feel every single minute inch of Maggie's body underneath him. Her breasts were driving him crazy. He had been cupping her face with his hands, but he moved one of those hands now to feel her breasts.

Oh, my God, thought Maggie.

She wasn't sure she hadn't said the words aloud into the open mouth of Jubal Green that still covered hers. She had never even considered the remote possibility that a man could touch a woman's breasts like that. She'd never felt anything so wonderful in her entire life. She heard funny little soft, kittenish sounds, and realized somewhere in her befuddled brain that they were coming from her own throat.

And she knew the low growls and groans of desire were coming from Jubal.

Maggie was whimpering with unrestrained desire and Jubal was just about to rip his clothes off and finish what they had begun when they both became aware of a voice hollering in the distance.

"Mrs. Bright! Jubal! Where are you?"

Jubal slowly withdrew his lips from Maggie's and heaved a gut-wrenching groan. He squeezed his eyes shut, gritted his teeth, and prayed for strength.

Maggie couldn't think. She could only stare up at him with eyes that looked completely dazed with passion. She was panting hard.

So was Jubal. With a monumental effort, he pulled himself off Maggie's wonderful body. Her arms fell away from his shoulders and landed on the bank when he stood up with one jerky movement. When he looked down at her, she was spread out like a sacrifice. His breath was coming in tortured gasps. His sex was so hard and throbbed so much he could hardly walk.

He got annoyed when Maggie didn't move but just lay there and stared up at him as though she didn't know what on earth had just happened to her.

"Get dressed, Mrs. Bright," he growled. His voice was harsh and ragged.

Then he cupped his hands around his mouth and hollered, "We're here! It's all right!"

Suddenly Maggie sucked in an enormous breath. She realized all at once where she was, and in what state of undress, and felt her face heat with embarrassment. She covered her naked breasts with crossed arms and drew her legs up.

Jubal could hardly resist the urge to carry her off into the trees like a caveman and make love to her until neither one of them could walk. But he did.

"Get dressed," he said again. "They're looking for us."

Maggie's brain finally jerked into gear. She sat up and grabbed for her fresh camisole in one fluid movement.

"I—I'm dirty again. I have to rinse off," she whispered. She found her voice didn't work very well yet.

Jubal finally tore his gaze away from her. He ran an agitated hand through his thick hair.

"Well, hurry it up. I don't want Dan and Four Toes to see you like that."

"No," Maggie said, with a wobble in her voice.

She quickly walked a little way into the creek and threw icy water over herself to wash away the dirt and grass that clung to her. She looked over her shoulder to find Jubal staring at her again.

"Turn around, Mr. Green," she directed in a high, strained voice.

Without a word, Jubal turned his back.

Even so, she went back to shore with arms crossed over her bosom. She dried herself off and donned her clean camisole and shirtwaist while Jubal continued to stare off into the trees.

She turned around when she took off her drawers, thinking that it would be more discreet to do that than to doff them in front of Jubal, even when his back was turned. She didn't see the agonized expression on his face when he peeked over his shoulder and saw her smooth buttocks, which looked as firm and silky as fresh peaches.

That's what you get for looking, he told himself with furious frustration.

"I think I'm ready now," Maggie said in a small voice when she had buttoned her skirt and pulled on her stockings and shoes.

She carried her dirty clothes with her when she stumbled back to camp, pulled along by Jubal Green.

Jubal and Maggie didn't say another word to each other until they had been on their way toward El Paso for a good two or three hours that night.

Maggie pretended to be occupied with keeping

Annie happy. She pointed out curiosities in the dry, dull desert landscape until it got too dark to see. Then she sang nursery rhymes to her until the little girl's yawns became too obvious to ignore any longer. Then she laid Annie down in the wagon to sleep.

Although the day had been hellishly hot, the night was becoming cold. Maggie made sure Annie was well protected from the elements and then fetched her own heavy coat to wear.

She realized Jubal didn't have anything but his shirt on and was stabbed all at once by a torrent of conflicting impulses. She finally decided that, while she might have made a blazing fool of herself with him this afternoon, that didn't negate her responsibility to him as one of God's creatures.

"Would you like me to bring you your jacket, Mr. Green?" she asked politely.

Jubal, who had been spending the last few hours trying to pretend Maggie Bright wasn't sitting next to him, ripe, womanly, and more desirable than any woman he'd ever known in his entire life, wished she hadn't spoken. It was easier to make himself believe he didn't want her when she wasn't being her usual kind self. Maggie was the first woman he'd ever met in his life who seemed to believe it was natural for people to take care of one another.

He finally decided he'd been enough of an ass for one day and it would be better to accept Maggie's offer gracefully than freeze to death. Already, his wounds were beginning to ache with the cold. He cleared his throat with some difficulty.

"Yes, please," he said. "Thank you."

"You're welcome."

Maggie brought him his jacket. She was obliged to

help him on with it, since he had to handle the reins. That necessitated her leaning over his back to hold the left sleeve at an appropriate angle for him to slip his arm into it. When she did that, her breasts pressed against his back, and they each experienced a few moments of embarrassment, but both pretended not to notice.

"Thank you, Mrs. Bright," said Jubal again.

"You're welcome, Mr. Green."

They were silent for another few miles.

Maggie was staring up into the sky, wishing she could see the stars better, when Jubal's voice startled her.

"I—I'm sorry for—for what happened back there, Mrs. Bright."

Maggie sucked in a quick breath and looked down at her lap. By the light of the millions of stars, she could just make out her hands as they kneaded themselves together nervously on her skirt. In spite of the full moon the desert spread out around them, an ocean of blackness.

"That's all right, Mr. Green. It wasn't your fault."

"Yes, it was. I shouldn't have done that. I'm sorry."

Maggie turned her head to look at Jubal's face. She could barely discern his profile, dark against the darker background of the night. Even so, she could tell he was a handsome man. She sighed and knew he had heard her when he flicked a quick glance at her.

"I—I guess I miss my husband, Mr. Green," she confessed. "I don't know what else could have got into me. It wasn't all your fault. It's all right."

Damn, Jubal thought sourly. Why does she have to make it all sound so reasonable?

It didn't seem reasonable to him. He'd never lost control of himself so completely before in his life. He

If you
have a passion
for great
historical
romance,
here's an offer
you'll love...

4 FREE NOVELS

SEE INSIDE.

Introducing
The Timeless Romance

Passion rising from the ashes of the Civil War...

Love blossoming against the harsh landscape of the primitive Australian outback...

Romance melting the cold walls of an 18th-century English castle —— and the heart of the handsome Earl who lives there...

Since the beginning of time, great love has held the power to change the course of history. And in Harper Monogram historical novels, you can experience that power again and again.

Free introductory offer. To introduce you to this exclusive new service, we'd like to send you the four newest Harper Monogram titles absolutely free. They're yours to keep without obligation, no matter what you decide.

Free 10-day previews. Enjoy automatic free delivery of four new titles each month —— up to four weeks before they appear in bookstores. You're never obligated to keep a book you don't want, and you can return any book, for a full credit.

Save up to 32% off the publisher's price on any shipment you choose to keep.

Don't pass up this opportunity to enjoy great romance as you have never experienced before.

Reader Service.

Indulge in passion, adventure and romance with your

4 FREE

Historical Romances.

realized he actually resented Maggie's jumbling him together in a neat little package with her dead husband. He sure as hell was no Kenny Bright, he told himself. Jubal would no more have taken a gentle creature like Maggie Bright into the uncivilized wildness of New Mexico territory than he would have sent a sheep out to tame lions.

The truth of the matter, that the gentle Maggie Bright had been surviving quite well in the territory before he'd been thrust upon her, didn't occur to him. He was a better man than Kenny Bright, and he'd prove it to Bright's widow or die trying.

He didn't respond to Maggie's comment, and she was embarrassed. It had cost her a good deal to admit to desiring a man. Desire was something proper ladies didn't admit to anybody, except maybe, once in a great while, to each other. She had been trying to make Jubal feel a little better about his boorishness. Besides that, it was the truth. Maggie had been missing Kenny more and more lately, for some strange reason. At least, she thought it was Kenny she missed. All at once she wasn't sure about that.

"Well," Jubal said at last, "I'm sorry."

Maggie sighed again. "It's all right."

They didn't speak to each other again during the long, black night. Maggie continued to stare at the stars and wish she could see them. Jubal continued to drive the team and try not to think about Maggie sitting next to him in the wagon.

The following day, the little band rested under some dusty brown outcroppings in the middle of the blazing desert.

"My goodness, I've never seen anything so empty before," Maggie said, as she surveyed the miles and miles of nothingness spread out before and around them. There didn't seem to be any vegetation at all but a dry, gray scrub that appeared to go on forever.

Dan was spreading his saddle blanket out to sleep on. "It's pretty ugly around here, all right," he agreed.

For the first time since that surge of excitement began to blossom within her when they were but a few miles away from her farm, Maggie's spirits started to droop. She hoped Jubal's ranch wouldn't look like this. She was used to green trees and water. This was the devil's land here.

She kept her opinion to herself, but Jubal noticed her mood and was sure he was the cause. He cursed himself.

"Here, Mrs. Bright," he said. "You and Annie better drink some water now. You have to keep drinking in this desert, or you'll dry up and blow away before you know it."

"Thank you, Mr. Green," Maggie said in a shy little voice. She took the cup of water from him, drank some of it, and held it to her daughter's lips.

The desert was a perilous place, and Four Toes rigged up a rope to keep Annie safe. One end of the rope was tied around Annie's waist, and the other was tied to his wrist. That way, if the baby got bored and wandered off while the adults slept, the rope would tug on his arm and he would wake up.

Maggie was impressed by his thoughtfulness. "Thank you very much, Mr. Smith. I really appreciate that."

"It's all right, Mrs. Bright. I grew up tied to the end of a rope myself."

He laughed when Maggie's eyes got round.

"It's the truth," he said. "There's all sorts of things around here that can hurt a child. Cougars find the little ones easy pickings. And a baby can wander off easy as pie. Anything tiny is hard to spot in this land, and if a body don't keep drinking, you can die in just a few hours. It's better to be tied to a rope than die, my family always thought." He grinned at Dan and Jubal, and they grinned back.

Maggie didn't understand that shared grin, but the words made sense and she swallowed hard. "I should say so."

It turned out that Annie wasn't much of a problem. She was happy to play with her nice new wooden toys while her mama and the men slept. It was too hot for adventures, anyway. When Maggie woke up a few hours later, Annie was sound asleep next to her. She herself was drenched in sweat, but there would be no bath today. There wasn't a creek or a stream or even a mudhole around for miles and miles.

All the adults were glad when morning found them rumbling along the dry, dusty streets of El Paso.

12

"*We're going to* stop at Garza's and get some supplies," Jubal told Maggie. "Then I have a couple of other stops to make."

"What's Garza's?" Maggie wanted to know.

"A big mercantile. They have dry goods and food supplies. I want to stop by the seed store after we stock up with flour and beans and such."

Maggie nodded. She guessed Jubal would know what they needed on his ranch.

When she stepped into Garza's Dry Goods Emporium she was overwhelmed. She'd never been in such a big store. Even the mercantile in Indiana, while tidier and more civilized-looking than this place, was tiny by comparison.

Jubal noticed her reaction and grinned to himself. He and Maggie were becoming more relaxed around each other, now that a day or so had passed since their encounter by Turkey Creek.

"Big place, isn't it?"

Maggie looked at him blankly. "Big?" she repeated. "It's huge."

She stood in the entrance of Garza's and tried to adjust her eyes to the bounty arrayed before her. She held Annie tightly. Annie, too, seemed amazed. The little girl's big brown eyes were wide and she stuffed her fist into her mouth, her habit whenever she was surprised.

Immediately in front of them was a long aisle that ended in the biggest, shiniest plank counter Maggie had ever seen. The shelves that lined the aisle were stacked with jars full of spices and patent medicines. There were spices Maggie had never heard of. She picked up a jar of allspice and wondered if it contained a combination of all other spices. Then she put it back and felt foolish.

She noticed three different brands of cod-liver oil. There were bitters, painkillers, magnesia tablets, tonics, seltzers, syrups, salves, and balms. She wondered what Appolinaris Water was good for. She liked the name. If she dared, she would have spent a few of her carefully saved pennies and bought Annie a bottle of cherry seltzer. But she felt intimidated in this new place and merely looked with awe at the vast array of goods neatly stacked around her.

It took her quite a while to walk down that one center aisle, she was so fascinated by everything. Once past that first intriguing lane, though, she gasped with pleasure.

"Oh, my, Annie, will you look at that."

Annie pulled her fist out of her mouth. "Look dat." She pointed a moist finger toward where her mother was staring, agape.

It seemed to Maggie as if she were looking at a mile's worth of fabric and notions, at the very least. Bolts and bolts of bright calicoes and ginghams tempted shoppers. Heavy denims, gabardines, and muslins lined a wall. There were wools for cloaks and coats, percales for sheets, and gauze for diapers. There were even satins, frilly laces, and tulles for wedding dresses and veils. A shelf laden with cotton batting, threads, cords, and braids took up an entire wall behind the cloth.

Maggie fingered several pretty fabrics and wished she dared buy something. She'd love to sew her little Annie up a dress out of a pink-checked gingham.

"I can't do it, though, Annie," Maggie said, as though she were apologizing to her daughter. "I don't know even where we're going to be pretty soon. I can't start spending our money foolishly, can I?"

Right before they'd left New Mexico, Jubal had handed her what seemed to Maggie to be a phenomenal amount of money. It was the reward that had been paid for French Jack's corpse, and he had given all of it to her in spite of her protests. In fact, it was his anger at her refusal that had finally shut her up about it. The mere thought of spending any of that money on frivolities made her feel guilty.

"I've never had so much money in my life, Annie," Maggie whispered now as she stared with longing at the bounteous display. She eyed the pretty pink gingham and then wondered if her notion was completely frivolous.

"Of course, baby," she said thoughtfully, "if I made me a dress too, it wouldn't be such a waste. We could wear them to church. There must be a church near Mr. Green's ranch." She looked around, wishing she could spot Dan or Four Toes in this amazing place. Maybe they could guide her in the proper way to go about buying fabric in such a fancy store.

A voice behind her startled her into squeezing Annie too hard, and the little girl uttered a chirping protest.

"Find anything you like, Mrs. Bright?"

Jubal had been watching Maggie eye the fabrics with a funny feeling swelling in his chest. Her wistful expression did not escape his notice. At first he wondered why she didn't just start yanking bolts off the shelf, as his mother or Janie would have done. Then he realized, yet again, that Maggie Bright was nothing at all like his mother or Janie. Maggie was a woman who appreciated how hard life was. She didn't take things like pretty fabric for granted.

Maggie turned quickly to find Jubal looking at her with a soft smile on his face. His green eyes, which were sometimes so hard and cool, were watching her with a tenderness that made her swallow and drop her own gaze to the floor.

"Mr. Green! I didn't know you were there. I—I've never seen anything like this store before. It's so big." Maggie's voice held awe.

Jubal chuckled. "It's big, all right. Garza's got the biggest place for hundreds of miles. There are huge spreads around this neck of the woods, Mrs. Bright, and they all come here for supplies. Pretty nearly all the people who live in the other small towns come here too. Garza has a regular mercantile empire in west Texas."

"I guess he has, all right." Her gaze swept the store again, and she shook her head.

Jubal cleared his throat. "You like that cloth, Mrs. Bright?" He nodded at the pink gingham.

Maggie could feel her face flush. She felt stupid because she didn't know how to buy something in this huge place. Every other mercantile she'd ever been in in her life was basically one small room with a proprietor never farther than a holler away. To Maggie, hollering in Garza's would be akin to hollering in church.

"Well," she said, "I—I was thinking about it."

"It would look good on you," Jubal said. Then he was embarrassed at having said something so inane.

Maggie looked up at him quickly. "Thank you," she said shyly. "I thought I'd make a dress for Annie out of it too."

Jubal nodded, as though he were considering her words carefully. In truth, he knew very little and cared even less about ladies' apparel. He just wanted Maggie to be happy.

"Good idea," he said.

"Do you think so?" Maggie asked with a lilt to her voice, obviously relieved to find somebody to advise her.

Jubal nodded again. "Sure," he said. "I'll get a clerk."

"All right," Maggie said. She didn't know what a clerk was.

She found out a minute or so later when an efficient young Mexican man accompanied Jubal back to her side.

"You'd like this gingham, ma'am?" the young man asked her.

"Yes, please," Maggie answered in a tiny voice.

The clerk had a pencil tucked behind his ear and carried a pair of scissors and an account pad in his waistband. He hefted the bolt of gingham off the counter and carried it to a cutting board. Maggie dashed after him, afraid she'd get lost if she didn't keep up.

"And how much would you like, ma'am?"

The question made her blush. She didn't know. She'd never bought yardage before. Her aunt had doled out fabric by the inch when she was growing up, and Kenny had brought her lengths of cloth from Lincoln occasionally. She'd made all of Annie's clothes out of leftover odds and ends she had at home.

"I—I don't know," she stammered.

The well-trained clerk didn't look at all disconcerted at her confession. Instead he just asked, "What do you intend to make out of it, ma'am?"

"Well, I guess dresses for my little girl and me," said Maggie.

The clerk eyed her critically for a few seconds. "I think ten yards will provide enough for both of you. If you'd like more for sunbonnets, you can get twelve yards for a dollar."

Jubal was watching Maggie closely. He saw that she seemed confused and realized she'd probably never done this before.

"Twelve yards sounds good to me, Mrs. Bright," he said, in an attempt to rescue her. He was unprepared for the swift look of gratitude she shot him. It hadn't occurred to him before how satisfying helping out Maggie Bright could be.

"Yes. Thank you. I'll take twelve yards."

"What about spool cotton?" asked the clerk.

"Yes, please."

The clerk pulled a spool of thread from the shelf behind him. "Do you need cardboard for the bonnets?" he asked.

Maggie's mouth dropped open. She'd always stiffened her bonnet brims by stitching layers and layers of fabric together, quilting them until her fingers ached from the tiny needlework, and then starching them until they couldn't have bent if they'd wanted to. The thought of putting cardboard into a bonnet's brim to hold it stiff had never occurred to her, but all at once she could visualize how one could do it. Lord, that would make her life easier. She looked at the clerk shyly.

"How much is the cardboard?"

Jubal wanted to curse and tell her he'd buy the damned cardboard. How much could it cost? He held his tongue, though. Maggie couldn't help her circumstances. And she couldn't possibly know that, all at once, just in the time he'd been standing with her at this dry goods counter, one of Jubal's major priorities in life had become seeing to her welfare.

"Two cents," said the clerk.

Maggie smiled with relief. "I'll take some, then," she said happily.

"Do you need edging? Lace? Ribbons? Buttons?"

Maggie thought hard. She had lots of lace scraps she'd rescued from old dresses and bonnets. She wasn't so sure about buttons, though. She wanted to make Annie's dress out of a pattern she'd saved from a *McCall's,* and it required a row of tiny buttons. The only buttons Maggie had were big and ugly.

"I'd like some small white buttons, please, about twenty of them."

The clerk scanned his notions shelf for a moment or two. "Here you go, ma'am, they come on papers of twelve each, so here are two of them. Genuine pearl buttons."

The buttons were shiny, pretty, and little, exactly what Maggie had hoped for. She beamed at the clerk.

"Thank you," she said.

"Thank *you*, ma'am," replied the clerk with a smile. "That will be one-twenty-seven, please, ma'am."

"Oh, yes." Maggie was momentarily flustered. She glanced quickly at Jubal.

"Will you please hold Annie for me, Mr. Green?" she asked.

"Why don't you let me pay for this, Mrs. Bright? It's the least I can do."

Maggie looked positively shocked. "Oh, no, Mr. Green. I could never let you do that."

She thrust Annie into Jubal's arms and opened the little bag that dangled from her wrist. Very carefully, she counted out the appropriate number of coins while Jubal, looking almost scared, held her daughter. Jubal couldn't remember ever holding a baby before, not even Sara. He eyed Annie with misgiving.

Annie smiled at him and reached for his face. "Ho, Juba," she said, and pulled his nose.

Jubal laughed. "What are you doing with my nose, Annie?"

"Juba's nose," affirmed Annie.

"Yes, that's Jubal's nose, all right. And this is Annie's nose." Jubal pinched Annie's nose, and the little girl giggled.

The clerk handed Maggie her package, carefully wrapped in brown paper and tied with string, and Maggie felt very sophisticated when she turned toward Jubal again. When she discovered him engaged in a nose-pulling match with Annie, her big-city airs dropped from her shoulders with a laugh.

"Here, Mr. Green, I'll trade you." She offered Jubal her package, and he gave her Annie, and they began to wend their way through the rest of the mercantile.

Maggie wandered from the fabrics to the toiletries counter. The sweet smell of fancy Paris soaps, sachets, bottles of toilet water, talcums, bath oils, skin balms, lotions, hair tonics, and pomades drew her like a magnet.

"Oh, my goodness, Mr. Green, I've never seen anything like this in all my life."

Jubal considered telling her she'd already told him that, but he restrained himself. He smiled as he watched her walk reverently up and down the aisle, her eyes wide and wondering at the vast selection of goods available for purchase. He noticed a little display of toilet waters and picked up a bottle of lilac fragrance. He wasn't exactly sure when or how he would give it to her, but he knew he would.

Maggie paused over some pretty hairbrushes. One in particular caught her eye. It was advertised to have come all the way from England. Its boar bristles were stiff, cream-colored, and new, and its wooden back was painted black and lacquered to a fare-thee-well. It was decorated with a pretty bouquet of flowers in pink, blue, and white on green stems, and Maggie thought she'd never seen anything so beautiful in her life. She picked it up very carefully.

"Oh, look at this, Annie," she breathed. "See the pretty flowers?"

"Fowers," Annie repeated. She reached for the brush.

"Better not touch it, Annie," her mother said. "It's not ours."

"Not ours," Annie said, her little voice mimicking her mama's regret.

Maggie placed the brush back on the counter with great care.

Jubal, strolling along behind Maggie and Annie,

waited until they had turned down another aisle
before he picked up the brush and tucked it under his
arm along with the bottle of lilac toilet water.
Suddenly he felt silly, hiding these things from the
woman he intended to give them to.

"Just about ready to go?" Dan asked, walking up to
them.

Maggie thought her head would start spinning if
she stayed in the huge mercantile any longer. "Yes,"
she said.

"I've got one or two other things to see to," Jubal said.
"You go on out to the wagon."

Dan nodded and guided Maggie through the maze
of merchandise and outside.

"I've never seen anything like that in my life, Mr.
Blue Gully," Maggie whispered when they were out in
the light of day once more.

Dan grinned. "Garza's takes some getting used to."

"I should say so."

Maggie began fanning herself with her free hand as
she peered around. It was hot again today. El Paso
didn't seem quite as hot as the bare desert had, but it
was plenty warm. There seemed to be a permanent
pall of dust hanging a foot or so above the ground,
stirred up by people and animals walking along the
dry street. Maggie noticed a couple of little funnel
clouds hovering in the distance, where the wind had
whipped the loose dirt into dust devils.

"It's real dry here," she said to Dan.

"Yes," he agreed, "it is that."

Neither one of them saw Jubal step out of Garza's,
take one look at Maggie fanning herself, and turn
right around and march back inside the mercantile.
When he emerged again, he carried not only Maggie's

bundle of fabric but a little paper packet of his own, as well as a pretty folding fan.

"Here, Mrs. Bright, you'll need this in my neck of the woods." He shoved the fan into Maggie's hand as he joined her and Dan. Then he turned immediately and stuffed his packages inside the wagon.

Maggie's mouth dropped open. "Oh, my, Mr. Green. I can't—"

"Yes, you can," snapped Jubal, interrupting her protest. "Now come along. We're going to the seed store."

He grabbed Maggie's arm and held on to it as he quickly walked the distance to the seed store. Maggie had to run to keep up.

Dan watched them race off down the street with a big grin on his face. He followed them at a more leisurely pace.

"Thank you for the fan, Mr. Green," Maggie panted when Jubal had yanked her inside the seed store and she could catch her breath long enough to speak.

"You're welcome."

Four Toes was already in the store. He'd been planning Maggie's flower garden while she'd been mooning around the mercantile. "How about some dahlias and cosmos, Mrs. Bright?" was his greeting. "They're pretty, and I think the colors will go together." He was contemplating the pretty illustrations on the flower advertisement printed up by the seed distributor.

Maggie had been reverently inspecting her brand-new fan. It was made out of stiff paper, separated by tiny stick ribs, and folded up tight. The paper was white, decorated with bright flowers.

She looked up at Four Toes, though. "Flowers?" she whispered in wonder. "You're buying flower seeds?"

"Well, we never got your flower bed planted on your farm. Jubal's got room for a dozen flower beds at his place."

"Oh, but I can't—"

Jubal was feeling really touchy now, although he couldn't have told anybody why.

"Will you stop saying you can't this and you can't that, Mrs. Bright?" he barked. "We came in and tore up your whole life and then dragged you away from your home. The least we can do is make your stay at my place pleasant. You saved my life, for God's sake. If you don't think my life's worth a few flower seeds, I sure do. If you want flowers, shut up and buy some seeds."

Maggie's mouth closed with a snap. Jubal felt like a big bully.

"Thank you both," she said humbly.

Four Toes had stared at Jubal with astonishment, as though his gruff outburst took him by surprise. But when he heard the quiver in Maggie's voice, he turned his attention to her. With one last puzzled glance at Jubal, he took her gently by the arm and led her over to look at the pretty flower poster.

By the time they left the seed store, Maggie had forgotten all about Jubal's grumpiness. She and Four Toes had selected seeds that would, with any luck and a good deal of tender care, produce huge purple and pink dahlias, pink and white cosmos, and lavender and purple petunias. Maggie's eyes were bright with excitement. "Annie, we're going to have pretty flowers," she told her daughter.

"Fowers," said Annie.

"I can't begin to thank you, Mr. Green," Maggie said to Jubal shyly.

Her eyes were positively shining. Jubal didn't guess he needed more thanks than that, but her words suddenly gave him the excuse he'd been looking for to get her to accept his next surprise without arguing with him about it.

"Yes, you can," he said.

Maggie sobered up in a second and looked at him with puzzlement. Oh, Lord. This was it, what she'd been waiting for. She knew it couldn't be this easy, just go with him to El Paso and be taken care of.

"I'll do anything I can, Mr. Green," she told him. She expected him to demand that she cook and clean for them while she stayed on his ranch. She had expected to do that anyway and had meant to offer to. "What would you like me to do?"

"You can come with me," Jubal said.

"Why, certainly. Where are we going?"

"To get you some spectacles." Jubal spoke the words as though he neither wanted nor expected any fuss from her.

Maggie, whose head was swimming with all the new things she had seen today, not to mention the prospect of new clothes and a flower garden, was slow to comprehend his words. When she did, she stopped dead in her tracks, stunned.

Jubal's arm, the one that was healing, jerked painfully when she stopped so suddenly.

"Ow!"

"Spectacles?"

"Spectacles." He let go of her and rubbed his arm. It was throbbing like a son of a gun, and he wanted to swear but didn't, out of deference to Maggie.

"I'm sorry, Mr. Green," she whispered softly, reaching out to rub his arm too. Her touch sent a thrill through

Jubal that surprised the hell out of him. "But—but you can't mean to buy me spectacles."

"I can too." He didn't trust that thrill he felt at her touch and jerked his arm away from it. That hurt even more.

"But that's just too much, Mr. Green. Spectacles cost a lot of money. I—I can't accept such a fine present."

Jubal was prepared for this.

"Yes, you can, Mrs. Bright. Your eyes are bad. There are people who want me dead, and because you helped me, they want you dead too. If you can't see the stars at night, you sure as hell won't be able to—to protect yourself and your daughter. You'll be in a new place in unfamiliar country, and the better you can see, the better you'll be able to stay alive."

Maggie didn't say anything for a moment. Her brain was whirling. Jubal's words made sense to her, but it didn't make any sense at all for him to pay for her eyeglasses.

"I guess you're right," she said at last.

"You're blamed right I am."

Maggie took a deep breath. "But you still shouldn't have to pay the expense for my spectacles. I have plenty of money since you gave me that reward for Mr. Jack. I can pay for them."

Jubal scowled down at her. He couldn't figure out why she was so irritating. Why did she just insist on arguing with him every time he wanted to do something for her?

"Blast it, Mrs. Bright, will you quit fighting with me? I'm going to buy you some eyeglasses, and I don't want to hear any more about it."

He yanked on her arm again. Maggie didn't want to make a scene in public, so she trotted along beside him. But she decided that, when the critical moment came and it was time to pay, she would reach into her handbag and use her own money. She wouldn't allow Jubal Green to pay for her spectacles. That was just too much to accept in one day.

Maggie was a little nervous since she'd never had her eyes tested before. She sat very straight in the examining chair and stared at Mr. Whitney with trepidation. He tried to put her at ease with the friendly banter he used with all his customers, but Maggie couldn't relax.

But when Mr. Whitney held up different combinations of lenses in front of her eyes and told her to read the big chart in front of her, Maggie was astonished at how much more clearly she could read the letters printed on the chart. She could hardly wait to look at the world through those lenses. She nearly cried with the wonder of it all.

Jubal watched her in alarm. He recognized that misty-eyed look. He held Annie on his lap during the examination and hoped like the devil that Maggie wouldn't burst into tears.

She didn't, but she was very disappointed that she couldn't wear her new spectacles to Jubal's home. Mr. Whitney kindly explained that it took time to grind the lenses and fit them into the frames, so it would be at least two weeks before she could take possession of them. Maggie was a-tingle with anticipation.

She didn't get the opportunity to put her payment scheme into operation at the end of her examination, though. Jubal recognized the look in her eye and forestalled her. Since both his mother and father had worn spectacles, he had established a relationship with the eyeglass man in El Paso a long time ago.

When the time came to pay, he merely said, "Send me a bill, Whitney."

"Sure thing, Mr. Green," Mr. Whitney replied.

And Maggie was left to gape at the two of them in surprise. She certainly wasn't about to fight with Jubal in front of the merchant, so she waited until they were headed back to the wagon before she said anything.

Then she told him firmly, "Mr. Green, when that bill comes, you give it to me and I'll pay it."

It didn't sound as though she planned to entertain any waffling on his part, so Jubal eyed her consideringly. "All right," he finally said. He didn't guess the gods would get him for one little fib.

Maggie continued to stare at him in concern for a second or two, but she didn't guess there was much she could do about it right now. She decided she'd just be sure to watch for the bill. Of course, she had no way of knowing that somebody from the ranch had to ride to town to pick up the mail.

She had expected to start out for Jubal's spread as soon as they left the optician, but Jubal had another idea in mind.

"It's been a long time since we've been to city, Mrs. Bright. Dan and Four Toes want to visit friends and relax for a few hours before we get on back to the ranch. And I want to do some scouting around."

"Scouting around?"

"Yes. I don't think Mulrooney knows we left for Texas, but if he does, chances are I'll be able to find out if I talk to a few people in town."

"Will—will we sleep in the wagon?" Maggie asked in a tiny voice.

She'd do whatever Jubal told her to do, but she

didn't relish the thought of bedding down in an open wagon in the middle of El Paso. Maggie had taken full note of the plethora of saloons lining either side of the main street. Although she hadn't spent much time in Lincoln, the only town of any size near her farm, she knew it was noisy all night long from the drinking and shooting that went on.

"The wagon?" Jubal looked at her as though she'd lost her mind. "Of course not. We'll stay at the hotel down the street."

Maggie followed Jubal's finger until her gaze landed on a building midway down the road. She couldn't read the sign out front, but the building had a tall false front and was painted a little more nicely than the rest of the shabby wooden structures that surrounded it.

"That's a hotel?" she asked.

"Yes. It's pretty nice, by El Paso standards."

Knowing how touchy Jubal was, she didn't dare ask how much it cost. But it somehow didn't seem proper for him to pay for her overnight accommodations.

Jubal saw her expression and was pretty sure it presaged an argument. He sighed. How on earth was he supposed to take care of this exasperating woman if she wouldn't let herself be taken care of?

He took a deep breath and said, instead of yelling at her, "You'll be able to take a bath there, Mrs. Bright. You and your little girl. You'll feel much better when you're cleaned up again, I'm sure."

"Yes," said Maggie. She licked her lips nervously.

Jubal saw that gesture and had a sudden, almost gut-wrenching desire to kiss Maggie's moist, tender mouth. He shut his eyes and fisted up his hands instead.

"Will—will I be able to fix us some supper in the hotel room, Mr. Green?"

Jubal frowned at her, and Maggie wondered what she'd said wrong this time.

"I'm sorry. I don't know what to do, Mr. Green. I— I've never stayed in a hotel," she added, to forestall any harsh words from him. She felt like a foolish little hick.

Jubal didn't notice her discomfort. "No, Mrs. Bright. You're not going to fix supper in the room. You're going to check in, take a bath, and get your little girl fixed up, and then I'm going to take you both to dinner in the hotel restaurant. It's the best place in town, and I'm paying for it, so don't even try to argue with me about it."

He sounded truly ferocious.

To the best of Maggie's recollection, she'd never been taken to dinner before. Oh, she'd served thousands of people in her aunt and uncle's chophouse in Indiana, and she'd eaten leftovers from those meals, but she'd never stepped out with a gentleman, dressed up, and had him buy her a meal. The idea appealed to her enormously. She especially liked the fact that the gentleman in question was Jubal Green. She forgot all about her awkwardness and smiled shyly at him.

"Well, thank you, Mr. Green. Annie and I will like that, I'm sure."

Jubal scowled at her, but he couldn't maintain his fierce expression in the presence of Maggie's sweet, bashful pleasure at the thought of dining in a restaurant. That touched him. In fact, Jubal was beginning to fear he was permanently touched—in the head.

Maggie was so intimidated by the elegant lobby of the El Paso Hotel that she didn't dare even open her mouth when Jubal checked in for all of them. He got a room for her and Annie and one for himself. Dan and Four Toes were staying with friends in town. The hotel didn't cater to Indians anyway, which shocked Maggie when Jubal told her about it later.

Jubal didn't care to examine why he insisted that he and Maggie have adjoining rooms. He told himself it was for her protection. Just in case.

Fortunately, Maggie wasn't around to hear him make the room arrangements. Jubal had left her staring in astonishment at the potted ferns next to the elaborate brocade sofa in the lobby.

Maggie was overwhelmed by the luxury of the hotel. Jubal heard her intake of breath at the first feel of the thick crimson Turkey carpet under her feet. He watched her brows lift in wonder as she gazed about. A small smile of appreciation curled his lips when she stopped in her tracks, looked around, and then turned at a sharp angle to make her way over to the potted plants. Jubal rightly guessed that she'd never seen an indoor plant before. He was beginning to anticipate her reactions to new things with rare pleasure.

Maggie stared at the lacy, fronded ferns. "Oh, my land, Annie, will you look at that. I've seen pictures of ferns, but I never hoped to see a real one."

The plant looked terribly exotic to Maggie and brought to her mind visions of tropical forests, naked natives, and thrilling adventures. She used to read a lot in Indiana, but she hadn't had access to many books after she and Kenny moved to New Mexico.

"Will you just look at that," she whispered again.

Annie didn't appear to be particularly impressed.

All at once, Maggie decided her daughter needed to feel the luxury under their feet. She had been carrying

Annie until now, worried that the hustle and bustle of
the rugged little frontier city might frighten her. But
Maggie didn't suppose anything could hurt her baby
in this magnificent hotel.

"Annie, you've got to feel this carpet, sweetie."

She swung her daughter down from her hip. She
didn't know that Jubal had finished booking their
rooms, and she didn't hear him pad softly across the
floor to watch her.

Annie looked up at her mama in surprise. Then she
looked down at the fuzzy red floor beneath her feet.
Carefully, she lifted one foot and inspected it. Then
she peered closely at the other. She'd never felt anything like the soft thick pile of a carpet under her feet
before. Then, being a baby and not understanding the
finer points of etiquette, she plopped herself down on
her tummy and dug her little fingers into the carpet
pile.

Maggie quickly shot a glance around the room,
torn between embarrassment at her daughter's obviously unsophisticated reaction to carpeting, and pleasure that Annie should enjoy the feel of it as much as
her mama did. She saw Jubal watching them with a
smile on his face and blushed.

"We've never been any place like this before, Mr.
Green," she said unnecessarily.

"So I gather," said Jubal. Then he wished he hadn't
said it because Maggie dropped her gaze and scooped
Annie up. She'd apparently taken his words as some
sort of censure.

"You like this place?" he asked her, in an effort to
smooth over his gaffe.

Maggie turned to him, and Jubal had the impression she was assessing his reason for asking.

He was right. Maggie didn't think he'd mock her, but she wasn't sure about anything anymore, especially as it pertained to Jubal Green and herself. She didn't want to look like a complete bumpkin. On the other hand, that was pretty much what she was, and she didn't suppose it would do her any good to pretend to be anything else. She opted for honesty.

"It's just about the prettiest place I've ever seen, Mr. Green. Thank you. If it wasn't for you getting shot and knocking at my door like you did, I'd never ever have seen such a wonderful place."

To her surprise, Jubal's response to those words was a shout of laughter.

13

Jubal saw Maggie to the door of her room. "I'm going to give you a couple of hours to get cleaned up and rested, Mrs. Bright, and then I'll come fetch you for dinner. Will that suit you?"

To his surprise, Jubal was extremely pleased that she seemed so excited about staying in a hotel. Before he met her, he didn't realize how satisfying it could be to introduce new things to a woman who expressed honest, open enjoyment of them. His experiences with women until now had led him to believe they were, at best, dissemblers all.

Maggie's eyes glowed. "That will be just fine, Mr. Green. Thank you." She was so agog she forgot to insist on repaying him for her hotel room.

After he left Maggie, Jubal quickly stashed his gear in his own room and went in search of Dan and Four Toes. He found them in a saloon down the road. It had been a meeting place for them for several years now.

When Jubal pushed open the swinging doors of the saloon and walked inside, he stopped short and looked around in some surprise. The room smelled rancid, of spilled beer, stale tobacco, and sweat. The smell was one of unpleasant maleness unrelieved by any trace of the softening influence of women. The only females present were heavily painted creatures who seemed oddly sad-looking to Jubal. A thick, constant pall of tobacco smoke had turned the once-white walls a dingy tan and lent a permanent acrid stench to the air. The seediness of the place both appalled and astonished him.

He shook his head. Jesus, guess I'm not used to saloons anymore, he thought sourly. It had been months since he'd been in one. He'd forgotten what wretched places they were.

A tinny piano, picked at by a reedy man with an incessant cough, tinkled away in a corner. A young woman with jet-black hair and a lot of paint on her face waved at Jubal, and he waved back without enthusiasm. He hoped she wouldn't come up and press her bosom against him. He used to look forward to Kitty's suggestive greeting. Now the mere thought of it made his skin crawl.

Sawdust had been sprinkled over the plank floor of the saloon in some long-gone-by day. It might have been clean once, but it was rank and filthy now and Jubal eyed it with disgust. Even walking on the stuff was unpleasant. The floor was sticky, and he didn't even want to hazard a guess as to what made it that way.

Dan and Four Toes were in a deep discussion with a couple of rough-looking men.

"What did you find out?" he asked.

They seemed to have expected this curt greeting. Dan looked up and gestured him into the scarred wooden chair next to him.

"Jeez, you could have chosen a cleaner place to meet, Dan," Jubal said, looking around with a grimace.

Dan grinned at him with real amusement. "We been meetin' here for years, Jubal. You never bitched about it before. Must be getting sissy, hanging around with a lady all this time."

Jubal shot a furious frown at his friend and then gave it up and offered him a reluctant grin.

"I guess," he said with a sigh. "It's funny what being around a woman will do to a man."

"Shit," said one of the men at their table. "Ain't funny a-tall." He spat onto the sawdust, and Jubal winced inwardly. Small wonder the floor looked like that.

"Don't spit on the floor, Hank," a shrill voice commanded.

A voluptuous woman whisked over a cuspidor and plunked it down next to the chair of the man named Hank. She was corseted tightly, and her ample white flesh spilled out over her dress in front. Hank gave her big rump a playful spank and ogled her bosom.

"Aw, Dolly, we was just talkin' about women. You know how itchy that kind of talk makes me."

Dolly winked suggestively at him. "Well, you know how to scratch that itch, don't you, Hank?"

"I'll see you later, Dolly honey," Hank promised.

Jubal watched their playful exchange with an odd griping in his gut. He recognized the banter as the same type he'd participated in hundreds of times. He couldn't figure out why it gave him such a lost and lonely feeling now. He shook his head one more time. He really was getting soft.

"Well, listen," he said. "I don't have much time. Have you found out anything?"

Hank drew his gaze away from Dolly's hind end and faced Jubal.

"Mulrooney's in his railway car on the way to Santa Fe," he said in a flat voice.

Jubal pinned Hank with a steady stare. "You sure?"

"I'm sure."

"Hellfire."

"The man himself," added Dan, just in case there was some doubt.

"Hellfire," said Jubal again.

"According to my contact in New York, Mulrooney left four days ago. Don't know whether he's found out you've left that farm in the hills yet or not."

"Well, look at it this way, Jubal," said Dan. "If he wasn't worried, he wouldn't leave his little nest. In a way it's good. You never could have got at him there. He was like a goddamned queen bee in a hive, protected on all sides. This way you have a chance to settle things once and for all."

Jubal stared at the filthy table in front of him. "Damn," he said softly.

"Hell, Jubal, it ain't so bad," said Dan. "We can even ride to Santa Fe and blow up the train, if it comes to that."

Jubal looked at Dan for a moment. He was very troubled about this turn of events. "He's probably got a damned army guarding that train, Danny. Besides, I can't do that. Not now. I can't do something like that without you with me. I don't trust anybody else, and I don't dare go away and leave Mrs. Bright and Annie with nobody around but hired hands. Our top priority is to keep the two of them safe."

Dan's eyebrows arched comically. "Well, now, did you hear that, Four Toes? Our priorities have changed all of a sudden."

Four Toes grinned at Jubal too. "I guess so."

"I didn't used to think there was anything on the face of the earth mattered to you more than killing P. J. Mulrooney, Jubal Green."

Jubal's crooked, rueful grin was that of a defeated man. "I didn't used to think so either, Danny."

Dan and Four Toes exchanged a wickedly gleeful grin.

While Jubal, Dan, Four Toes, and their spies discussed Prometheus Mulrooney in the saloon, Maggie was trying to get used to the amazing luxury of her hotel room.

"Shoot, Annie, I'm afraid to touch anything," she told her little girl. Everything was shinier, prettier, and newer than anything Maggie had ever seen before.

Annie was too busy toddling around on the carpet in her bare feet to notice her mother's awed reaction to their surroundings. The little girl liked the mattress on the big bed, too. It was nothing like the prickery tick mattresses at home. Not only that, but the frame holding it was springy, and Annie discovered the joy of bed-bouncing for the first time in her young life.

"Oh, my land, baby, don't jump on the bed."

Maggie snatched her daughter up and carted her into the bathroom. There were even more amazements in store for them there, because the hotel was equipped with faucets. Maggie had never seen a real faucet before, although she had seen pictures in a magazine Sadie Phillips let her borrow.

With a trembling hand she reached out and turned the tap handle. The immediate gush of cold water made her jump back in alarm.

"Wa!" shouted a delighted Annie. She pointed at the cascade of water pouring into the sink.

Maggie giggled. "It sure is, honey. It's water, all right. Right here in our own room. Whatever will they think of next?" Maggie sneaked up to the basin and turned the tap off quickly, afraid she would flood the place if she let it run much longer.

A brisk rapping at the door to their room startled her.

"Who on earth can that be?" she wondered aloud. It certainly wasn't time for Jubal to be back yet.

Maggie wasn't sure what to do. If it had been her own home, she would have walked over to the door and flung it open. But this was a fancy hotel, and she'd never been in a fancy hotel before. She tiptoed up to the door and stood in front of it, clutching Annie tightly.

"Who is it?" she called in a shaky voice.

"Room service, ma'am. Mr. Green requested hot water for a bath in this room."

Hot water for a bath? She opened the door a crack. Then, when she saw an army of hotel staff, all holding buckets of steaming water, she stepped back and opened it all the way.

The bellboy smiled at her and swept an arm out to usher in five uniformed maids. They trooped in one after the other, headed straight into the bathroom, and, with clocklike precision, dumped two bucketfuls of water apiece into the bathtub. Each one gave Maggie a little curtsey before she left. The bellboy touched his cap and shut the door behind him on his way out.

"Thank you," Maggie whispered to the closed door. "My Lord in heaven," she murmured when she went back into the bathroom.

The water was a little bit hot, so she added cold water from the tap, and then she and Annie had a delightful bath. She even washed their hair and rinsed it under the cold running water. They were both laughing by the time they were clean, and then Maggie dried them off with the fluffiest towels she had ever seen.

"I swear, Annie, I think I've died and gone straight to heaven."

Two hours later, when Jubal tapped at the door of their room, Maggie and Annie were both clean as a whistle and dressed in their Sunday best. Maggie had surveyed them both critically and come to the conclusion that their best clothes weren't any too good, but it couldn't be helped.

Jubal had spiffed himself up some too. He appeared at Maggie's door shaved and washed and wearing a new pair of trousers and a coat he'd bought at the dry goods store after he left Dan and Four Toes in that dismal saloon down the way.

Jubal couldn't help but notice Maggie's happy, bright eyes when she opened the door to admit him. A warm feeling of contentment spread through him. He was almost getting used to that warmth, even though it was something he'd never felt before he'd met Maggie.

"You're looking mighty pretty tonight, Mrs. Bright."

Maggie flushed and picked up Annie to hide it.

"Thank you, Mr. Green. So are you."

Jubal grinned and Maggie got flustered.

"I mean, you're not pretty. You look—you look very handsome."

"Thank you." Jubal's smile broadened, and he offered her his elbow.

Maggie reached for it and then got even more flustered when she realized she'd forgotten something. She put Annie down and whirled around, dashed over to the dresser, and snatched up her hat.

It was her very finest one. She had ordered its bare skeleton out of a catalog and decorated it herself with flowers she'd made from scraps of material and then stiffened with starch and quilting. She tied the ribbons under her chin, scooped up Annie again, and rejoined Jubal at the door.

"I almost forgot my hat," she said unnecessarily.

Jubal didn't quite know what to say, so he opted for, "It's very pretty."

He felt really good when Maggie beamed at him. Then she tucked her gloved hand in his elbow, and he led her and Annie downstairs to the restaurant.

Jubal had dined in relatively good restaurants, by Texas standards at least, with his mother and sister-in-law, but he'd never taken a lady out to eat like this before. He had a vague notion that this was courting behavior, but he didn't care to examine that notion closely. He could, after all, have had food taken to Maggie's room if he'd wanted to. But he was deriving a great deal of enjoyment out of watching her react to all the new things to which he was introducing her.

He had a rebellious thought that there were one or two other new things he'd like to teach her too, but he tried to tuck that thought away behind his nobler motives. It popped out again, however, at odd times during their meal.

"I'm nervous as a cat," Maggie whispered in his ear as they reached the threshold of the restaurant.

She clutched his arm tightly, and Jubal suppressed the urge to pat her hand. He had made reservations, and the host led them to their table with a stiff-backed, pompous air that made Maggie's eyes widen.

Jubal had also thought to make arrangements for Annie, in the form of a chair equipped with a cushioned bolster. Maggie clearly didn't know what to do with the contraption.

"Here, let me," said Jubal. He took the baby from her mother's arms and carefully set her on the seat.

"There you go, Annie. You've got your own little chair now." He grinned at Annie and patted her cheek, and she smiled back at him.

Maggie would have thanked him, but she realized all at once that the host was holding out a chair and looking at her imperiously. She quickly sat down.

"Thank you," she whispered.

Jubal watched her looking around the restaurant and felt himself go soft inside. The interior reminded him very much of a whorehouse he'd visited in San Antonio once, but he didn't tell Maggie that.

"I declare, Mr. Green, this is the prettiest place I've ever been in."

Maggie felt very rustic and ignorant in the grand restaurant. The walls were covered with striped crimson wallpaper, flocked to perfection. Thick crimson carpet covered the floor here, as in the lobby, and each table was adorned with a squat cranberry-colored crystal lamp, in which a real beeswax candle burned. No nasty, heavy tallow smell marred the ambiance *here.*

A waiter appeared, and Jubal ordered a bottle of wine. He hadn't intended to do that, but Maggie's pleasure had suddenly become very important to him. And she was enjoying this new experience so much he wanted to do everything he could to make the evening special.

Maggie's reaction to his generous gesture was everything he could have hoped for.

"Why, Mr. Green, I've never tasted wine in my whole life. This is such a—such a—such an exciting day."

For a minute, Jubal was afraid she'd cry, but she didn't, and he breathed a gentle sigh of relief.

"Well, Mrs. Bright, I figured you might enjoy a real night out."

It was a little lame, but he couldn't think of anything better to say. Maggie was neither a stuffy matron nor a brazen light skirt, both types he'd had a good deal of experience with. Instead she was a sweet, pretty lady who'd had a hard life with no frills and had saved his life. That was worth a bottle of wine, at the very least.

"Thank you very much," she said, this time to him.

Jubal felt his insides suddenly go soft again at Maggie's gratitude. Then he caught the warm glow in her eyes, and the unruly male part of him went hard. He hoped he'd be able to get through this evening without doing something rash. He hadn't had a woman for a really long time. For not quite that long a time, he had considered the idea of relieving himself with a prostitute with something close to revulsion. It was becoming almost painfully obvious to Jubal that he wanted Maggie Bright and nobody else.

He studied her face in the light of the candle as it flickered in its little round globe on the table. The red accents in the room created a pink glow that did wonderful things to Maggie's vivid features. Her cheeks weren't as thin as when he'd first met her, Jubal noted, and she didn't have those circles under her eyes. He felt good about that.

"You look really pretty tonight, Mrs. Bright," he said tenderly.

Maggie looked at him quickly. He had already told her that once, up in her room, but the way he said it now was different somehow. The words were gentler, softer. They caressed her and sent a little river of warm feelings flowing through her insides. His eyes looked deep and mysterious to her.

"Thank you," she whispered.

She didn't look down as she usually did when she felt shy around him. Instead, she stared into his beautiful green eyes and, for the first time since Annie's birth, wished her baby elsewhere. Much to her surprise, she wanted to be alone with Jubal Green.

He was nothing like Kenny, she thought. Kenny had been sweet and soft and maybe a little bit dumb. There didn't seem to be a sweet, soft, dumb bone in Jubal's body. He was hard and sharp and strong. And he'd already made her feel things she'd never even imagined she could feel. As she peered into his eyes, she wondered what else he could make her feel, and her cheeks went hot. She knew she was blushing, but she still couldn't look away.

Jubal saw the slow blush creep into Maggie's

cheeks, and his resolve not to do anything rash began to wobble. Oh, Lord, he thought.

The waiter brought the wine and took their orders. Maggie was adorably confused when asked what she wanted to eat. She finally begged Jubal to order for her, so he did. Annie was being a very good girl. She usually was a very good girl, Jubal realized. Maggie was a very good mother.

As the evening advanced, a spell began to weave around Jubal, and he didn't even notice until it was too late. The magic started with his undisciplined sex, which didn't surprise him much. But it grew and spread from there, upward, until it had spun little tendrils that were sneaking into his very soul, and they disturbed him more than he could ever remember being disturbed before.

Maggie forgot to be nervous after a little while, and her candid, unspoiled charm sent those whispery little magic tendrils creeping closer and closer to Jubal's heart until he couldn't have stopped them if he'd tried. Before he even knew what was happening to him, he was caught. He realized that for him to get free again would require more effort than he had in him. Not only that, he didn't even want to. He shook his head in amazement. He'd not only gone soft, he'd gone completely daft. He loved her.

Jubal was never quite certain whether he groaned out loud or not when the truth hit him, because Maggie was paying attention to Annie at that particular moment.

The baby was yawning as their enchanted meal ended. Jubal carried her up the stairs to Maggie's room. Maggie held his arm tightly. She felt secure when she was holding on to him.

"Thank you so much, Mr. Green. That was the nicest evening I've ever had in my life," she said in a whisper-soft voice as she unlocked the door.

"I'm glad."

Maggie turned to take Annie from him, but Jubal walked the now-sleeping baby into the room. There was only the one bed in the room, so he laid her down there.

"I think I'll just take her shoes and dress off. She can sleep in her chemise," Maggie decided as she looked tenderly at her baby.

Jubal watched Maggie with hungry eyes. He kept glancing at the door that separated his room from hers and wished he had a glib tongue and a way with women. He was dying to feel Maggie in his arms, but he wasn't about to grab her and scare her to death. She didn't deserve that. She was as poor as a church mouse and as unsophisticated as her own baby daughter, but she was the greatest lady Jubal had ever met and he wasn't about to ravish her.

She must miss that part of her life, he thought, in spite of his noble resolve. Hell, she's young and healthy.

Still, he held back. After all, Maggie was a marrying kind of woman, and until this second, marriage had never even occurred to him. He was watching very carefully as Maggie finished getting Annie tucked into the big bed. She folded her daughter's little dress up into a tidy square and laid it on top of the shabby carpetbag that held their clothes and the baby's clean diapers. She put Annie's tiny shoes there, too. Jubal noted they were scuffed and old-looking. They looked suspiciously as though maybe Mrs. Phillips had given Maggie a pair of the twins' castoffs. His heart gave a little lurch, and he wished he had thought to pick up some kid's clothes in Garza's today.

When Maggie was through with seeing to her baby, she stood and looked up at Jubal with eyes that nearly glowed with happiness. She held her hands clutched together in front of her and appeared endearingly shy. Jubal knew she was going to thank him again, and he wished she wouldn't.

Hell, he thought, *I* should thank *her.* He couldn't remember an evening ever giving him so much pleasure before.

"Mr. Green, I—"

Jubal interrupted her.

"Don't thank me, Mrs. Bright. I enjoyed it. I'm glad you had a good time."

Maggie's soft smile almost sent Jubal over the edge.

"Oh, I had a wonderful time, Mr. Green."

She reached up, put her hands on Jubal's shoulders, and gave him a very quick, light kiss on the lips. Then she blushed furiously.

It took Jubal all the restraint at his command to say, "Thank you, Mrs. Bright," with barely a tremor in his voice and to turn to the door separating their rooms, unlock it, and walk inside.

As Maggie watched him enter his room and shut the door, she was assailed by a huge throb of regret. She wanted to run after him, to beg him please to stay and to kiss her again the way he had on the banks of Turkey Creek. Maggie had never been kissed like that before. She put her fingers to her mouth and remembered the feel of him, hot and hard and insistent.

She sighed deeply.

"I must really miss Kenny," she mused. Then she

told herself to quit lying. "It's not so much that I miss Kenny. It's that I want Jubal Green."

It surprised her when she finally admitted the truth to herself. She hadn't even enjoyed that part of her marriage very much. Kenny was a sweetheart, and he loved her to distraction, but he had been a rather clumsy lover.

"Lover," Maggie murmured, as she slowly shed her best dress. The word held such mixed connotations to her.

She wondered if she were a wicked, fallen woman to want a man who wasn't her husband. She sighed. "I guess I am," she whispered. "Wicked, fallen, and disloyal. Poor Kenny."

As she brushed out her hair, she wished again that she had a stronger character.

She stripped to her chemise. It was her prettiest one, and she had worn it in honor of the evening. It was made of simple muslin, but she had embroidered the yolk with delicate pink flowers. She smoothed the fabric over her body, closed her eyes, and thought with longing about how Jubal's hands would feel doing that. After she put on her one and only bed wrapper, she stepped hesitantly to the door. She stood there for what seemed like hours, her heart slamming against her ribs.

Maybe he wouldn't mind just talking to me for a little while, she thought.

Maggie could barely hear her own timid tap at his door. As soon as she tapped, she prayed that Jubal wouldn't hear it at all.

Jubal had already shed his shirt and shoes. He still wore his trousers and had been poised on the other side of the door with his hand raised, trying to work

up enough courage to knock. As soon as he heard
Maggie's timid rap, he opened the door. When he saw
her standing there, clutching the neck of her wrapper,
her honey-colored hair tumbling around her shoulders and her big blue eyes looking up at him, frightened
and uncertain, he drew in a huge breath and knew he'd
just been sucker-punched.

"Mr. Green, I—"

Maggie hadn't been sure what she was going to say,
and she didn't get the chance to find out.

Jubal muttered, "Aw, hell, Maggie," pulled her into
his arms, and covered her mouth with his before she
could utter another word.

Maggie only had time to gasp in pleasure before her
arms wrapped around Jubal's shoulders and she
found herself kissing him back.

Kenny hadn't been much of a kisser, Maggie realized, as Jubal taught her things to do with her mouth
and did things with his own that she'd never experienced. As he had done by the creek, he tasted her lips
with his tongue, and this time Maggie didn't even hes-
itate to open her mouth. She wanted to feel what he'd
done before. Jubal obliged her.

He was almost wild. He'd never felt himself to be
so near to losing control. He'd been wanting to do this
for so damned long.

"Oh, God, Maggie, I want you so bad," he said in a
ragged voice.

Maggie couldn't believe it was her own voice that
answered him. "I want you too, Jubal," it said, husky
and strained.

She knew ladies didn't say things like that. She
would have been terribly embarrassed if she had the
time to think about it. But she didn't.

Jubal didn't seem to mind, though. With a low growl, he picked her right up off the floor, laid her down on his bed, and joined her there immediately. Then he took her face in his two hands and kissed her deeply, sweetly, drinking her as he had earlier drunk the restaurant's fine wine. She tasted better.

Gently, gently, he untied the neck of her wrapper and eased it back from her shoulders.

"Lord God, Maggie, I've dreamed of this for months," he whispered.

"Yes, Jubal," she whispered.

He slid the wrapper off her body and threw it toward the foot of the bed. Her skin felt like the finest silk under his calloused palms.

At the first touch of his hands on her bare skin, Maggie got gooseflesh all over. When he cupped her breast and stroked his hard thumb across her nipple, she pressed into his palm with a whimper of desire.

"Oh, God, Maggie," he groaned.

Her breasts weren't big, but they were a perfect handful, and her nipples were hard as ripe cherries. He was sure he was going to die if he couldn't taste them soon.

"Please, Maggie, please let me take this off you." Jubal lifted the hem of her chemise.

Kenny had never asked her to remove everything. Maggie was sure this was improper, but she didn't care about propriety right now. What Jubal was suggesting sounded incredibly good. She had a vision of her tender, sensitive breasts pressed against his broad, hairy chest.

"Oh, yes!" she whispered.

Jubal slid Maggie's chemise up her legs and over her head, using the experience to maximum effect.

His warm hands and lips caressed their way up her
silky thighs and across her smooth abdomen and up
over the twin globes of her breasts, following the fabric they pushed up and loving her every inch of the
way. By the time he pulled the gown over her head,
Maggie was completely at his mercy.

"Oh, Lord." She sighed. "I never felt like this before."

Her words were music to Jubal's ears. He was tired
of hearing her constantly refer to her dead husband.
He wanted her to think only of him right now. He
kissed her again, hard, while he quickly unbuttoned
his trousers and shed them. Then he began to trail
kisses down her slender neck.

When his tongue flicked her rock-hard nipple,
Maggie thought she was going to die. When his hand
slid down to the silky triangle between her thighs, she
wasn't sure what she was supposed to do, because
Kenny had never done that either, but her body
responded for her so it didn't matter. She nearly
screamed with pleasure when Jubal's skillful fingers
slid inside and found the center of her building need.

"Oh, my Lord," she whispered in ecstatic agony.

Jubal needed all his strength to keep from plunging
into Maggie's sweet, ready femininity. But he was
sure he'd explode immediately if he did. He wanted to
know that Maggie's pleasure was complete first. The
best and quickest way to assure that complete pleasure was chancy, because Maggie was a proper lady.
But Jubal was about to bust, so he decided it was
worth the risk.

Whispering sweet endearments the entire time, he
kissed his way from her breasts to her belly to her
thighs, and then to her precious womanhood. Very
carefully, he risked a brief kiss there. When he glanced

up from between her thighs, he saw that Maggie's eyes had opened in astonishment.

"It's all right, Maggie," he whispered, praying she wouldn't rebel.

His gratitude was impossible to measure when she sighed a soft, "Oh, yes!" and closed her eyes, and he felt her hips arch under his lips. He dipped his tongue into her honeyed depths once more, heard her low moan of pleasure, and was momentarily afraid that he would burst even before he was inside her.

Maggie hadn't realized it was possible to feel the sensations that shot through her body as Jubal's lips and tongue pleasured her. Her skin was on fire, and she had never felt so alive. Liquid heat coursed through her body, and the pressure built and built until she thought she was going to shatter into a million pieces.

And then she did. Suddenly, in one gasping, shimmering wave of pleasure, she exploded in a burst of light. She was sure the scattered fragments of herself would never float to earth again.

For some time Maggie had been dimly aware that the tiny gasping, mewing noises she was hearing were coming from her own throat. With the incredible surge of energy that Jubal sent coursing through her body, she nearly screamed. A ragged cry of pleasure tore from her throat and ended in a gasping sob.

She was still feeling the rippling spasms of her orgasm when Jubal lifted his body over hers and thrust inside.

Maggie received him with something close to reverence. She had never experienced such ecstasy in her life, hadn't known it even existed on earth.

"Oh, God, Maggie, you feel so damned good," Jubal groaned in her ear. She was still contracting with residual spasms of fulfillment, and Jubal felt as though his very life's essence was being sucked out of him.

It had been so long, and he was so hot, and Maggie felt so good, that four or five deep, exquisite thrusts sent him hurtling after Maggie into the most amazing bliss he'd ever experienced.

When he eventually came back down to mortal soil, he wasn't sure he'd ever recover. He didn't want to. Maggie's body felt like sleek satin underneath his. His face pressed into the hollow of her throat, and he wanted to drink of her forever. His spasms of pleasure subsided only slowly.

When he became aware of his surroundings, he was surprised to find himself murmuring sweet words into Maggie's ear. "Oh, God, Maggie, I didn't know it could be so good."

Maggie herself was sobbing. Jubal became aware of that fact only gradually, and when he did he was aghast.

He lifted his head and looked at her with terrible concern. "Maggie, are you all right?" He stroked her hair back from her damp face. "Did I hurt you?"

Maggie took a deep breath and sobbed, "Oh, my Lord, Jubal Green, I didn't know anything on earth could feel that good."

She didn't even try to stop crying. Rather, she flung her arms around Jubal's sweat-soaked shoulders and held him to her so hard Jubal feared she'd be crushed.

Still, he was a happy man. He had been afraid his own needs were so overwhelming that he hadn't given Maggie the full measure of pleasure she deserved. Apparently, he needn't have worried.

When Maggie finally stopped sobbing, she rained ecstatic kisses over Jubal's face. She traced his high, chiseled cheekbones and his beautiful, sensual mouth with her fingers.

"My Lord, I know this is a sin, but I don't even care right now. And I know a real lady would never say such a thing, but thank you. I didn't know it could be like that."

"It's not a sin, Maggie. And you *are* a real lady. You're the finest lady I ever met. And I wanted you to feel it. God knows, I wanted you to feel it."

Jubal kissed her again, so hard and so thoroughly that his manhood began to stir once more. He figured he'd better stop that right now, or Maggie would probably get scared. He didn't know very many women who wanted it more than once a month or so, much less twice in one night, though he hoped Maggie would be different in that regard as she was in so many others.

It wasn't only concern for Maggie, however, that stopped him. His healing wounds were beginning to object seriously to this strenuous exercise. His right shoulder in particular was throbbing from holding up his weight, and he rolled off Maggie with a groan of regret.

Maggie sighed when he left her. But then Jubal wrapped his strong arms around her and hugged her close to his body, and she smiled and cuddled up next to him. Jubal decided this was a nice way to end a perfect evening.

He did, however, wake up once during the night. Delighted to find himself entangled with sweet Maggie Bright, and since his muscles no longer throbbed from their earlier exercise, he decided it would be worth experimenting with a few kisses. Maggie responded immediately, and they made slow, sleepy, languorous love together. He took care that his own needs didn't overpower his goal, which was to take Maggie to deeper depths and higher heights of pleasure than he had before.

She cried even harder the second time.

Jubal wasn't sure he'd ever get used to her reaction to the pleasures of his touch, but he planned to try very, very hard and practice as often as he could in the endeavor.

14

Prometheus Mulrooney was livid with rage when he arrived in Santa Fe, only to discover it was no mean trick to get from there to Lincoln County. His heart was set on personally watching Maggie Bright's farm burn down.

"What do you mean there are no rail tracks to Lincoln?" he yelled at Ferrett, who cowered before him, flinching at each word.

"I'm s-sorry, s-sir," Ferrett stuttered. "They haven't laid any tracks yet, sir. In order to get there, you have to take a jerky through Apache territory."

"Apaches?"

"Yes, sir."

"There can't be a place that uncivilized still left in the United States," said Mulrooney, who had lived in New York City all his life.

"Well, sir, technically, New Mexico is a U.S. territory, sir. I—I guess different rules apply."

Mulrooney skewered Ferrett with a scowl and then stood there quivering in impotent fury for a full two minutes. It looked as though he was having a terrible time comprehending the fact that he, Prometheus J. Mulrooney, a man wealthy beyond measure, could actually be thwarted in his schemes by the realities peculiar to New Mexico Territory. By something as trivial as transportation, for heaven's sake! His face turned a deep purple.

"What's a jerky?" he asked at last.

Ferrett, whose eyes had been shut in anticipation of a huge explosion, opened them and peeked uncertainly at his employer.

"It's a mercantile wagon, sir. No springs."

Mulrooney's frown deepened, but his color lightened. "You can't possibly expect me to ride two hundred miles in a mercantile wagon, you imbecile."

"No, sir."

"Well then?" roared Mulrooney, setting Ferrett's knees to trembling furiously.

"Well, sir, Mr. Pelch has looked into the purchase of a wagon for your use, sir. It will be incommodious and uncomfortable, sir, at best, and you'll need many guards to protect you from the wild Indians that roam the territory between here and there, sir, but it will be more to your liking, I'm sure, than the jerky. I—I don't know what you wish to do, sir," he admitted.

Mulrooney pinned poor Ferrett with a glare. "Toad!" he spat. Then he sat down and proceeded to think.

While Mulrooney thought, Ferrett attempted not to squirm. It was an effort destined for failure, since Ferrett had a naturally squirmy disposition, but he tried very hard to confine himself merely to wringing his hands in anguish.

Finally a satanic smile spread itself slowly over Mulrooney's face. Ferrett saw that smile and was not comforted.

"Buy the wagon and hire the guards, Ferrett. I'm going to see that harlot's farm burn, even if it means a delay in getting to El Paso."

"Yes, sir," Ferrett whispered, relieved that this torture would soon be over and he'd be allowed to leave his boss's presence.

"Well?" thundered Mulrooney. "See to it, you blithering fool!"

"Yes, sir."

Ferrett propelled himself out of Mulrooney's railway carriage as though he'd been shot. His retreat from his employer's presence was so hasty that he crashed flat into Pelch, who had been hovering at the door of the next carriage, waiting to comfort poor Ferrett upon his eventual release from Mulrooney's custody.

"What did the devil say, Mr. Ferrett?" Pelch asked breathlessly.

"He said to buy the wagon and hire the army, Mr. Pelch. We're going to Lincoln. He's set his heart on seeing for himself that the poor woman's home is destroyed."

Pelch shook his head in dismay. "He's a devil, Mr. Ferrett," he said glumly. "He doesn't have a heart."

"A scab over his liver is more like."

"Well, I suppose I'd better get on it before he starts to yell again," Pelch said with a deep sigh.

"I suppose," muttered Ferrett.

The two men walked slowly through the carriage that was used by them as an office. They made their way to the front of the train, where they began to debark.

Suddenly Ferrett grabbed at Pelch. His skinny fingers trembled as they gripped his friend's arm.

"Mr. Pelch."

"Yes, Mr. Ferrett?"

"Do you see that little saw?"

Ferrett's gaze was fastened on a metal saw that hung on the wall of the engineer's cabin.

"Yes, Mr. Ferrett, I do."

Ferrett's little eyes sought Pelch's face. "Do you recall that our employer enjoys standing outside his carriage on the observation deck?"

"I do, Mr. Ferrett, yes."

"When the carriage is in motion?"

"I do recall that, Mr. Ferrett."

"Do you recall that he often leans against the wrought-iron railing as he smokes his foul cigars?"

Pelch didn't answer Ferrett's question immediately. His eyes opened wide, and he, too, sought the saw on the wall.

"I recall that as well, Mr. Ferrett," he whispered at last.

"That's the last car on the train, and Mr. Mulrooney is a large man."

"He is indeed, Mr. Ferrett. A very large man."

"That little rail has to support a good deal of weight when he leans against it, Mr. Pelch."

"That's very true, Mr. Ferrett."

The two men stared at each other for several nerve-racking seconds.

Ferrett cleared his throat. "Perhaps it would be best to purchase our own saw, Mr. Pelch."

"I believe that would be a wise precaution, Mr. Ferrett."

The two men bounced against each other in their hurry to get into town to find a hardware store.

*   *   *

When Maggie woke up the next morning, she felt just wonderful. She'd never quite gotten used to sleeping with Kenny, but she fit exactly into the cradle Jubal's body made for her, and her head tucked perfectly beneath his chin.

It wasn't until her eyes fluttered open that she realized she was still in Jubal Green's arms, and in his bed, and she remembered exactly what her wicked, weak character had led her to do the night before. She nearly groaned in dismay.

That was before she realized how very, very good she felt. Then she sighed with a puzzling mixture of contentment and shame and wished she didn't have to get up and face the day and the awful embarrassment it would bring.

I just hope embarrassment is all I have to face, she thought with a sigh. Lord, I am a fool.

She didn't for a second believe that Jubal had anything in mind but a carnal interlude. She couldn't imagine being loved by more than one good man in a lifetime, and she'd already had Kenny.

They had not closed the door that separated Maggie's room from Jubal's, and Maggie knew she'd have to get up and see to Annie soon. Annie wouldn't wait for her foolish, fallen mama's heart to quit soaring and come back down to earth.

With a soul-deep sigh, Maggie eased out of Jubal's arms. She kissed him lightly on his forehead before she reached for her chemise and wrapper.

I love you, Jubal Green, she thought as she gazed down at him. She guessed it was all right to admit it to herself now, after what they'd done the night before, even if the admission did cause her tumbling emotions to jangle even harder.

I loved Kenny, too, I'm sure I did. Her love for sweet Kenny Bright, though, didn't hold a candle to the feelings she had for Jubal Green. All of a sudden she felt disloyal and mean.

The sensation that he'd lost something precious made Jubal wake up a few seconds later with a worried clenching in his chest. As soon as he saw the rumpled place beside him and knew that Maggie wasn't there, he realized what he'd lost. He sat up, his half-awake brain in a panic for fear she'd somehow slipped away from him and wouldn't ever come back. He couldn't let that happen. He needed her.

A hearty sigh of relief escaped him when he noticed her merely tiptoeing to the door of her room.

Maggie heard him and glanced back over her shoulder with an embarrassed smile. "I need to check on the baby," she whispered.

"Bring her in here." Jubal's voice was raspy in the morning and Maggie liked it. Still, she was surprised at his words.

"You really want me to?"

"Sure. Bring her in here." Jubal figured if she did that, he could be with Maggie longer.

Maggie smiled brightly at him. "Thank you, Mr. Green."

"Call me Jubal, Maggie," he commanded gruffly.

Maggie flushed. "Thank you, Jubal," she whispered, and fled into her room.

Annie was just beginning to stir. Maggie picked her up, changed her diaper, and carried her, still sleepy, into Jubal's room. When she laid the baby down beside Jubal, he smiled because he couldn't help it.

Asleep or awake, Annie was a darling little girl.

"Kiss me, Maggie," he demanded of Annie's equally darling mama.

So Maggie did. She felt her face turn a fiery red, but she kissed him.

She had intended it to be a discreet peck on the lips, but Jubal would have none of that. Clamping his hand to the back of her head, he drew her deeper and deeper into the kiss, until Maggie thought for sure she was going to drown.

It was Annie's sleepy question that finally separated them. "Mama? Dat Juba?"

Maggie flushed and pulled away from her lover. Jubal took a deep breath, peered at the baby, and smiled at her.

"It sure is Jubal, Annie honey," he said to the little girl, and added a tickle.

Jubal's tickle induced a spate of giggles in her baby, and Maggie thought this must be the happiest morning of her life so far, even if she was beyond redemption.

Jubal yawned and stretched. Then he sat up and gave Maggie another quick kiss. "Well, I guess we'd better get dressed. We'll get to my spread this afternoon if we start this morning."

"I'll get us ready, then," Maggie told him with a sigh.

She didn't want to leave this hotel now and spoil the perfect communion that seemed to have spread about them like syrup over hotcakes, bathing all three in its healing sweetness. She picked up Annie and headed back to her room.

"I'll come get you for breakfast," said Jubal, watching with regret as Maggie walked farther and farther away. He knew it was silly, but he didn't want her out of his sight. "Will a half hour be enough time?"

When Maggie looked back at him over her shoulder, her face was a picture of delighted surprise.

"Oh, my, what a treat! A half hour will be plenty, thank you." Maggie had never eaten breakfast out. Having breakfast in a restaurant sounded almost more decadently luxurious than eating dinner out did.

At her expression of honest delight, Jubal felt like a love-struck schoolboy. He wanted to do things for her and still wished she wouldn't thank him every time, but he was beginning to understand. Maggie just truly appreciated things that other people took for granted. He hated it when the door closed behind her.

While Maggie got herself and her daughter ready to face their day, both her heart and her head were in a whirl.

"Annie, your mama may have made a real big mistake last night, but I don't think I'll ever regret it, no matter what happens. Jubal Green's a good man. And I swear I won't be a burden to him. I won't cling and whine and make a fuss. After all, I wanted him just as much as he wanted me." Her face got hot all over again when she admitted that out loud.

Then she thought better of confiding these things to her daughter, even a daughter as young as Annie. "What kind of mama am I?" she asked aloud, shaking her head in distress.

Annie was busy with her corncob doll and didn't seem to notice.

Soon they joined Jubal and walked down the street with him. Maggie was holding Annie on her hip, absolutely fascinated by the busy, dirty little border town. She was gazing with interest at the magnificently tooled leather goods in a saddler's shop when Annie startled her with, "Fo' Toes, Mama, Fo' Toes!"

The little girl was leaning out of her mother's arms and reaching for the tall Indian by the time he joined them, with Dan close behind. He grinned broadly at Annie's enthusiastic greeting.

Jubal watched Four Toes and Annie, noticed Maggie's pleasure at their friendship, and felt an irrational surge of jealousy. Damn, I've got it bad, he thought.

The little Mexican place where they all ate breakfast was nothing like the grand hotel restaurant where Jubal had wined and dined Maggie the evening before, but Maggie didn't mind. She was still basking in the rosy glow of freshly discovered love and would have been enraptured with anything. Not only that, but their chubby waitress was delighted with Annie and made a big fuss over her. Anybody who praised her baby was all right in Maggie's book.

The rest of the trip to Jubal's ranch was accomplished with very little talk on either Jubal's or Maggie's part.

It was not merely her determination to keep from burdening Jubal with her love that kept Maggie silent. What had begun as honest puzzlement about his intentions grew as the day progressed until she was certain he must consider her no better than a floozy. She didn't have any idea what she'd do if he ever wanted to bed her again. He'd certainly expect her to capitulate, but she knew she shouldn't, no matter how much she wanted to.

If I were a proper lady, she told herself I never would have done that. Time after time that day, when shivers of remembered ecstasy gave her gooseflesh, Maggie was almost glad she wasn't a proper lady. Then she'd sneak a peek at Jubal and wish he could love her as she loved him, and her heart would squeeze in dismay.

As for Jubal, he'd never been in love before and didn't know what to do about it. He half hoped he'd get over it soon, sort of like a bad cold or a bullet in the arm. He had nothing at all against Maggie. If he had, he wouldn't be in love with her. But he wasn't used to caring so hellishly much about another human being, and he found the sensation unnerving. It played absolute havoc with the settled order of his life.

Still, he wished Maggie would talk to him. She didn't jabber and prattle or sulk and whine like the other women he'd known in his life, and he always found her unstudied, ingenuous observations refreshing. But she didn't seem inclined to want to talk at all today.

He wondered if she were embarrassed about last night. He got hard immediately and decided he'd better not think about last night at all. Anyway, even if she didn't talk to him, he enjoyed listening to her dealing with Annie.

The weather was hot, although it was nowhere near as hot as it had been when they'd been forced to travel at night. Still, the sun was strong, and Maggie found it difficult to keep Annie occupied and cool. Her own face was soon flushed and dripping with the heat.

She wished Jubal would say something, but he didn't seem to want to talk. Her heart clutched in pain, but she sternly told herself not to fuss. The man had a job to do. And he was actually helping her keep her resolve by remaining aloof. Her heart didn't quite listen to her mind's reasoning, though. It ached for his attention.

Maybe he wants me for his mistress! That sudden, awful thought nearly brought tears to her eyes until she realized, with a dismal frown, that it's just what a woman in her situation should anticipate.

What did you expect? she asked herself bitterly, already having condemned Jubal for her own base supposition.

By the time they stopped for a rest and lunch in the early afternoon, Maggie was resigned to her fate. She would refuse Jubal's further advances, if he made any, and try her best to repair her fallen dignity.

When Four Toes lifted little Annie out of the wagon, Maggie was feeling stronger and was able to smile at him with real gratitude. They had found a small stream that hadn't yet dried up, surrounded by a stand of stunted trees that offered a little bit of shade.

"Thank you, Mr. Smith," Maggie said, glad for the respite some time out of the wagon would afford them.

"Sure thing, Mrs. Bright. I got Annie something in town while we were there. I thought it might be a good idea to save it for this afternoon, since it's a long trip and everybody's itchy to get home."

Maggie beamed at him, completely forgetting her status as wicked woman, when he held up a little gourd doll. It was pear-shaped and brown and was clothed in calico. Its face was painted comically, and yarn hair adorned its head. But the most exciting thing was that when you shook the doll it rattled. Annie was enchanted.

"Mr. Smith, you're a pure wonder! You should have children of your own."

Four Toes looked at Maggie with a rueful smile. "I'd love to, Mrs. Bright, if they could grow up free like Annie, here."

Maggie wished she hadn't said anything. Her heart ached when she considered the tall Indian's plight.

"He adopts every kid he sees, Mrs. Bright. He's got kids all over the territory," Dan told her with a laugh.

As he took care of the two mules, Jubal watched and listened. He fed each animal a handful of meal, gave them some water in a bucket, and frowned the whole time. He'd never considered this particular aspect of his friend's life before.

"Hell, Four Toes," he said at last, "why don't you just move in with Danny and me? My spread's big enough for three families easy."

Maggie smiled at him with such tenderness that Jubal was astonished.

Dan quirked a brow. "Three families, Jubal?"

Jubal scowled. "Why not?" He sounded kind of grumpy. "It's big enough, isn't it?"

Dan smiled and hauled down another sack of meal from the wagon. "Just wondering where all these families are going to come from is all," he said innocently.

Jubal gave him a hard frown and didn't answer. Nor did he look at Maggie. Jubal Green might have grudgingly admitted to himself that he loved Maggie Bright, but he was nowhere near ready to admit it to anybody else. Dan laughed when Jubal stomped away without a word.

They ate lunch quickly and continued their journey without resting long. Luckily, Annie settled down with her new toy and was content to rattle it, play Mama, and laugh until she finally wore herself out. She'd been sleeping for an hour or more, and Maggie figured it must be getting on toward four in the afternoon, when she decided she'd risk asking Jubal a question.

She'd had a long time to consider the way the two of them had spent the night. Ever a realist, Maggie didn't suppose brooding would pay any dividends. So she determined that the best course for her to follow would be to act as though nothing at all had changed, even if her world was now teetering perilously. No matter what, she didn't want to be a burden.

"Mr. Green?"

His head whipped around and he glared at her. "I told you to call me Jubal," he said harshly. It really annoyed him that she was back to calling him "Mr. Green." Hell, hadn't last night meant anything at all to her?

Maggie was dismayed. She hadn't meant to irritate him. "I'm sorry, Jubal," she began, and was even more dismayed when he became instantly exasperated with her.

"Will you quit apologizing?"

Maggie's mouth dropped open and she nearly apologized for annoying him by apologizing before she thought better of it. She took a deep breath and tried again. Her aunt's constant admonition about not making people angry sang off-key in her mind, and she phrased her words carefully.

"Um, well, I just wondered when we'd be getting close to your land, Jubal." Recalling her resolve not to cling and her worry about his intentions, Maggie tried to phrase the question so it wouldn't smack of impatience. Lord, it was tricky business, trying to stay off this prickly man's toes.

But Jubal wasn't angry. He was surprised. "Hell, Maggie, we've been on my land for three hours now."

Maggie was astounded. Her mouth gaped open and she looked at the landscape surrounding them as though she expected to see some sign.

"Oh. Well . . ." She finally gave up trying to express herself and laughed.

Maggie's laugh was so enchanting it made Jubal's insides ache with hunger for her. He watched in appreciation as her eyebrows lifted into two incredulous arches above her pretty blue eyes. His uncivilized masculinity reacted by instantly thickening up.

"I thought you knew," he said.

Maggie was still laughing. "How on earth could I know that Mr.—Jubal? I've never been here before."

"I guess not." Jubal wasn't sure why she thought this was so funny.

"I didn't know anyone could own so much land," Maggie admitted with an awed shake of her head. "I guess I'm kind of naive, Jubal, but three hours' worth of Texas is a whole lot of property to belong to one person."

That innocent, wondering comment finally made Jubal's unsettled mood smooth over. "I guess it is," he said with a grin. "But if you ride in the other direction, you can go for days and still be on Green land."

"Oh, my." That was impressive indeed.

At the moment, Jubal was driving the wagon along the base of some stony foothills that angled out from Mount Franklin, which had spawned El Paso in one of its low passes. He pointed to the top of a rise.

Maggie's gaze followed the line indicated by his finger, but she couldn't really see much except the brown hills, even when she squinted hard.

"I don't know if you can make him out, but one of my men is posted at the top of that hill over there."

He waved, and Maggie could just make out a glint of light as the late-afternoon sun struck the guard's rifle barrel when he waved back.

"Oh, I see something now."

Jubal was still squinting at the top of the hill. "I think that's Ramón. I have men posted everywhere. Mulrooney's people can't get at us here, Maggie. See him up there?"

Now Maggie was *really* impressed. He even had guards on his land. "No, I can't see him," she admitted. Then, with a thrill in her voice, she added, "But as soon as my eyeglasses are ready, I'll be able to see him and everything else too."

She actually gave herself a little hug of pleasure. Jubal wanted to hug her too, but he had to drive the wagon. His grin got bigger, though.

"That's right. You'll be able to see everything. I just hope you like what you see."

A sudden unpleasant thought struck Maggie like a blow, and she eyed Jubal uneasily. She swallowed hard. "It'll be real nice to be able to see clearly," she said. "But—um, I don't believe I've seen too many ladies wearing spectacles."

Jubal had never particularly thought about it before. "I don't guess I have either," he said. He appreciated observant people and chalked up one more point for Maggie Bright.

"I—I don't guess spectacles will improve my looks any."

Maggie ventured that observation with a tiny little laugh that trickled out uneasily. She was still watching Jubal out of the corner of her eye, keenly studying his face for any sign that might ease her worry or confirm it.

Jubal turned his head to look at her. "Do you worry much about your looks, Maggie?"

Now she felt embarrassed and wished she hadn't

gone on this stupid fishing expedition. You are what you are, Maggie Bright, she told herself firmly. You can't help it that you need spectacles—and you can't help it that you want to look pretty for Jubal Green either.

She had to clear her throat before she answered him. "I—I don't guess I worry, exactly. But—well, I want to look nice, yes," she said shyly. She couldn't look at him now. She knew she was blushing.

"I think you're pretty, Maggie," said Jubal. "I think you'll be pretty with eyeglasses too."

He looped the reins in one hand and reached out the other to nudge her under the chin so she'd look at him. He was surprised to see tears glittering in her eyes when she turned her face toward his.

"I think you're about the prettiest lady I've ever met, Maggie." He didn't know if it was the truth or not, but he did know she was the only one he'd ever loved.

"Oh, I'm not," she whispered, stunned. Nobody but Kenny had ever said such sweet words to her, and she hadn't believed them then. She didn't believe them now either, but suddenly she really, really wanted to.

"Don't argue with me, Maggie Bright." He squeezed her chin. Then he leaned over and kissed her on the lips.

"Thank you," she murmured.

She couldn't look at him any longer, because his eyes were making her melt all over, the way she had the night before. Instead, she stared into her lap and blushed furiously.

Jubal was rather pleased at her reaction to his words and touch. Maybe he could get used to this love stuff. He clicked gently to the mules and turned his attention back to his driving.

They arrived within sight of his ranch house a half hour or so later. His father had built the place near a branch of the Rio Grande that ran beside a little nest of hills. It was, therefore, much greener in Green's Valley than in most of the surrounding desert lands.

Jubal pointed the ranch out to Maggie long before she could see it. He could tell they were almost there because his own eagle eyes had picked out the spreading sward of green and the dark pinpoints that indicated treetops. Cottonwoods and willows lined the stream, and it wasn't long before Jubal began to see the distinctive white gleam of the roofs of the outbuildings and the ranch house itself.

He discovered to his surprise that he was getting nervous. Until this moment, he hadn't realized how much he wanted Maggie to like it here. He didn't want her to pine for that stupid, dumpy farm of hers; he wanted her to think of her home as where he was.

Maggie was straining to see Jubal's place in the distance. When she thought she could finally discern a darker patch against the vast sandy brownness that lay in front of them, she nearly jumped off the wagon seat.

"Oh, Jubal, I think I see it." Her whisper was a burst of happy excitement.

He smiled at her, glad for her enthusiasm. "I hope you like it, Maggie."

"Oh, I'm sure we will."

Jubal didn't miss that "we."

"When we get close, I want Annie to see it too," she added.

"Well, let her sleep for now. Distances are deceptive out here. It will be an hour or so before we're there."

"A whole hour?"

"Afraid so."

She sighed heavily. Her disappointment was relieved somewhat when Dan and Four Toes rode up to the wagon.

"Gettin' close Jubal," Dan called.

Jubal waved at him.

"Want us to ride on ahead to warn Codfish and have Beula get a room set up for Mrs. Bright?"

Jubal didn't answer right away. He hadn't actually considered sleeping arrangements yet. All sorts of scenarios, some of them quite appealing, flitted through his nimble brain before he finally said, "Okay. That's probably a good idea."

Jubal had never been hasty in his life. And while he admitted he loved Maggie Bright, sort of the way he'd admit to having a bum knee or a broken arm, his instinct was to go slow. If luck was on his side, he'd get over it before it settled in and became a permanent condition.

The two Indians rode off in twin puffs of dust, and Maggie watched them with interest.

"Who are Codfish and Beula?"

"Codfish is my foreman, and Beula is his wife. She sort of keeps house for me."

"Is his name really Codfish?"

Jubal chuckled. "Nah. It's Henry. He's from Maine. Some of the hands began calling him Codfish decades ago, and it just stuck. He still talks funny, like an Easterner. Calls himself a Mainiac."

Maggie giggled. She wasn't too sure of her ground here, but she did know that she wanted to be as useful as possible while she and Annie were living at Jubal's. She also much preferred to offer her own suggestion as to how she could earn her keep rather than wait for any unsavory propositions Jubal might make. In fact, she was pretty sure any such proposition would go far toward breaking her heart. In a tentative voice, she said, "I'd be happy to help keep house, Mr. Green—I mean, Jubal."

She peered at him nervously. She never quite knew how he was going to take things. Sure enough, his forehead began to wrinkle up and his eyebrows knit together in a frown.

"I don't want you working hard here, Maggie," Jubal told her tersely. "You've worked hard all your life." He shot her a brief scowl before he returned his attention to the desert in front of him.

"Oh." Maggie didn't know what to say. She opted for "Thank you" and hoped he wouldn't get fussy at her for that. Then she contemplated her folded hands and hoped against hope he wouldn't suggest that she become his mistress. The possibility made her want to cry, but she braced herself.

He didn't. Instead, he just growled, "You're welcome," and flicked the reins.

It was another forty-five minutes before either of them spoke again. Then Jubal told her, "I think it's time to wake Annie up."

Maggie had been nodding on the hard wooden seat with her eyes closed. The sun was barely visible above the hills now, the worst of the heat had burned itself out, and she was feeling sleepy and oddly happy. Jubal's words snapped her awake, and she was amazed to see that they had driven through a steep-sided rocky gorge and out into a lovely green valley.

Her gasp of pleased surprise was music to Jubal's

ears. He grinned and peered at her out of the corner of his eye.

"I had no idea, Jubal! This is wonderful. I expected it to be all brown and dry like the rest of the land around here."

"I know," he said. "My pa always used to say that the first time he saw this stretch of land, he knew this was where he was going to make his heaven on earth."

"What a pretty thing to say," said Maggie, impressed by the poetic nature Jubal's father apparently hadn't handed down to his son.

Jubal snorted. "Sure. Well, his intentions were good, but it didn't exactly work out that way, thanks to Mulrooney and my mother."

Maggie glanced at him and saw that his face had gone hard. "I'm sorry," she said softly.

She turned to lean over the back of the wagon seat to wake her daughter.

"Annie, we're here. Wake up, sweetheart, we're at Jubal's ranch. You can meet his dog Rover. And there's a man named Codfish, and a lady named Beula. It's pretty here, honey. There's a river and trees and—" Maggie glanced up. They were in view of the ranch house itself now. It was so big and pretty, Maggie gaped in astonishment. "Oh, Annie, the house is beautiful!"

Jubal heard the awe in her voice and his grin broadened. He was very proud of himself all of a sudden.

Annie had been sleeping soundly and obviously wasn't convinced that waking up was a good idea. She grumbled and whimpered and ground one little fist against her sleepy eyes. Her face puckered up, and it looked like she might be winding up for a good wail when Maggie remembered her new dolly. She leaned over to pick it up and rattled it in front of Annie's unhappy face.

"Look, Annie, your dolly likes it here. This will be her new home too, for a while."

"Mine," Annie announced. She snatched the doll out of her mother's hand and hugged it hard to her little chest. Then she glared at her mother. Maggie sighed.

"Oh, my. I wish there were some children around for you to play with, baby girl. You need to learn to share."

"She just doesn't want to wake up," Jubal said with a grin. "I get like that too, sometimes."

Maggie considered telling him she'd be sure to keep that in mind, but decided she'd better not. Instead, she said, "Well, it sure would be good for her to have kids to play with. Sadie and I used to get her together with the twins as often as we could, but I didn't have much time."

Jubal wondered how Maggie would take to the idea of having one or two children with him, but it was definitely too soon to be asking her that. Instead, he said thoughtfully, "Codfish and Beula have a couple of kids. I think they're about four and seven."

"Really? Oh, how wonderful," Maggie said. "Did you hear that, Annie? You'll have playmates here."

She hugged her sleepy baby tightly to her breast while the wagon rumbled nearer and nearer to their goal. As they approached, things began to take on definition for Maggie. She saw the stream and the lacy willows weeping on the bank. The cottonwoods had leafed out after their winter rest and dappled the fresh spring grass with early evening shade.

The ranch house was a sprawling one-story affair, built on square Spanish lines with a patio in the middle. A smaller house, fashioned of the same whitewashed adobe, squatted to the west of the main house with a tidy picket fence around it. Flowers bloomed in a little bed, and Maggie figured that house for the home of Codfish and Beula.

"Flowers," she breathed. "Oh, look, Annie, flowers!"

She pointed the flowers out to her daughter and then offered Jubal a perfectly heavenly smile. His heart quit beating for a second. The first thing he was going to do, he told himself, was dig this woman a flower bed. If she got that dewy-eyed over a couple of black-eyed Susans, he couldn't wait to see her reaction to a bed full of those tall pink things Four Toes called dahlias.

"I don't know how you can stand to be away from here for so long at a time, Jubal," Maggie said as she gazed around her. It was the loveliest place she had ever seen.

"Well," he said with a chuckle, "I hadn't planned on being away for quite this long."

Maggie looked over at him with chagrin. "Of course not," she said. "I don't know how I could have forgotten."

Jubal laughed out loud at that. "Hell, I don't know either, Maggie. I turned your life upside down and inside out."

Maggie gave him a soft smile that ate up the rest of his heart. "I guess you did at that."

He cleared his throat. "Well, anyway, I've got a good crew. And Codfish is a mean son of a buck. He makes sure everybody does his job, believe me. Nobody shirks work around Codfish. Not even me."

Jubal drove the wagon past what seemed like miles of fences. Maggie guessed they were corrals. It looked to her as though a whole herd of horses was residing in one green fenced pasture. She pointed them out to Annie with a thrill of excitement. Beyond, Maggie noticed a huge meadow that seemed to have only one big, surly-looking, long-horned beast lodged within its fenced confines.

"Why is there only one cow in that pasture, Jubal?"

"That's not a cow, Maggie," Jubal told her with a laugh. "That's Cannibal. He's my stud bull."

"Oh!" Maggie blushed.

Jubal grinned, amused by her reaction. "He likes his job."

Maggie shot him a quick look and then she grinned too. "I just bet he does. Why do you call him Cannibal?"

"He's mean as hell. Don't ever let Annie get near that fence. Any bull is unpredictable, and that particular Texas longhorn is about the sorriest-disposed bastard I've ever seen."

Maggie immediately imparted that important piece of information to her daughter. "Did you hear that, Annie? You see the bull in that field? Don't ever go in that field, Annie. That bull is mean and will stick you with his horns."

Annie looked curiously at where her mother pointed. "Boo stick Annie," she said. She glowered at the bull as if daring him to try it.

Jubal laughed again and continued. "The bunkhouse is over there by the stable. There's a hog wallow and chickens out back behind the barn where the smell can't get to the house. I think you'll like Beula. She likes to grow things too."

A friend. Maggie would have a friend. Except for Sadie, who wasn't entirely satisfactory because her flair for the dramatic sometimes interfered with her honesty, Maggie had never had a friend. She had not been allowed friendships when she was growing up, and Bright's Farm was too far away from anybody but the Phillipses to make the luxury possible once she was married.

Jubal was appalled to see a tear slide down Maggie's cheek when he turned to see why she'd gone so quiet all of a sudden.

"Are you all right?" he asked in alarm.

Maggie turned such a glowing gaze upon him that he would have stopped the wagon and scooped her into his arms, except that the welcoming committee had already formed and such a display of emotion would be embarrassing.

"Oh, I'm just fine. I'm just fine, thank you," she whispered.

15

The first two people Maggie spotted in the small crowd that surged toward them from the ranch house were Dan and Four Toes. They were both waving and grinning as Jubal drove the two tired mules to a plodding stop in front of the white fence.

Jubal decided to show his eager ranch family that he was fully recovered from his injuries by bracing his right arm on the wagon and bounding out of his seat. He immediately realized that this decision was foolish. His right shoulder felt like fire, and the jolt to his left thigh when his feet hit the ground nearly made him holler. He gritted his teeth and managed to keep from making a total fool of himself only with great effort.

He almost got mad when Maggie, horrified at his move, leaned over the driver's side of the wagon and said, "Oh, my land, Mr. Green, you shouldn't have done that! Are you all right?"

But she looked so sweet and concerned that he didn't get mad. Instead he grinned up at her and said, "I'm just fine, Maggie," and, in spite of his throbbing shoulder he reached up to take Annie out of her arms.

Maggie let him have the baby and then Four Toes helped her down. Suddenly she was standing in the middle of a welter of strange people, wondering what to do.

An ecstatic spaniel was leaping on Jubal and barking energetically, and Jubal was smiling at Annie and pointing at the dog. Maggie assumed the beast was Rover and hoped it wouldn't frighten the baby.

She didn't have time to worry for long, though, because she suddenly found herself crushed into the largest, softest bosom she'd ever encountered.

"You must be Miss Maggie!" cried the owner of that bosom. "You saved our Jubal's life. Dan and Four Toes told us. You're so brave!"

Maggie feared she was going to be smothered and wondered if it would be rude to struggle. Fortunately, the hugging stopped before it became imperative to make the decision. She staggered back to behold a large woman with flaming red hair knotted on the top of her head and freckles everywhere. Freckles danced across her nose and over her cheeks and down her arms and, Maggie was sure, covered the rest of her body as well. Right now, her friendly, freckled face was shiny with tears, which she brushed away impatiently with the back of her hand.

"I'm Beula Todd, Mrs. Bright. I'm so glad to meet you." She stuck out her hand and Maggie shook it.

Maggie smiled. "It's nice to meet you."

Beula beamed at her. "Now you have to meet my husband, Henry."

She tugged Maggie over to a person who looked, if she had seen him on a street in El Paso, to have blown in by accident on the end of a hard gale. Codfish Todd was exactly like Maggie's idea of Captain Ahab. He was tall, sunburned, wrinkled, and old, and had thick stark-white hair and a white beard. A tattered sailor's cap perched on his white head, and a black pipe was stuck in his mouth. The pipe, at this moment, was wreathing his head with a halo of fragrant smoke. All he needed was a sou'wester and a harpoon. Maggie figured him for at least fifty-five, though Beula didn't look much more than thirty.

"It's nice to meet you," she said meekly, and held out her hand for him to shake.

Codfish paused for a moment to remove the pipe from his mouth before he very slowly shook Maggie's proffered hand. Then he grinned and said, "Ayup."

Maggie didn't have time to ponder this oddly matched pair because Dan caught her by the arm and swung her around to meet the rest of the household crew. He introduced her to Julio Mendez, a tall Mexican wrangler who seemed quite shy; Jesus Chavez, another Mexican man with a wrinkled face, yellow teeth, and a kind smile, who did carpentry work around the place; and Sammy. Sammy Napolitano was a young Sicilian who had washed up on the shores of the United States and found himself a job with the army, fighting Indians in Texas. Sammy was out of the army now and in charge of Jubal's security forces.

Maggie was sure she'd forget everybody's name. She hadn't met so many people in one place since she'd come with Kenny to live in New Mexico Territory, and she felt almost dizzy with the introductions.

Then Beula said, "And here are my children."

Maggie snapped back to attention to discover she had been clinging like a vine to Jubal's arm. She glanced up at him nervously, worried that he'd be angry, but he was looking down at her with a tender, almost possessive expression on his face. She smiled a brief, flickering, nervous smile at him and turned to meet Beula's children.

She nearly laughed to behold a miniature Beula standing before her. A little butterball of a girl, seven years old, with red hair and freckles and a chubby little body that foretold a buxom future, held out her hand and introduced herself as Connie.

Henry, Jr., was four years old. He was lean and small, and he too had red hair and freckles. They were really rather handsome children, if one overlooked the freckles. Maggie herself had never found freckles unattractive, although she knew a proper lady would probably be aghast and advise Beula to rub their skin with coconut milk or witch hazel or something.

"How do you do?" She smiled at the children and shook their hands. Connie curtsied, and Maggie thought that was about the sweetest thing she'd ever seen.

She took Annie out of Jubal's arms and introduced her to Connie and Henry. Annie looked uncertainly at the little boy and girl from the safety of her mother's arms. Then she stuffed one fist securely into her mouth and gripped her new dolly tightly with the other hand. She studied the two children with solemn brown eyes for a long time before she pulled her fist out of her mouth with a moist pop, held out her gourd dolly, and said, "Mine."

Maggie sighed and looked at Beula, who smiled at her and winked. Maggie appreciated that wink. She decided she liked Beula Todd.

"Well, I guess you'd both better meet Rover before he busts a gut," said Jubal with a chuckle.

He took Annie back from Maggie and knelt down. Annie seemed a bit uncertain about the rambunctious spaniel. When Rover gave her a huge, slurping lick on the cheek, she tucked her little head into Jubal's shoulder and flung her arms around his neck, and Jubal suddenly felt like a father.

At least he thought that was what he felt like. But it was sort of like being in love. He'd never felt that way before and didn't quite know what to do about it. It was bewildering, all these new emotions. He peered up at Maggie and discovered that every single employee on his spread seemed to be watching him with huge, eager eyes. He stood up in a rush and thrust the baby into her mother's arms.

"Let's get inside," he said gruffly.

Then he turned quickly to see who it was that had snickered. He pinned Dan Blue Gully with a piercing glare, but Dan just grinned back at him and snickered again.

Ferrett and Pelch stood in the flickering shadows, huddled together for solace. They watched as the soaring flames splayed unsteady light across the florid, fat, unpleasant features of their employer.

Prometheus Mulrooney was beside himself with glee as greedy tendrils of fire gobbled up Maggie Bright's farmhouse.

The ride down to Lincoln from Santa Fe had been one of unrelieved agony for Mulrooney's underlings, and he himself had been petulant and uncomfortable during the entire two-hundred-mile trek. There was simply no easy way to get here, a fact Mulrooney took as a personal affront. Even after special alterations, he found the wagon in which he rode hellishly uncomfortable.

The weather was miserable too. During the day, the sun scalded Mulrooney's pink face underneath his sparse yellow hair until he looked like a tomato, even when he wore his big wide-brimmed sombrero. Rivers of perspiration soaked his clothing and then dried so that when his fat thighs rubbed against each other, they chafed. Ferrett had not thought to purchase talcum, so he was on Mulrooney's blacklist, a circumstance that made poor Ferrett's life even more terrible than usual.

What with the heat and the sweat, everybody riding with Mulrooney smelled bad too, and there was no way to bathe. He hadn't realized life could be so damnably awful.

"Serves that bastard Green right," he muttered to himself as he dabbed a scented hankie to his heated brow. "He deserves this hellish place."

Then, at night, Mulrooney nearly froze to death. He confiscated everybody's blankets to keep himself warm.

"What do you mean, you can't build a fire?" he had roared to the buckskin-clad man Pelch had hired to guide them through Apache territory.

"Indians," the laconic guide had replied, as if Mulrooney should have known that.

Mulrooney started to berate the guide, but the man, who didn't care who Prometheus Mulrooney was, just rode away, leaving him to splutter and flap at the cold night air. Mulrooney took his unrelieved fury out on Pelch.

"What do you suppose he expected, Mr. Ferrett?"

poor Pelch asked his friend as the two of them shivered on the cold ground, trying to get through the miserable night without freezing into solid lumps. They had thrown woolen serapes over their shoulders and sat on saddle blankets, but their efforts were not paying particularly warm dividends.

Ferrett shook his head. "I don't know, Mr. Pelch."

Even though they were practically touching, neither man could see the other. The night was black as a raven's wing.

Pelch peered up into the inky heavens. They didn't look like any heavens he'd ever seen before. His heavens had always been pocked by the friendly glimmer of gas streetlamps and the warm yellow glow of light streaming from hundreds of cozy windows. These territorial heavens were alien, black, and very cold. And they hid mysterious, frightening things that made strange, terrifying noises.

A coyote yipped and then gave a piercing, high-pitched howl in the distance, and Ferrett clutched at Pelch's arm.

"Oh, my word, Mr. Pelch," he whispered unsteadily.

Pelch sucked in a shaky breath. "Aren't there supposed to be stars in the sky, Mr. Ferrett?" he asked uneasily. "Even in New Mexico Territory?"

"I believe so, Mr. Pelch," Ferrett responded in a frightened whisper.

Both men nearly had heart failure when a chuckle came to them out of the blackness.

"You fellers will see stars pretty soon," a voice said, following closely on the tail of that chuckle. "It's just gone on to dark. Pretty soon there will be stars enough."

The voice proved to be telling the truth. As Ferrett and Pelch sat in silence, both cowed at the thought that unknown persons could hear them speak, the stars began to twinkle in the sky. It wasn't very long before a sparkling blanket of splendor grew overhead until it seemed to reach into infinity.

Ferrett gaped in wonder at the amazing display above his head.

"My goodness, Mr. Pelch, will you just look at that," he whispered solemnly.

"I'm looking, Mr. Ferrett, I'm looking," Pelch said in awe.

Their unseen friend chuckled again. "Told you so," he said. Then he tossed a thick wool blanket over to the two men. "Here. You two city fellers probably need this."

"Th-thank you," murmured Ferrett. He was so unused to such kindness that he almost cried.

"Sure thing," said the voice.

All that could be discerned then was the sound of shuffling feet and the slither of blanketed bottoms as Ferrett and Pelch rearranged themselves underneath their benefactor's largesse.

"Thank you very much, sir," Pelch said after they had settled down.

"Yes, this is much warmer," added Ferrett with gratitude.

"No problem, gents," said the voice.

Silence reigned for a few minutes as Ferrett and Pelch occupied themselves with staring up at that incredible sky. They were both startled when their friend's voice broke into the blackness once again.

"Purely don't know how you two fellers tolerate that man you work for."

Ferrett and Pelch looked at each other. They could just see under the canopy of stars.

Ferrett sighed morosely.

"He's a devil," Pelch whispered.

"Agreed," said the voice. "Don't you fellers get sick of his bellyachin' and hollerin'?"

"Oh, my, yes," Ferrett mumbled.

"Indeed," agreed Pelch.

"Why don't you just up and quit?"

Neither man spoke. How did you say that one did not resign from service with Prometheus J. Mulrooney and expect to live past the front door on the way out?

Finally Pelch cleared his throat and said, "It is not considered—uh—healthy to quit."

That news was greeted by silence.

Then the voice muttered, "Well, maybe an Apache will stick an arrow in him for you." The voice did not speak again during the night.

Those cheery words buoyed Ferrett and Pelch's spirits briefly, even into the following day. Eventually, however, they understood that Mulrooney's hired guards were much too alert to allow such a quick and pleasant end to their troubles.

It was now evening of the day after their adventure under the stars. As they watched cinders from Bright's Farm fly up into the night sky, illuminating the diabolical face of their employer, both men were very depressed.

"It was such a homey little place, Mr. Pelch," mourned Ferrett.

"We're responsible for this too, Mr. Ferrett," said Pelch in an undertone. "If only we were bolder."

Ferrett nodded.

"That poor woman," Pelch muttered. "All she did was help a fellow human being in distress."

Ferrett only stared straight ahead into the inferno that had been Maggie Bright's home.

Finally he said, not even trying to sound hopeful, "Well, there is still the saw, Mr. Pelch."

Pelch nodded unhappily. "Yes," he said. "There is still the saw."

Beula had prepared a special dinner in honor of Jubal's return home with the woman who had saved his life, and Maggie was not allowed to help cook it, serve it, or clean up after it.

"I feel useless," she announced, and Jubal got the distinct impression that she didn't like the feeling one bit.

He asked her to take a little walk with him after dinner. She agreed somewhat reluctantly, hoping he wouldn't suggest any kind of unsavory alliance. Somehow, he didn't seem the kind of man who would keep a mistress, but since Maggie didn't really know what the keeper of a mistress was like, she didn't know how she'd come to that conclusion.

"I want to show you around the place, since it's going to be your home now—for a while." He added that last part because he didn't know what the future held. It had become very difficult for him to imagine life without Maggie Bright, but he wasn't ready to admit that yet, even to himself.

His words sounded innocuous enough to her, not at all like the preamble to an illicit offer. "Wait until I get Annie settled, please; then I'll be happy to walk with you."

"All right."

Then he decided to go with her and help. Actually,

he didn't know how to tuck a child in bed, but he had a sudden interest in learning. It occurred to him that this new fatherly urge might be getting out of control, but he didn't care.

Beula had fixed a room up with a bed for Maggie and the Todd babies' old crib for Annie. Jubal wondered briefly why Beula had chosen the only other bedroom in the wing where he slept, but Dan had probably told her which room to use. Good old Dan, maybe he did always know best. At any rate, Jubal could hardly stand the wait until he could have Maggie to himself again.

Annie settled down slowly. The last few days had been full of unaccustomed activity for the little girl, and she was reacting by being uncharacteristically cranky. Maggie hoped she'd calm down and be her usual pleasant self after a couple of days spent in one place. In the meantime, she made sure Annie's gourd dolly went to bed with her. Then she sang her a couple of lullabies.

Jubal listened to Maggie's gentle dealings with her baby, and his heart began to feel a longing so acute that it ached. He didn't remember his mother ever being sweet and gentle with him. He didn't remember ever hearing a lullaby in his life until he'd ended up in Maggie's bed, shot blame near to death. He'd always wondered why people spoke so respectfully of their mothers. As far as Jubal was concerned, his own mother hadn't been worth a plug nickel. But Maggie! . . .

He stood in a corner and shook his head with wonder while he watched her and listened to her. Lord above, he could get used to this.

When Maggie thought Annie was sleepy enough

not to fuss, she tiptoed over to Jubal. He was almost disappointed when they quietly left the room.

"You're a real good mother, Maggie," he told her in a husky voice as he guided her outside onto the patio.

Those words came as a complete surprise to Maggie, who wasn't used to thinking of herself as much good at anything. She looked up at him with a quick, amazed smile and a little blush.

"Do you really think so?"

It was Jubal's turn to be surprised now. "Of course, I do. Why on earth do you think I'd lie about that?"

Maggie blinked. This man could be so touchy. "Oh, dear." She sighed. "I didn't mean to say I thought you'd lied to me, Jubal. It's just that it's—it's been so hard, raising Annie alone. There was always so much work to do that I didn't have as much time with her as I would have liked to have had. That's all."

Jubal took her arm and put it through the crook of his elbow. "Well, you won't have to do that much work here," he told her firmly.

Maggie looked up at him again. "No, I guess I won't have to work that hard until I go home again." Then she looked away quickly, not certain she wanted to see his reaction to those words.

The truth was, Maggie didn't know her own mind, any more than she knew Jubal's. Her heart knew she loved him, but she didn't know what he felt about her, and she sure didn't want to give up Kenny's farm. It had been his dream and had become hers, and she aimed to keep it alive. She didn't think she even had words enough to explain all that to Jubal.

It was probably just as well she wasn't looking at him, because Jubal's scowl had become positively ferocious.

There she goes, talking about her goddamned home again, he thought. Pretty soon she'll be running on about that damned dead husband of hers. Jubal didn't know whether he was more angry or hurt.

"Yes, well, you can think about that later, after we've taken care of Mulrooney," he finally said, almost in a growl.

That was fine with Maggie. She was too busy looking at the patio to think about anything else at the moment. Two torches lit the big square, casting shadows over a scruffy, dirty, tiled walkway and a bare dirt middle. Work on a stone fountain had been begun and abandoned in the center of that dirt patch a long time ago. The patio had the makings of a perfectly idyllic place.

"Oh, Jubal, this is lovely."

Jubal looked around and wondered what Maggie could see here that he couldn't. "Looks mighty bleak to me," he said at last.

"Oh, but just imagine what it *could* look like," Maggie whispered. Her voice was hushed with the visions her imagination had already begun to spin for the place.

Jubal grunted. "I guess. My father had plans for it. But Mulrooney and my mother killed them and him before he could do much."

"Mulrooney and your mother?" Maggie's voice was shocked.

Jubal led her over to a carved stone bench, one of the few amenities his father had been able to provide before the worries of his life took over and prevented his plans for the patio from reaching completion.

"Sit down, Maggie. As long as you're involved in all this, you might as well hear the story." Jubal sounded weary, as though he himself was sick to death of telling it.

"Thank you."

So they sat on Jubal's father's patio, underneath the wide Texas sky, in the flickering light of a torch, and Jubal talked. He told her the story of his parents and Prometheus Mulrooney, and how it had put an end to Jubal's father's plans and had followed Jubal's father's sons right on down to this day. That story had sent Jubal's brother to an early grave and left Jubal alone on his father's ranch wondering what, if anything, was worth a bucket of warm spit in this life. He didn't say exactly that, but Maggie understood what he meant.

Halfway through his recitation, Maggie put her arm through his and hugged him tight. She wanted to cry when he told her about the two little boys who had been born to Benjamin and Marianna Green and then left, bewildered and alone, to fend for themselves because their parents were too distracted to love them. Jubal was a year older than Benny, and Maggie could tell he'd never forgiven himself for failing to protect his brother.

She found out how Dan Blue Gully and Jubal became friends. She heard how a Mescalero band had camped on Jubal's father's land and how Jubal's father had not paid any attention to them because he'd been too preoccupied with Mulrooney and his own failing wife. She learned how Dan's father had been wounded and left behind by the Apaches when they ran, and how Dan's mother had stayed with her husband and welcomed Jubal and Benny into their camp.

Then when Dan's mother and father had succumbed to the rigors of their hard life, Jubal's father had let Dan live at the ranch house with them. The three boys, Jubal, Dan, and Benny, had grown up together and formed a bond of brotherhood that was stronger than the bond between the Green children and their parents. Dan had become as involved in the Green-Mulrooney feud as either Green son.

Somewhere along the way—Jubal couldn't even remember when—Dan had brought home a wounded Mescalero child, abandoned in a wild fight between whites and a renegade band. Dan and Jubal had bound up the boy's foot and nursed him until he was healthy again. Jubal said they called him Four Toes as a joke, because of the nature of his injuries and because he'd been too little to tell them his real name.

"I think it was a year or more before my parents even realized they'd adopted another Indian kid," Jubal said with wry amusement.

Maggie didn't think it was funny. Surreptitiously, she wiped away a tear. She knew Jubal would frown if he found out she was crying.

At first she felt a vague sympathy for Marianna Green. She envisioned Jubal's mother as a beautiful, fragile creature, brought to the rugged west Texas frontier by Jubal's father. She must have been a weak woman, unprepared for the hard life that awaited her here. Then, when Mulrooney began to torment the couple, her spirit had died completely, leaving her the hysterical, shadowy, wraithlike woman her son now remembered only with scorn and a deep, deep hurt that Maggie could tell he'd never dealt with. Maggie figured it might be too painful to acknowledge such a pain, and she wondered if anyone could ever truly recover from a loveless childhood. She herself had only a shimmering, flickering memory of her own mother, but she held that golden memory close to her heart because her mother had loved her. She knew it.

She watched Jubal's hard face in the wavering torchlight and decided, vague sympathetic stirrings aside, she'd never forgive Marianna Green for what she'd done. No matter how hard her own life had been, she should have loved her sons. In Maggie's book, there was never a good excuse for shirking one's responsibility to one's children.

She had died a suicide. Maggie flinched when Jubal told her that. She poisoned herself one day after a month-long pout. Then Jubal's father had been killed a week or so later as he was riding on the vast range. Nobody knew why he went out alone. He knew better.

"So that's it," Jubal finally concluded. He stared off into the unfinished middle of the patio as though he were still walking down those long, painful, arid years. His voice sounded tight.

Maggie didn't know what to say or do. She stared at the fountain with him and hugged his arm to her breast.

Finally she said, very softly, "I'm sorry."

Jubal put an arm around her shoulder and squeezed her to his side. He knew better than to think anything as fine and good as Maggie Bright would stay with him now that she knew about him. But he could offer her his protection in the meantime, until she went away. By then, maybe he'd be over this love problem. He had a depressing feeling that he was indulging in wishful thinking. Maggie Bright might walk out of his life, but he didn't expect she would leave his heart any time soon.

"May I try to fix up the patio, Jubal?" Maggie whispered.

He looked down at her with real surprise. That suggestion sounded mighty permanent. Maybe she wouldn't leave him after all. He tried not to feel too optimistic.

"Sure. Dan and Four Toes can help with the fountain. My father had pipes laid from the river. I guess you and Four Toes can plant stuff," he added vaguely.

Maggie laughed softly. "I guess we can."

Jubal cleared his throat. "Maggie," he ventured hoarsely, afraid of her answer, "will you sleep with me tonight?"

Maggie peered at his profile. He was still staring at the unfinished fountain, as if he didn't want to look at her. She couldn't swear to it in the dim light, but he looked almost afraid. She wondered why. She didn't say anything for a good few moments. At least he hadn't asked her to be his mistress, to pay her way with her body, even if he hadn't offered anything else.

"I don't reckon I should," she said at last, and dropped her gaze quickly.

"Why not?" Jubal finally looked at her. He was surprised at her answer. He'd expected a flat-out no, and maybe even a slap, now she knew all his sordid secrets.

"Well, because we're not married or anything," she said, in such a tiny voice that he could barely hear her.

After the merest hint of hesitation, Jubal said, "Well, we could change that." Then he swallowed hard and wondered what on earth had come over him to make him completely suppress his better judgment and speak so rashly. And to a woman, of all people. What if she said yes? Worse, what if she said no?

But Maggie only looked up at him in astonishment. "You—you want to marry me?" she asked incredulously.

Jubal cleared his throat again. "Well—I've been thinking about it."

"Oh, my goodness," breathed Maggie, stunned, after the first soaring burst of happiness shot through her heart. This amazing turn of events surpassed her wildest imaginings. "I don't know what to say."

Jubal was getting grumpy now. Hell, he'd asked her to marry him and she didn't know what to say?

Maggie saw his brow furrowing and swiftly added, "I mean, I—I have a farm and all, and a baby, and—oh, I just don't know." Oh, Lord, why did everything have to be so darned complicated? If she didn't have the farm, if she didn't have Annie, if sweet Kenny Bright weren't buried up there in the New Mexico mountains, she'd marry Jubal Green in a second. Less than that.

Jubal sighed. There was the damned farm again. He was sort of surprised she hadn't also mentioned her dead husband's grave. Then he decided, Aw, to hell with it.

"Well, at least you can kiss me," he said.

And before Maggie could say another word, he had her in his arms and was kissing her. Maggie was amazed at how quickly her body responded to Jubal's touch. It was as if it anticipated the joys to come and ran on ahead, leaving her brain behind to deal with the morality of the issue.

Jubal grunted. Her reaction triggered his, and he was hard as a rock in a second.

"Oh, God, Maggie, I thought once I had you, it would be over, but now I just want you more." He hadn't meant to confess that, but it slipped out.

Maggie didn't even hear him. Her ears were ringing with the sudden rush of heat, and his tongue was driving her wild. Her arms tightened around his shoulders, and she pressed herself against his broad chest as if she wanted to climb inside his body. She knew she had it backward. He was going to be in hers. She didn't even bother to fight it. She loved him.

Jubal broke the kiss with a deep groan. But he didn't let go of Maggie. Instead, he scooped her off the stone bench and marched her back inside the house. He didn't even notice if anyone was around to watch as he carried her down the hallway to his bedroom.

He held Maggie with one arm as he pulled the covers away from his pillows. Then he laid her down in the middle of his bed and stood up. His hands already tearing at the buttons on his shirt, he told her raggedly, "Take your clothes off, Maggie."

The day before, when Jubal had first carried her to his bed, it had taken Maggie a while to feel the insistent, scorching pressure build inside of her. But today her body was primed. She was already about to explode with desire. Her fingers trembled as they unfastened the buttons of her shirtwaist.

Jubal watched with greedy eyes when she shrugged the garment off her shoulders and began to unbutton her skirt. When she kicked that off and was left in her chemise and drawers, he said hoarsely, "Let me."

His big, calloused hands sent shivers of anticipation shimmering through Maggie's body as he quickly tugged her chemise over her head. Then he untied the tapes to her drawers and pulled those off. That left her naked to his eyes and the cool night breezes, except for her black stockings that were tied with pretty pink garters.

Jubal was naked as a jay himself. He stood beside the bed, eating Maggie's body with his eyes, while her own eager gaze feasted upon the treat he made.

"Lord, Maggie, you're a picture."

"So are you, Jubal," Maggie whispered. Her hand reached out to stroke those massive thighs. "When I first saw you naked, I was afraid you'd die. I never thought I'd get to see you healthy and perfect like this." Her fingers touched the ugly, scarred indentation left by French Jack's bullet and stroked it lovingly.

"Perfect?" Jubal's chuckle was hoarse with desire and surprise. "I've got scars in places people don't even talk about."

"I think you're perfect," she murmured. She was now staring at his rigid manhood, stiff, hot, and huge, and her fingers tentatively lifted from his thigh to stroke it. He gasped in pleasure.

"Aw, shoot, Maggie."

Jubal couldn't stand it any longer. He dove into the bed next to her and crushed her to his chest. Her perfect breasts smashed against his hardness, and he felt her nipples press into him like bullets.

He entered her with one deep thrust that made him shudder when he was finally buried up to the hilt in her tight sheath.

"Oh, Lord," whispered Maggie. Her legs wrapped around him in response to his invasion, and she lifted her hips high to receive him, body and soul, into herself.

Jubal had his head buried in the hollow of her shoulder, trying to hold on. When he thought he could move without exploding, he began to kiss Maggie's neck. He tongued the thrumming pulse at its base and almost lost control again at her gasp of pleasure. He didn't understand it. He'd never had this reaction to a woman before. It was because this was Maggie. He knew it. She just wasn't like anybody else.

"You feel so good," he murmured into her hair.

His hands left off where they were cupping her face and trailed down to feel her wonderful breasts. And then he started to move in her.

Maggie couldn't help herself. She knew she was behaving like a wanton, but she'd never felt anything like the way Jubal made her feel. She arched herself against him, trying to take more and more of him. She realized she was whimpering, but she couldn't find it in herself to care. Her nails raked his shoulders and her legs lifted even higher and wrapped around him so that her hips cradled him perfectly.

Jubal knew he was going to burst soon. His hand left off teasing her hard nipples and moved to her precious secret core.

When his finger began to stroke her there, her reaction was so electrifying she nearly bucked them both off the bed. Her nails dug into his back, but Jubal didn't mind. She was sobbing even before her shattering climax rocked her this time, and when she exploded, she clung to Jubal as if to life itself.

Jubal was sure his end had come when he felt Maggie's body tighten around him and begin to squeeze him until he couldn't hold back any longer. With one wild, reckless plunge so deep he feared he might have pierced her womb, his seed burst from him. He knew the cry that tore through the room had come from him, but he couldn't have held it in if he'd tried.

His release complete, he lay in Maggie's arms, breathless and weak. He knew he must be heavy on her, but she was clutching his back so tightly he couldn't have moved if he'd had the strength, which he didn't.

His breath was coming in ragged gasps and he was only dimly aware that he was whispering into Maggie's ear.

"Oh, God, Maggie, it's so good. You're so good. You feel so damned good."

Maggie was crying. Jubal had expected that. He still wasn't entirely sure what, if anything, to do about her tears, but when he was able to breathe again, he eased his body away from crushing hers and peered down at her with real tenderness. He had the feeling she was trying to stifle her sobs but was having no success. Her lips were ripe and swollen with his kisses, her eyes were smoky with passion, and her expression, in spite of her tears, was one of bliss.

He watched her sob for a few seconds and then lowered his lips to hers once more. She kissed him greedily, and he smiled with satisfaction. He'd done this to her; it made him feel good.

Jubal smoothed the hair away from her damp cheeks. "You always cry afterward, Maggie."

He didn't want her to think he minded, although it did confuse him some. But he sort of wondered why their sexual encounters, which were so overwhelmingly wonderful for him, made her cry. He caressed her tears away with a hand.

Maggie sniffled, swallowed hard, and covered his big warm hand with hers, holding it to her cheek. "I c-can't help it," she confessed. "I've just never felt anything like this before. It's—it's just so wonderful."

Jubal's grin began to take on a slightly arrogant cast. "I think it's wonderful too."

"It was never like this with—with K-K-Kenny." Maggie began to sob again, and Jubal rolled over onto his side and hugged her close.

He stroked her back, long comforting strokes that began at the nape of her neck and slid all the way down her damp spine to her pretty round buttocks. He tucked her head under his chin and let her cry.

"It's all right, Maggie."

"I h-hope so, Jubal," Maggie said. "I feel so funny about it. I never felt like this with Kenny. It was never anywhere near like this."

Jubal thought he knew the reason for that, but vanity made him ask, "Is it better with us, Maggie?"

Maggie's slender body shuddered with another huge sob. "Oh, yes!" she whispered. "It's so much better, it's almost like we're not even doing the same thing at all."

Jubal was positively gloating by this time. He felt so good, he wanted to shout. "It's all right, Maggie," he whispered. He tried to keep the arrogant satisfaction out of his voice.

Maggie sniffled again. "But I feel so guilty."

"Guilty?" Jubal drew his head back to look at her face. Sure enough, Maggie looked as though she had stolen all the cookies out of the cookie jar and just been found out.

She nodded. She had to swallow again before she could talk. "Yes," she whispered.

"Why do you feel guilty, love? Do you think what we're doing is betraying your marriage vows or something?" He guessed he could understand that, although it aggravated him.

"Well, kind of," she confessed. "But it's more like—like—oh, Jubal, I tried so hard to be a good wife to Kenny. I really did. I tried and tried." Her voice had taken on a miserably unhappy tone that made Jubal feel bad.

"I'm sure you did, Maggie. It's your nature. I know you were a good wife."

Maggie shook her head. "And, Jubal, I loved him. I know I loved him. I really, really did. He was so sweet I couldn't help but love him. But—but it was never like what I feel now." Maggie's unhappy wail was muffled in Jubal's muscled flesh, and her tears mingled with his golden-brown chest hairs.

Jubal was sure his heart was going to rocket right out of his body. He cradled Maggie in his strong arms and murmured sweet hushes in her ear and stroked her tenderly.

"It's all right, Maggie," he whispered, emotion making his words quaver. "You gave him everything. You know you did. You were the best wife that man could ever have had. I know it."

Maggie sniffled one more time. "I really tried, Jubal. I really tried."

By this time his eyes had shut tight and he didn't feel arrogant anymore. He felt almost as if he wanted to cry himself, but he didn't. He rocked Maggie for a good five minutes before he dared to ask her what he wanted to know.

"Maggie?" he whispered, when he thought he could speak without his voice cracking.

She wasn't sobbing anymore. Her eyes were closed and she had snuggled her head against him. It felt so good there, so solid and secure, that she didn't want him ever to let her go again.

"What, Jubal?" she asked in a breathless whisper.

"Do—" Jubal stopped, wondering if he should ask this. He was afraid of the answer. He finally took a deep breath and just blurted it out. "Do you love me?"

Maggie swallowed hard. She didn't want her love

to be a problem for him. But he'd asked. She guessed she owed him an honest answer.

"Oh, yes, Jubal," she whispered. "I love you to death."

Jubal felt as though all the burdens of hell had been lifted from his shoulders. It took him a couple of minutes to recover his composure, and when he did, he said, "Well, then, everything's all right. Everything will be just fine. I swear it."

He squeezed her tight, and Maggie sighed, and they both drifted off to sleep.

16

Maggie knew in her mind that she and Annie were in the middle of a gruesome feud. But in her heart she had never been so happy. The next week was like a dream come true for her.

The morning after her confession of love, Jubal had hugged her hard, kissed her soundly, and bounded out of bed feeling like a new man. Then he made it his business, before he even rode out to check his stock, to ask her exactly what he could do to make her happy.

Maggie stared at him in blank astonishment. Nobody had ever asked her that before, not even sweet Kenny Bright. She blushed.

"I—I don't know, Jubal. I guess I think it would be nice to fix up the patio."

"Done!" Jubal cried. He threw on his clothes. "Now don't you try to do anything yourself, Maggie," he commanded. "All you have to do is plan it and tell Four Toes what you want done. He'll see to the work."

Maggie was laughing by this time. "But, Jubal, I've got to have something to do. You don't want me to sit around and get fat, do you?"

As Jubal grinned at her, he remembered something. He stooped to rummage around in his bureau drawer for a second. When he stood up, he was holding a very elegant enameled hairbrush. It had a black-lacquered back with flowers painted on it.

"Here, Maggie. You can brush your hair."

Maggie looked at the brush wide-eyed. "Oh, Jubal, how pretty," she whispered. "It's just like the one I saw at the big mercantile in El Paso." She lifted her gaze to him, and found him nodding with supreme male satisfaction. "It's the same one, isn't it?"

"Yes, it is."

"Oh, Jubal!" Maggie flung herself out of bed and into his arms. "Thank you so much!"

Jubal couldn't stand holding a naked Maggie Bright without his body undergoing changes that were difficult for him to control.

"Don't do that, Maggie, or I'll never get to work."

Maggie let go of him, but she couldn't stop herself from reaching up with the brush and running it through Jubal's thick, sun-streaked hair. The gesture was incredibly sensuous, as she had to stand on her tiptoes, rubbing her belly against his rock-hard erection and making him groan. He finally reached up, grabbed her by the wrists, and drew her away from him.

"God, Maggie, don't do that," he growled.

She smiled at him, a little embarrassed at her own wanton behavior. Still, she was pleased by his reaction to her charms.

"Well, all right, Jubal. I'll let you get to work. But I still don't know what I'm supposed to do with myself all day long if you won't let me work at anything."

"You can help Beula."

Then he kissed her so soundly he nearly didn't make it out of the bedroom, especially when she began to press herself against him as though she wanted him too. But he'd been away from home for a long time and had lots of catching up to do. So he went out to fetch Four Toes and Dan for a consultation.

"I want you to talk to Maggie and find out what she wants to do with the patio today, Four Toes. Dan and I will see to the cattle."

Four Toes was delighted. "Great. I'd love to see that place cleaned up. It could look real nice."

Jubal smiled. "You sound just like Maggie."

Dan laughed. "I notice it's 'Maggie' now, not 'Mrs. Bright,'" he said slyly. "This is quite a departure, isn't it, you takin' a good hand away from cow work to play in the yard?"

Jubal couldn't decide whether to take offense at his oldest friend's words or not. He finally decided it wouldn't do him any good. Dan knew him too well. He chuckled softly.

"You're right, Danny," he said. "You're right. It's all over. I can't help it. She's got me."

"It's about time," Dan said. Then he slapped Jubal on the shoulder. "I told you so, Jubal. I told you so when you were lyin' on your damned back, near dead. I told you so."

Jubal tried to frown. "I don't remember."

"Well, I did, whether you remember or not. I knew it." Dan turned to Four Toes. "Didn't I say so, Four Toes?"

Four Toes nodded. "He said so."

"Well, all right. You can quit gloating. We've got a lot of work to do. Four Toes, you and Maggie get me up a list, and when I take her into El Paso to pick up her eyeglasses, we can get the materials you'll need to finish the fountain and lay new tiles or whatever you need to do."

"Tell you one thing would help right off," said Four Toes.

"What's that?"

"Cow shit."

"Fertilizer?" Dan asked.

"Right."

"Well, hell," said Jubal sourly. "I'm willing to do a lot of things for Maggie, but I'll be damned if I'll carry a sack of cow shit around with me all day while I ride the range."

Four Toes laughed. "Damn, I'd like to see that. No, I think I can get the Todd kids to help us. I can send 'em out into the pasture with a couple of sacks and pay 'em a penny to fill 'em up. Maybe even little Annie can help."

The thought of little Annie Bright dragging a sack of cow patties around was so comical that Jubal couldn't help but laugh. He also couldn't help but compare this lighthearted conversation with the last one they'd had here on his ranch, right after his brother Benny had been killed and they'd set out in pursuit of French Jack. He shook his head in wonder.

"Lord almighty. Four months ago when we left Green's Valley, did either one of you think we'd be doing this today?"

Both foster brothers shook their heads too.

"No," said Dan with a wry smile. "Four months ago things were pretty grim, all right."

"Real, real grim," amended Four Toes.

"Things were hell," Jubal said.

"They're a lot *bright*er now," said Dan with a wink.

Jubal eyed him with a pained expression on his face.

"But I get the feeling they're going to be *green* pretty soon," Four Toes added.

Jubal grinned. "Lord above, you two are really reaching. Let's get busy."

This was to be the first time since he'd been shot that Jubal would have to ride for any length of time, and he wanted to start early and get as much done as he could before his newly healed wounds could stop him. So he and Dan left for the stable to saddle up, and Four Toes went off to the kitchen to find Maggie. She and Beula had fixed breakfast together and were now taking care of the washing up.

Beula had commanded her two children to watch Annie, who seemed to be over her sulk this morning. She even held out her gourd dolly and smiled shyly when Connie, who took after her mama and was a very motherly child, grinned and praised it. Annie even let Connie hold it while she named its various body parts.

Maggie couldn't help laughing at Annie's firm "Haiw" when she pointed at the doll's yarn topping, and Connie's considerate "That's right, Annie. That's the dolly's hair."

Maggie figured her baby would do just fine here.

"Honest, Beula," she was saying now. "I can take care of these men in here. You have a family to care for."

Beula eyed Maggie doubtfully over a tub of soap-suds, as though she wasn't sure such a little thing could handle three men and a baby all by herself.

"Well, I don't want you to overdo it, Maggie," she said. "I'm pretty used to it, you know."

Maggie laughed at that. "Lordy, Beula, I been running my farm single-handed since Kenny died. Feeding four people and a little kid is nothing compared to that."

Beula's expression was incredulous. "You ran that farm all by yourself?"

Maggie, ever honest, looked slightly abashed. "Well, it wasn't much of a farm. And I did have one hired hand. 'Course he was drunk most of the time and didn't do much. But I'm used to hard work." Her eyes got sort of dreamy. "After Mr. Green got shot and showed up at my door, and Mr. Blue Gully and Mr. Smith came to stay, it was ever so much easier."

Beula was astonished. "Easier? With three men to feed, one of them gun-shot, and them villains shooting at you all the time?"

"Well," Maggie admitted, "getting shot at was sort of scary. But, Beula, I never had anybody work like those men worked around my place. It looks better now than it ever did."

"Do you 'spect you'll go back there after all this is over, Maggie?"

For some reason Maggie's heart clutched painfully. Did she plan to go back?

"Why—why, I guess I will, Beula. Don't know what else I'd do," she said, after the barest pause.

Beula eyed Maggie with a slight frown. Then she shook her head and dunked a pot into her tub and began to scrub it vigorously.

"Humph," she said. "'Pears to me Mr. Green might have something to say about that."

Maggie blushed. She didn't want to, but she couldn't help it. She tried to hide behind the big platter she was drying. "Mr. Green's been mighty nice to me," she muttered.

"Nice!" said Beula with another *humph*. "I should say he pretty well ought to be." She pinned Maggie with another sharp stare. "Of course I might be wrong about this, Maggie Bright, but it seems to me that Jubal Green has taken quite a shine to you. And it don't look to me as though you object to him any too much, neither."

Maggie couldn't meet Beula's eyes. She was embarrassed to death. "Well," she said, "I don't know about Mr. Green liking me. I—I like him just fine."

Her face felt so hot now she expected it to burst into flames. She busied herself by putting the platter away on a shelf where it looked like it might belong.

Beula apparently decided her conversation with Maggie was more important than the pot she had just dunked. She wiped her hands on her apron, settled her fists on her hips, and gave Maggie a steady stare.

"Now, I know it ain't none of my business, Maggie Bright, but you been married before, ain't you?"

"Of course," said Maggie.

Beula nodded. "Were he a good man?"

Maggie's eyes opened wide. "Oh, yes. Kenny was wonderful."

"And I bet he loved you too, didn't he?"

Maggie swallowed and looked down. "Yes, he did," she said very softly.

"And you loved him."

"Yes."

"And you were happy."

Maggie looked up quickly and nodded fervently. "Oh, yes."

"But did you get a quivery feeling in your belly like you were sick all the time and like you didn't care how many other men there were on earth, that he was the only one you ever wanted to be with as long as you lived and you'd die if he ever went away, and you didn't know what to do when he wasn't around?"

Maggie didn't have to think about it, but she was overwhelmed by such a feeling of betrayal that she didn't answer Beula's question immediately.

Beula's eyes narrowed. "Well?" she asked.

"Kenny was a wonderful man, Beula," she whispered.

"I believe you, Maggie," Beula said, "but that don't answer my question."

Maggie dropped her gaze. "No," she murmured.

Beula sniffed and resumed scrubbing her pot. "Didn't think so," she said with a nod of satisfaction. "But you feel that way about Jubal, don't you?"

Maggie felt absolutely awful now. She realized with horror that her eyes were welling up, and she swiped a stray tear away with her dish towel.

"Yes."

"I thought so," Beula announced. "I could tell."

Then she dropped her pot into the water tub once more with a big splash and turned around to face Maggie.

"Maggie Bright, like I said, this ain't none of it my business, but I can tell you this: when you find the right man, you know it, and you better grab him while you can, because you might not ever get another chance in life. When I found Mr. Todd, I didn't even pause to consider. I just up and grabbed him. I know he's older than me and I know he's a dratted Easterner, and I know my ma and my aunts like to flayed me alive, but I knew, Maggie. I *knew* he was the only man on the face of the earth for me. And I was right."

Beula ran out of breath and stopped talking.

Maggie didn't know what to say. She had a suspicion that Beula was right. But Maggie didn't have only herself to think about. She had Annie to consider, and she had Kenny Bright's memory and Kenny Bright's farm. Her farm. And she loved Annie and that memory and that farm with a passion she couldn't even begin to explain.

"Thank you, Beula," she said at last. "I really do thank you for your concern."

Beula didn't look as though she was entirely satisfied with Maggie's response to her lecture. She shook her head again.

"Well, you just think about what I said, Maggie, is all," she finally muttered.

Maggie was still feeling subdued and more than a little beleaguered when Four Toes found her in the kitchen.

"Mrs. Bright, Jubal sent me in here to fetch you out to the patio. He says you're finally going to finish it."

Maggie flushed with pleasure. "How nice of him. I'd really like to do that."

"It's a wonderful place," Four Toes said. "All it needs is a smack o' love."

Maggie looked at the tall Indian closely. She was touched by his words. It surprised her that a man who had been saved from a violent death as a boy by three other boys, none of whom had known more than a lick or two of love in their lives, seemed to have so much love of his own to give. Sometimes the human spirit absolutely astonished her.

She and Four Toes spent a productive morning on the patio, where she made a list of all the things they decided to do and Four Toes inventoried supplies on hand at the ranch. When he was through with that, Maggie was to write up a shopping list.

In the meantime, she discovered that the tiles that had been laid nearly three decades earlier, and then left to collect layers of dirt and Texas dust, were absolutely beautiful. Apparently Jubal's father had imported them from Spain.

Maggie was nearly quivering with excitement when Four Toes came back with his inventory report.

"I've never done anything like this in my life, Mr. Smith," she confessed with glee. "I've never seen anything as pretty as those tiles. I can't wait to clean them up. And I can't even imagine going to town and buying a bunch of new stuff and just fixing up a place like this. Even when Kenny was building the farm, we had to make do with old stuff or stuff he mixed himself. He cut the trees for the logs and then he built the shelves on the porch out of old barn siding."

Four Toes was smiling at her. "Well, Jubal's got lots of money, Mrs. Bright. His father left him pretty well off—financially, at any rate—even if he didn't pay no attention to him or Benny. I guess Mr. Green and Mr. Mulrooney made a fortune in New York before they split up and started feuding."

Maggie stopped smiling. She'd almost forgotten about that cursed feud. "Isn't that something?" she said softly.

Four Toes read her mood and might even have read

her thoughts. "It'll be all right, Mrs. Bright. Jubal, he'll win this war. He ain't like his pa. He cares about this place and he cares about his people. His pa—well, Jubal's pa, he wasn't prepared for the pounding life give him. He just seemed kinda lost."

"I don't know how you boys grew up to be so good, Mr. Smith," Maggie whispered. "You're all so good."

Four Toes colored up. He hadn't done that for a long time, and Maggie was surprised. "Thank you, ma'am. I think that's Jubal's doing too. Him and Dan's ma and pa, but I don't remember them much."

Maggie decided she'd better change the subject pretty quickly or she'd end up bawling. "Well, anyway," she said briskly, "I've got me a shopping list here that will probably just about curl Mr. Green's hair."

Four Toes chuckled. "I don't think he'll mind, ma'am."

Jubal and Dan spent a profitable day out on the range, surveying Jubal's vast cattle empire. Jubal had forgotten just how wide open these Texas spaces could be. It felt good to breathe in the clean air and to look around and see miles and miles of nothing but his own land. The thought of Prometheus Mulrooney— or anybody else, for that matter—trying to wrench all this away from him hit him with such repugnance that Dan had to ask if something was wrong.

"Nothing's wrong," Jubal said with a grim smile. "It's just that I'd almost forgotten how much I have to lose."

"You aren't going to lose anything, Jubal."

Jubal nodded. "They'll have to kill me to get it, Danny."

"They'll have to kill me first," his friend replied.

The two men came home earlier that day than they would have under normal circumstances. But circumstances were still far from normal, as far as Jubal's body was concerned. By the time he rode through the ranch house gate and over to the stable, his face was white and pinched with pain, and his thigh felt as though somebody had jabbed him with a red-hot poker and was now jiggling it around just for fun.

His arm didn't hurt too much. Maybe the exercise he'd been getting with Maggie helped to strengthen it. He hoped so, because he planned to do some more of that as soon as he possibly could.

"Watch it, Jubal," Dan called to him when he slid off Old Red and his legs nearly gave out under him. "Why didn't you wait for me, you fool man?" Dan was smiling but he shook his head, too.

"Aw, hell, Danny," Jubal said through clenched teeth. "I can't stay an invalid forever."

"A couple of months ain't forever, Jubal. You damn near died, remember."

Jubal was grimacing now while he tried to get his legs to work right. "No, thank God, I don't remember that part of it."

Dan laughed. "It's just as well. You were a rotten patient."

All at once Jubal stopped stock-still as a sudden flash of something just on the edge of being a memory assailed him. The flickering, shadowy image of something ethereally angelic passed before his mind's eye. His face crunched up with the effort of concentration.

"What is it, Jubal?" Dan asked, eyeballing him oddly.

Jubal didn't answer for a second or two. He was trying with all his might to capture the shimmery, whispery tatters of thought that played so tantalizingly close to his consciousness and yet wouldn't allow themselves to be caught. He finally shook his head with disgust.

"Hell, I don't know. There's something I can't remember."

"There's lots of stuff I don't remember," Dan said.

Jubal gave him a crooked grin. "I guess," he said. Then he took a big step, leading out with his left leg, and very nearly ended up in a heap. Dan caught him just before he hit the ground.

"Lordy, Jubal, you shouldn't have ridden so long with that leg wound so fresh. You could still open up your thigh, you know." He grabbed Jubal by the shoulder and, in spite of his friend's grumbling protests, supported him from the stable to the house.

Jubal let Dan help him, but he made him let go when they got to the house. He wasn't about to advertise the fact that he was a cripple.

Once in the house, he started looking for Maggie. He limped into the parlor. No Maggie. He peeked into his study, where he kept all his books. Not a soul in sight. He made a hopeful tour of his bedroom and then checked out Maggie's room. No luck. He finally made his way to the kitchen, only to find Beula stirring a big pot of stew.

"Maggie said she was going to be cooking for you men, but she's been working so hard today, I made her let me cook your stew tonight," Beula told him.

"Working?" Jubal's frown was so ferocious that Beula actually looked almost frightened.

"Yes, sir," she stammered. "She's been working like a dog all day long."

"Damn." Jubal swung out of the kitchen and stomped out to the patio as fast as his throbbing leg would allow.

Sure enough, there she was. On her hands and knees with a bucket of frothy water by her side and a stiff-bristled brush in her hands, her face gleaming with sweat, Maggie Bright was scrubbing tiles for all she was worth. Jubal didn't notice that her sweaty face was beaming with happiness or that she was humming a merry tune. He also didn't notice that Connie Todd was supervising her brother and little Annie as they spaded manure into a plot of dirt behind the fountain. He didn't see the fountain itself, either. It had undergone a rather startling transformation while he'd been out checking fences and counting cows.

"What the hell do you think you're doing?"

Jubal's furious bellow startled Maggie into a full-fledged scream. The stiff-bristled brush slithered soapily out of her grip and her hand flew to her bosom. Connie shrieked too, little Henry clutched his sister's skirts with muddy hands, and Annie began to cry.

Maggie had to swallow her heart again before she could answer him. Then she did so with a horrid, sinking droop to her spirits.

"My Lord, you scared me to death," she whispered. Then she glanced over to the children. "You scared the kids to death too. It's all right, babies. It's just Mr. Green."

She looked up at Jubal with such an expression of dismay on her face that Jubal could have kicked himself. If it wasn't for my damned leg, he thought, I could squat down next to her and hold her tight. But he was sure his leg, if it bent at all, would never allow him to stand up again. Instead, he walked up close to her and whispered furiously, "I thought I told you not to work today!"

Maggie's initial fright was rapidly being replaced by irritation. "But, Jubal, you said I could fix up the patio." She eyed the children and added in a low voice, "There's no need for you to holler, either. If you're mad at me for something, tell me. Don't shout in front of the children."

Jubal was embarrassed now. "I'm sorry I hollered at you, Maggie." He glanced over at the children, too, and looked back at Maggie and said, "Of course you can fix the patio. That's what I told you. But *you're* not supposed to do the work. You're supposed to get Four Toes and tell him what you want done and then he'll get people to do it for you. *You're* not supposed to do it. You're supposed to rest. I'm taking care of you now, damn it, remember?"

Maggie's expression began to clear up when his words penetrated. She never was any good at holding on to her anger, anyway, and the fact that he was upset because he was worried about her working too hard was purely sweet.

As a matter of fact, her face began to get a downright tender look to it as she gazed up at him. She realized he was still trying to scowl at her for all he was worth, even though he was obviously abashed at his initial roar, and she smiled.

"Oh, Jubal!"

She got up off her hands and knees and wiped her hands on her apron. She would have hugged him, except she didn't think an overt display of affection would be proper in front of the children.

"Thank you. But Four Toes has been working on the fountain, and the kids wanted to help, and I'm just washing these tiles. They're real pretty when you get the dirt off. See?"

Jubal didn't want to see. He wanted to pull Maggie close to his chest and kiss her until she squealed with joy. Instead, he was left to frown after her when she stepped over to the three children and knelt down to comfort them. Annie ran into her arms and sobbed. Henry, Jr., looked uncertainly from her to Jubal. But astute little Connie had it all figured out, apparently, because she just smiled and said, "Hi, Uncle Jubal. We're going to plant a garden."

Jubal's expression remained defiant for another couple of seconds, but he finally admitted defeat and gave Connie a crooked grin. "A garden, huh?"

A huge smile lit up Connie's face. "Yes. Mrs. Bright said we can plant flowers here, 'cause it's the patio. We don't have to plant carrots and cabbages and such here. And she said maybe we can even have a rose-bush."

"You want a rosebush, Maggie?" Jubal asked. His forehead creased up and he looked worried. He hadn't even thought about roses when he'd been buying seeds for her. If anybody had mentioned a rose to him, he'd have bought one right off. Or two or three. He couldn't think of everything, could he?

It took all the control Maggie could command not to wrap her arms around him and kiss him. He looked so adorably concerned for her.

"We can plant a rosebush later, Jubal," she said gently.

Annie had stopped crying now, but she was still frowning. She looked mad, in fact, and her little fist was crammed into her mouth, a sure sign that all was not well with her. When her mama stepped up closer to Jubal, she pulled her fist out of her mouth and pointed a dirty finger at him.

"Juba mad," she announced. She didn't sound any too pleased with the fact.

Jubal felt bad.

Then Annie said, "Juba bad," and he felt even worse.

He looked at Maggie and saw she was watching him with a mixture of amusement and tenderness that was completely irresistible. He finally let out a heavy sigh and chuckled. "Jubal's not mad anymore, Annie honey," he said. Then he took her out of Maggie's arms. "Boy, you don't let a guy get away with anything, do you, you little chipmunk?"

That comment got young Henry's attention. "I'm your little chipmunk," he reminded Jubal. The child seemed mighty offended that Jubal could have forgotten that "chipmunk" was an endearment reserved for him alone.

Jubal looked down at Henry and sighed again. "Good God," he muttered. "I never realized being a—an uncle would be so much trouble." He had been going to say "father" but thought better of it.

"I guess Annie will have to be something else, Jubal," Maggie said with a giggle.

"How about a parsnip?" Jubal eyed Annie narrowly. She was listening to the conversation with interest. "You seem like a parsnip to me, Annie. How about it? Will you be my little parsnip?"

"Powsup?" Annie asked, looking rather dubious.

Jubal's grin broadened. "Close, Annie. Will you be my little parsnip?"

Annie eyed him doubtfully for another second or two, but when he continued to grin at her, she relented. First she nodded. Then she threw her arms around his neck and laid her head on his shoulder and hugged him.

Maggie and Jubal just looked at each other for a few moments. Then Maggie said, "Looks like you got yourself a parsnip, Jubal Green."

Jubal wished he could kiss her. "Looks like I do," was all he said.

For the next two weeks, Jubal pulled so many strings that he felt like a puppet master. But at last he maneuvered circumstances so he could have Maggie all to himself when he went to El Paso.

It was not difficult getting Beula to agree to take care of Annie for the duration. Beula was on his side.

"It's about time you found yourself a good woman, Jubal Green. Haven't I been telling you?"

Jubal cast his gaze toward the heavens and prayed for patience. "Yes, Beula. You've been telling me. But near as I can figure you haven't yet come up with a solution to the problem of Prometheus Mulrooney trying to murder anybody who even so much as smiles at me. How the hell am I supposed to keep a wife?"

Beula scowled at him. "Well, you just better figure that one out yourself pretty darned soon. I'd be mad as fire if anything happened to Maggie Bright." She was hanging out her washing as they spoke. To emphasize her point, she gave Codfish's union suit a hard flap, splattering Jubal with water.

Jubal jumped back. "Jesus, Beula, you don't have to

drown me. I'm not about to let anything happen to Maggie."

Beula *humph*ed. "Well, just see that you don't."

She stabbed two clothespins onto the shoulders of Codfish's underwear and turned around to finish her lecture. She wasn't through with Jubal yet. Her fists sank into her ample hips and she glared at him hard. Beula's eyes were brown, but when she was feeling intense about something, they took on an amber cast. They were really, really amber now.

Jubal knew he was in for a good, hard, impassioned lecture. He sighed and stood his ground bravely, hoping she wouldn't yell at him for too long.

"And not only that, Jubal Green," she began, "but you'd better do something pretty darned quick about making an honest woman of her."

Jubal's brows shot up. "An honest woman of her?" he bellowed.

"Yes," said Beula, apparently not at all intimidated by his hollering. "I know good and well you've taken her to your bed. Now, Maggie Bright is a good woman. She wouldn't do something like that with just anybody, and I'm not going to let you get away with trifling with her affections." Beula looked like an ornery mule as she said this.

"Trifling with her?" Jubal couldn't believe his ears.

"Trifling with her, yes. I don't care if you do own this ranch, Jubal Green. I won't have it."

Jubal was so mad now, he tore his hat off his head and slammed it into the dirt. A puff of dust swirled up around their feet, but Beula didn't back off an inch.

"I'm not trifling with her, God damn it!"

"Well, then, just what do you aim to do to save her

honor?" Beula's enormous bosom was heaving with every agitated breath.

"Save her honor?"

Jubal couldn't believe his ears. He glared back at Beula with terrible ferocity. She didn't budge.

"Well?" she said.

Jubal stooped to pick up his dusty hat, slapped it against his left thigh before he thought about it, and nearly bellowed again when it stung his barely healed bullet wound.

"I'm waiting for an answer," Beula said through stiff lips.

"God damn it," Jubal said again.

"Blasphemies won't get you anywhere," Beula announced primly.

"For Lord's sake, Beula, I asked her once."

"Well, what did she say?"

"She sort of didn't answer."

"Now, just what on earth does that mean? Just exactly what is 'She sort of didn't answer' supposed to mean?"

"Well, she's worried about her damned farm."

Jubal felt really sulky. Until Beula's words shattered his happy fantasy, he figured nobody else knew about his nighttime activities with Maggie. It was truly a blow to discover he had no secrets from his little ranch family.

Beula's face relaxed a touch.

"I'm sure a bright man like you can figure out some way to ease her mind about her farm, can't you." It wasn't quite a question.

Jubal glared at her in defeat. During the past two weeks, he'd pretty much come to the conclusion that he wasn't going to get over this problem of loving

Maggie Bright any time soon. But since his first fumbling, tentative mention of marriage, he had been postponing an actual honest-to-God proposal because it seemed so permanent. Marriage sounded so final. It was such an endless condition. Sort of like consumption: once you got it, there was no getting over it unless one of you died. He just hated having his hand forced as Beula was forcing it now.

He gave her another good solid glare before he said, "Sure, I guess I can do something about her damned farm."

Beula beamed at him. "Good." And she went back to hanging out her wash.

Jubal thought about proposing to Maggie that night in bed, but he got distracted.

"Your leg still hurts, Jubal, I know it does," Maggie said softly.

"I don't care how much it hurts. I've got to make love to you or die, Maggie." He had an awful thought then. "Don't you want to?"

Jubal looked so forlorn that Maggie giggled. "Oh, yes, Jubal. I want to. I just don't want you to hurt. You've been on that fool horse every day for almost two weeks now, and each time you come home, you can barely walk, and I know it hurts."

"I don't care, Maggie. I need to make love to you."

"You need to?" Maggie smiled at him with infinite love.

Jubal was lying on his back, with his condition stiffly evident. He was caressing Maggie's arms, and his hands were making occasionally forays over to her breasts, where he would lovingly massage her rigid nipples.

Every time he touched her, Maggie felt as though lightning were throbbing from his fingers straight to her core, her reaction to his touch was so strong. Her nipples were so sensitive that every caress sent gooseflesh shooting down her arms.

Right now she was running her nimble fingers through his curly chest hairs. She absolutely loved to feel his chest. It was so hard, and the way his hair sort of thinned out into a straight, dark line that pointed right smack to his sex drove her to distraction. In fact, her hand began stroking lower and lower on Jubal's belly until he groaned deep in his throat and growled, "God, Maggie, take me in your hand."

So she did. "I just don't want to hurt you," she whispered.

"There's no way you can hurt me by doing that," came out in a ragged croak.

Maggie had begun feeling bolder as the days progressed. Tonight, she had an almost killing urge to kiss him in places she wasn't sure were supposed to be kissed. She sighed. She'd never dreamed, even in her wildest, wickedest imagination, that people could do the things she and Jubal had been doing these last few nights. She was sure Kenny hadn't even known about most of them.

She leaned over and kissed his belly button, and Jubal sucked in a quick breath of pleasure.

"Oh, yes, Maggie. Kiss me."

So she kissed him there. When Jubal shut his eyes and groaned in ecstasy, she took it as a good sign and moved a little lower. In fact, she made a little wet trail of kisses down his belly and right to the curly brush of hair that grew around his manhood. Then she decided that since she was already there, she might just as well taste what it was that had been driving her to such incredible peaks of ecstasy these past few days.

When she began to nibble his shaft, Jubal thought for sure he was going to die. When she began to lick it with long, delicious strokes, he groaned. When she took it into her mouth and began to love it very much the way he had loved her with his own tongue, he just about lost his mind.

Maggie was delighted with his reaction. Knowing how much pleasure she was giving him increased her own longings too, until she was sure she was going to erupt into flames of desire. Her own hips began to rock in the rhythm of love even before she straddled him and impaled herself.

"Oh, my God, Maggie. Oh, my God," Jubal whispered. He was just about to burst. But he didn't want to finish before Maggie did, so he sneaked his hand between them and stroked her lovingly until he heard her gasp and felt her tighten around him.

Maggie had been spiraling higher and higher as she rode Jubal. She had never felt so powerfully in control. Then when his fingers began to work their magic, she soared. Her climax was shattering. She thought for sure she was going to get lost in the burst of ecstasy that overwhelmed her.

She collapsed on Jubal's chest and could feel him pouring burst upon burst of his seed in her. She knew by now that Jubal wasn't quite sure what to do when she cried after they made love, but she couldn't help it. It was so wonderful. Her tears soaked his chest.

But Jubal didn't mind anymore. He was getting used to her reaction. He anticipated it. He was proud that he could do this to her. He held her tight as he tried to catch his breath.

"It's just getting better, Maggie," he whispered when he could talk. "It's just getting better and better and better."

17

Prometheus J. Mulrooney had to spend a couple of days at a hotel in Santa Fe, recuperating from the rigors of his uncomfortable journey back from Lincoln.

Ferrett and Pelch took every moment they had away from his presence to hie themselves over to his train carriage and try to saw through the wrought-iron railing on his private observation deck. It was slow going.

"I don't think we've even made a dent, Mr. Pelch," said Ferrett, wiping his forehead with a red bandanna he'd bought at a local mercantile. He had never owned a red bandanna before. It made him feel very Western.

Pelch sighed and stared at the railing. "I'm afraid we're going to need more blades, Mr. Ferrett."

Ferrett eyed the now-dull blade mournfully. "I believe you're right, Mr. Pelch."

"I shall fetch them, Mr. Ferrett, if you will continue to saw."

"That's a wonderful idea, Mr. Pelch. We still have two hours left to work before the devil wants us back."

"I'll hurry, Mr. Ferrett."

"Thank you, Mr. Pelch."

They worked for hours and hours every day while Mulrooney rested. By the end of the fourth day, Ferrett believed he could see a tiny indentation where the saw blade had nicked the metal, but Pelch seemed dubious. Both men were very unhappy that their plan didn't seem to be working as well as they had hoped.

"If this doesn't work, Mr. Pelch, I don't know what to do," admitted Ferrett.

"I don't either, Mr. Ferrett," said Pelch.

They sat and stared into the starry sky for a few moments without speaking. They had been sawing for hours and it was late.

Pelch sighed. "Still," he said. "You did have this one idea. It was a good one, and it isn't your fault that the iron is difficult. Perhaps you'll have another idea, Mr. Ferrett." Pelch's voice was bracing, as though encouraging his friend to think hard.

Ferrett sighed too. "I thought it was a good idea at the time, Mr. Pelch. I guess it wasn't, though."

"Well, we don't know that yet, Mr. Ferrett. We can still work on it."

"I guess so." Ferrett didn't sound exactly pleased at the thought.

"And you might well think of another good idea too, Mr. Ferrett."

"Maybe," said Ferrett glumly.

Pelch sighed again, deeply.

"Yes," he said.

*   *   *

Even though Jubal had finagled Maggie to himself while in El Paso, he had to take guards with him on the road. It was more than a seven-hour drive in the wagon, and although most of the travel was across his own land and he hadn't heard from Mulrooney for a long time, he didn't believe for a moment that he and Maggie had faded from his enemy's mind. And anybody who remained on Prometheus Mulrooney's mind remained in danger. If Mulrooney's hired thugs chose to attack Jubal on his own land today, it wouldn't be the first time.

Still, the journey was a pleasant one. Maggie's attention was unfettered by concerns for Annie, and she was no longer shy around Jubal—or at any rate, she was not *very* shy around him. Maggie hadn't yet figured out exactly what Jubal Green wanted from her, even though he had proposed marriage. At least she thought he had. It wasn't altogether clear. And she hadn't yet decided what she wanted from him either. She was happy, though. She was very, very happy.

She sat close to Jubal and held his arm. Since it was his right arm she was clutching, she made sure her grip wasn't tight, and she smoothed his flannel shirt every now and again as if to rub away any aches. Jubal smiled at her concern.

"It's all right, Maggie. I like it when you hold me."

"Well, I don't want to squish you. Your shoulder is still too tender for that."

"I don't think you could squish me if you tried," Jubal said with a chuckle.

Maggie pinched one of his large biceps just to test it. It was remarkably hard. "I think you're right."

Her gaze swept the landscape and she hugged Jubal's arm again. "Oh, Lordy, Jubal, just think. When we go home tomorrow I'll be able to see all this. I mean, I'll *really* be able to see it, 'cause I'll have on my new spectacles."

Jubal smiled at her excitement. He felt good too. It did not slip his notice, either, that Maggie had referred to his ranch as "home."

She still hadn't said she'd marry him. Of course, she hadn't said she wouldn't. Then again, he hadn't asked her except that one time, and he wasn't altogether certain that counted since he hadn't actually come right out and said point-blank that he wanted her to be his wife. For the rest of his life. For the rest of her life.

Jubal wasn't sure why the thought of marriage held such terror for him. Probably an heirloom left over from his parents' example, he figured.

As they bumped along in the rough ranch wagon, Maggie chattered happily about the patio and about how much she enjoyed being around Beula. Jubal was surprised that he didn't find her chitchat annoying. He usually didn't enjoy listening to women gab. In fact, he hated it. But Maggie was different. She didn't blither.

After a while, though, Maggie fell silent. She sat on the hard seat and hugged Jubal's arm and looked around her. Jubal noticed that a sigh escaped her occasionally.

After about the fourth sigh, he began to worry about them.

"Is everything all right, Maggie?"

She was a little taken aback at his question. "Of course everything's all right. Everything's just fine."

Jubal frowned slightly. "Then why aren't you talking anymore?"

Maggie looked up at him in surprise. "Why, I don't know. I guess I don't have any more to say."

Jubal scowled down at her. "Then why are you sighing?"

Maggie eyed him for a second or two before answering the question. Then she sighed again.

"I don't know. I guess I'm just thinking about how nice it is to be at your place and to be fixing up your pretty patio and having a friend and Annie having friends and all that. And—and being with you. It's going—well, I guess it's going to be real hard to leave it all." She swallowed hard after that admission.

Jubal's scowl was growing more ferocious by the second. There she went again, rattling on about that blasted farm of hers. At least she'd stopped mentioning her dead husband every other second.

"I wish you'd stop talking about going back," he said grumpily.

Maggie opened her mouth and then shut it again. Her brow furrowed, and she looked a little bit confused.

"Well," she finally said, "I don't guess there's anyplace else I *can* go, is there?"

She sighed again. Of course, she might be willing to consider staying with Jubal Green, if he'd ask her. Maggie had tried and tried to remember what exactly it was he'd said to her the night they arrived, but she couldn't quite put her finger on it, no matter how hard she tried. She was absolutely certain, however, that he hadn't looked at all happy when he said he'd been thinking about marrying her. And he hadn't said it again.

The thought of marrying Jubal Green actually appealed to her a great deal, but she'd be roasted in hell before she'd make him marry her if he was reluctant to do it. Besides, she really did have to go back to Kenny's farm. She was honor-bound to go back. It was Kenny's dream.

Maggie felt ashamed of herself when she realized just how far away from being her own dream Kenny's farm had slipped. In fact, the thought of returning to that place was becoming downright depressing. She sighed yet again but knew she had to do it. The farm was not merely Kenny's dream, it was Annie's legacy.

"Will you quit that?" Jubal was near to shouting now.

"I'm sorry, Jubal. I don't mean to fret you." Tarnation, this man was touchy. Maggie tried to keep her annoyance tamped down.

"And stop apologizing, damn it!"

Maggie didn't know what to say for a second. Then she gave up trying to figure out what he wanted and cried, her voice brittle, "Jubal, I can't help it! I really don't know what to do. I don't want to leave you. I can't give up my farm. I've got to make a decision that I'm going to hate one way or the other. And you won't even let me apologize for making you mad!"

She was kneading her hands together and looking up at him with such a poignant combination of emotions playing on her features that he couldn't stay angry. He realized she was unsure of her future and knew it was his fault. That made him feel bad and he wanted to reassure her. But although he wanted to, he didn't think it was appropriate to declare his intentions right this minute, as they sat together on the hard plank seat of a rough wood wagon, bouncing along through the dust devils on the dry dirt road toward El Paso.

"Aw, Maggie, I didn't mean to be crabby. It just drives me crazy when you talk about leaving me."

Maggie tried to smother the raw pleasure that Jubal's confession evoked. She was afraid he would take the look of glorious relief in her eyes amiss. In her heart of hearts, she was virtually positive that her honor would make her return to that poor farm, but she was ever so pleased to know he'd miss her. She'd miss him for sure. In fact, the thought of living the rest of her life alone on that miserable farm without him was so painful she couldn't even bear to think about it. At least she'd have Annie. She held that thought close to her heart.

"Thank you, Jubal," she said at last. "I'll miss you something awful."

God damn it, thought Jubal. He didn't dare say anything for fear he'd holler her right off the wagon.

Maggie was not reassured by the glare he shot her. It was so full of angry frustration that she was afraid for a moment that he was going to begin yelling at her again, so she decided it would be best not to say anything.

Jubal came to that same conclusion. His own emotions were confusing the hell out of him. At the moment, he was so frustrated he wanted to kick something. He hoped he'd have everything all figured out by tonight.

They rode along in silence for a while, with only the slow crunching of the wheels and the *clop-clop* of the mules to keep their tumbled thoughts company. Maggie squinted into the dry countryside and knew that tomorrow, on her way back to Jubal's ranch, she'd be able to see everything clearly. She tried to concentrate on that happy thought and not on the roiling emotions she felt and the unpleasant decisions she knew she'd have to make once this terrible feud was resolved.

Finally, in order to ease the tension that had begun to weave around them in the dusty warmth of the morning, Jubal said, "When we get to town, I'll check us into the El Paso Hotel and go to the post office while you freshen up. Then I'll take you to Garza's. We can buy most of the things you need for the patio there."

He looked over at Maggie, hoping those promises would perk her up. She'd stopped sighing, but now she was staring straight ahead of her, and she didn't look happy.

"Will that be all right?"

Maggie smiled at him with love shining in her eyes. She'd miss him so darned much, she just wanted to burst into tears. She wouldn't do it, of course. He'd hate that.

"That would be just fine, Jubal. Thank you." He was so nice to her.

Her answer and the way it was given eased his mood a good deal. "Fine. That's fine." He felt better.

As soon as they got to El Paso, Jubal was as good as his word. He checked them into the same wonderful hotel they'd stayed in before. This time, since they were alone, he registered them as Mr. and Mrs. Jubal Green. He didn't ask for Maggie's permission. Besides, he figured, he might just as well get used to it now as wait until they were officially married. The practice surely couldn't hurt.

Maggie was a little shocked when they went upstairs. "We're sharing a room, Jubal?"

He frowned at her. "Shoot, Maggie, we've been sharing a room for two weeks now."

"But nobody knows about it." Her face flushed delightfully.

He grinned at her. "The hell they don't. I got a blistering lecture from Beula just yesterday."

Maggie's mouth dropped open, and her color deepened. "Oh, my land," she whispered. "Oh, my land. Oh, my God, I've never been more embarrassed in my life."

"It's all right, Maggie." Jubal took her gently by the shoulders. "Beula doesn't mind. She understands."

"How on earth can Beula understand when even I don't understand?" cried Maggie. "We're not married. We're not even promised! I'm so ashamed."

Jubal didn't like the shimmer in her eyes. It worried him. That shimmer looked perilously close to tears. He was also irritated by her words.

"What do you mean, you're ashamed? Just what does that mean? You're ashamed to be with me, is that it? I'm not good enough for you? Just what is it you're ashamed of anyway?"

Maggie's surprise at Jubal's suggestion smothered her embarrassment in an instant. "Not good enough for me? What are you talking about, Jubal Green? You're a rich Texas rancher. I'm just poor Indiana trash who was lucky enough to marry a good man who loved me and gave me a farm in the territory and a precious baby. *I'm* the one who's not good enough."

"What?" Jubal's shout made Maggie flinch. "What the hell are you talking about? What in holy hell does that mean, you were lucky enough to be married to a good man who gave you that dratted farm? I'm sick of hearing about how wonderful Kenny was, Maggie. He's dead, damn it."

"I know he's dead, Jubal." At the thought of her sweet dead husband, a painful ache started throbbing in her heart.

"Well, then, quit telling me about him! I'm really tired of it."

Maggie wanted to wipe away the treacherous tears that burned her eyes, but she wasn't able to because Jubal still held her by the shoulders and she couldn't lift her arms.

"Stop squishing my shoulders, Jubal! And I'm sorry. I didn't know you minded."

Jubal squeezed his eyes shut in frustration. "Will you stop apologizing to me every other second?" He was yelling again.

Maggie finally just gave up. She didn't understand any of this. She found her emotions so unsettling that she forgot all about her aunt's admonitions not to make people mad and started hollering. "I'm sorry, Jubal! I'm sorry I'm sorry. I can't help it. I can't help missing Kenny, either. He's the first person on the face of the earth besides my mother who ever loved me. He's the first person on the face of the earth besides my mother who ever cared whether I was happy or not. And I don't even remember my mother half the time!

"Kenny was the first person who ever told me I was worth more than—than a slave. Him, and then Mr. Blue Gully, when I was nursing you. Those are the only two people on the face of this earth who ever said I did anything right! I can't help it if I miss Kenny. I'm sorry if you don't like it, but I can't help it!"

Maggie gulped down a big breath of air. "Kenny

loved me, Jubal!" she cried out. Then she couldn't say anything else, because her words couldn't swim out past the tears that had dammed up behind her anger.

Jubal stared down at her while her words lashed at him, and he suddenly understood Maggie Bright. His hands slid down from her shoulders and around her back, and he pulled her to his chest. His little Maggie.

Jubal wasn't a fanciful man, but all at once his mind's eye painted a vivid picture of what Maggie's life must have been like before Kenny Bright married her. Her aunt and uncle had resented the care of her and used her as an unpaid servant. He could imagine a sweet-tempered little Maggie trying in vain to win a smile or a nod from either one of them, working herself to a frazzle in the attempt, only to be rebuffed time and time again. Small wonder that she apologized for everything. She'd probably grown up apologizing for living. No wonder Kenny Bright had been a saint in her eyes.

Kenny loved me! Her words lacerated Jubal's heart. Kenny loved her. That one fact, all by itself, was enough to bind Maggie to him forever.

"He isn't the only one, Maggie," he said in a gruff whisper.

"Yes, he was."

"No, Maggie. He wasn't."

Jubal took a deep breath, expelled it before he could use it, then swore viciously at himself, called himself every kind of coward, and berated himself for a fool. When he was through doing that, he sucked in another huge breath and said, before he could lose his courage again, "I love you, Maggie. Kenny Bright wasn't the only one. I love you too."

Maggie didn't hear him. She was so upset she could

only shake her head miserably against his chest and run through the catalog of her sins, sins Aunt Lucy had drummed into her head until Maggie sometimes wondered why the good Lord let her live, she was so awful.

Jubal wondered why she was shaking her head and wondered if she'd heard him. So he said it a little louder. "Kenny wasn't the only one, Maggie. I love you too."

His words penetrated her misery very slowly. In fact, she was so busy telling herself how unlovable she was that at first she was sure she hadn't heard him correctly.

Then he said it yet again.

"I love you, Maggie. I tried to get over it, but I couldn't. I love you so much I can hardly stand it. I love you so much it hurts."

She pulled away from him a little bit and noticed the big wet spot on his shirt. She brushed her hand over it as if to wipe it dry. Her hand, of course, had no effect at all on his shirt, so she used it to swipe at her wet cheeks.

"You—you what?" she whispered. She was still sure she couldn't have heard him right.

But Jubal didn't want her looking at him right now. This was hard enough without having her stare at him while he made such a difficult confession. He yanked her to his chest again and put his big hand over her head to hold her there.

Maggie didn't mind. Her arms went around him and she squeezed him tight.

"At first I didn't know what was wrong with me," he said. His voice was hoarse and he had to keep clearing his throat. "I figured it was just because I was gun-shot and weak. I thought it would go away, this funny feeling about you. But it didn't. It was while we were eating in the restaurant downstairs that I finally figured it out."

He stopped talking. But Maggie wanted to hear it again. She wanted to be sure he'd said what she thought he'd said.

"What"—she had to clear her throat too—"what did you figure out, Jubal?"

Her head was tucked neatly under his chin, but he drew it back a little bit so he could look down at her. He thought she was teasing him. When he saw her tear-stained face, swollen eyes, and expression of utter incredulity, he realize she wasn't teasing. He hugged her tight again.

"I figured out that it wasn't just being gun-shot and weak and sick. It was love."

In spite of her recent fit of anger and tears, Maggie couldn't help giggling a little bit.

"You mean loving me was like being sick?" Her voice was shaky.

Jubal's brow began to furrow. "It's not funny, Maggie. I'd never been in love before. I didn't know what it felt like."

Maggie's heart soared like the proverbial eagle. She tightened her arms around him so hard that Jubal grunted. Then, out of deference for her beloved and because she didn't want to annoy him, she tried not to laugh. She wanted to shout and sing and holler. He was in love with her! Jubal Green loved her, Maggie Bright!

"Do—do you really mean it, Jubal?" she asked in a quivery voice. She realized that was the wrong thing to ask when he scowled at her.

"I'm sorry, I didn't mean to doubt you." Then Maggie remembered how much he hated her to apologize, and she blurted out, "I didn't mean that. I'm not sorry. I'm—oh, I don't know what I am. I'm happy! That's what I am. I'm happy, Jubal Green. I'm happy."

And she burst into tears again.

Jubal sighed and hugged her hard. He'd never understand women as long as he lived.

He did, however, know what to do with a woman when she was in his arms, particularly when the woman was Maggie. Her breasts were crushed against him and driving him crazy. She was such a perfect little armful. He decided that now they had the issue of who loved whom out of the way, it was time to offer a little demonstration.

Maggie slowly became aware that the way he was holding her had undergone a subtle change. Instead of holding her tight, as if to comfort her, his hands began to make delicious swirling caresses on her back and down her arms. He reached up and slid his fingers through her hair, loosening all the pins. His fingers sent tingling shivers ricocheting from her scalp to her toes. He pulled her hairpins out one by one and laid them on the bedside table.

"I love your hair down, Maggie." Then he remembered something that had been shimmering in the recesses of his consciousness for a month or more. "I remember seeing you standing by the window brushing your hair when I was so sick. I thought you were an angel."

Maggie's laugh was a little watery. She used Jubal's shirt to wipe her cheeks. It was already sopping wet; she didn't suppose it mattered much.

"You asked me if I was an angel," she whispered.

Her smile was terribly tender as she unbuttoned his shirt.

"What did you say when I asked you that?"

Jubal was working on her shirtwaist buttons while she unfastened his shirt. His chest went all over gooseflesh with the feel of her hands on his skin.

"I told you I wasn't an angel, just a poor widow woman who was trying to help you get better."

Jubal shook his head. His warm hands sent shivers of pleasure shooting through Maggie's body when he smoothed her shirtwaist over her arms. Then he slipped the straps of her chemise down. When his hands covered her breasts, Maggie groaned with delight.

"You were wrong, Maggie. You *are* an angel. You're *my* angel."

"Thank you, Jubal." Maggie sighed. She began to nibble her way across his broad chest, to the accompaniment of his growl of pleasure.

When she tentatively tongued his hard nipple, he decided it was time to get down to business. He quickly unbuttoned her skirt and untied the tapes to her petticoat and drawers. They lay as they fell when he picked her up and deposited her on the bed. Then he quickly shed his boots, trousers, and underwear and joined her.

Maggie didn't know anything about being an angel, but she was pretty sure that making love with Jubal was as close to heaven as she'd ever get in this lifetime. His touch sent her soaring, and when they were joined in the timeless rhythm of love, he rocketed her higher and higher until she exploded in a starburst of pleasure. She called out to him just before she went over the edge into bliss, wanting him to join her there.

He did. He'd never experienced anything like it, this loving with Maggie. The confession of love he'd made to her, the one wrung out of him against his will that he had been sure would weaken him, instead seemed to free him. He was free to give her all his passion and all his love, and to receive all hers with joy. When he heard her call to him and felt the ripples that meant she was almost there, he couldn't hold back any longer. He soared with her, knowing it couldn't get any better than this.

It took them a long time to recover. Maggie's contractions seemed to go on forever. Every one of them was an affirmation of love to Jubal. She was his. She was his and nobody could take her away from him. Not Prometheus Mulrooney, not society's restrictions, and not the dead though admittedly good Kenny Bright. She was his. The knowledge made his heart swell until he was sure it would burst with the fullness of emotion.

Maggie, of course, was crying. This time, though, she was also trying to talk to him.

"Oh, Jubal, I love you so much. I didn't think I could ever love anybody again. I didn't think I could ever love anybody like this. I didn't know what it was like."

At least, Jubal thought that's what she was saying. It was hard to understand her words, since they were drowned in tears and being muttered in between the breathy kisses she was tattooing onto his chest and cheeks. Her hands were almost convulsively gripping his muscled arms. Jubal smiled when he realized that, even through her haze of passion, Maggie was very, very careful not to touch his bullet scar.

"Oh, Maggie, I love you so much it hurts," he whispered into her hair.

She kissed him passionately.

It was a funny thing, but now that he had finally admitted to having succumbed to the weakness of love, it didn't bother him anymore. In fact, he found that he enjoyed speaking the words to her. Of course, the way she reacted when he said them helped some.

"I love you, Maggie," he murmured once more.

She kissed him again.

He grinned with satisfaction. This love stuff might not be so bad after all.

"Better start thinking about our wedding, Maggie Bright, because we're getting married as soon as I can arrange it."

The glowing smile Maggie gave him nearly knocked him flat. She was an angel. He didn't care how absurd it sounded. He knew she was an angel. His angel. His very own personal angel.

"The patio," Maggie whispered. "We can be married on the patio. With flowers."

It took Jubal a while to get dressed to go to the post office, since he and Maggie had a lot of hugging to do before he left, but he finally managed to get himself out of the hotel room. He stopped by the front desk to order a bath for Maggie before he went to the restaurant and arranged for their evening meal. It was to be their engagement party, for just the two of them, and he intended it to be special.

As for Maggie, she washed and dressed slowly. She had to stop what she was doing every once in a while just so she could think about the astounding turn her life had taken.

"I'm sorry, Kenny," she whispered. "I loved you. I

really did love you. I still do. You were so wonderful to me. I hope you don't mind that I love Jubal too."

Maggie wasn't a philosopher; her life had held no room for such impracticalities. But she did harbor a deep respect in her heart for the spirit of her departed husband. She'd always sort of savored the idea that Kenny's spirit was still around somewhere, looking after Annie and her.

It might have been her imagination that whispered reassurance to her in the hotel room, so softly she couldn't really hear. It might have been her hopeful heart, telling her that Kenny was happy for her, that he was glad she had found somebody to take care of her and Annie. But Maggie didn't think so.

"Thank you, Kenny," she murmured through her happy tears.

18

Jubal felt like the lowest kind of snake. He didn't know how on earth he was going to tell Maggie that her farm was gone and it was because of him. He walked slowly back to the hotel, wondering if there wasn't something he could bring to her, some gift he could give her, that might soften the blow.

Even before he completed the thought, though, he knew what the answer was. There was nothing he could do but simply tell the truth. Anything less would be a lie. Anything more would be a bribe.

God, please help me, he thought. It was the first time in years that Jubal had uttered a prayer.

His heart ached when he opened the door to their room and saw her. Maggie had bathed and washed her wild-honey hair and was dressed in the best dress she owned. Jubal was surprised at the sudden ferocious impulse he felt to snatch her away with him, find the best dressmaker in El Paso, and buy her pretty things. He knew she'd never had anything, and he found himself wanting to make up for a lifetime of poverty and want right now, this minute. He knew he was being irrational.

Maggie ran into his arms. Until now, she hadn't known it was possible to be this happy to see somebody who'd only been gone an hour or so. She felt renewed, having made her peace with Kenny. Now she wanted only to begin her new life, free and happy, with Jubal Green.

When she was finally willing to let him go, she stepped back and looked up into his face, and her shining smile dimmed. "What's the matter, Jubal?"

Her heart began thudding in a painful cadence. She recognized that look. It was a bad-news look, and it frightened her.

"Is everything all right?"

Frantically, she ran through the possibilities, trying to determine what could have put that look on Jubal's face. She knew everybody on the ranch was all right. They'd just left them this morning. She wondered if he had any relatives she didn't know about who might have died. Maybe a stock-market crash had affected the price of cattle.

Jubal cleared his throat. "There's a letter from Sadie Phillips for you."

Maggie's sudden golden smile almost broke his heart. She grabbed the edge of the envelope, but Jubal didn't release it.

"I have to tell you something first." He figured Sadie would have written Maggie about the fire.

Maggie looked up at him uncertainly. This was odd behavior for Jubal. He usually wasn't hesitant about things. He got happy fast and he got mad fast and he got over it fast.

"What's the matter, Jubal?"

Jubal cleared his throat again. "It's your farm, Maggie," he said softly.

Maggie's eyes widened, and the expression that crossed her face made Jubal want to shut his own eyes against it. It was an expression of heartbreaking fear, and if he didn't already hate Prometheus Mulrooney for everything else he'd done, he would have hated the man for making Maggie's face look like that. He figured he'd best just get it over with.

"Mulrooney burned everything down."

Maggie's mouth dropped open. Jubal released the letter, and she blinked up at him for a second or two. Then she walked numbly to the bed, sat down, opened the envelope with great care, and read Sadie's words without uttering a sound.

Jubal knew enough about Sadie Phillips to realize that the letter was probably chock-full of exaggeration, and he swallowed hard and tried not to be angry with her.

Maggie read the letter twice. Sure enough, the farm was gone. Even when she took into consideration Sadie's extreme emotionalism and love of drama, Maggie could tell that her farm was lost forever. Kenny's farm. Kenny's dream. It had been burned to the ground. The newly repaired chicken coop, the brand-new goat pen, the shed, the fence, the house itself: everything was gone.

She could picture the little clearing in her mind, but she couldn't make herself envision the charred remains that must be all that was left of her former life, an ashen pile of rubble sitting alone and forlorn in the pretty green woods. Bright's Creek would still be bubbling and splashing as it rambled merrily along past the blackened ruins of her home.

A tear slid down her cheek as she stared with unseeing eyes across the room. She didn't see the hotel wall, decorated with its elaborately framed painting of Niagara Falls. She saw Kenny's farm, bright in the sunlight of an early spring morning, always warm, always welcoming, no matter how tired she was, no matter how worn down or discouraged, the first real home she ever had.

Jubal watched her for what seemed like forever. Then he couldn't stand it any longer. He took a step toward her and she looked up at him.

God damn Prometheus Mulrooney to eternal hell; the words passed through his mind. And God damn me for making Maggie go through this.

When Maggie saw the look on Jubal's face, she was afraid he would be angry because she was sad that her farm had burned down. She didn't want him to think she loved him less because his enemy had hurt her. She wanted to apologize to him.

"I'm sorry—" she began.

Then she stopped. He hated apologies too. Maggie didn't know what to say. She just sat still and silent as tears flowed down her cheeks. She had never felt so helpless, worthless, and unhappy. Practically everything she had ever loved had been burned to the ground and now lay in ashes, and she didn't know what to do or say or think.

"Oh, God, Maggie," Jubal whispered, as he bent to hold her. When Maggie shook him off, he was sure his heart would break. He wanted to cradle her in his arms and rock her as one might rock a hurt child.

"No, Jubal. Please don't touch me right now."

So he backed away from her. His chest ached with the longing to love and comfort her, and dread began to coil up from his belly like a venomous black snake.

Oh, God, Maggie, don't turn away from me now. Not now, when we've just found each other.

He didn't know how long they stayed like that, Maggie sitting on the bed, staring at the wall in front of her, and Jubal leaning against the far wall, watching her, wanting her, aching for her. Every now and then, a shudder would ripple through her body, and Jubal's fists clenched with each one of those shudders, as if he longed to slay the monster of unhappiness that had invaded their room.

They both became aware of Jubal's muttering at the same time. Jubal hadn't realized he'd been speaking, and Maggie hadn't been listening.

But slowly his words penetrated the fog of unhappiness that surrounded them. "I'm sorry, Maggie. It's my fault. I'm so sorry. I'm sorry."

Maggie couldn't stand to hear him sound so unhappy. She looked up at him. Poor Jubal, she thought. He wants so much to help.

But there wasn't any help he could give her. There wasn't anything he could do that he hadn't already done. The reality of her life, that she was back to having nothing but herself and her baby, settled like a cloak of mourning around her shoulders.

"It's not your fault," she whispered.

Jubal didn't know what to say. He wished like the devil that he possessed a glib tongue. But he didn't.

Finally he said the only thing that he could think of: "Please let me hold you, Maggie."

His words, propelled by infinite love, managed to

slither through tiny cracks in Maggie's wall of loneliness. It occurred to her that perhaps she wasn't as alone as she had at first felt herself to be. She gave him the tiniest of smiles.

"It's not your fault," she whispered again.

He seemed positively angry at that. "It is too, Maggie. If it weren't for me, you'd still have your pretty little farm. You saved my life, and this is the result."

"But if you hadn't come to my door, I'd never have loved you, Jubal," she said softly. Then she gave him a real smile and patted the bed next to her.

Jubal said a prayer of gratitude before he slowly covered the space between them and sat down next to her. Very carefully, he wrapped his arms around her and felt her slump into his embrace. He couldn't remember the last time he had cried, but tears stung his eyes now.

"Will you marry me, Maggie? Will you marry me today, right now? I swear to God I'll never let anything else ever happen to you."

"Thank you, Jubal."

That didn't sound like a "yes" to him, and he glanced at her sharply. His heart was still doing crazy things in his chest, and a sudden horrifying thought that she was going to say no surged through him. She couldn't leave him now. He wouldn't let her!

"Well?" he asked. It came out as a demand.

Maggie took a deep, shuddering breath. "You don't have to marry me, Jubal."

His eyes widened. "What?" He was sure he'd misunderstood her.

With another deep sigh, Maggie said, "You don't have to marry me."

He drew away from her a little bit so that he could

look at her face. He couldn't quite believe she'd said what he'd just heard. "What do you mean?" This didn't make any sense to him. None at all.

"Oh, Jubal, please don't feel guilty. You couldn't help what happened any more than I could. It's not your fault, and I'm not going to marry you just because you feel guilty. I—I couldn't do that."

"*What*?" The word was sharp and ricocheted in the room like a bullet.

Maggie winced, and he squeezed her again and tried to calm down.

Very carefully, he composed himself so he wouldn't yell and said softly, "I don't want to marry you because I feel guilty, Maggie. I want to marry you because I love you. I can't even stand to think about living without you." Upon another deep, calming breath, he said, "Please marry me, Maggie. Please marry me because I love you and you love me." He was very proud of himself for sounding so calm when he wanted to shake her until her teeth rattled and then holler at her.

Maggie drew back a little bit and gazed up at him, doubt clouding her expression. He looked sincere. In fact, he looked very sincere. He also looked as though he wanted to strangle her. The combination actually made her want to chuckle.

She thought about asking if he truly meant it. Then she remembered how touchy he was and decided that for once in her life, and in spite of Aunt Lucy's many lessons to the contrary, she'd believe something nice that somebody said to her. The good Lord knew, she wanted to believe Jubal Green right now.

"All right, Jubal. I'll marry you. I'd love to marry you. Thank you."

She had begun to stroke his chest lightly, sending bolts of heat through him, and he tried to suppress his uncivilized reaction to her touch. It didn't matter. He was hard as an oak log in a second.

Her words did make him feel better, though, and he no longer felt like shaking her. "Good," he whispered.

"But I want my baby to be there, Jubal, and Dan and Four Toes and Sadie Phillips, and Beula. I want to marry you on your pretty patio after it's fixed up. I—I never had a pretty wedding. I always sort of dreamed about it."

Jubal was frowning at her, and she got a little worried.

"Do you mind?" she asked in a tiny voice.

Jubal didn't answer her for a minute. When he did, his voice was rough with emotion. It was a voice Maggie had never heard before.

"I don't want to wait, Maggie. I want you to be my wife as soon as we can get it done. If anything happens to me, I want to be damned sure you're taken care of."

The sudden surge of fear that shot through Maggie at the thought of something happening to Jubal made her forget his wound. She squeezed his arm so tight that he grunted in pain. Then she let him go and rubbed his sore scar gently.

"Nothing will happen to you, Jubal," she whispered, as though she hoped it was true.

"You don't know that. It's not an idle consideration." Jubal's voice was fierce. He wanted to quell any arguments she might come up with. "Mulrooney burned your farm down because of me. It's me he wants. He could kill Dan and Four Toes and me, and then you'd be left all alone with Annie and no place to call home, no money, and nobody to take care of you. I can't let that happen. I *won't* let that happen." He held her close to his chest as though afraid she'd bolt if he let her go.

As Maggie sat next to Jubal, her thoughts whirred and stumbled over one another. She'd never lived through such an emotionally crazy day in her life. Her fingers stroked his cheek, and she felt the stubble of his quick-growing beard. She inhaled a deep breath and smelled him, warm and male and wonderful.

"All right, Jubal," she whispered.

She still needed to go back to her farm, but she didn't have the energy now to deal with that problem. Besides, she was sure Jubal wouldn't understand this particular need of hers: to see her home, to apologize to it, to say good-bye, to look for one last time upon the earthly resting place of her beloved Kenny.

Jubal expelled a huge sigh of relief. "You'll marry me? Right now?"

"Yes."

He held her close and rested his chin on her head. It took him a little while to realize he was breathing a prayer of thanks. It was the third prayer he'd uttered this day.

"Jubal?" Maggie's voice was so soft, he could barely hear her.

"Yes, love?"

"Even though we get married today, can we still have a ceremony on the patio when it's ready? Sort of a party or something, and ask our friends?"

Our friends. Jubal smiled at that. Until he'd met Maggie, he'd never even considered himself as having friends. She'd made both his heart and his eyes open wide, though, and he realized just how blessed he was, in spite of the feud that still threatened everything he was and everything he had.

"Yes, Maggie," he said, with an almost painful welling of love in his chest. "We can have a party on the patio and invite our friends."

She snuggled up closer. "Thank you."

"But we'd better get this over with right now, or we're never going to get out of this hotel room."

Jubal set Maggie on the floor very gently and stood up. She straightened her hair and pinned it back into a knot on her head while he tucked in his shirt and tidied himself up some. He put on a vest and a black string tie and wished he'd thought to bring along a better-looking jacket. He consoled himself with the thought that he'd dress up properly for his bride when she held her party on the patio.

Once they were ready, they located a judge and secured a license. Then Jubal said they'd have to find a wedding band.

"We can use this one, Jubal," Maggie said, fingering the thin gold band she'd worn for the past four years. It was worn down from hard work, but Maggie loved it and knew she could never let it go completely.

"You're going to be *my* wife now, Maggie," Jubal told her. He was making a great effort to hold his annoyance at bay. Maggie's feelings were still too fragile to contend with his anger; he knew that, but it was a struggle to behave himself.

He sucked in a deep, calming breath and continued.

"I'm not going to tell you to stop caring for Kenny Bright. I know you loved him. But I'll be damned if you're going to wear his ring on your finger after today."

Maggie turned Kenny's ring around and around on her finger and stared at it for a long time. Jubal held his breath. Finally, she looked up at him and smiled.

"All right, Jubal."

She hugged his arm tight as they strolled along the dusty plank walkway that had been laid to protect the ladies of El Paso from having to slog through sloppy mud on rainy days.

Jubal directed them into a jeweler's shop that wasn't very far away from Garza's mercantile establishment. The jeweler was a Chinaman, which Maggie found fascinating. She'd never seen an Oriental in the flesh before, and the deep gash of sorrow in her heart was forgotten momentarily in her interest at this phenomenon.

When Jubal told the merchant the nature of their errand, the man offered them a silky smile and brought forth a tray of rings.

Maggie stared at the dazzling display of gold before her for so long that Jubal finally had to nudge her.

"What do you think, Maggie?" He picked up an elaborate model that was bedecked with diamonds. "You like this one?"

Maggie gazed at the ring with awe. It looked like a cluster of infinitesimal stars shimmering between Jubal's big brown fingers, and it was entirely too splendid.

"I can't imagine wearing that, Jubal. It's too fine."

When her beloved's forehead crinkled up and she saw a frown forming, she hastened to add, "It's not that I don't like it, Jubal, it's just that I'd feel funny wearing anything so—so big. I'd like something simpler. I'd be worried to death all the time if I wore that one."

Maggie shook her head, envisioning herself on her hands and knees scrubbing tiles on the patio and wearing the elaborate work of art that was presently clutched tightly in Jubal's fingers. That ring was meant for a princess, not for Maggie Bright—Maggie Green, she corrected herself, with a surge of real pleasure in her heart.

"I want to get you something nice, Maggie," Jubal told her fiercely. "I can afford it, and you're worth it," he added, just in case she had any questions about either of those circumstances.

"Thank you, Jubal." She gave his arm a quick squeeze and went back to eyeballing the tray. It was odd, she thought, how happiness and sorrow could live together in a person's heart, neither emotion interfering with the other.

Her eye kept straying back to one particular ring, and her fingers hovered over it. She felt funny about boldly picking it up to scrutinize it. She wished she had her eyeglasses, but Jubal wanted to get married before they did anything else in town. The jeweler spared her the decision.

"Very pretty ring," he announced, and plucked it out of its velvet sheath and held it before her.

"You like that one?" Jubal's expression was mighty dubious as he eyed the ring. It seemed awfully plain to him. It was fashioned out of three thin, flat bands of gold woven together. That was all. No diamonds sparkled from its braid. No jewels glistened from its coils.

Maggie peered hard at the band, wishing again that she had her eyeglasses. "Yes," she said. "I like that one a lot."

"You're sure?"

He was a little disappointed. He'd been hoping she'd
go for something more flashy. He realized that was
silly of him, though. This was Maggie. This wasn't
any other woman he'd ever known in his life. He
decided he approved and took the ring out of the jeweler's hand and slipped it onto Maggie's finger. It fit
perfectly, so he took it right off again.

"Sold," he told the man.

Maggie almost fainted when she heard how much
the ring cost, but Jubal handed over the fifty-five dollars without so much as a flinch. She found herself
wondering just how much money Jubal Green had
that he could part with such a sum without batting an
eye.

Then they went back to the judge's office. Maggie
surreptitiously slipped Kenny's ring off of her finger,
pressed it once against her heart, and put it into her
skirt pocket. She was unprepared for the sudden
aching pang she felt. But the spirit of Kenny Bright,
or her imagination, gently told her everything was all
right. She wasn't being disloyal.

Fifteen minutes later, she and Jubal were strolling
along the plank walkway to Mr. Whitney's arm in
arm, Mr. and Mrs. Jubal Green. All thoughts of dis-
loyalty gone from her heart, Maggie stared at the
beautiful new ring on her finger until she stumbled.

Jubal laughed. "Better watch where you're going,
Mrs. Green," he said. "I can only hold up one side of
you on a public street."

Maggie blushed and smiled up at him. "Mrs. Green,"
she said with a sigh. "It sounds so strange."

Jubal was surprised at how wonderful he felt when
he looked down into her pretty blue eyes and realized
she was his, now and forever. His wife. His Maggie.

His hand closed over hers where she held his arm.

"I love you, Maggie," he whispered into her ear.

Mr. Whitney seemed pleased when they told him their news. "Why, congratulations, Mr. Green. It's a shame your parents can't be here to meet your bride."

Jubal's smile soured a little bit. "Yes," was all he said.

Mr. Whitney seemed to take special care when he tested the fit of Maggie's eyeglasses. The wire branches tucked snugly behind her ears. Jubal was afraid they'd hurt her, but she assured him they didn't. Still, he commanded Mr. Whitney to be absolutely certain that his wife's tender ears wouldn't be pinched by the wires.

"That's why we put rubber tips on them, Mr. Green. See?" Mr. Whitney held up the spectacles with a smile that told Maggie he wasn't offended by Jubal's concern.

"Well, all right." Jubal bestowed a frown upon him to let him know he'd be held personally accountable if Maggie's ears began to hurt.

Maggie thought her heart might just burst when she stepped out of the optician's store with her new spectacles perched on her nose. She could see! She looked at the town and then she looked at her ring and then she looked at her husband.

Jubal eyed her with concern. "Don't go to crying on me, Maggie. Not here on the street."

"I won't, Jubal. I promise."

And she looked around some more. She was surprised at how scruffy the place looked now that she could see it. Before, all of life's rough, ragged edges had sort of blurred together softly. Now she could see every scarred board, every filmy window, every bullet-pocked wall in the rough frontier town. It was beautiful, though. She loved it all. She didn't allow the painful thought that she would never be able to see Bright's Farm clearly take root and spoil her mood.

She was squeezing Jubal's arm tightly as she peered around, and he was hard pressed to keep from laughing in delight. His Maggie. His little wife.

She only came up to his shoulder, and even though she wasn't as bone-thin as she'd been when he'd first collapsed into her life, she was still small. Her shiny, dark-honey hair was knotted up on top of her head, and she had an absurd little flowered hat pinned to the knot. Her wire-rimmed spectacles perched upon her pretty nose so sweetly that he wanted to kiss the tip of that precious nose.

Maggie's gaze swept the town before her once more, and when she looked up at Jubal she was positively beaming.

"Oh, Jubal, it's all so wonderful."

"Good."

An expression of concern suddenly crossed her face. "Do I look funny, Jubal? Tell me if I look funny. I don't want you to think I look funny."

Jubal wanted to pick her up and swing her around, she was such a darling. "You look beautiful, Maggie. You're perfect."

"Oh, I'm not," Maggie cried in delight. She blushed and smiled with embarrassment.

They spent a long time in Garza's. Maggie was so thrilled at being able to see clearly for the first time in her life that she spent a lot of time just looking at things.

Jubal didn't mind. In fact, he was so pleased with himself, her, the day, and life in general he couldn't stop smiling. He just let her roam. Any time it looked as though she especially liked something, he bought it for her. He didn't let her know that, of course, or she would have objected. He just motioned to a clerk, who gladly followed the couple on their rounds through the store, carrying the items Jubal pointed out over to a counter and keeping a running tally of the prices.

Jubal understood that fairy story now, the one about the prince and the beggar maid. Not, he reminded himself firmly, that Maggie was a beggar maid, far from it. His little Maggie was as tough as uncooked grits and he loved her to death. Still, it felt so good to be able to buy her things that he wasn't about to deny himself the pleasure.

As they meandered around the huge store, Jubal saw something that struck him as exactly what Maggie needed. It hit him like a flash, and the thought of it both pleased him and made his heart ache a little bit. But he knew it would make Maggie happy, and that's what counted. He picked it up, but this one item he didn't hand to the clerk.

By the time they were ready to leave, Jubal made an excuse to leave Maggie for a moment. He left his wife mulling over fabrics while he paid for everything. Then he tucked that one particular item into his shirt pocket and arranged with the clerk to have the rest of his surreptitious pile of goods sent to his ranch. When he rejoined Maggie, he was feeling like the cat in the cream pot.

"Your patio is going to look so pretty," Maggie told him with excitement quivering in her voice, as they left the store.

She was clutching a brown parcel full of green calico

that Jubal had forced her to buy because she liked it. She planned to make dresses for Annie and Connie Todd with it. She thought the green would look fine with Connie's red hair.

"It's *our* patio now, Mrs. Green," he reminded her.

Maggie glanced up at him with such love that he nearly keeled over under the force of it. "That's right, it is."

They shared a beautiful dinner at their hotel. Jubal ordered a bottle of iced champagne.

"I've never had champagne before," Maggie confessed.

Somehow that didn't surprise Jubal any.

"To us, Mrs. Green." He tipped his glass toward his wife and she clinked hers to his.

"It tickles," she said with a giggle, after her first sip.

Jubal only smiled at her. Maggie had left her spectacles in the hotel room because she wanted to look pretty for him, and the soft candlelight in the restaurant was dancing in her blue eyes. The flickering flames gave her face a soft rosy glow, and Jubal didn't think he'd ever seen anyone as lovely as his new bride was this evening. And her loveliness had nothing to do with the presence or absence of spectacles.

She was all he'd ever wanted. That knowledge hit him like a punch in the gut. Maggie was all the softness and goodness and love he'd never had, and he only now realized how much he needed it. He shook his head with the wonder of it all.

"Are you happy, Maggie?" he asked softly.

"Oh, yes, Jubal."

"So am I."

Jubal had been saving his next surprise, the surprise he had found in Garza's. He decided this was

the time, in the soft light of the evening candles and
their love. A little clumsily, he reached into his breast
pocket, took out a little box, and handed it to her.

"What's this?"

Maggie had never been given so many things in her
life, and she felt funny about it. Still, she couldn't stop
her flush of pleasure.

"Open it, Maggie. It's for you." Jubal felt silly after
he'd said that. Whom else could it be for?

So Maggie did as he commanded, opened the tiny
box, and peered at the slender golden chain that lay on
its velvet bed. Then she looked up at Jubal, curiosity
making her eyes shine.

"It's lovely, Jubal." She wasn't sure what she was
supposed to do with it.

Jubal cleared his throat. "I thought you could put
your old ring on it and wear it around your neck."

"Oh, Jubal." Maggie couldn't whisper more than
those two words because her throat closed up with
emotion. Her fingers trembled when she picked up
the chain and slipped Kenny Bright's ring—the ring
she had tucked into the pocket of her evening dress—
onto it.

Jubal felt awkward when he pushed his chair back
and surged to his feet, but he wanted to clasp the chain
around her neck.

"Here, Maggie," he said gruffly. "Let me."

Maggie was embarrassed by two tears that trickled
down her cheeks. She tried to wipe them with her
napkin before Jubal could catch her crying yet again.

"Thank you so much, Jubal."

His fingers were warm on her shoulders as he clasped
the chain, and she instinctively brushed her cheek
against the back of his hand.

"I'm sorry about your farm, Maggie," Jubal whispered into her hair before he returned to his chair.

Maggie's heart gave a flinch of pain that lasted only an instant. Her farm. She still needed to go back to her farm. The smile she gave him was wistful.

"I have you now, Jubal," she said. "I have you and Annie. I guess I don't need that old farm." She fingered her golden chain adorned with Kenny's ring and smiled at him with so much love that Jubal felt an unfamiliar sting behind his own eyes. For a minute the appalling thought that he might burst into tears assailed him. He didn't, though.

Instead, when their wedding meal was over, he took his wife upstairs and they consummated their marriage with sweet and tender passion. Jubal loved Maggie until she thought she was going to shatter into a million pieces with the splendor of it. He was sure he'd never walk again.

"I love you, Maggie Green," he whispered as they cuddled into sleep.

"I love you too, Jubal."

"I wish there was something we could do about it, Mr. Pelch," said Ferrett miserably. He chewed on his fingernails and looked as though he was about to cry.

"So do I, Mr. Ferrett," whispered Pelch. "But if we send a warning, we're sure to be found out. You know we can't do anything without that devil finding out about it."

Ferrett shook his head sadly. "That's so, Mr. Pelch."

The two men sat in silence and listened to the wheels of the train as it sped through the night, away from the New Mexico Territory on its way to the state of Texas. They would be in El Paso the following day.

"I feel like a murderer, Mr. Ferrett," murmured Pelch.

"So do I, Mr. Pelch."

"If there were only some way we could warn them!" cried Pelch.

Ferrett seemed to be barely holding his tears in check. "How many saw blades did we buy, Mr. Pelch?" he asked.

"Fifteen, Mr. Ferrett."

"And how many do we have left?"

"Twelve."

Ferrett sighed. "I wish we could see some progress, Mr. Pelch."

"So do I, Mr. Ferrett. So do I."

19

The wagon full of Jubal's gifts for Maggie, as well as a note from him telling his ranch friends about their marriage, arrived before Maggie and Jubal did. When they got home, Maggie was nearly over-whelmed with the greeting they received.

Beula and Codfish Todd stood at the gate, with lit-tle Connie and Henry, Jr., flanking them. Beula held Annie in her arms. The children were spanking clean, as Beula had scrubbed their freckled faces until they gleamed in the afternoon sunlight.

Dan Blue Gully and Four Toes Smith were dressed in identical blue suits with identical black string ties. Julio Mendez, the wrangler, wore clean denim trousers over his lean bowed legs, and even old Jesus Chavez had dressed for the occasion, in loose-fitting white cotton trousers and shirt with a colorful serape thrown over his shoulders.

Sammy Napolitano looked elegant in his black suit and hat. His security forces, those who weren't out on the range guarding the ranch, were lined up in a double row beside him. They stood at attention with their rifles held at their sides and looked extremely well organized and official.

Garza's mercantile wagon sat like a load of treasure beside the gate, awaiting the arrival of Mr. and Mrs. Jubal Green.

When Jubal's own wagon pulled into view, the cheering started, and it didn't stop until he had reined the mules to a stop in front of the hollering throng. He looked frightfully abashed. Maggie was blushing. Her new eyeglasses twinkled in the sunlight and seemed to fascinate Annie when Beula handed her up to her mother.

"All right, what's going on? Who's doing the work if you all are standing around out here?" Jubal tried to sound grumpy, but he didn't quite succeed.

Dan, Four Toes, and Beula only laughed.

"I swear, I didn't think that man would ever fall, but now it looks as though he's taken about the biggest tumble I've ever seen," said Dan with a huge grin to the company in general. He walked up to the wagon and all but pulled Jubal out of it, shook his hand so hard that Jubal flinched, and then hugged him.

"Take it easy, Danny. I'm a wounded man."

"Like hell." Dan turned to help Maggie out of the wagon.

"Congratulations, Mrs. Green," he said with a grin.

"Thank you, Mr. Blue Gully." Maggie was very happy when Dan lifted her to stand beside her new husband. She didn't even mind when Annie's busy little fingers smeared her new spectacles.

"What did I tell you?" Beula nearly smothered Annie with a hug to her bosom.

Jubal shook hands with everybody and thanked them. He was not used to thanking people any more than he was used to apologizing, but he did it with grace and goodwill.

"We're going to have a party as soon as my wife fixes up the place," he announced.

"Looks like you got the goods to do it," said Dan wryly as he nodded toward the wagon.

Jubal was a little self-conscious. "That's Maggie's wedding present," he mumbled.

"What?" Maggie hadn't even noticed the mercantile wagon loaded to the top with goods. She stared at it now with amazement.

She was embarrassed to death. She was also so pleased she could hardly speak when she realized what her husband had done.

"My Lord in heaven, Jubal Green, what on earth did you get all that for?"

In spite of a flash of embarrassment, Jubal was pleased as punch. "I wanted to surprise you, Maggie."

"Well, you did that, all right." She laughed.

Her view was marred by two little fingers, as Annie again poked at her glasses.

"Stop that, Annie."

Annie's little mouth puckered up, and Maggie was ashamed of herself. Here she had gone away and left her baby all by herself with a bunch of strangers and then she'd come back married, and now she was getting mad at Annie for wondering about the two shiny pieces of glass sitting atop her mama's nose.

"I'm sorry, baby. These are Mama's new spectacles.

You musn't touch them, because they help Mama see," she explained.

"Speckles," said Annie. She removed her fingers from the lenses and merely pointed at them.

Jubal laughed. "That's right, little parsnip. Those are your mama's spectacles."

Annie had apparently forgotten all about Jubal. But when he spoke to her she seemed to decide she needed him to hold her. She held out her chubby little arms to him and said, "Juba!"

"Yes, Annie." His voice sounded a little choked.

"Jubal's your pa now, Annie," Connie announced. Connie had her mother's definite way about her, and her voice was firm.

"Pa?" Annie eyed Jubal speculatively. "Dat Juba," she said with a frown.

Jubal hugged her. "I don't care what you call me, parsnip," he said. "Just as long as you and your mama are happy."

Maggie hugged him hard. "We're happy," she said.

"Happy," echoed Annie.

"They might be happy, but Jubal's gonna have to build another house to put all this stuff in," Four Toes said as he and Dan unloaded Garza's wagon later.

"I swear, men," was all Beula Todd said as she watched them. But she said it with a big smile on her face.

The wagon was stuffed to the brim with china, chairs, tables, mirrors, silver boxes, handkerchiefs, garters, parasols, atomizers, window shades, hats, hairpins, fabrics, shawls, children's shoes and stockings, bonnets, andirons, candlesticks, and even a brass feeding dish that Maggie had thought would be sweet for Rover.

It was like Christmas and all the birthdays in the world rolled together into this one glorious wagon. Maggie had never seen anything like it. She and Beula Todd spent a wonderful afternoon poring over everything. Their children got mighty fed up with being called into the house every few minutes to try on new bonnets and shoes and jackets.

While the women enjoyed themselves and tormented the children, Jubal, Dan, and Four Toes went into a huddle as soon as the wagon was unloaded.

"Mulrooney will be in El Paso any day now," Jubal told them.

"Hell. Who knows what he'll do now?" grumbled Dan.

"All I know for sure is that he's sneaky and smart and he wants my hide and everything I own." Jubal pulled the telegram Mulrooney had sent him out of his breast pocket. "He burned down Maggie's farm."

"Aw, no!" Four Toes was aghast.

Jubal nodded grimly. "To the ground. Burned it to cinders. Even bragged about it." He waved the telegram in front of his friends.

"Bastard," growled Dan.

"Whatever he does, and whatever happens, I want Maggie to be safe," Jubal announced. "We're married now, and I visited the lawyer to change my will. If Mulrooney does kill me, at least she'll be taken care of."

"I don't like to hear you talk like that, Jubal." Four Toes looked troubled. "I never heard you talk about dyin' before."

Jubal sighed. "I never talked about love before,

either, or taking a wife." He grinned sheepishly and shrugged. "But there you go. Life plays tricks on you."

"Well, just don't let any of them tricks catch you off guard again, is all," said Dan.

"Right. That's what I want to talk to you two about. I want to get Mulrooney before he has a chance to settle in El Paso. Hank's agreed to send me word as soon as his train is spotted. You know Mulrooney. He doesn't travel light. We'll know before he hits town.

"You," he said, pointing at Four Toes. "I want you to guard Maggie and Annie. Don't let them out of your sight. Dan and I will get Sammy to organize the guards so there will be no way for Mulrooney's men to sneak past them."

"Right," agreed Four Toes.

"Then what?" Dan looked vaguely disappointed, as though he'd been hoping for a more aggressive plan.

"Then you and me are going to ride to El Paso and I'm going to kill that son of a bitch. I just don't want the filthy snake to slither in through the cracks before I can do it."

Dan smiled grimly. "Good."

Prometheus Mulrooney took ironic satisfaction in the knowledge that he was staying in the same hotel that Jubal Green had vacated just the day before.

"If I'd only known, I could have had a surprise waiting for him," he said with a chuckle. Then he glared at Ferrett and Pelch, who stood before him with their heads bowed. "But I'll get him anyway," he went on. "He can't escape me. Especially not now. How deliciously pleasant to discover that even Jubal Green's hirelings can be bought. He's a man who inspires disgusting loyalty in his men as a rule." Mulrooney was obviously disgruntled over that last fact.

"Well, sir, you have to admit that it wasn't actually *his* people who were disloyal."

The words tumbled out of Ferrett's mouth before he could stop them, and they drew an astonished gasp from Pelch. Ferrett himself visibly blanched as he realized he had actually dared to call his employer's statement into question.

Mulrooney's piggy eyes scrunched up ominously. His bulbous nose turned purple and his jowls quivered. He leaned into Ferrett as though a hurricane were blowing at his back. Ferrett tilted away from him until he had to take a step to keep himself from falling over backward.

"What did you say?" Mulrooney's voice was very soft and slow, which made both Ferrett and Pelch swallow convulsively.

Ferrett's teeth chattered when he answered. "Well, sir, I—I was just—well, venturing to point out to you, sir, that Mr. Green's man Mr. Napolitano didn't know the new men he hired were your people. Sir." His eyes squeezed shut as he waited for his fate, which he was sure would be painful. He hoped it would be quick.

When nothing happened to him, Ferrett began to tremble. Since his eyes were still shut, he couldn't see the expression of infuriated loathing that passed over Mulrooney's face, leaving in its wake an evil smirk, as Mulrooney realized how frightened Ferrett was.

Mulrooney glanced at Pelch and discovered that his eyes were darting from him to Ferrett and back again as though he were watching a furiously paced tennis match. Mulrooney shook his head, and his jowls wobbled like the wattles on a turkey cock.

"Imbeciles!" he cried.

Then he reached out a blubbery hand and poked Ferrett with the sharp stub of his finger. Ferrett stumbled backward and was only saved from falling over by bumping into the wall.

"If you ever question my words again, you miserable wart, it will be your last act on earth. Of course, you already know that." Mulrooney sounded positively jolly.

"Y-yes, sir," whispered Ferrett. His face was white.

"Now get out of here, both of you!"

Mulrooney's roar elicited a tiny scream from Ferrett. Pelch's knees gave way as he ran toward the door, and he embarrassed himself by falling down and crawling the last few feet.

Without pausing to confer, the two men ran down the elaborate crimson-carpeted spiral stairway into the hotel lobby, dashed out the door, and made a beeline to the train station. They hurtled onto Mulrooney's private carriage and out to the observation platform in the rear.

Until very late, furious sparks could be seen as the two men sawed frantically at the wrought-iron railing of Mulrooney's deck. They broke four more saw blades that night alone.

Ferrett couldn't hide the tears in his eyes when they finally trudged wearily back to the hotel, where they were sharing the least luxurious room the El Paso could provide.

"It's no use, Mr. Pelch." His voice broke on a sob. "Nothing is going to get those bars to break."

"Don't despair, Mr. Ferrett," said Pelch, "or all will be lost."

"I'm afraid all is already lost, Mr. Pelch," his friend answered sadly.

"Don't say so, Mr. Ferrett. Please don't say so. After all, if we don't have hope, we don't have anything."

Ferrett looked at Pelch, and his face spoke the words he didn't have the heart to utter aloud.

Maggie had never had such a streak of uninterrupted good luck before. It was true that her farm had been burned to the ground, and she knew she had to go back there again one day. But that one unhappy circumstance was very nearly overwhelmed in her heart by the good that now surrounded her.

She moved her things into Jubal's big bedroom and then set about to soften the masculine room with curtains that she made out of one of the bolts of chintz Jubal had bought. Then she fixed up the room that she and Annie had shared for Annie's sole use. She made Annie and Connie each a dress out of the green calico and had enough left over for bonnets.

"I swear, Maggie, I don't know how you can find time to sew for my little girl with everything else you're doing around here," Beula told her.

Although Beula sounded gruff, she had tears in her eyes when Maggie showed her the pretty green dress and bonnet. Maggie had trimmed the bonnet with some white cotton lace, and there was enough extra lace for the sash to the dress as well. Connie's freckled face glowed when she tried on her new finery.

Maggie only laughed at Beula's concern. "I'm having a wonderful time, Beula. It's no bother at all. I've never had—" Maggie struggled for words. "I've never had so much. I've just never had so much." She shook her head with the newness of it all, and her spectacles sparkled on her nose. "I've never been so happy," she admitted shyly, with a slightly guilty feeling.

Beula smiled.

The fact that Maggie could see her surroundings so clearly made her new life all the more exciting. It took her a long time before she stopped wanting to inspect every little thing in her world.

"I've never really seen it before, Jubal," she told her husband in a hurt voice when he laughed at her for going into raptures over the cottonwood they sat beneath one evening. "I can make out every little tiny leaf," she added with awe as she stared up into the branches above her head.

Jubal couldn't help it. He laughed again. Then he hugged her hard and hauled her up to sit on his lap.

"My little blind wife," he said, nuzzling her honey-colored hair.

"Not anymore," she said firmly.

"No. Not anymore."

Maggie loved Jubal to death. It nearly broke her heart when he rode away every morning, and she wanted to cry with relief when he came back to her, safe, every evening. She did try very hard not to cry, even though it was her natural reaction to almost anything. She knew how much Jubal hated to see her in tears.

She wrote to Sadie Phillips, giving her the happy news of her marriage, and Sadie wrote back a letter so full of surprise and exclamation points that Maggie giggled for an entire evening. She longed to visit

Sadie and see what was left of her former life, and to tell Kenny that she and Annie would be all right now, but she didn't want to hurt Jubal's feelings.

Someday, she promised herself.

Not only did she have a wonderful husband, a beautiful home, enough money to see to her baby's future, and friends, but she also could look forward to her monthlies without dread.

She'd had one flux since she and Jubal had begun sleeping together, somewhat to her dismay, but the fact that she no longer feared a brain-shattering headache cheered her up considerably. Never again would she be forced to endure a week of having to function through a thick, gummy fog of pain, of trying to take care of her baby properly while she had to blink back double images, of having to cook when the very smell of food made her sick. Maggie couldn't even begin to explain to anyone how blessed she felt for the gift of Dan Blue Gully's aunt's headache bark.

Still, she harbored a secret terror, tucked away in a corner of her heart, that Prometheus Mulrooney would somehow snatch all this happiness away from her. Maggie wasn't used to good things sticking around for very long.

Four Toes Smith was seldom far from her side. He guarded her closely. Since they were working on the patio together for many hours every day, Maggie didn't realize that he had been set to watch out for her. She only figured him for a dear friend, just as he was a wonderful friend to the children.

Four Toes gave Annie unlimited horsey rides. He told Henry, Jr., that he was too big for horsey rides, but he carried the little boy around on his shoulders everywhere they went. He also helped Connie plant the garden, and he finished repairing the fountain.

Maggie, Beula, Connie, Henry, Jr., and little Annie all shrieked with glee when Four Toes opened the lines and water began to splash into the renovated pool at the fountain's base. Water splattered up like diamonds in the sunshine, and if she looked at it from just the right angle Maggie could even see a rainbow. She made the whole household eat supper outside on the patio that evening.

"I didn't know the place could look like this," Jubal said as he peered around the beautiful, candlelit patio.

He wondered why his mother hadn't done this. Instead of worrying and fretting and making everybody's life a living hell, she could have been using her energy to make it nicer. His heart ached with love as he watched his pretty little wife putter around her kingdom.

Maggie was really excited when little green shoots began to appear where she and Connie had planted dahlia seeds.

"Oh, my land, look at that! We're going to have flowers, Connie!"

Four Toes smiled at the two of them. "You should have a whole garden full come summer. That's when you ought to hold your wedding party."

Maggie thought that was a perfectly splendid idea.

The gourd dolly that Four Toes had given Annie was her favorite toy, and she carried it with her everywhere. Maggie had to glue its yarn hair back on twice in the ensuing few weeks, and she made it a change of clothing out of scraps of green calico. Annie was ecstatic.

"Look, Juba," she said when Jubal came home to supper. "Mama make dolly dress like mine."

Jubal was mightily impressed with Annie's sentence. "Your mama's a wonder, isn't she?"

"Mama's a wonder," Annie repeated with a nod.

Maggie laughed at them, but she was pleased that her husband seemed to appreciate his new family.

Jubal himself hadn't realized how sweet life could be. Until now, he had lived under the curse of a feud that had drained the humanity from his parents and colored every aspect of his growing up and everything he did and was.

He never even dared to imagine that there was such a person as Maggie in the world for him. He was, therefore, totally unprepared for his every bitter barrier crumbling before Maggie's unstudied goodness. She didn't try to be good. She just was. It amazed him. He couldn't have remained unaffected if he'd tried. Every day, his heart softened a little more. He looked into his shaving mirror in the morning and barely recognized the man staring back at him. It had never occurred to him that love could be a part of his life.

"You're turning me into mush, Maggie," he told her when they went to bed one night.

"You don't feel mushy to me, Jubal Green," Maggie said as she touched him. She never even imagined she'd be able to tease like this and not feel wanton. But she didn't feel wanton with Jubal. She just felt good.

"I'm not mush *there,* wife," Jubal growled into her ear. He nibbled on her lobe and dipped his tongue into her ear.

"That's what I said." Maggie gasped under his gentle assault.

"I'm mush in my heart, wench," her husband informed her. His words were muffled because they were spoken as he nibbled his way down her neck and over her shoulder and across her collarbone to her delectable breasts, where he stopped to suckle greedily.

"Oh, Lordy, Jubal. You can be as mushy as you want as long as you keep doing that to me."

Maggie's body reacted to Jubal's ministrations with an electric tingling that shimmered over her in waves. She groaned with desire and her hand sought his hardness. She loved the feel of him. He was so hot and silky, and pulsing with life. Maggie wanted him to give her body that life. She wanted to have his baby, to have a family with him. It would be a family for both of them, for neither one of them had ever really truly had one.

Before she met Jubal, she didn't have much experience with the physical side of marriage. Kenny had been sweet and gentle. Now she was learning he had been rather inexperienced. Not so Jubal Green. Every night was a marvel of newly discovered pleasure for Maggie.

It astonished her that this facet of marriage could be so delightful. She'd always submitted to Kenny with love and resignation. She'd never objected because she was so grateful to him, but she'd never really enjoyed it much, either. Now she spent all day waiting and longing for bedtime so she could love Jubal some more.

She told Jubal that.

"Oh, God, Maggie. I can't even think about my work anymore because I'm always thinking about you. I want to be in you. All day long, all I can think about is coming home and doing this."

"Don't you dare think about me when you're supposed to be keeping yourself alive, Jubal Green. If you get killed by that awful man, I'll never forgive you."

Jubal couldn't stop the deep chuckle that rumbled out of his mouth and into Maggie's as he covered her lips with his. His tongue followed his laughter and sparred with Maggie's. When their bodies finally joined, he uttered a deep, guttural hiss of satisfaction.

"Lord, Maggie, I'll keep safe. I promise. I promise I'll keep safe for you, for this. Oh, Lord."

Maggie could only gasp in response.

"Oh, yes, Maggie. Oh, God, yes!" And Jubal followed her to the fantastic land they had discovered together, in which nobody else was allowed. It was theirs, and it glittered and sparkled with their love.

Sammy Napolitano was worried, not particularly about Prometheus Mulrooney, but because there seemed to be an epidemic rampaging among his security forces.

"They're all getting sick, Mr. Green," he complained one morning, about three weeks after Jubal and Maggie had returned to the ranch. "Every morning another couple of them wake up puking their guts out."

Jubal grimaced at Sammy's vivid description of his little army's condition.

"Should I send for Doc Haskins?" Jubal didn't want anything to weaken his forces. He needed every one of his men.

"Well, I guess it will be all right. It only seems to last for a day or so. Then they're weak, but it doesn't take long for them to be on their feet again. I've hired a couple more men to pick up the slack."

"Be sure to let me know if you think it's getting serious, Sammy. I don't want to let down my guard now. Mulrooney's in El Paso. Dan and I are going in tomorrow."

Sammy nodded. He knew the plan. His boss and Dan Blue Gully were going to make their move the following day. Jubal and Dan planned to make their circuitous way to El Paso, being very careful to elude any sentries Mulrooney had on the watch for them. Once they got to El Paso unobserved, they planned to kill Mulrooney, any way they could.

Too many lives had been lost for either side in the long feud to feel compelled to act honorably. Of course, honor had never been a consideration for Prometheus Mulrooney. Jubal had once believed he should fight Mulrooney fairly, face-to-face. It wasn't very long, however, before he realized that Mulrooney never fought face-to-face—or fairly.

So tomorrow Jubal Green planned to sneak up on him and murder him before he had a chance to so much as blink. Jubal didn't even care if Mulrooney knew what hit him. He used to think he'd like Mulrooney to know who had sealed his doom. Now Jubal only wanted him dead and he didn't care who did it or how. He wanted no further danger to himself or those he loved.

It was difficult to keep from becoming too excited now that he could see an end to a generation's worth of misery. But he knew he needed to be completely, methodically, coldly in control of himself or he would fail.

"We've got to keep calm, Danny."

Dan eyed him with a wry grin. "I'm not the one you have to remind of that, Jubal."

Jubal sighed. "You're right."

"Just try to think about the job, Jubal. Don't think about Maggie."

"It's hard not to, Danny. I've never had so much to lose before."

"I know." Dan's words were solemn with compassion. "I know."

20

Jubal didn't tell Maggie what his plans for the day were that morning when he was getting dressed. For her sake, he tried to act normal, as if it were going to be just another day. He didn't want her to worry. Still, he couldn't help grabbing one last kiss and making it a deep, lasting, memorable one.

"My, Jubal, you'd better not do any more of that or you'll never get out of here." Maggie rubbed herself against his body, glorying in the feel of him.

Jubal groaned. "Would that be so bad?"

Maggie's voice was soft as a summer cloud. "I'd love it, Jubal Green. I'd purely love it."

Her whisper elicited another deep groan. Jubal tore himself away from her only with difficulty. But, he told himself, if the day went the way he and Dan planned, he'd never have to leave her again. Not like this, with his life and hers in the balance.

"Tonight," he promised her. "I'll make it up to you tonight."

"I'll hold you to that."

Maggie caressed his cheek and wondered why it was so much harder for her to let him go this morning than it usually was. With a sigh, she yawned and figured it was just because her monthlies were almost upon her. She always got emotional right before her monthlies. Thank God for Dan's magic bark. She'd take emotions over those killing headaches any day.

This morning she and Four Toes were going out onto the desert to look for plants. He had suggested placing some prickly desert plants in front of the ranch house for decoration. Maggie had been skeptical at first.

"You mean those prickly pears and cactuses and things? Aren't they real thorny?"

Four Toes laughed. "Sure, they're thorny, but they can be pretty if you do it right. You can put flowers and things in between them. You can eat the fruit too, and if you use plants that are used to growing around here, you won't have to be forever haulin' water out to the yard."

Maggie had looked at him thoughtfully. The idea had a certain merit, to be sure.

"All right. It will be fun to go out for a picnic, anyway." Maybe it would take her mind off worrying about her husband.

She fixed a lunch and packed it into a wicker basket Jubal had bought when she admired it at Garza's. Every time Maggie looked at one of her many wedding gifts, her heart glowed. Nobody had ever bought her things before.

Kenny would have, if he'd had any money, she

reminded herself a little guiltily. Then she realized that it was all right; Kenny wouldn't mind that she was happy now. She'd make sure of that when she returned to the farm. Someday.

Connie and Henry, Jr., seemed to be suffering from the same malady that had been plaguing Sammy Napolitano's little army. Maggie didn't like the idea of having a nice picnic on the desert without taking Connie and little Henry along.

"You just go along with Annie," Beula told her. "You can have a picnic another day and take my kids along then. They both know you'd take them today if you could. Life isn't always fair, you know, Maggie. The sooner they learn that, the better."

Although Maggie agreed wholeheartedly with Beula that life wasn't always fair, she had serious doubts about whether children needed to be initiated into that sad fact at such a tender age. She didn't argue, though.

The picnic basket was already in the wagon, and Annie was outfitted in her sturdy new shoes and pretty checked sunbonnet. Maggie and Annie and Four Toes set out on the wagon to go exploring, with two of Jubal's guards riding shotgun.

They weren't the men who usually accompanied Maggie whenever she and Four Toes or Jubal went out wandering. Those two were victims of the mysterious stomach ailment that seemed to be making its way through the ranch denizens. They had been hand-picked by Sammy Napolitano, so they must be capable, but Maggie couldn't account for the feeling of uneasiness that assailed her when she observed the two new men.

They look rough, she thought. Then she decided

she was being fanciful. These men were supposed to be rough. Jubal had hired a whole band of rough men to protect the ranch.

Maggie also knew it was necessary to have guards when she went away from home, but it still made her uncomfortable. Every now and then, when she was working in the house or digging in the garden or reading on the patio, she could forget about the threat that Prometheus Mulrooney posed to everything she loved. But with two armed men riding alongside the wagon, that blissful forgetfulness was impossible. She chalked up her particular uneasiness today to her impending monthly flux.

"We're going on a picnic, Annie," Maggie said.

"We go picnic," Annie told the gourd dolly she hugged to her chest.

Four Toes chuckled and flicked the reins. The two mules jerked the wagon forward and ambled into a sluggish walk. The rifle Four Toes always carried with him lay on the floor at his feet, in easy reach in case of danger.

Maggie tried to keep her mind on their conversation as the mules bumped the wagon along. Four Toes was talking to her about plants. But for some reason, Maggie kept looking back at the ranch today. She hated to see it getting smaller and smaller as they drove away from it.

The early June day was pleasant. Recent rains had blessed the normally dry desert so that it was greener than usual. Wild flowers bloomed in clumps of yellow and purple. This time, since she wore her new spectacles, Maggie could discern the tiny lavender blooms that she hadn't been able to see on the first ride to El Paso. Her heart constricted at the memory, and she mentally uttered a little prayer of thanks for her new husband and for whatever kind spirit had brought him to her door. She pointed the purple flowers out to her daughter now.

When she looked over her shoulder again, she felt a terrible uneasiness as she realized the ranch was out of sight. She shook her head, wondering what the problem was. Her heart just seemed to be stuffed full of foreboding.

"Maggie, are you all right?" The question penetrated her thoughts and made her jump.

"Oh, I'm sorry, Four Toes. I don't know what's wrong with me. I feel funny."

He looked at her curiously. "What do you mean by 'funny'?"

"I don't know." Maggie sighed. "You'll think I'm being stupid. I feel—I feel—I'm worried. I guess that's what it is. And I don't know why."

Four Toes eyed her with concern. "Anything in particular you're worried about?"

Maggie shook her head. "No, there's nothing. It's probably just stupid." She tried to smile at him but achieved only a crooked grimace.

"Maybe we ought to go back," said Four Toes. "I don't scoff at premonitions, Maggie. People don't usually feel uneasy for no reason, even if they can't put their finger on what the reason is."

Maggie did smile then. "Do you really think so? I feel so silly for thinking we'd be safer back on the ranch. There's just something about being away that makes me nervous today."

Four Toes pulled up on the mules. "We're going back," he announced. "We can picnic on the patio."

The two guards had ridden up next to the wagon.

"What's going on?" one of them asked.

He was a surly-looking man with longish black hair and a droopy black mustache. Maggie was sure she was being silly for the revulsion she felt when she eyed the man, since Sammy Napolitano never hired anybody who didn't have good references. She looked at the second guard, a small fellow with light brown hair and milky blue eyes, and realized she didn't feel any better about him.

"We're heading back to Green's Valley," Four Toes said.

The dark-haired man looked across Four Toes and Maggie to the light-haired man. Maggie saw him give what she thought was a slight nod, and suddenly her heart clutched with fear. When she saw the light-haired man nod back, she frowned.

"I thought you was goin' on a picnic," the dark-haired man said. He sounded as though he was trying to be pleasant.

"We were, but we changed our minds." It was Maggie who spoke this time. The sharp edge to her voice surprised her.

She noticed that Four Toes had narrowed his eyes, and her fear surged higher.

"Mrs. Green wants to go back to the ranch now, so we're going," Four Toes said. He raised the reins to slap the mules' backs.

"I don't think that's a good idea," said the black-haired man.

With one fluid movement, Four Toes picked up the rifle and lifted it to his shoulder. But when he saw the black-haired man's gun, cocked and aimed at his chest, he slowly lowered the rifle.

"Damn," he whispered. Maggie heard the frustration and defeat in the word, and she squeezed Annie tight.

Annie had nearly fallen asleep while Maggie and Four Toes had been talking, but with her mother's convulsive hug, her big brown eyes flew open. She rubbed her eyes with a tiny fist, looked at the dark-haired man, and frowned.

"Mama, dat man has a gun!" she said. She obviously did not approve.

"Shhh. I know it, baby."

Maggie didn't want to do anything that might get her daughter hurt. She wasn't sure what was going on, but she suspected the unthinkable: that Jubal's security forces had been breached and these men were traitors.

"Why are you pointing that gun at us?" she demanded. "My husband employs you to protect us, not point guns at us."

The black-haired man spit a jawful of tobacco juice into the desert and Maggie watched dust puff up around it. It seemed to her that things were happening very slowly.

"He don't pay as good as Mulrooney though, ma'am," the black-haired man said with a yellow-toothed grin. He seemed to be the spokesman for the pair.

"You traitors." Maggie's furious whisper cut through the warm June air. "You damned traitors."

"I guess you got a right to call us anything you want to, ma'am. But we still got to take you to Mulrooney's train."

"Train? I thought he was in El Paso."

"Not no more, he ain't. When he heard your man and his Injun buddy was headin' to El Paso today, he got on his train. We're goin' to take you and meet him along the way."

"I'm not going anywhere with you," Maggie said firmly. She was holding Annie so tightly the little girl began to whimper.

"I'm afraid you got no choice, Mrs. Green," the man said.

Maggie glared at him, and hate radiated from every pore of her body. "I've never seen a real live traitor before. You're a hateful man, mister, you and your friend."

"Oh, we ain't friends, ma'am, just employees."

Maggie shook her head. She couldn't think of anything foul enough to say to them.

"You'd better just go along with them, Maggie."

Maggie stared at Four Toes in horror.

"Four Toes Smith, we can't just go with them!" she cried. "They'll use us as hostages to draw Jubal to that horrid man. I'd sooner die than lure my husband to his death."

The look Four Toes gave Maggie then stopped her words and dried her mouth and made her heart begin to thud with dread.

"It isn't 'us' they want, Maggie, it's you and Annie. I'm afraid this is the end of the road for me." Four Toes looked at her kindly, as if he knew his words would make her cry.

He was right. Maggie's mouth dropped open and she couldn't talk. Tears pooled in her blue eyes until the irises looked like sapphires glinting in a brook.

"You can't mean—" She gasped in horror.

The Indian put a brown hand on her cheek. Then he stroked Annie's soft curls.

"I don't want to scare Annie. Please don't scream or anything. This is all right. You know, I grew up with Jubal and Dan on the ranch. But Dan taught me enough about being an Indian that I know one or two things. These men are nothing. Jubal and Dan will rescue you. They'll get Mulrooney. I feel it in my gut. I knew I wasn't going to live very long. It's something I grew up knowing."

Four Toes seemed to be more concerned about the tears that were now flowing freely down Maggie's cheeks than he was about his own destiny.

"It's all right, Maggie, really. I've had a good life, thanks to Jubal and Dan. As my people say, it's a good day to die. The main thing is not to frighten Annie."

Maggie nodded numbly. She couldn't stop her tears. Little Annie was beginning to cry too, because her mama was crying and Four Toes seemed so somber and those bad men were pointing guns at them.

"Better come with me, Injun." Those were the first words the light-haired man had spoken since guns were drawn. They weren't said unkindly.

Four Toes leaned over and kissed Annie. "I love you, Annie," he said. Then he kissed Maggie on her tear-drenched cheek. "Take care of Jubal and Dan for me. They're my brothers."

Maggie was shaking her head. "You can't just go off with that man, Four Toes. You can't." Her whisper was incredulous and miserable at the same time.

Four Toes shrugged and got down from his seat. "Got no choice, Maggie. Only gun I got is that rifle." He pointed at the floor of the wagon. "I can't risk getting you and Annie hurt." He grinned ruefully. "We lost this one, Maggie."

"Oh, my God," Maggie whispered. "Oh, my God."

She watched as the black-haired man dismounted and tied his horse to the wagon. Then he got into the driver's seat and whipped up the mules.

Maggie lurched off her seat, but the black-haired man shoved her back onto it, hard. Her glasses flew off her face and landed on the desert floor. Maggie could barely see them: two bright circles of glass reflecting the sun. Her stomach clenched.

She looked over her shoulder as they drove off. Four Toes smiled at her. She knew her heart was breaking. He waved at Annie.

"Bye-bye, Annie," he called.

"Bye, Fo' Toes," Annie called back. She sounded puzzled. Then she turned to her mother. "Where he go, Mama?"

But Maggie couldn't answer her daughter's question. Her throat was tight and aching, and her tears would have drowned any words she might have spoken. She just shook her head and sobbed.

The two men at least spared Annie and Maggie from seeing Four Toes murdered. The light-haired man and Four Toes were out of sight by the time Maggie heard the gunshot. It sounded muffled, as though it had to travel over many lifetimes to reach her ears. She couldn't stop the ragged cry of grief that tore from her throat.

"How could you? How could you? How could you?" she asked the black-haired man, over and over. She sobbed into her baby's pretty bonnet.

"It's not personal, ma'am," he told her. He sounded a little bit sorry about it all.

"Not personal?" The words stumbled out of Maggie's throat thick and sad.

Maggie remembered Dan Blue Gully's words from what seemed like a century ago as he knelt beside her in the kitchen of her house and tried to calm her down. He told her then it wasn't personal. Maggie knew she'd never understand as long as she lived why this had to happen. It was the most personal thing she'd ever experienced.

She didn't even try to stop crying, though she knew it would upset Annie. She couldn't help it.

Four Toes Smith was the kindest man she'd ever known in her entire life, and the best friend her little girl would ever have. She couldn't even stand the thought of him lying there, dead, under the merciless desert sun. And she was here in this wagon, being driven as a hostage to a crazy man she'd never even met, and she couldn't do a thing for Four Toes. She couldn't even bury him, for God's sake.

Not personal! Maggie couldn't stand it.

When Jubal and Dan got to El Paso and found out Mulrooney had left, they knew something had gone incredibly wrong.

"There's no way he would have left unless he knew we were coming for him," Jubal told Dan as they tore away from the town and back toward Green's Valley. "Mulrooney never moves unless he has to. Something's wrong."

"Jesus, Jubal, do you think Maggie and Four Toes are in any danger? They were going out for a picnic in the desert today."

"Sammy sends guards with them whenever they leave the ranch."

Dan eyed Jubal through the dust that the pounding hooves of their horses spewed up. "He's had to hire new guards, since everybody's been getting sick. If Mulrooney knew about our coming to El Paso, that means somebody on your spread is being paid for information. Mulrooney must have infiltrated your forces, no matter how careful Sammy's been."

Jubal's face was pale as death under his hat. His lips were pressed together and his expression was drawn with worry.

"I know that, Dan." His words were clipped. "I already know that."

They rode back to Green's Valley as fast as they could.

"So this is Mrs. Green."

The black-haired man, whose name, Maggie learned, was Sloane, had led Maggie by the arm through the five-car special to the very last carriage and deposited her in front of an enormously fat man. The light-haired man, Potts, had rejoined them before the wagon reached the train.

Maggie couldn't even look at Potts, the villain who had murdered Four Toes. She held Annie tightly in her arms.

It made her feel sick to her stomach when a mousy little man gave Sloane and Potts a wad of money and the two thugs left the train, which immediately started up again, and rode away across the desert. She wondered if kidnap and murder was their usual line of work.

Prometheus Mulrooney stood near the little open observation deck in his luxurious private railroad carriage and beamed at his prisoners. His voice was slick with pleasure, and his big stomach rippled when he laughed. He was so pleased with himself that his fat face fairly glowed.

Maggie was petrified, but she swore to herself that

she would not allow Prometheus Mulrooney to witness her terror. She noticed that two men, one of them the mousy man who had paid off Sloane and Potts, were cowering at Mulrooney's side. They kept eyeing Mulrooney as though to assess his mood.

The two were obviously underlings of Mulrooney's, and they both seemed like truly miserable human beings. Maggie didn't understand how people could allow themselves to be so downtrodden as to let their better natures be so completely subverted. Yet that was apparently just what these creatures had done. Their cowardice repelled her. Unwittingly, they gave spur to her own courage. She sucked in a deep breath.

"Yes, I'm Mrs. Green. And *you* must be Prometheus Mulrooney."

Maggie spoke to the huge man as though he were a freak in a circus sideshow. To the contempt in her tone of voice she added a glare that took in the fullness of Mulrooney's person, from his broad shoes to his enormous, sparsely covered head. Maggie's supercilious stare did not miss his huge belly or his watermelon thighs. She tried very hard to make her expression as full of loathing and disgust as she could. It was not a difficult task.

Ferrett and Pelch looked at each other in horrified astonishment.

Mulrooney's smile soured some at Maggie's tone of voice and frosty glare.

"The same, madam," he said, "and I suggest you treat me with the respect I deserve." He spoke smugly and rocked back on his heels, a man supremely pleased with himself.

"Respect?" The word flew out of Maggie's mouth

and slapped Mulrooney on the cheek as surely as if she'd used her open palm. "*Respect?* You don't know the meaning of the word. You're a filthy murderer. You—you—you horrible man. You're a beast! A criminal! Respect? I'd respect a rattlesnake before I'd respect you." Maggie's gaze raked Mulrooney's blubbery body once more. "You, Mr. Mulrooney, are a truly disgusting creature."

Mulrooney had already turned a deep red. Nobody had talked to him like this in forty years. He made it a point to see that no one he dealt with had any spirit. But this honey-haired woman, who was at most a quarter his size, was actually daring to vilify him—and in front of his underlings, no less.

His huge body quaked with outrage.

"I suggest you shut your mouth, Mrs. Green. Perhaps you don't realize just exactly how tenuous your position is."

"My position? Tenuous?" She spat at him.

Maggie's courage had been overtaken by anger, and she wasn't even thinking any longer. Her one goal was to let Prometheus Mulrooney know how much she hated him.

"Tenuous? I don't even know what that word means, mister. If you're trying to tell me you're going to kill me and my baby, why don't you just say so? That shouldn't be too hard for you. God knows you've murdered better people than me in your filthy, depraved life."

Mulrooney's pig eyes bulged in his florid face. "Ferrett!" he roared.

"Yes, sir," Ferrett whispered.

"Take this miserable creature away from me."

"Yes, sir."

Maggie whirled on Ferrett. He still stood next to Pelch, not daring to move, and both men were eyeing Maggie with awe. They had never heard anybody stand up to Prometheus Mulrooney before.

"And you!" Maggie shrieked at Ferrett. "What do you do all day long, just quake in your boots while this horrid man makes you pay the people who murder for him? How on earth can you live with yourself?"

Ferrett reached a tentative hand out to pat Maggie's arm and try to calm her down. His own timid nature would never allow him to buck Mulrooney, and he was sure Maggie was destined for a cruel, perhaps immediate fate if she didn't stop yelling soon.

"Take your cowardly hands off me, you miserable thing!" Maggie cried at Ferrett, wrenching her arm away from his touch. Poor Ferrett shrank back against Pelch, who put a comforting hand on his shoulder.

"Ferrett! Pelch!" Mulrooney's face had by now turned a deeper purple than either man had ever seen it.

Maggie spun to face Mulrooney again.

"Ferrett! Pelch!" Her voice was a mockery of Mulrooney's furious rumble. "You filthy pig! You murdering devil! You surround yourself with weaklings and toadies and make them do your horrid butchery. You slime! You burned my house! You murdered my friend!" Her voice caught at the mention of Four Toes, but she took a deep breath and went on. "You tried to murder my husband! You awful, fat, disgusting—greasy lard pudding!"

Maggie couldn't think of words terrible enough to express to Mulrooney exactly what she thought about him, but she was doing a fair job of getting her point across. The expressions on the faces of the room's occupants testified eloquently to that truth.

At the word "fat," both Ferrett and Pelch looked at each other with alarm. When she called him a "greasy lard pudding," both men gasped. Nobody ever mentioned Mulrooney's obesity in his presence. It was an unspoken rule.

"Enough!" Mulrooney roared.

His piggy eyes were lost in his purple face, and his hands were balled into enormous fists at his sides. He reached one of them out now to push at Maggie, who was leaning toward him. He'd never had to lay a hand on an enemy before, but Maggie showed no sign of going away, and Ferrett and Pelch seemed immobilized by surprise.

Annie chose that moment to frown, point at the quivering man, and say, "Dat's a bad fat man, Mama."

"He's a *terrible* bad fat man, Annie," Maggie said furiously.

Mulrooney's roar was deafening, but it only fired Maggie's fury to a pitch unknown to her before.

When Mulrooney's hand reached out to her, Maggie rebalanced Annie on her hip in an instant and slapped the enormous, porky fist as hard as she could. He drew his hand away with a gasp of pained surprise. Nobody had ever dared strike Prometheus Mulrooney. He actually took a step back.

Maggie, who knew nothing of battles or the element of surprise, instinctively pressed her advantage and followed him. She stalked Mulrooney like an infuriated cat attacking its prey.

"You vicious, depraved, disgusting thing. You don't even deserve the word 'human.' You're too foul. How many people have you murdered in your miserable life? How much did it cost you to burn my house? It wasn't worth it, believe me. That poor place barely kept us alive, yet you must have spent hundreds of dollars to burn it down. And how much did it cost you to have Four Toes Smith murdered? As good a man as ever walked the earth, and you killed him!" Maggie's voice cracked again, but she pushed on, her rage giving her strength. "And you did it all out of pure meanness. You're a freak, Mr. Mulrooney. You're a fat, disgusting freak of nature. Why are you doing this? Why?"

Maggie's shriek might have shattered glass if the door to the observation deck was shut, but it wasn't. She had backed Mulrooney out the open door of his carriage by this time.

"Why?" Mulrooney roared in harmony to Maggie's screaming. "Because that damned Marianna Potter wouldn't marry me, that's why! The fool married Benjamin Green instead. I'll teach her! I'm going to wipe the Greens off the face of the earth!"

He was trying to sound ferocious but he was, in truth, frightened. Nobody had ever yelled at him or come at him the way Maggie was doing. She'd even slapped him! And his men weren't bounding to his rescue either.

"She wouldn't marry you." Maggie's voice dripped with sarcasm that seemed acid enough to eat through metal.

"She wouldn't marry me." Mulrooney was whining now.

"That's the reason for all this butchery?"

"I prefer to call it justice," said Mulrooney.

"Justice? You prefer? *You prefer?* You disgusting idiot!"

"Well, she wouldn't marry me."

"Why should she marry you? You're a disgusting, filthy, grotesque pile of lard! You're a horrible person! Who on earth would want to marry you?"

Mulrooney uttered an incoherent bellow of rage.

Maggie had by this time pressed Mulrooney across his observation deck to the wrought-iron railing of the platform. When he leaned his bulk against the rails to get away from this violent, screaming termagant who wouldn't stop following him, Ferrett and Pelch looked at each other with wide eyes. They were probably the only two people on the whole moving train who heard the ominous groan of overtaxed metal.

"Oh, my Lord, Mr. Pelch," whispered Ferrett.

He looked out the window of the carriage to discover that the train was, at this very moment, crossing a bridge that spanned a deep—a very deep—rocky gorge. Ferrett tapped Pelch on the shoulder and pointed out the window. Pelch gasped.

"Good heavens, Mr. Ferrett."

Pelch crept to the deck and stood in the doorway to stare as Maggie pressed closer and closer to Mulrooney and Mulrooney leaned harder and harder against the delicate railing. Ferrett joined Pelch, and they watched, wide-eyed, as Maggie continued to confront her husband's tormentor.

"You vicious fiend! You actually created all this misery just because a woman wouldn't marry you? No woman on earth would want such a stinking, filthy, fat, disgusting blob! I can't believe you murdered all those people just because a woman spurned you. You're not even a man. A man would have accepted his fate and gone on with his life. But not you. No. You had to get even. Like a little baby, you had to get your 'revenge.' You're crazy! You're a maniac! You may kill me and my little girl, you filthy pig, but I'll be damned if I'll let you do it before I tell you what I think of you."

As the train crossed the bridge there was a hollow rattle and a loud cracking of the iron railing as it gave way.

Pelch reached out a hand to grab Maggie's arm before she could follow Mulrooney through the gap that opened up as the bolts fastening the metal railing to the carriage wall gave way. Mulrooney's roar of alarm and his sudden wide-eyed look of horrified surprise stopped Maggie's tirade in mid-shout. Her mouth was open to spew more bile onto Prometheus Mulrooney, but suddenly he wasn't there anymore. She saw his fat hands reach desperately at the broken railing and saw the jagged metal bend and slice his palm open as his hands slithered off the bar. The metal was too weak to hold the enormity of Mulrooney's evil bulk.

After Pelch steadied her, Maggie found herself alone all at once, as both Pelch and Ferrett dashed past her to the new opening in the railing. They clutched each other convulsively and leaned carefully over to peer into the gorge. She heard a terrified bellow that seemed to get weaker and weaker as Mulrooney neared the rocky bottom of the valley.

"Will you look at him flail about, Mr. Pelch," Ferrett murmured in an awed voice.

"I've never seen the like, Mr. Ferrett," whispered Pelch.

For several moments the only sounds Maggie heard were the rumble of the train and the frantic wail that drifted up from the gigantic hole in the earth. Then that faraway wail stopped abruptly, and both Ferrett and Pelch flinched.

"My goodness gracious!" breathed Ferrett.

Pelch shook his head. "Burst like a melon," he murmured.

Maggie clutched Annie closely. "Oh, my God," she gasped.

"Where dat bad man go, Mama?" came the puzzled voice of her little girl.

Maggie swallowed hard. "To the devil, I guess, baby," she whispered.

"And did you notice where it broke, Mr. Pelch? It wasn't even where we sawed."

Ferrett's voice held vast astonishment as he fingered the ragged iron and eyed it closely. The bolts had ripped away from the wall of the carriage, apparently unable to bear the gigantic weight pressed against the railing.

Pelch nodded in bemusement. "We could have just loosened the bolts, Mr. Ferrett."

Ferrett looked at Pelch blankly. "I guess it doesn't matter now, Mr. Pelch."

"I guess not, Mr. Ferrett."

Suddenly the two men grinned wildly and grabbed each other, causing Maggie to back up and squeeze Annie. And she was sure they had lost their minds when they began dancing up and down Mulrooney's elaborate carriage to shrill cries of "We're free! We're free!"

21

Jubal's heart just about broke when he and Dan found the spot where the abduction had taken place. The tracks were plain to read, as was the sickening black stain on the desert made by Four Toes Smith's dried blood. The old, floppy-brimmed hat he always wore lay brim up next to the blood.

"Oh, God, Danny," Jubal breathed. He leapt off of Old Red's back and ran over to the hat, hoping against reason that he would find Four Toes somewhere, anywhere, still alive.

"Leave it be, Jubal," Dan told him, when Jubal made as if to begin to search for their missing friend.

Jubal turned his haunted gaze toward him. "We can't just leave him out here, Dan. He's our brother."

Dan's expression was grim. "We'll come back for him, Jubal. I ain't going to leave him here forever without lookin'. But you know as well as me that if he lost that much blood, it's too late."

Jubal couldn't speak.

"You know what probably happened, Jubal." Dan's voice was thick.

"Yeah. I know." But he couldn't say it out loud. A cougar or a coyote dragged the body off. That was what happened out here. He knew it and Dan knew it.

Jubal whispered as he walked back to Old Red, "We'll be back for you." He hooked the hat over the horn of his saddle.

Then he spotted Maggie's eyeglasses. They were unbroken and lay as they had fallen, two bright ovals of clear glass, shimmering in the heat. He picked them up and stared at them.

Dan didn't say a word. His lips were pinched tightly together, and his face was set in grim lines.

Jubal folded the glasses up carefully and put them in his shirt pocket.

When he swung his leg over Old Red's back, he felt as though his soul had died. He couldn't see anything for a few seconds; the world had gone blurry. He passed his gloved hand over his face and didn't realize the moisture the soft leather picked up from his cheeks was his own tears. He nudged Old Red's side and the horse began to trot again, following the trail left by the ranch wagon.

Dan scrutinized Jubal with sad eyes. "Maggie's probably still all right, Jubal."

"Sure."

The two men rode on in silence for another few minutes.

"He knew it was his time, Jubal. He told me. He'd been feelin' it."

Jubal couldn't look at Dan. His pain was almost too

big for him to speak. "Well, he didn't tell me." His voice cracked, and his throat ached from trying not to bawl like a baby.

Dan gave him a bitter grin. "You been busy with your wife, Jubal. Besides, you ain't Indian."

"Hell," was all Jubal said to that.

They were surprised when, an hour or so later, they came upon the special train Prometheus Mulrooney had hired, stopped dead on the railroad tracks halfway to Amarillo. They were even more surprised when no gunfire erupted as they boldly stormed up to the engine.

When they climbed aboard and discovered the engine had been abandoned by the engineer, and heard the sounds of celebration coming from a back carriage, they were flabbergasted. They eyed each other uneasily.

"I don't like this, Danny," said Jubal. "What the hell's going on?"

Dan shook his head. "Beats me."

Guns drawn, they crept stealthily from the engine to the next car, which had also been abandoned. That car was apparently the kitchen. Another empty carriage was obviously where Mulrooney's hired help slept. It was from the fourth carriage that all the noise was coming. They heard whoops of laughter and even jolly, out-of-tune, masculine singing. They stared at each other in bemused wariness.

Jubal carefully opened the door of the carriage. Dan was right behind him. Both men's guns were cocked and ready for use, and Dan made sure his knife was within easy reach. They stood just inside the open door and stared in astonishment at the scene in front of them.

Ferrett and Pelch were still dancing. Mulrooney's other hired help, among whom were the train's engineer and his mechanic, were toasting one another with opened bottles of champagne. The bubbly wine had foamed over the bottles' mouths and was sloshing over the floor, walls, and furniture. Maggie and Annie sat on a cushioned bench in a corner. Maggie appeared to be a little ragged around the edges. She wasn't smiling, and her eyes seemed empty. Annie was laughing and clapping her hands at the antics of the men in front of her. She saw Jubal and Dan first.

"Look, Mama. Juba!" she cried.

Maggie looked up numbly. She still felt vaguely unsettled about her part in Mulrooney's demise, although she was glad he was dead. But her heart ached so painfully for Four Toes that she wasn't sure she could stand it.

When she realized it was her husband standing at the door, she leapt to her feet with Annie in her arms. She didn't even notice people scatter out of her way when she ran.

"Jubal! Jubal!" Maggie wasn't numb any longer. She felt as though someone had ripped a gash in her heart and she was crying now, full force. "Jubal, they killed Four Toes! They murdered him! Then Mulrooney fell off the train and into a gorge and he's dead and I did it, and—oohhh!"

Jubal barely had time to holster his gun before Maggie and Annie hit him in the stomach. He staggered back with a grunt and wrapped his arms around them. He tried to say something, but his throat was too tight.

"Mulrooney's dead?" Dan's incredulous words didn't penetrate anyone's consciousness for a second.

Ferrett and Pelch and the engineer and mechanic had all stopped dancing and singing. They were standing still now, and their stupid grins looked as though they had been painted on their faces. It was Ferrett who spoke first.

"He's dead," Ferrett confirmed in a high-pitched voice.

Pelch nodded.

Then Ferrett picked up a pile of papers and threw them into the air. "He'd dead! He's dead! He's dead!" he shrieked, as though he were ringing in a new year or celebrating the end of a war.

Jubal had buried his face in Maggie's hair, but he lifted it when he realized what Ferrett had said.

Maggie took a huge breath and drew her wet face away from Jubal's shirt.

Annie smiled up at Jubal and held out her gourd dolly.

"They killed Four Toes, Jubal," Maggie whispered. She swallowed hard.

"I know, baby. We found the place." Jubal brushed his lips across her hair again.

"How did Mulrooney die?" Dan hadn't been able to follow Maggie's ragged explanation before she collapsed into Jubal's arms, and Mulrooney's staff didn't seem to be of much help.

"Mama yell at dat fat man and he fall," little Annie told them all, in her longest sentence to date.

"Your mama made him fall?" Dan pinned Maggie with bright black eyes.

Annie nodded seriously. "He bad man."

Jubal gave both of his women another squeeze. "He was a *real* bad man, parsnip," he said to Annie in a ragged whisper.

"But he gone to da devil now," Annie told him solemnly, as though she figured that circumstance might make him feel better.

Jubal and Dan ultimately restored order to the little train and supervised Ferrett and Pelch's cleanup of Mulrooney's papers. Both men from Green's Valley wanted to read them to make sure Mulrooney hadn't planned any further treachery that might sneak up on them later.

Then Jubal made Maggie sit down and tell him exactly what happened from the time Sloane and Potts kidnapped her and killed Four Toes Smith to Mulrooney's fall through the broken railing of the train platform. At the mention of Sloane and Potts, Jubal shot a quick glance at Dan, Dan nodded, and Maggie knew Four Toes would be avenged. She wasn't sure whether she was glad or not. There had already been so much bloodshed.

She didn't have too much time to think about it, though, because just then Jubal remembered he had her spectacles in his pocket.

"Here, sweetheart, you probably miss these." He tried to wipe the lenses off on his flannel shirt.

"Oh, Jubal," Maggie whispered. "I thought they were broken." And she burst into tears once more.

Jubal looked at Dan with resignation while he comforted his wife yet again. Dan just chuckled at them and shook his head.

Ferrett and Pelch managed to find some food for everybody, and then Jubal made Maggie lie down and rest. Annie was already napping.

"We'll see that the train is tidied up, sir," said Pelch,

who had already transferred his subservience to Jubal.

"Indeed we will, sir," added Ferrett. "And we'll be absolutely certain that nobody makes a loud noise and wakes the lady." He spoke of Maggie with reverence.

Jubal nodded at the two men. Then he took Maggie's glasses off her nose, laid them carefully on the table beside her sleeping head, and kissed her.

Once she seemed comfortable, Jubal and Dan mounted up and nudged their horses alongside the rails, backtracking. They rode silently through the still desert; neither one of them felt like talking. No wind stirred the air. The June sunshine gleamed against mica-crusted rocks, and lizards scurried out of the way of the horses' hooves. They walked their mounts slowly until they reached the bridge over the gully. Then they dismounted, tied up their horses, and began to walk across the trestle.

About halfway over the span, Jubal stopped and gestured to his friend. They both leaned over and squinted down into the deep gorge. The sides of the gorge were steep and slick and glinted in the sun. Jagged rocks lined the bottom of the gully, and a thin, silvery thread of water snaked between the huge boulders at the bottom. Although not a breath of air stirred above the huge hole in the earth, they could hear the wind moaning like a malevolent ghost through the deep valley beneath them.

"Shoot, that's a long way down," muttered Dan.

"Can you see him, Danny?"

"I can see what's left of him. It ain't much."

"Maggie said she could hear him yelling for a long time. I wonder how long it took before he hit those rocks."

"Long enough, I reckon."

"Sweet Lord above, I didn't think this feud would ever end." Jubal's voice was a study in amazement, frosted with relief and a soul-deep sadness.

"It was Maggie who ended it." Dan was smiling a little bit as he peered into the gorge.

"She hollered him right through the railing." Jubal smiled a little bit too.

"Hope she don't never yell at you like that."

"I'll do my best never to give her cause." Jubal was only half teasing.

"You better." Dan wasn't teasing at all.

Jubal shook his head. "I'm sorry she had to go through all this."

Dan pinned Jubal with a steady gaze. "I told you a long time ago she had a strong spirit. It's strong enough to get her through this."

Jubal grinned. "I know you did, Danny. And I know you're right." His grin faded. "I guess the worst of it was when those bastards got Four Toes."

Dan looked down into the gully again. "That was the worst of it for all of us, I reckon." His voice was deep and still in the breathless day.

Neither man spoke for a minute as they peered into the gorge.

"Should we pick Mulrooney up?" Jubal didn't sound as though he were thrilled at the prospect.

"Hell, no. Just tell the authorities in El Paso there's been an accident. Let them deal with the bastard. With any luck, the buzzards will have picked his bones clean by that time."

Jubal shuddered in spite of himself. "I guess he'll feed the buzzards for a long time. Maybe even a coyote or two."

"I guess."

The two men were silent as they rode back to the train.

Jubal drove Maggie and Annie in the wagon back to Green's Valley, with Old Red tied behind. He wanted to put his arm around them both, but he had to drive the mules so he couldn't.

Dan rode a little way away from the wagon, obviously not willing to talk, too busy thinking his own thoughts. He fingered the medicine pouch that hung on a leather thong around his neck, and his eyes looked as though they weren't seeing the landscape around him but were focused on something in his memory.

Maggie was sitting as close to Jubal as she could get, so full of confused emotions she couldn't even begin to voice them.

Worst of all—worse than being kidnapped or watching Prometheus Mulrooney fall to his death or being afraid she and her baby would die—was the knowledge that Four Toes was gone. Murdered.

Annie was wearing his floppy hat as they drove home. It was so big it swallowed her head whole and rode on her little nose, but since she was sleeping soundly in her mother's arms it didn't matter. Every now and then Maggie would look at that hat and feel like bawling.

All of a sudden she was glad she had been instrumental in Mulrooney's death. She felt as though, for once in her life, she had accomplished something worthwhile.

Her Aunt Lucy had always told her that anger was

bad. She had drummed it into Maggie's head that she was weak in character because every now and then, when pressed beyond endurance, she flared into anger. For her entire short life, thanks to Aunt Lucy's training, Maggie had tried never to get mad.

She wondered about that now. She wondered if anger might not serve a useful purpose in life. Maybe her character wasn't as weak as she'd always believed it to be. She thought about it for an hour or more before she felt she'd sorted her thoughts out enough to ask Jubal about it.

"Jubal?" The word was a near whisper. Her throat still felt tight.

Jubal, whose own thoughts were as muddled as Maggie's, didn't even hear her at first. He was still numb about Mulrooney's death. It hadn't quite settled into his gut that the feud—the struggle that had spanned decades, miles, and way too many lives—was over. More clear to him was the fact that he had lost another brother. He wasn't sure he could stand it.

"Jubal?"

She said it with more force this time, and it startled him. He looped the reins in one hand for long enough to give her a squeeze.

"Yes, Maggie?"

Although she had been thinking about this for an entire hour, she still fumbled a little bit when she asked, "Do—well, I mean, Aunt Lucy—Oh, Lordy." She took a deep breath. "Jubal, do you think I have a weak character?"

If his own emotions had not been so raw, his own thoughts so tumbled, he might have gotten mad and yelled at her. As it was, it took him a moment or two to take in her question. He couldn't believe she'd asked it, and he had to turn on his seat and stare at her for a second before he realized she actually seemed to expect an answer.

"Maggie, I've never met a woman in my life who had a stronger character than you. My mother—well, my mother had a weak character. But there's not a weak bone in your body. Your Aunt Lucy was a bitch. Don't even think about anything she ever said to you. She was wrong. She was mean and wrong and she hated you because she resented you. Forget her."

Maggie stared at him as he spoke, listening for all she was worth. For once in her life, she wasn't allowing her mind to interfere and filter Jubal's words through a lifetime of Aunt Lucy's training. She allowed them to settle in so she could think about them.

Jubal wondered why she didn't respond after he said his piece, but he was too occupied with his own unhappy thoughts to question her.

After what seemed like another hour, Maggie said, "Thank you, Jubal. I think you're right."

They rode the rest of the way home in silence.

Except for the rumbling of the wagon and the *clop-clop* of Old Red and Dan's horse, the ranch was silent when they made their way through the gate and lumbered into the yard.

"I'll take care of the horses." Dan's voice sounded raspy and it cracked a little bit, as though it had dried up in the desert.

"I'll make some tea." Maggie didn't wait to be helped down from the wagon but handed her daughter to Jubal and scrambled down over the big dusty wheel.

Jubal adjusted Annie against his shoulder and carefully climbed down from the wagon. Then he put a hand on Maggie's shoulder. "I'll put Annie in bed while you do that, Maggie."

On the way home, he had decided that Annie was his daughter. He knew he hadn't fathered her in the literal sense, but she was his daughter now, and he was her father, and he wasn't going to fight it any longer. All the fatherly urges he'd been feeling since he'd met these two females weren't a weakness. They were a strength, like Maggie's character, and he was going to enjoy them. To hell with anybody who thought otherwise.

Beula Todd met them before they got to the kitchen door. Her face was red. She was wiping her hands on her apron, and she looked as though she had been crying.

"Oh, thank God you're back!" she cried out as Maggie and Jubal stepped toward the door. "I was so worried about you. But Doc Haskins says he's going to be all right. It's a miracle!"

Upon those words, Beula burst into tears that looked suspiciously hysterical to Jubal.

With a very few quick steps, Maggie covered the distance between them and wrapped Beula in her arms. "It's all right, Beula. Everything will be all right."

Maggie thought she heard Beula say, "I know, I know," but she wasn't sure, because the words came out waterlogged, soggy, and heavy with tears.

"What's Doc Haskins doing here?" Jubal's question was sharp.

It took a while for Beula to compose herself enough to sniff back her tears and answer him. "Why, it's Four Toes. When that man brought him in, we thought he was dead, but Doc Haskins was passing by, and he dug the bullet out, and he says that if we're careful he'll live." She took another watery sniff and repeated, "It's a miracle."

Heedless of the sleeping child in his arms, Jubal whirled around and yelled as loud as he could, "Dan! Dan! Come here right now!"

Everything seemed to freeze. Later, Maggie couldn't even remember what she'd been thinking during those seconds. Or even if she'd been thinking at all. She was too stunned.

She couldn't believe it was her husband's voice that croaked a ragged, whispery, "He's alive!" when Dan came running hell for leather up to them. Then she couldn't believe it was the same two men she knew and loved who first threw their arms around each other, then opened their little circle to include her. Then she stood there in that circle and every one of them cried like babies.

In all the years she'd known Dan Blue Gully and Jubal Green, Beula Todd had never seen either of them even close to shedding a tear. She was wiping her own streaming eyes with her apron when they finally quit embracing each other and ran toward the house, the horses Dan had been going to take care of clearly forgotten.

It was much later, after the doctor had left, when they were sitting at the kitchen table drinking tea, that Beula told them the story.

"It was the strangest thing," she said. "Oh, I didn't think anything about it then because I was too worried about Four Toes. But now I think about it, it was really strange.

"This man showed up with Four Toes propped in front of him on his horse. I don't know how he knew where to come. Four Toes was unconscious."

"What was his name?" Jubal was going to be damned sure that the good Samaritan was well rewarded for saving his brother's life.

"Well, that's the strange thing, Mr. Green," Beula told him. "We don't know. We were busy fussing over Four Toes for the first little while. And then, when we went to see to the stranger, he was gone. As if he'd never even been here. Didn't say a word. I felt bad because I wanted to thank him and feed him, but he was gone. And nobody remembers ever seeing him before." She shrugged and shook her head.

"Maybe he went on to El Paso," said Jubal. "What did he look like? I'll try to find him."

"Oh," said Beula, smiling at the memory, "he was the nicest man. Had the sweetest smile and the prettiest brown eyes I ever seen. Curly brown hair—a pretty brown, like Annie's. He was tall and sort of gangly. Wore a blue plaid shirt and a denim jacket. I remember that jacket because it had a pretty patchwork flower sewn onto the pocket. Like a sweetheart had made it for him or something. Had a ring on his finger. Guess he's married."

Maggie had been staring at Beula with an odd expression on her face. Now she uttered a strangled gasp. Beula and Jubal looked at her.

"You okay, Maggie?" Jubal gave her a squeeze. He had put Annie to bed at last, and the little girl was sleeping soundly, Four Toes Smith's hat gracing one of the posts at the foot of her bed.

Since she didn't trust herself to speak, Maggie only nodded.

It was impossible. She knew it was impossible. Things like this didn't happen in real life. In books, in fairy tales, in dreams they happened. But they didn't *really* happen. Maggie knew that.

"Did he say anything at all?" Jubal asked.

Beula sighed, remembering. "Said as how he found Four Toes in the desert. Padded the bullet wound and wrapped it up, got him on his horse, and brung him here. Didn't say how he knew where he lived."

"Well, it happened on my land. Guess this is the closest place to bring him." Jubal was frowning into his tea, trying to make sense of it, wondering how the man had gotten past the guards. "He must have followed the wagon tracks."

But Maggie knew that wasn't it. She couldn't say so because her husband and Beula would think she was crazy beyond hope, but she knew that wasn't it.

The man Beula had described was Kenny. Kenneth Anthony Bright, Maggie's dear, sweet, dead husband, her guardian spirit for all these months, had found Four Toes and brought him home. It even sounded crazy to her. But they'd buried him in that jacket. The man was Kenny.

"Did—" Maggie fought hard for her voice and managed, with an enormous effort of will, to keep from shrieking her question. "Did he say anything else? Anything else *at all*?"

This was important. She wanted to know. Needed to know.

Beula thought for a moment. She seemed to be collecting the fragments together into some kind of sensible whole.

"Yes. That was a little odd too, come to think on it. He looked around him after Codfish and Sammy took Four Toes into the bedroom. Then he smiled, said something like, 'This is a good place. Good place to raise kids. Good place to be happy.' Something like that. Then he said, 'Tell the lady of the house I'm happy for her.'" Beula nodded at Maggie and Jubal. "I remember that especially because it seemed so strange."

Maggie lurched from the table, overturning her teacup, and ran blindly toward the window. It was dark outside now, and she didn't see a thing but her own memories as she stared out the window. They were almost indecipherable through the tears that blinded her and the roaring in her head.

"Maggie? Maggie, are you all right?" Jubal surged to his feet and followed her, concerned.

When his warm hands touched her shoulders, Maggie turned and flung herself into his arms.

"I'm fine, Jubal," she sobbed, her words almost impossible to understand through the tears choking her. "I'm fine. Everything is just fine."

And it was. She knew that now. Everything was just fine, and it always would be. She had been given a sign. Kenny had told her so.

Jubal sat beside Four Toes on one side, and Dan sat on the other. It was difficult for either man to tend to business while their brother remained so sick. But today, Four Toes was conscious, and they dared to talk to him.

"You damned Indians and your 'good day to die' shit," Jubal grumbled with the grin he was using to cover the emotion he felt. "You don't know so damned much at all."

Four Toes was almost too weak to respond to that grin, but he did it anyway.

"Maggie told you that, did she?" Four Toes looked a little bit embarrassed, in spite of his weakness.

"She sure did." Jubal shook his head, his heart too full to say anything else, even though he longed to rib Four Toes some more for scaring them all and almost dying.

"Hell, Jubal, we can't be right all the time. Besides, it *was* a good day to die. I guess it was just a better day to live." Four Toes gave him the biggest grin he could summon up. It was crooked and teetered on the edge of his lips for only a second or two before he couldn't maintain it any longer.

Jubal almost gave in to the tears that threatened to overwhelm him when he said, "I'm sure as hell glad you weren't right this time, you fool Indian."

"Amen to that," added Dan.

Sammy Napolitano felt responsible for Four Toes Smith's injuries, and he made it his personal business to deal with Sloane and Potts. He left the ranch right after he and Codfish settled Four Toes into his sickbed and was gone for days.

When he came back, he was mighty disgruntled that he hadn't been able to find the two men and exact the appropriate retribution, the kind of retribution he remembered from his childhood in Sicily.

Maggie didn't tell a soul that she was glad he had failed to kill the two villains. There had already been too much blood spilled during the years of the horrible feud. It was over now, and she was glad it had ended with no more deaths.

Life at Green's Valley Ranch gradually settled into a smooth routine. In any other household, it might have been said that things were getting back to normal. But normal in Jubal Green's life had always meant a perilous balancing act between running his ranch and staying alive. It seemed odd to him, not having to look over his shoulder all the time to check for predators.

"I'm jumpy as a frog on a hot rock," he confessed to Maggie one warm July night as they undressed for bed.

Maggie smiled with infinite tenderness at her husband. She loved him so much she could hardly stand it. And she felt so free, now she knew Kenny approved.

She still hadn't told anybody about how he had saved Four Toes. That was between the two of them. She expressed suitable remorse when Jubal returned from El Paso disgruntled that he hadn't been able to find the charitable stranger who had saved his brother's life, but she knew before he set out that he was tackling an impossible task. How could a human being, even one as skilled at tracking as Jubal Green, track down a guardian angel?

Nor had she told anybody yet what she was now sure of: that she was expecting Jubal's child. For some reason, the knowledge that she was pregnant was making her think of her farm again, and she knew now was the time. She had to go back to see it again, to say good-bye. And Kenny's grave—she needed to visit Kenny's grave one last time. She had some things to tell her dead husband, and she had been trying hard to think of a way to ask Jubal to take her there.

"You'll get used to it," she said now. "You know, Jubal Green, it's really more normal *not* to have people trying to murder you all the time than the other way around."

Maggie smoothed back her husband's hair from his forehead as he sat on the edge of the bed. He had doffed his shirt and boots but still wore his trousers. As ever, Maggie was impressed by his muscular shoulders and arms. She loved looking at him. His big brown hand caught hers and drew it to his lips.

"I guess so," he said.

He looked up at her. Maggie had brushed her hair out and taken off her spectacles, and her smiling face was angelic in the candlelight. Jubal's breath caught when he looked at her.

"God, Maggie, I love you so much. Don't ever leave me."

His fervent whisper surprised her. "I'll never leave you, Jubal." She kissed him on the forehead.

"You left me when I was sick. I remember. I thought you were an angel and you kept going away."

Maggie laughed softly. "I only went away to get you tea or water or medicine. I never left you, and I never will. And I'm not an angel, either."

"Yes, you are," Jubal said, and it didn't sound as though he planned to entertain any arguments about that. "You're my angel."

Maggie looked down into his eyes and saw the love in them, and she wanted to cry. She shook her head.

"Why are you shaking your head, Maggie?"

"Because I'm so silly. Every time anything happens I want to cry."

Jubal smiled up at her. "That's not silly, Maggie. That's you. I love it."

That really did make her cry.

They made beautiful love then. Maggie didn't understand how it could keep getting better, but it did. His every touch made her body surge with longing. That night he took her over the edge of ecstasy to a place she didn't even know existed.

They lay side by side in each other's arms afterward, relishing the quiet night and the peace that had settled over their life together. That peace was hard-won, and they appreciated it all the more because of it.

"Will you take me back to see my farm, Jubal?"

Maggie whispered her request tentatively. She didn't want to hurt his feelings, but her growing womb seemed to tug at her to go back there again, to say a last good-bye to her old life, to Kenny Bright. She had to. Someday had come.

Jubal didn't answer her for a minute. He had just been experiencing an incredible and completely unfamiliar sense of peace and happiness, but Maggie's words made his chest constrict painfully all at once. She wanted to go home. His heart plummeted and he felt as though somebody had just sprinkled salt onto his raw, bleeding soul.

His mouth was dry when he said, "You want to go back to New Mexico to live?"

Maggie heard the fear and worry in his voice and felt bad. She put a comforting hand on his chest.

"Just to say good-bye, Jubal. I never really got to say good-bye."

Jubal turned to look at her. He could barely make out her face in the moonlight. She looked pale and ethereal to him, and he had a momentary thought that she was his only temporarily, that she was destined to be snatched away from him as suddenly as she had come to him. He tried to shut his heart against that dreadful thought.

"That's all? You just want to say good-bye?"

Maggie nodded. "That's all, Jubal. Honest."

He looked mighty worried to her, and that bothered her a lot. She didn't want to hurt him.

"It's the first place I was ever happy, Jubal. I—I just want to see it again."

Jubal was silent for a couple of seconds. "It's not even there anymore, Maggie. Mulrooney burned it down."

Maggie sighed. "I know, Jubal. Please?"

Jubal felt his heart constrict painfully when he said, reluctantly, as though the words were being dragged from his toes, "All right."

Maggie took Annie with them, and Dan rode alongside the wagon. Four Toes was still too weak to make the journey. It took three days to get there, and they rode at night again because it was now full summer and even hotter than when they'd made the trip from New Mexico to El Paso in the springtime. Jubal's spirits drooped lower and lower the closer they got to the little clearing near Bright's Creek. He didn't speak at all for the last dozen miles or so.

When he heard Maggie's gasp of dismay as she finally saw the charred rubble of her home, he frowned.

"Oh, my God," Maggie whispered. "This is the first time I've ever been able to see the place—really truly see the place—and look at it. It's all gone." Tears trickled down her cheeks as she scanned the clearing through her spectacles.

Jubal only grunted. Dan helped her get down from the wagon. Then she carried Annie through the clearing toward the blackened heap that used to be their home. Annie looked around the rubble with eyes that were as solemn as her mama's.

Jubal watched his wife and daughter pick their way

through the mess, and his heart ached. Maggie was examining everything closely, peering at the charred remains with minute care.

She was remembering everything as she looked around and tried to determine exactly where it all had been. With a distant, aching fondness, she recalled the years she'd spent here as Kenny's wife. More clear to her was the memory of that bleak February day when she was in the throes of a vicious headache and a gun-shot stranger banged at her door with the butt of his rifle. She shook her head.

The clearing smelled acrid, like old burned wood, and her heart hurt. She recalled when she used to stand outside her door, breathing the crisp mountain air that always seemed to have an overlay of clean, freshly chopped wood. She loved that smell. Those days were gone forever, she guessed. Or at least until unstoppable nature took over, healing the scars stupid men had left behind, softening the rubble with vegetation, creating new life on the ruins of the old.

"Life is really strange, the way it works, Annie," she whispered to her little girl.

Annie didn't respond.

Maggie walked slowly to where the back of the house would have been and tried to determine where the woodpile used to be. She remembered finding Ozzie Plumb draped over it, and a little burst of left-over fear shot through her and almost immediately dissipated. That had been a terrible night, to be sure.

When he watched Maggie slowly pick her way over to Kenneth Anthony Bright's grave and squat down beside it, Jubal thought his heart had just been hacked in two.

But she didn't linger there. She whispered a soft, "Thank you, Kenny Bright. Thank you for saving Four Toes. And you were right. Annie and I are going to be fine now. Jubal's ranch is a wonderful place for us both. You were so good to us, Kenny, and I'll always love you." She sighed when she said, "I wish I could keep up your grave for you, but Annie and I have to go back and live in Texas now. I just came to say good-bye."

She knelt there for another minute or two and then said, "I guess it's all right. I guess you don't confine yourself to this silly little piece of dirt anyway." She smiled at that happy realization.

Kenny's spirit—or maybe it was her imagination—whispered to her soul that it was indeed all right. He was happy for her, and he would always love them both. Maggie smiled again.

Then she picked herself and her daughter up and strode firmly toward her husband. She smiled at Dan, who helped her back onto the seat of the wagon and then remounted his horse.

"Thank you, Jubal," Maggie said pleasantly. She felt really good now.

Jubal blinked at her. "That's it?"

Maggie nodded. "That's it. I just wanted to say good-bye."

Jubal didn't figure he'd better argue. He was too relieved. He just shook the reins, and the two mules began a slow turn-around in the clearing.

Annie waved good-bye to the remains of her first home as the mules began the weary trudge back to El Paso. Maggie looked back at the clearing until it was out of sight. Then she sighed.

"Well, that's that."

Jubal eyed her suspiciously. He wasn't used to good things lasting any more than Maggie was, and he didn't altogether trust her "that's that."

Maggie noticed his uneasy glance and smiled at him. She reached out to caress his cheek.

"I guess since we're going to be starting a family at your ranch pretty soon, I just needed to say good-bye to my old life, Jubal. It sort of came on me sudden-like, the need to come here."

Jubal grunted and turned his attention to the mules. Annie was sleepy, so Maggie laid her down in the wagon bed to rest. They had ridden nearly another mile before Jubal realized what Maggie had said. Then his head whipped around and he pinned her with a hard stare.

"What?"

Maggie was startled. "What what?"

"What did you say?"

"About wanting to say good-bye?"

"No. Back there. About a family."

Maggie smiled wickedly. "Oh," she said with a soft, sly little smile, "did I mention that?"

"Mention what?" Jubal was glaring at her now.

"Mention that Annie is going to be having a little brother or sister in about eight months?"

Jubal could only stare at her for several seconds. Then he whispered, "Oh, my God!" dropped the reins, and grabbed his wife.

Dan rode up at a dead run, scared to death because the mules were wandering. When he saw Jubal and Maggie in a fierce embrace, he seemed torn between anger and amusement.

"What the hell's going on with you two?" he hollered.

Jubal reluctantly let go of Maggie and turned to his oldest friend with an expression on his face Dan had never seen before.

"What's going on?" Dan asked again. He sounded confused. "What's wrong?"

"Not a thing," said Maggie.

"Not a goddamned thing, Danny," Jubal confirmed. "Everything's just perfect."

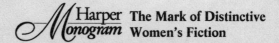